REBOUND

Also by Heather Justesen

The Ball's in Her Court

REBOUND

HEATHER
JUSTESEN

CFI
Springville, Utah

This is a work of fiction. The characters, names, incidents, places, and dialogue are products of the author's imagination, and are not to be construed as real.

ISBN 13: 978-1-59955-363-4

Published by CFI, an imprint of Cedar Fort, Inc., 2373 W. 700 S., Springville, UT 84663
Distributed by Cedar Fort, Inc., www.cedarfort.com

LIBRARY OF CONGRESS CATALOGING-IN-PUBLICATION DATA

Justesen, Heather, 1976-
  Rebound / Heather Justesen.
    p. cm.
  Summary: Lily Drake must deal with her husband John's arrest for fraud and identity theft.
  ISBN 978-1-59955-363-4
  1. Mormon women--Utah--Fiction. 2. Swindlers and swindling--Utah--Fiction. 3. Domestic fiction, American. 4. Christian fiction, American. I. Title.

  PS3610.U883R43 2010
  813'.6--dc22

             2009046548

Cover design by Angela D. Olsen
Cover design © 2010 by Lyle Mortimer
Edited and typeset by Heidi Doxey

Printed in the United States of America

10 9 8 7 6 5 4 3 2 1

Printed on acid-free paper

Praise for Heather Justesen and *Rebound*

Heather Justesen's unique turns of phrase bring to life a story of family relationships, the search for belonging, and a bit of romance along the way.

Tristi Pinkston,
author of *Agent in Old Lace*

Rebound is a great, second edition in the series, starting with *The Ball's in Her Court*. If you liked *The Ball's in Her Court*, you're going to love *Rebound*. The story keeps getting better and better.

Keith Fisher,
http://thecampcookinyourbackyard.blogspot.com

I was drawn into *Rebound* from the very beginning. Heather does a great job giving just enough information to make you want to know what happens next. It's a perfect mix of intrigue and romance—you won't want to put it down.

Kimberly Job,
author of *I'll Know You by Heart*

Justesen weaves a touching tale about strength, family relationships, and what it's like to start over. This heart-wrenching story comes with a side of wry humor that will have you crying, laughing, then gasping as the romance grips your heart. *Rebound* is a page turner you won't want to miss.

Nichole Giles,
author of *The Sharp Edge of a Knife* and
Mormon Mishaps and Mischief

Rebound is the perfect title for this tale about Lily—a young mother left to start over after her husband commits fraud and is sent to jail—and Curtis—a wannabe pro basketball player, searching for his birth family. Together, Lily and Curtis help each other through the unexpected twists their lives take. *Rebound* is perfect for anyone who loves to curl up with a book, hoping for a dose of good, clean romance.

Danyelle Ferguson,
book reviewer (www.QueenOfTheClan.com)
and author of *(dis)Abilities and the Gospel*.

For all of the patient and enthusiastic English teachers who helped me on my way, with special thanks to Carolyn Stevens, and in memory of Olive Robison and Verlene Phillips. These ladies touched my life in so many ways.

CHAPTER ONE

John tuned out the babbling of the other realtors from outside his office door and focused on the computer screen. If things went well that evening, he'd have to buy himself a celebratory present. The Baccarat Tornado Vase on the screen in front of him was exquisite and worth every dollar of its nearly $3,200 price.

It's a pity I'll have to tell Lily I picked it up at a yard sale or something. She's far too straitlaced. Naïveté works for her, though. Thankfully, it works for me too.

He whistled as he bookmarked the page for later.

The phone rang and he snatched it up, modulating his voice. "Hello, this is John Drake."

"Mr. Drake," the receptionist said. "There's a man here to see you. Aaron James. Do you have a few minutes?"

After a quick glance at the clock on the computer screen, John figured he had five. "Just a few, but I'll be happy to speak with him until my next client arrives." It wouldn't do to turn down a possible commission. After all, one never knew when five minutes could turn into that Rolex he'd been looking at online.

With a sigh, John closed the Internet window and shut down his laptop. Self-conscious, he ran his fingers lightly over his bleached-blond hair, pulling out the mirror he kept in a desk drawer to make sure he looked perfect. In his job, his name was his brand, so it was important to always make a good impression. He smiled brightly into the mirror to make sure nothing was stuck in his orthodontist-perfected teeth.

After stashing his laptop and a file with his day's paperwork into his briefcase, John stood and walked out to the reception area.

The man facing him was dark haired, hard-eyed, and several inches shorter than John's own height of six-foot-one. He wore a suit and was well groomed, so it was likely he made a decent income, even if his outfit was off the rack.

"Hello, I'm John Drake. How can I help you this morning?" John extended a hand in greeting.

The man's grip was firm, his expression flat, unimpressed. "I'd like to speak with you in private for a few minutes, Mr. Drake. Could we go into your office?"

A flicker of warning lit up inside John's chest, and he forced his most charming smile into place. "I'm expecting a client shortly, but I have a few minutes." *Best to act calm and innocent. Just because he practically screams cop doesn't mean he knows anything.*

The man nodded but said nothing. A man John hadn't noticed stood from his seat in the corner and joined them. The flicker of warning grew into a small blaze, but he shoved it away. Businessmen often traveled in pairs. The fact that they hadn't introduced themselves yet was strange but might mean nothing.

John turned to the receptionist and smiled reassuringly. "When my clients arrive, please have them take a seat and offer them refreshments. I'll be right back."

No one spoke as John took the men to his office. He glanced back at the tall, heavy-set man behind him and widened his smile into his most charming salesman grin. When they reached his office, both men stepped in, and one closed the door behind them.

"Now, how can I help you?" John indicated that the men should sit, then leaned back against his desk, grasping the lip of the desktop to hide the way his hands shook.

Ignoring the offered chair, Aaron James reached into his pocket and pulled out some papers. "John Sebastian Drake, these papers include a warrant for your arrest, and another granting us permission to search your home, cars, and office."

John felt the color drain from his face but tried to brazen it out. "Come now, gentlemen. What's going on here? Is this a joke?"

"No, Mr. Drake. We're arresting you for fraud. Identity theft is serious business, and we have evidence you've been actively engaged in it for some time now. You may want to get someone else to take care of your clients this afternoon. You won't be going anywhere except with us."

Her call went to his voice mail again.

In frustration, Lily Drake flipped her cell phone closed and ran her fingers distractedly over her son Stephen's soft, damp locks. His head was warm, heating her collarbone where it lay. His fist curled at the base of her throat as she adjusted the overloaded diaper bag on her shoulder and headed out of the babysitter's house toward the car.

Her prenatal checkup had gone well enough, though the doctor had been concerned about her stress levels and how they were affecting her baby, who was still eight weeks from full term. She shifted her attention back to the child in her arms. "Played too hard at the sitter's, huh? Maybe you'll stay down while I work on dinner then." She brushed her lips over her two-year-old's soft head and inhaled his sweet scent. "Mom could use a nap too." Her back ached, and her arms were tired from hitching Stephen over and around her swollen belly.

The day was warm for mid-January. The sun shone and the latest snow was disappearing into the grass. Before she knew it, early spring flowers would bloom. If it weren't for the dratted dinner party she had to host in a few hours, she would've spent the afternoon puttering in the yard after her nap. The roses needed pruning, and a few other between-season chores ought to be done before the crocuses decided to show themselves. Her advancing condition was another reason to get to the yard as soon as possible. Instead, she mentally checked off a list of preparations and felt the tension grow in her shoulders. She used to enjoy entertaining.

As she tried to one-handedly maneuver the car key out from the dozen on the ring, she wondered again where John was. She reviewed her preparations for dinner. Her signature cheesecake and special strawberry glaze sat in the fridge. Hors d'oeuvres of cream-cheese on herbed Melba toast and stuffed mushrooms were prepped and ready for assembly—and the house sparkled.

Doubtless John would find something to keep him from being satisfied with the evening's preparations, but Lily couldn't think of anything else to do. Still, the fact John hadn't called to grill her was unusual, concerning even. He often let voice mail pick up her calls when he was with clients. However, it was strange for him to be so quiet when they were having people over.

It took only a couple minutes to get Stephen settled in his car seat, untangle her long brown hair from his fist, and slide behind the steering wheel of the new Lexus John had bought her the previous spring. The car was comfortable, had lots of safety features, and, most important to John, announced he was making plenty of money.

Pushing thoughts of her husband aside, Lily turned her mind to something else. She considered the new flowers she planned to put in the yard and mused over raised-bed designs she'd seen in a magazine.

Her neighborhood roads wound around natural hills and valleys, making a confusing, twisting trail she had long ago learned by heart. She came around the last bend, slowing as she neared her home.

The surprise of seeing three dark sedans parked in front of the house and the front door standing open slowed her reflexes, and she nearly hit one of the cars. Just in time, she twisted the steering wheel to pull around them and into her parking space.

Her heart pounded and blood rushed in her ears as she tried to decide what to do. Could she go in when there were obviously strangers in her home? Should she call the police? It wasn't like whoever was inside had bothered to hide their presence. Did that mean they wouldn't be aggressive, or did it make no difference? Before Lily could decide what to do, a man came out and walked over. He stood tall and sturdy, his politely curious expression capped by a shock of dark hair.

Lily rolled down the window only a few inches and locked the doors. She looked into his eyes as he leaned over to speak into the window opening. "Can I help you, ma'am?"

"This is my home. What are you doing in it?" She heard her voice quaver but tried to pretend she wasn't disturbed by the questions swirling inside her.

"You're Lily Drake? Wife of John Sebastian Drake?" he asked. When she nodded, the man reached into his pocket and pulled out a black leather cover, flipped it open, and showed her his FBI badge. "I'm Agent Melton. I'm glad you've come home. I need to speak with you."

Lily felt her brow wrinkle as she tried to make sense of his request. Why would he want to speak with her? What were they doing in her home? "What's going on?"

"Please get out of the car so we can talk and I'll tell you."

Lily hesitated for only a moment before withdrawing her key from the ignition. She heard the doors unlock automatically, and Agent Melton opened her door and then moved away. Lily shut the door behind her and leaned back against it. "What's going on?" She turned her head to steal a glance at her son and saw him through the window, still sleeping peacefully. *Small miracles*, she thought as she wrapped her arms around her growing middle, suddenly cold, though the sun beat on her head.

The man stuck his hands in his pockets and put an understanding expression on his face. Lily distrusted him immediately.

"Mrs. Drake, what can you tell me about your family finances?"

That was one question she was not prepared for. Lily blinked. "What does that have to do with . . . anything? I . . . ." She trailed off, not sure how to answer.

He came to the point. "Are you aware of your husband's fraudulent activities?"

It took several seconds for her mind to verify he had really spoken those words; then she shook her head. "You must be mistaken. My husband would never be involved in fraud." Her knees felt weak.

The agent must have sensed her need to sit down because he suggested, "Let's take this discussion inside, shall we?" Without waiting for an answer, he opened the back door of the car and removed Stephen from his car seat. Too numb to object, her mind reeling, Lily followed the man through the arched entrance, across the cobbled patio, and into the spacious foyer of her home. Agent Melton led her to the buttery soft dark leather sofas in the great room.

"Let me put Stephen to bed. I'll be right back." Lily took her son, using the moment to try and gain control over her emotions. The sight of two men going through John's office drawers only increased her tension. She turned to look back and saw Agent Melton watching her. He moved closer and stood at the bedroom door as she put Stephen down.

"What's this all about?" Lily asked when she was seated across from the agent again. She was sure she'd heard something wrong outside. The man couldn't be accusing John of fraud.

"For some time, we've been working to track down a man we suspected to be involved in fraud in Utah and Salt Lake counties. Your husband, Mrs. Drake, is that man. I have a search warrant if you'd like to see it." He pulled a paper from the breast pocket of his jacket and handed it over.

Lily took the paper, though reluctant to look at it. She was afraid that seeing it would make this become real and not just a mistake. She unfolded the sheet and noticed her address, John's business address, and both cars listed as being covered by the warrant. A judge's signature flourished across the bottom. Her hands began to tremble as she returned the sheet. "You've made a mistake."

"I'm sorry to say we have not. In addition, although we have no substantial evidence against you at this time, it's hard to believe you could be completely unaware of your husband's activities." He looked around him at the solid mahogany tables and entertainment center, the Tiffany lamp in the corner, and the china hutch filled with pretty trinkets. "You've certainly been living well."

"My husband is very successful," she answered, irritated with his insinuation. Lily could hear the sounds of men moving around down the hall and deep voices speaking in tones she couldn't distinguish. It seemed unreal.

"Not this successful. I saw your tax returns from last year. It was a good income, yes, but not nearly equal to this lifestyle. How much do you pay your gardener a month?" He turned his head toward the window. "I saw this place last fall when there were still late flowers in bloom. You've got a real setup out there."

Last fall? They've been watching a long time. "I'm the gardener around here. Other than the mowing, which John insisted we hire a boy to do."

This brought a faint smile to his wide mouth. "You're very accomplished. It's clear you do more than help charge up the credit cards."

Lily knew he was probably just trying to put her at ease, and for whatever reason, she found it helped. She let out a slow, deep breath. "There was an inheritance a few years ago. John was able to buy most of the furniture, as well as my car, with the proceeds. It's enabled us to live a little more comfortably than we otherwise would have. His folks have also been very generous. This sofa set was a wedding gift from them." She rubbed a hand over the sofa. Her in-laws were a little too generous, she admitted to herself. It made her uncomfortable.

He stood and walked over to the china hutch and inspected the pieces on display.

"It's mostly glass or flea market finds. John is a pro at that. He picks things up every time he makes a trip out of the area." Lily was hasty to explain the beautiful collection John had steadily added to over the past several years.

Agent Melton sent her a look of disbelief, then opened a door and picked up one of the two candelabra on the top shelf. They had medallion bases and intricate serpent-looking sticks. Tiny crystals hung all around them with cylinders of etched crystal surrounding the candlestick. Lily had to admit the pair was exquisite. She hadn't been surprised when John told her he paid a hundred dollars for the set. The workmanship was so incredible; she couldn't argue that they were worth it.

"That looks like Baccarat to me." He set down the candelabra and picked up a small porcelain box. "And the pill box, I would swear it was Limoges. They certainly fit the descriptions we have of items that were purchased with the fraudulently obtained credit cards."

Lily had only heard the brand names in books. Though John made a good income, they had never shopped anywhere that sold anything so expensive. "You must be mistaken. They're beautiful, of course, but John wouldn't spend several hundred dollars on a pair of candlesticks."

"Fine crystal artistry," Agent Melton corrected her. "Or so my wife calls it. And the candlesticks that were purchased with the credit cards cost several thousand dollars, not several hundred." He replaced the porcelain pill box and shut the glass door.

She tried to convince herself the man was simply wrong. But the longer they spoke, the less certain Lily was. There were too many little things over the years that she couldn't completely disregard. He walked over to stand near the sofa, his hands tucked into his front pockets.

"So I must ask you again: is there anything you'd like to tell me about your family finances, or anything you might know about your account balances? Your credit cards are well charged up. You might have wanted a way to keep spending when you hit your limit. That kind of thing happens all the time."

"I don't know what you're talking about. I only have one credit card, and John pays it off in full every month." Dread sat heavy in her stomach, however. She'd never seen the bills, had she?

His eyebrows winged up. "One credit card? Mrs. Drake, you have no fewer than six in your name, with a combined balance of something around thirty-thousand dollars."

Lily felt like she'd been punched in the stomach. "You can't be right. I've only applied for one card in my life, and I know John said he was keeping it paid off. I only use it for groceries if I forget to bring my checkbook, and then I give him a check for my charges, so it can be covered at the end of the month. My household allowance is plenty for the bills I pay."

"You mean the power, gas, water, telephone, fuel for your car, baby expenses, and food items. Occasionally you purchase clothing for yourself, though not as much as I expected."

She blinked. "Have you been studying my spending habits?"

"This is an FBI investigation. I could tell you what ice cream you buy, the number of diapers you go through in a week, and which flowers you've purchased online for your garden this summer."

His admission made a lump rise in her throat, but she managed to ask, "Are you arresting me?"

The man lifted a dark brow and considered her for a long moment. "Not right now. If there's evidence that you're involved, I will find it. And if you truly didn't know about those other credit cards, you're as much a victim as anyone. Unfortunately, it may be hard for you to prove you didn't know anything about them—you do live here, after all."

Lily clutched the arm of the sofa. Could John really have charged nearly thirty-thousand dollars on credit cards she hadn't known existed? "Where's my husband?"

Another man entered the room, carrying a large garbage bag, and Agent Melton approached him. They spoke in low tones for a moment, and then Agent Melton took the bag and returned to her. "He's in custody. I wouldn't be expecting him home anytime soon. Bail will likely be set somewhere around the half-million mark."

"Ha-half a million?" Even the bond on that would be far beyond her ability to raise. She sat on the sofa in shock. John's father might pay it, but she couldn't imagine even he had that kind of cash available.

That thought reminded her of the dinner party and the clients her father-in-law had referred to his son. "My father-in-law—does he know? We have clients coming for dinner. John's parents will want to know."

"His father knows. Someone from our office spoke to him earlier this morning."

It probably never occurred to him to call me.

After a few seconds passed, Lily heard men walking down the hall toward the door. They had boxes and bags in their hands. "What are they doing?"

"It's either evidence or items they want to look through. Don't worry—anything unrelated to the case will come back." The man reached into the bag he held and pulled out a gallon-size zippered baggie full of credit cards and picture IDs.

He held them out so she could see them better. Lily lifted her free hand and touched the bag, tilting the contents toward her. There were cards from every imaginable bank with the names of people she had never heard of. Gilbert Louder, Samuel F. Caldwell, Samuel A. Bishop—the list went on and on. One ID card had her husband's picture and description but the name Jacob Lewis.

That ID dissolved the last of her hope that this was all one big, horrible mistake. Her hand dropped from the bag, and she leaned back against the sofa while the men continued to remove items from her house.

"We've got to return to the office. I'll need you to come in for questioning. If you could get your son, I'll move his car seat to my vehicle."

Lily thought she heard a buzzing in her head and then realized it was her cell phone. She fumbled to pull it out. It was Denise, her best friend. She set the phone down without answering it. What could she say?

"I'll get my son, though he probably needs a diaper change."

He nodded and gestured for her to precede him to Stephen's room. The tread of feet through the house quieted, and she heard one car start up and back down the drive.

The few minutes it took her to change Stephen gave Lily a moment to think, to consider all of the times John had shown up with a new trinket, or what she had thought of as trinkets. She hadn't grown up in a home where those kinds of extravagances were common. Her parents provided well enough for her and her three sisters. Her childhood home had been steady and safe, not fancy or large. Though she liked beautiful things, she never thought she'd ever have them. John had grown up in a completely different situation. He was the only child, the model son who put himself out to gain his father's favor. He was driven to do better, be better, and gain more. And he'd been able to gain the best without her realizing what he was doing. She still couldn't quite believe it, even though she'd seen the evidence.

Lily tossed the dirty diaper into the pail in the corner and restocked her diaper bag. Agent Melton stood in the hall, following her with his eyes. When she returned to the great room, she walked past the curio again, stopping to allow her fingers to brush the glass between her and the candlesticks that cost a small fortune. How had she been so blind?

She picked up her bag and headed for the front door. As Lily sat in the agent's car, her cell phone began to vibrate. It was Denise again.

"Answer it if you like," the agent told her.

Lily didn't know if she wanted to. What would she say? She wasn't sure she believed it herself.

CHAPTER TWO

When Agent Melton finished interrogating Lily about her husband's actions and what she knew about his various purchases, he finally let her go. Two hours had passed and both she and Stephen were cranky.

Lily checked her missed calls when she left his office and noticed Denise had called twice more, as had Lily's sister Shelly. Remembering she didn't have a car, she sighed and picked up her cell phone. She didn't want to talk to anyone, but there wasn't much choice. "Denise," she said when her best friend answered. "I need a favor. Can you come get me?" She gave the address, then promised to explain everything when Denise arrived.

Fifteen minutes later, after the agent brought her car seat from his vehicle to the front door where Lily waited for her ride, she asked him, "What's going to happen now?"

He glanced at the little boy in her arms and nodded. "The evidence is overwhelming. You need to face the fact that your husband won't be coming home for several years. Your car is in your name, so the government can't take it unless you're implicated. But every account and asset with his name on it will be seized by the courts. They won't seize your home until everything's settled, so you should have a few months to figure things out."

A car pulled in front of the building, and Lily fought back the tears forming in her eyes. She had nine hundred dollars in her personal checking account and a car. What was she going to do? She glanced over to see Denise's graceful frame emerge from her car. "Thank you," she said, without looking back at him.

He pressed a card into her hand. "Call me if you think of anything else you can tell us. And if I were you, I'd contact the credit card companies right away. You'll have several messes to work out." He turned and walked back down the hallway. Lily picked up the diaper bag and waited for Denise to reach her.

"Hey, I've been trying to call you all afternoon. I wondered if something was wrong." Denise came over and gathered Lily into her arms, sandwiching Stephen between them. "What's going on?"

Lily leaned her head on her friend's shoulder and burst into tears. How was she supposed to deal with this mess? When she pulled away again, Denise snatched up the car seat and guided Lily to the passenger door.

Wiping at her face, Lily settled into the front while Denise secured Stephen's seat, then put him in it before climbing into the driver's seat herself. "Where's Cameron?" Lily asked about Denise's eleven-month-old son.

Denise turned the key in the ignition. "Play date at the neighbor's." She pushed her pixie-cut dark hair back from her face and set a hand on Lily's arm. "I wasn't sure what I'd find when I got here. What's going on?"

"Start driving and I'll fill you in. Just get me out of here." Lily spilled the whole story, crying the tears she'd held back through her earlier interrogation. "And even more than that, he's charged up something like thirty thousand dollars in credit card debt in my name. I didn't even know he had those cards. I didn't sign for them. I don't have a job. I have a toddler and a baby on the way, and I'm going to be homeless in a few months. My husband is going to be in prison for years. What do I do?"

They pulled in front of Lily's home, and Denise wrapped Lily in her arms and let her cry it out. Lily saw her look at Stephen, who sat watching his mother cry. Denise smiled at him, his confusion and worry apparent. "Don't worry, Stephen. Mommy has an owie, but it'll feel better soon," Denise said.

Lily pulled back. She had nearly forgotten he was in the back seat and realized she was upsetting him. He had tears in his eyes.

"Where the owie? Why sad?" Stephen asked, pointing to his mother. She went around to his door and released him from his car seat. He touched the tears on Lily's cheek, and she picked him up and held him tight. "I hurt here." She touched her chest and then pushed the hair back from his face. "It'll be better soon." She lied to her son without compunction. If he'd been older, she might have told him bits of the truth, but he wouldn't under-stand, so it was best to keep him calm. "Do you want pizza for dinner?" She couldn't face the steak and potatoes she'd prepped for that night.

"That's a great idea. I'll call and order one. We can pick it up on the way home. You come stay the night with us and maybe we can help you work through this. We'll just pack an overnight bag," Denise said as she led Lily to the front door, leaving Stephen's seat in the car.

"Oh, I don't want to get in the way, I mean—"

Denise took Lily by the chin and looked her in the eye. "You won't be in the way. Besides, Rich will charge up here like an overprotective lion if you don't come over, and you know it." Denise's husband, Rich, was also Lily's cousin.

Accepting her friend's words, Lily nodded. "I'm not spending the night, though."

"Just pack a bag. You can always bring it back if you decide not to sleep over." Denise took the keys from Lily's limp hand and opened the front door. Then she led the way back to Stephen's room "I need to call Rich, and then I'll pack the tyke's stuff. You pack for yourself."

After Denise picked up her son from the neighbor's, they walked into her house, a steaming pizza in her hand. "You can put your things in the blue room," she told Lily.

"I'm not staying the night," Lily said, taking the overnight bag from her shoulders and dropping it in the corner. Stephen ran circles around them. Cam laughed and jabbered at Stephen every time he passed by.

"Of course you are, but we can argue over that later. Rest for a few minutes if you'd like. Stephen, go into the kitchen and we'll eat soon."

Stephen raced for the kitchen shouting, "Pizza! Pizza! Pizza!" in a dis-organized chant while Cam crawled lightening-quick behind him. Denise sighed and followed, still carrying the pizza. Giving in, Lily flopped into an easy chair in front of the television. She rested her head back and let the tears flow while she listened to Denise settle the boys into a high chair and booster seat. She just felt numb. The day seemed utterly unreal as she thought back over the past few hours. She wasn't sure where to go from here.

A few minutes later, Rich entered through the front door and paused when he saw Lily. He came around the chair so he could see her face. "Lils, what's going on? What happened? Denise said John was arrested."

"I'm still in shock." She looked up at her tall, dark cousin.

He sat beside her and slid an arm around her shoulder, holding her tight. They had been close since childhood, almost like brother and sister. She told him everything she had already told Denise, starting to feel like a broken record.

He didn't interrupt or ask questions. He just let her get through the whole mess, allowing her to blubber on his shoulder. "Wow, that's a barrel of fun to deal with," he said when she finally wound down. "I'm so sorry this is happening to you."

She sniffled and reached for the box of tissues Denise had brought over earlier. "I just can't believe I was so wrong about him. How could I have made such a huge mistake?"

"Are you sure they're right?"

"I don't want to believe it. I want to think there's some reasonable explanation, but the evidence seems too strong to be wrong. What was he thinking?" Though she would have thought she couldn't eat, she found her stomach growling.

"I guess you'll have to ask him." Rich must have heard the grumble because his lips turned up at the corners in a half-hearted smile. "Come and eat. You need to feed that little one inside you." He helped her stand and slid an arm around her shoulders as he led her into the kitchen.

In no time they were settled at the table and Lily started eating—she was hungrier than she thought. When she started to feel full, she pushed her plate away. "I still can't believe it. It's like one of those horrible nightmares that you wake from at night, still breathing heavily. The kind that keeps you awake for an hour afterward. I just can't put it all together."

Rich reached over and squeezed her shoulder. "I understand how you could feel that way, but it'll all work out. Eventually."

"Gee, thanks for the reassurance. Eventually I'll feel peace of mind from that." Lily rolled her neck to loosen her tight shoulder muscles and stood from the table. "I'm way past ready for sleep. I have a big dinner sitting in the fridge at home. You guys game to join me tomorrow night? I might as well cook it instead of tossing it." She pulled a very tired Stephen from the extra booster seat Denise kept around for visits and carried him to the sink to wash up.

"We have that game of Curtis's tomorrow night at the Y." Denise looked apologetic at the reminder. "He's coming back to stay with us for a few days. Maybe we could join you for Sunday dinner instead?"

Lily nodded. She remembered Denise talking about the game. Curtis was Denise's biological half brother, and they seldom saw each other during the basketball season because playing for Utah State University sucked up so much of his time. "That would be fine. The meal was planned for four people anyway, and the munchkins will probably be happier with mac and cheese. Won't you, kiddo?" She directed the last comment to her wet-faced son.

"And cheese!" he called out. He splashed water in the sink, then wriggled to be set down.

"Well, that sounds perfect. You can stay here through the weekend if you like." Rich stood and hauled his son to the sink for a cleanup as well. Both boys had nearly as much tomato sauce on them as in them.

"No, you don't have that much room to spare. Besides, I have to face it all again." She put on a determined smile, or at least she hoped it looked determined. Her main emotion at the moment was despair, followed closely by confusion. "I'll stay the night, then get out of your hair tomorrow before the game. You'll want to spend as much time as you can with Curtis."

"We can get out of it. Curtis will understand if you need us." Denise slid an arm around Lily's back and pulled her close.

Lily rested her head against Denise's shoulder for just a moment, before moving away. "Thank you. I know you would cancel everything if I needed you to. But no, it wouldn't be right. I'll see you in the morning."

"There are clean towels for you on the nightstand. Let us know if you need anything." Rich held Cameron back as he watched Lily turn away.

"Thanks. You guys are the best." Lily disappeared into the hallway, pulling Stephen by one hand. She shouldered the bags she had left by the front door and headed for the room she knew would always be held open for her if she needed it.

She sank onto the bed. It wasn't long before she was tucked next to her toddler under the covers, ready for the peaceful oblivion of sleep.

Unfortunately, sleep wasn't quick in coming. She stared at the ceiling, trying to forget everything that had happened that day. Just a few hours of unconsciousness were all she wanted right now. Still, sleep didn't come.

The longer she lay there, the more upset and angry she felt at her husband for causing this whole mess. Finally she decided she wasn't going to sleep anytime soon, so she got out of bed and padded down the hall in bare feet to the office.

Denise was a computer programmer who also did online research for adoptees who were looking for their birth families—a talent she had developed in the years before her own family search. There were always notebooks and pens available in Denise's office.

Lily hit the jackpot when she slid the first drawer open. She took the notebook and pen over to a comfortable arm chair in the living room to write. Agent Melton mentioned it might take a few days to get clearance for a visit, especially since it was the weekend. But there was so much she wanted to say to John. She figured maybe if she wrote him a letter, she would be able to settle down to sleep. She flipped the pen around in her fingers for several minutes, trying to figure out how to word it, what to say. Then she decided just to write. There was no reason she had to send it if it came out unintelligible, after all. It was only paper.

John,

You can't imagine my shock when I came home today to find the FBI at our house. I don't understand. How could this have happened? I saw the evidence right in front of me, but I can't quite believe it's true. I thought we had something special, that we could do anything together as a team. The FBI agent told me you were doing this before we married, though. Has it really been going on so long? How could I not have noticed? I have no idea what to do now, how I'm going to provide for our children while you are in jail. How do I explain to Stephen that his daddy isn't coming home? We need to talk. Please write me back, call, something.

She ended the letter and felt slightly better, even if nothing had changed. After a moment she ripped the page from the notebook, then stood and returned to her room. Sleep teased and taunted her, but she felt it drawing closer. When it finally arrived, it wasn't very peaceful.

The next morning, Lily woke feeling every bit as tired and wrung out as she had at bedtime. If Stephen hadn't been crying for breakfast and a diaper change, it would have been all too easy to roll over for a few more hours of sleep.

Denise stood at the stove, cooking, when Lily walked into the kitchen with Stephen. "Good morning," Lily said, though she wondered if she had ever experienced a worse morning.

Denise turned to look her friend over and then shook her head. "Did you sleep at all? You look worse than you did after coming off the grave-yard shift."

Lily pulled a face at the memory of her nights spent stocking a toy store during college. "Gee, thanks. I slept—some. You look like you could use a little more sleep yourself." She noticed the dark circles under Denise's eyes and the wan look on her face.

"I had a lot on my mind last night." She shrugged.

"I'm sorry about that." Guilt layered itself over all of Lily's other con-fused emotions.

"None of it's your fault. And if you hadn't called me, I'd have had to kill you. You were there for me when things looked pretty bleak, and you are my best girl friend, so if you need something, you call. Okay?"

Lily nodded and rubbed her face with her free hand. She settled Ste-phen on the floor with some blocks and moved to the cupboards to help set the table. Cameron was already smashing banana pieces on his high chair.

They finished setting the table and put the food on it as Rich came into the kitchen. He paused to speak some baby nonsense to each of the boys, brushed his lips across Lily's cheek, then lingered over a kiss with his wife. When he pulled away, he glanced back at Lily. "How are we doing this morning?"

Lily forced a smile, but she knew he didn't buy her bravado. He could read her too well.

Rich sat down at the table and gestured for Lily to do the same. She wasn't sure how much food she could stomach this morning, but she sat anyway.

She managed to eat some toast and a few bites of egg, but nothing tasted good.

"Did you really have no idea? None at all?" Rich asked.

"None, though the clues were there staring me in the face—hindsight and all that. Obviously, I'm a fool. Sweet, naïve Lily. I knew we lived well, but the mortgage payment was really low because of his inheritance, and I know he does well at work. His sales have been so good we've had plenty of money. Or at least, that's what he's been telling me—and I believed it all this time." She played with the napkin by her plate. "Where will Stephen and I go when the courts seize the house?"

Her list of worries grew. "I'll need to get a job and day care, and summer's coming up. There'll be no teaching jobs during the summer. I'll have to renew my certification since I haven't been teaching. Then there's the baby." She touched her hand to her bulging middle as worries swirled through her mind, making her light-headed.

"Slow down, Lily. Let's take one thing at a time." Rich rested a hand on her arm. "If the evidence is as bad as you said, you'll have to make some plans. You can move in here for a while if you need to, but find out what your options are. Once you know what to expect, we'll take things from there. Would you like one of us to go with you to see the FBI agent again?"

"I can tell my boss I have a family emergency," Denise added. "I'm working ahead of deadline anyway, and I hate to think of you facing all of this alone."

"No," Lily shook her head. This was her problem, and she was going to deal with it—somehow. Denise and Rich were already doing enough for her. "I'll take care of it. I appreciate your offers, though. It helps to know you're there for me." She pushed the half-full plate away from her and swallowed the last of her juice. "I guess I should get cleaned up, go home, and start some laundry and whatnot. I'll see you both tomorrow."

Nausea swept over Lily as she showered and changed for the day. Stephen played independently, if not quietly, on the bed with the little truck she gave him and she put up a prayer of thanks as she hurried through her morning routine. Before she left to return home, Denise brought her a house key. "Keep it. You're welcome here any time."

"Thanks." Lily blinked back tears and forced a smile. "I appreciate it."

CHAPTER THREE

Lily walked back into her home to the sound of the phone ringing. She dumped her bags on the floor and pulled Stephen in behind her, then hurried to pick up the phone before it went to voice mail. "Hello," she said, breathless.

"Hello, is this the Drake residence? Is this Lily Drake?" a woman's voice asked.

"Yes. Can I help you?"

"This is Carly Simson with Channel 5 News, and I wondered if I could ask you a few questions about your husband's alleged activities."

Lily felt her stomach drop, and she gripped the edge of the kitchen counter. The media knew about John's arrest. And they had her name and number. "I have no statement." Not giving the woman a chance for a rebuttal, she hung up the phone, closing her eyes in despair.

Everyone was going to know. Everyone. How could she explain it to others when she didn't understand herself?

"Mommy, pway outside?" Stephen asked, tugging on her pant leg.

Opening her eyes, she put on a smile that felt like plastic and looked down at her son. "Not now, sweetie. In a little while." Stephen loved to play in his sandbox while she worked in the yard, and the weather was still nice. Needing a distraction, Lily flipped on the television to a local station and let the morning show fill the silence.

She remembered the meat had been marinating since the previous morning. Hoping the flavor wouldn't be too strong, Lily emptied the liquid from the bag of steaks, then returned the bag to the fridge and took stock of the other ingredients. The potatoes were ready to pop in the oven, and the cheesecake was done and sitting in the sub-zero refrigerator's top shelf, a masterpiece waiting to be devoured. She hoped the extra time wouldn't affect the flavor.

She glanced at the answering machine and saw several messages waiting for her. The caller ID told her they were mostly news agencies, so she decided to put off listening to them.

Lily turned back and looked at the long island of butcher block and the gleaming copper pans hanging above it. If she were forced to leave the house, what would she be allowed to take with her? What would the government confiscate to cover John's fraud debts?

A news blurb came on the television, drawing Lily's attention. "This Highland man was arrested last night for alleged identity theft. Learn more on the news at noon." John's face flashed across the screen, and Lily felt her knees grow weak. She turned the television off and wrapped Stephen in his winter coat. She had to get out of the house.

Once in the privacy of the back yard, Lily took her frustration out by trimming back the rose bushes and Russian Sage and clearing away yard debris.

When Lily arrived at church the next day, she slid into her seat in sacrament meeting just as the opening song began to play. After the meeting ended, she hurried off to leave Stephen in nursery and then hid in the bathroom until her class was beginning before she took a back seat.

All the while, she remembered seeing John's face on the television screen the previous evening when she had been unable to quell her morbid curiosity and had decided to watch the segment and see what they would say. The details had been sketchy in the program, but her whole ward had to know about it by now.

She knew she shouldn't be embarrassed; she hadn't been involved in his activities—hadn't, in fact, had even the tiniest glimmer that he might be doing something illegal. But this knowledge didn't clear her conscience but rather made her feel guilty. And stupid. How could she have been so blind? She kept her eyes on her scriptures and refused to glance up to see if others looked at her.

When she arrived in Relief Society, she noticed a few furtive glances in her direction. Some women whispered, peered at her, and then looked away. Lily had to tell herself to stop being paranoid. Still, she sat along the aisle in case she needed a quick escape.

The Relief Society president, a blonde woman only a few years older than Lily, greeted her and took the seat beside her. "Lily, I'm so sorry to hear about your husband. Is there anything we can do for you?"

Feeling a muscle twitch in her cheek, Lily tried to put on a smile. "How did you hear?"

"It was in all the papers this morning. There isn't any truth to it, is there?"

A glance told Lily several women were straining to hear and not being very subtle about it. "Since I haven't read the newspaper, I'm not sure what they said." She felt her fingernails dig into her palms and the heat of a deep blush on her face.

The woman put a hand over Lily's and gave it a gentle squeeze. "Know if you need anything, you can come to me. I'll be happy to do what I can for you."

"Thank you." Lily blinked back tears and felt relief swamp her as the woman stood and returned to the front. When she looked around the room a few minutes later, she could see the speculation in people's eyes. It was a relief when, shortly after the opening song, the nursery leader brought Stephen in for a diaper change, so Lily was able to get up and leave the room.

She didn't go back.

The phone rang like crazy that afternoon until she took it off the hook, but she wasn't able to reach her family. It was well into the afternoon before Lily remembered her parents had taken advantage of the school holiday to go visit Rich's family in California and then head down the coast to Disneyland that week.

She was undecided whether she should bother them with her news when they were on vacation. It had been ages since her parents had been able to go on a nice trip, and her two youngest sisters had talked about it for months. She knew that wasn't what stopped her, however. They were out of state, and no one would tell them before they returned home. Maybe by then she would have a plan. Or, better yet, she could wake up and find the whole thing was a bad dream.

"Don't be stupid," she muttered under her breath as she dialed her Aunt Charlotte's house in San Jose. When she learned her family had already left, Lily chatted with her aunt for a bit before ending the call and dialing her dad's cell phone. He didn't always carry the phone, and rarely checked his voice mail, but she left a message, and hoped he would get around to it soon.

When the doorbell rang several hours later, Lily was relieved to find Denise, Rich, and Curtis on the other side, rather than some curious neighbor or enterprising reporter. With a tiny shake of her head, Lily pushed the thought away and welcomed everyone into her home. "Please, ignore the mess. Stephen's been running wild while I worked in the kitchen."

"Then Cameron will feel right at home." Denise set her son down beside Stephen and handed him a little truck. The two boys began making engine noises.

Curtis looked at the food on the coffee table as he folded his six-foot-seven-inch frame onto one of her sofas. "Do you always lay a spread like this? If so, we've been having far too many of our activities at Denise's." He ducked and grinned when Denise reached out and bumped his shoulder with her fist.

"You better watch out or I won't invite you over ever again," Denise told her brother.

Lily smiled despite herself. She loved watching the siblings when they got together. It was obvious how much they enjoyed each other. It was even more pronounced whenever Curtis's twin joined them. "You just got lucky this time. Cream-cheese herbed Melba toast and stuffed mushrooms were on John's list of favorites. I had them ready for his . . . business dinner." She had lost steam by the time she reached the end of the sentence. She didn't really need the reminder of why she had all this food sitting around.

Everyone looked a little uncomfortable, but when Lily's gaze strayed to Curtis, he nodded. "I was sorry to hear about everything."

"Yeah, me too." When she felt her eyes glossing over with tears, she excused herself to the kitchen to check on dinner.

"Can I help?" she heard a few minutes later.

Lily looked up in surprise, pausing as she flipped over the steaks. She expected to see Denise or maybe Rich in here offering assistance, but she never thought Curtis would volunteer. "No, the table's set and the pota-toes and veggies are ready."

"And you have the steak well in hand." He moved further into the room and leaned back against the counter.

Though she'd never considered herself especially short, her five-foot six-inch height felt tiny when she stood beside him. "Yeah. I appreciate the offer, though. I heard your game went well last night, exciting down to the last minute. Nice job."

He grinned at her. "Thanks." He glanced around the room, and Lily saw it through his eyes, remembering what she thought the first time she walked through it.

A cook's paradise. Chrome gleamed, sunlight streamed from big banks of windows, and twin sinks deep enough to soak half a dozen pans flanked the island stove top.

She loved the kitchen more than the showy elegance of the great room. All of the crystal and antiques were nice, but the kitchen was more efficient and useful.

"It's a nice place." He shoved his hands in his pockets and watched her.

Lily shrugged. "Yeah." *I wish I still believed John had earned it.* As that thought was too depressing to continue, she changed the subject. "Well, this'll be ready any minute." She turned to the twin ovens on the wall behind her and opened the top one. After slipping on an oven mitt, she dropped the baked potatoes into the china bowl nearby and handed it to him. "Could you set that on the table and let Denise and Rich know we'll be ready soon?"

He grinned. "Dismissed. I'll see you in a bit then." He took the dish and walked out.

Lily found herself smiling as she turned off the stove top.

After working around the house in quiet desperation, Lily finally managed to track down Agent Melton on Monday afternoon to arrange a meeting. When she walked into the reception area, the man at the front desk took her straight back to the agent's office.

"Mrs. Drake." Agent Melton stood to shake her hand. "Have you learned anything, thought of anything that might help us?"

She lifted her brows and settled Stephen on what remained of her lap with a book, praying he would read quietly for a few minutes. She ached all over but was determined to ignore the discomfort. "Not really. I wondered if there have been any new developments and what I should expect for the future—my future, Stephen's, the baby's."

"We're trying to get your husband to agree to a plea bargain. I think he's got information that could help us stop the person who sold him the identities. If the information's good enough, we might get him worked down to three or four years' confinement before his first parole hearing. If he plea-bargains, it could cut your time in your house short a bit, maybe down to a couple months."

"I can't even afford the utilities right now." She ran a hand through her hair and tried to keep her head from reeling. There was too much to figure out. She was completely overwhelmed. She pressed her fingers to her eyes, then looked back at him.

"You'll be allowed to take a few pieces of furniture with you. We took pictures of everything in the house on Friday before you arrived, so we'll know if you sell or take off with anything valuable, but the kid's crib and stuff will probably be granted you by the court. We're not out to ruin you, though I imagine it feels that way. You brought some furniture and things into the marriage with you, didn't you?"

"Very little, and we've gotten rid of most of it. I was a starving college student, and most of my stuff was secondhand. I wouldn't worry so much about starting over if it was just me." She rubbed her cheek over Stephen's silken head. She straightened and asked, "What about John? I'd like to see him. He hasn't even called. When I contacted the jail this morning, they told me I wasn't cleared to visit, either."

His gaze softened as he looked at her. "Clearance for calls takes time. It's a process that has to be initiated by the inmate, and then you'll put money into an account for him to use to place the calls. I would think a visit would be easier at this point."

"But they won't let me in. Can you help me?"

"What about his lawyer?"

"No one will even tell me who it is." Her frustration grew. Everyone was trying to pawn her off on someone else. Why wouldn't someone just help her?

He pressed his lips together and flipped through some papers. After jotting something down, he handed her a sticky note. "This is the name of the law firm he's using. You'll have to call and see what they'll tell you. I don't have jurisdiction over the jail, but I'll see what I can do." He spoke a bit more about what to expect on the proceedings and promised he would try and arrange for her to see John as soon as possible but he told her not to hold her breath.

She left the office more frustrated than when she'd arrived.

CHAPTER FOUR

Lily lived in a fog. Taking care of Stephen kept her grounded, but she could hardly think past the shock of her life twisting out of control. She stayed home and wallowed. She told herself she was going to sort through the boxes the FBI had left in the basement to separate out her things from John's. Mostly she just sat on the couch while Stephen played and a series of Disney movies blasted in the background.

This was how her bishop found her Tuesday evening when he appeared on her doorstep. Lily was embarrassed by her messy hair and voluminous sweatshirt—though at this point in her pregnancy most everything she wore was huge. Still, she smiled woodenly at the tall, graying man and directed him to a seat in the parlor while she collected Stephen from the great room.

Toddler under one arm, Lily shoved a lock of hair back from her face and sat across from the bishop. She settled Stephen next to her on the floor. "So what brings you here today?" she asked with forced brightness.

"Lily, I apologize for not getting here sooner. I've been out of town the past couple of days. I wanted to see how you're doing. Knowing the situation you're in, I wondered if there was something I could do for you. What's going on?"

There was little Lily wanted to discuss less than her husband's activities. Still, she felt it necessary to give her bishop the highlights. When she finished, she retrieved Stephen from the hall where he had pushed his fire engine. "I don't know exactly what to do. I can't focus yet, but I've been told I've got some time to figure things out."

"And what about your marriage? Have you talked about your future plans with John?"

She played with her fingernails, focusing on anything but his face. "I still haven't spoken with him. He hasn't called or written, and it takes a while to get clearance to visit an inmate." That word still left a nasty taste in her mouth. *Inmate.* Her husband was an inmate. "I have no idea what I'm going to do. My parents have recently moved into a tiny apartment while they build their new house. There's definitely no room there. They've been out of town this week on vacation, but they're supposed to return in a couple of days."

"And John's family? Can you turn to them for help?"

Stephen stood and held his arms out to Lily, asking to be picked up. She sighed and pulled him onto her lap. "His dad knew before I did, and I haven't heard a word from either of his parents. We've never been close, but I'm sure they're struggling to deal with everything. I'm not counting on any help from them, though I suppose they might surprise me." *Unlikely,* she thought. They had never seemed to like her, not from the first time John introduced them. And they hadn't returned her calls yet.

His brows lifted, but he didn't comment on it. "And how are you set financially?"

Untangling Stephen's hand from her hair as he got fussy and tugged on it, Lily held in the groan she wanted to let out. "The government has frozen everything with his name on it. I have nine hundred dollars in my personal checking account. That's it. My car's in my name, so I should be able to sell it, but I don't know what I owe or what it's worth. I could be totally upside down on the loan. I have no idea. The house and most of the contents will be sold by the courts. No point worrying about the mortgage when I don't actually own the house anymore and can't sell it—not to mention the fact that I don't have enough money to make a single payment. With my food storage, the money in my account should last six, maybe eight weeks if I'm lucky."

"Just long enough for your baby to be born."

"Yeah. Maybe by then I'll have some idea what I want to do about everything. I'm so torn." Tears began to flow, and Lily turned around, pulling a tissue from the box on the table behind her. "I believe in my covenants, but do I stand by someone who could do this? Do I know him at all? I'm still in shock. I can't figure out what I should cook for dinner tonight, never mind the course of my future."

"It's admirable that you take your marriage vows so seriously. I advise you to wait for now. You don't have to make any firm decisions tonight. I want you to consider your options, your job skills, what you need to get by. Pray, read your scriptures, and see what answers come to you. How about if you come by my office Sunday evening, say six-thirty?"

The phone rang Thursday morning, and a glance at the caller ID showed her parents' number. Finally. "Hello, Mom."

"Lily, what's this I heard? Someone sent us a link to the newspaper online. What happened?" Darlene Cox sounded more than a little frazzled.

Lily broke into tears and told her mother everything from the moment she found the FBI agents in her home to her conversation with Agent Melton earlier that week. She wondered about the cell phone, then learned her father had forgotten to bring the charging cord.

"Honey, how are you going to pay for everything? You should come home while you try to get on your feet again."

"Mom, I appreciate your concern, but you have a two-bedroom apartment and four people living there. There's no room for me and Stephen right now, never mind the baby."

The call resolved nothing, but at least Lily felt better when she hung up more than an hour later.

Lily took Stephen to church again Sunday but only stayed for sacrament meeting. The pointed looks and hurried whispers she caught were enough to send her heading home when the first meeting ended. She couldn't stay there. She doubted the people in her neighborhood were trying to be mean, but they didn't really know her.

Part of that was because she held herself back, feeling out of place in the posh neighborhood. Another part was John's insistence that she be home when he called, expecting her to take care of everything he needed, when he needed it. That had isolated her from her family and friends— whether it had been his intention or not. Over the past week she started to wonder if it had been his plan all along.

John's constant harping on her minor inadequacies made Lily more dependent on him, reducing her feelings of self-sufficiency. She hadn't noticed it at the time, but now she looked into the future and saw nothing but question marks. She wondered what happened to the self-assured college student she had been before she met John. Had she been over-confident of her abilities before?

On Monday she managed to reach Agent Melton on the phone. When she asked for any news, he said, "Your husband has worked out a plea bargain."

Lily gripped the phone tightly in her hands, her knuckles turning white. "What does that mean, exactly?"

"His court date for the hearing has been moved up. He'll go before the judge in a couple weeks. At that time, the judge will set another date for sentencing about a month out. After sentencing, all of the frozen assets will likely be seized. You'll want to make alternate living arrangements before then. I'm sorry."

"Yeah, me too." Six weeks until sentencing. Well, since she wouldn't be taking much with her, she wouldn't have to worry about packing up the whole house. That was a good thing, considering her aching back and swelling ankles—never mind her bulging middle. Yet she still felt overwhelmed. Now the question was where to move and how she would pay her bills. Who was going to hire a woman who was seven months pregnant? If only she could speak with John.

"There's one more thing. Your husband has chosen to refuse the bail his parents offered to pay."

That brought her attention back from her own troubles. "What? Why? Why would he do that?"

"It happens sometimes. Maybe he doesn't want to face people. The man seems to be very wrapped up in appearances. Due to recent media coverage, he won't be able to return to a normal life between now and sentencing. Also his time now will count toward the total, so maybe he's just trying to get it over with. He might be counting on county jail being better than the federal prison they'll send him to."

"Right," Lily said, though she hardly knew what she thought of the agent's theory. She wanted to talk to John—needed to talk to him. He still hadn't contacted her, and she didn't know where to go from there. "Have you made any headway in getting me in to see him?"

"Yes, clearance should go through in a day or two. You'll get a notice in the mail, along with directions."

"Thanks, Agent Melton. I appreciate it."

After she hung up, Lily leaned back against the kitchen counter. That was it: six weeks and she would be homeless. John hadn't bothered to contact her in all the time he'd been in jail, though Agent Melton told her he could have if he wanted to. She had sent him the letter she wrote that first night, along with a second one, but hadn't received a response. Now it would still be two more days—maybe longer—before she could talk to him. Why wouldn't he write her, call, or something? Was she really so unimportant? Were his children so unimportant that she didn't rate any contact?

Her whole life was being turned upside down, and her husband, the man who had promised to protect and love her for eternity, didn't even have the decency to write her back. Feeling helpless, Lily threw the extra pillows from the sofa across the room, one after the other in quick succession. She felt a gleam of satisfaction when one hit a curio and there was the slight tinkling of glass as the items inside jiggled slightly. Out of ammunition, she crumpled onto the sofa and buried her face into a pillow as sobs tore through her. She beat on the cushions repeatedly, wishing she could take out her aggression on the person responsible for her pain.

Tuesday morning Lily decided it was time she took charge of her life, instead of sitting back and pretending it would all go away. The first big hurdle for the day would be getting a key to the mailbox and emptying it. John always checked it at the post office and had never seen a need to give her a key. She hardly ever got mail anyway, and he took care of all the bills. Now she understood why he wanted to be the one to collect the mail.

The woman at the front desk of the post office handed over her letters and promised to have a key ready for Lily by Monday. When Lily returned home, she began checking through the scant paperwork left behind by the FBI to see what bills she needed to take care of. After an hour of searching through her mail in tears, she gave up and called Denise.

"Hey, how are you doing today?" Denise asked when she picked up. They had been in nearly constant contact since John's arrest.

"I need a favor. I have no idea what bills I need to take care of, what creditors I owe money to, or if my car even has a loan on it. I know they have those free credit report agencies, but I don't have a computer anymore, and I don't know where to start." How had she ever let her life get so out of control? Shouldn't she know who they paid regularly, where they owed money?

"No problem. Hold on a minute."

Lily heard clicking with a few pauses, and then Denise started asking for her social security number and other pertinent information.

"Holy cow!" Denise said after a moment. "Hold on—I'm adding all of this up. You mentioned he had taken out credit cards in your name, but I had no idea."

"Do you see anything that looks like a car loan on there?" Lily asked as she schlumped into the kitchen to look for something chocolate. This was not what she needed.

"No, though I could be wrong. Did you sign paperwork for the car loan?"

"No, but I didn't sign on any of those credit card forms, either, so that hardly makes a difference." Lily dug into the baking cupboard and found a bag of chocolate chips. A moment later she opened it with a knife and dropped a couple of sweet morsels in her mouth. It wouldn't compare to a Lindt truffle, or a Dove chocolate bar, but the chips did qualify as chocolate, so they would have to do, since nothing else happened to be handy at the moment. "Can you print it all off for me? I'll swing by there later and pick the papers up. I suppose I should contact someone about our utility bills too."

"So what are you going to do about the car?" Denise asked.

"I'm not sure. Maybe I'll contact the lot where John bought it and see if they have any record of who they sent the title to." She tossed another small handful of chocolate chips into her mouth.

"Let me know if you need anything else," Denise said.

"Yeah, thanks." Lily hung up, then pulled out the phone book. She paused for a moment and then decided she needed to get out of the house. Besides, she would be less likely to get the run around if she showed up at the dealership in person. Maybe they would take pity on the poor little pregnant woman.

Fifteen minutes later, she pulled into a parking space at the car lot where the Lexus had been purchased. She took the registration papers in with her—just in case there was any question about which vehicle it was. Stephen had been clingy and whiney all day. Actually, he had been more clingy than usual since a day or two after John's arrest. He missed his father. *And isn't that lovely, since John won't be returning anytime soon?* she thought gloomily.

All of the employees seemed busy when she walked in, but after wandering for a moment, she found someone on the phone at a desk. She hung back until he ended the call, then approached with a smile. "Hi, I have a question."

The balding older man smiled up at her. "Yes, I'm Larry. How can I help you?"

Lily held tight to Stephen's hand and walked closer to the desk. She would have sat in the chair provided but was afraid of not being able to stand again. "I have an odd request. My husband bought a car for me here last spring, and well . . ." How did one ask this? "I need to know if you would have kept a record of whom you sent the title to. I don't know which bank provided the loan, so I'm not sure where to make my next payment."

He gave her a puzzled look. "You don't know who the lien-holder is?"

"My husband is . . . unavailable at the moment, and I really need to know who to contact about making payments. I brought in the registration paperwork. Can you track it according to the VIN number?" She gave him her most pathetic pregnant woman expression and saw his resolve begin to crumble.

"Well, yes, but I can't give that information out to just anyone. Do you have identification?"

She produced her ID, which was quite a feat to do one-handed, but Stephen seemed determined to make a break for it if she let go of him. When Larry compared the registration information and ID and saw they were both her, he nodded and headed for a computer terminal in the next room.

Several minutes passed as Lily allowed Stephen to drag her around part of the show room. When the man returned, he smiled broadly. "Good news for you. He paid cash for that transaction, so there is no loan. Unless he's used it as collateral since he took it home, you own the car free and clear."

That was a relief, anyway. "Oh, that's so kind of you to check for me. Thank you so much!" She scooped Stephen up and adjusted her purse strap over her shoulder. "I really appreciate it." She took the registration paperwork back from him and hurried out the door. So she owned the car—of course, she had no idea what it was worth, and she had credit card bills she never knew about before to take care of, but this was something, anyway. She would need to call and verify when the next insurance payment was due, but that was for another day.

Half an hour later she studied the sheets Denise had printed off for her. It was worse than she expected. As she uncovered the truth, the lies John had been telling her piled on top of each other until Lily felt like she was suffocating. When would the nasty revelations end?

CHAPTER FIVE

"What did you say to my son to convince him to stay in that horrible place?"

That was the first thing Lily heard when she opened the front door on Thursday afternoon. Elizabeth Drake—not Liz, never Eliza, and certainly not Beth—wore a sour expression and one of her standard dress suits in a muted shade of plum. She clutched her Louis Vuitton purse in her perfectly manicured hands.

Holding back a sigh, Lily gestured for her mother-in-law to come in and followed her to the sofa set. She was surprised to see the woman—despite Lily's having left a couple of messages on their phone. There had been no contact from either Elizabeth or her husband, Ross, since the arrest.

"I haven't spoken with John at all," Lily began, "nor has he responded to my letters or questions through his attorney. I have no idea what his reasons are. When I see him, I can try and ask him for you if you like."

Elizabeth picked up Stephen and pressed her lips to his cheek, then deposited him on her lap before turning back to her daughter-in-law. "What do you mean you haven't spoken to him? You're his wife."

"Yes, but he has to initiate calls—something he hasn't done. If you're even receiving information through his attorney, you're doing better than I am." Lily's tone showed more bitterness than she intended. Taking a deep breath, she tried again. "I'm working on a face-to-face visit with him. The FBI agent who came here is helping me get in to speak with him, since John's attorney isn't working with me at all. I understand you haven't seen him either." She watched Stephen wiggling, trying to get away while Elizabeth's mouth firmed into a frown, and Lily braced herself for a temper tantrum. One would think Elizabeth would know that toddlers were wiggly.

"No, we haven't seen him, but we spoke to him on the phone. John called us twice in the past week. We had to provide money for the calls too." Elizabeth's eyes narrowed. "What, did you two have a fight? What kind of demands did you make this time?"

Lily bit back her anger, and the hurt that speared through her that John had called his parents but not his wife. How could he ignore her? She ground her teeth together as Stephen began to wail. "No, we didn't fight."

Elizabeth looked down at Stephen in disdain and released him to the floor with an expression that said he was an ingrate—never mind the fact that two-year-olds tend to forget people they rarely see, and it had been months since his grandparents had bothered to stop by. "I suppose now my son isn't around to bring his children by for visits, I'll never see them. Stephen's my only grandchild, you know." She sent the defecting grandson a dirty look as he ran up to his mom. "I'd like to see the baby when it's born too."

Lily bit back the resentment the words brought up and heaved Stephen onto her lap. "Not that you've ever made an effort to come see Stephen, but I'm not stopping you from visiting your grandchildren. I'm sure they'll need to have you around sometimes. If you'll let me know when we can come by, I'll do what I can."

Elizabeth's eyes flicked over Lily. "Of course you will." Her tone stated otherwise. "Just like you always accepted our invitations to dinner and other family gatherings. Don't think I'm going to simply forgive and forget your past behavior." She stood. "And don't think for a moment that you're going to squeeze one penny out of us. You may have sweet-talked my son into fraud to satisfy your never-ending need to have the best, but we're not so easily taken in."

"I have no idea what you're taking about. *Your* invitations? What about my invitations to you? You never came over when I invited you." She lifted a hand to stop her mother-in-law from interrupting her. "And don't start me on John's actions. Your son made all of his choices without any help from me. The pressure to prove himself started long before he and I ever met." She threw a significant look at her mother-in-law.

"Well, I never!" Elizabeth grasped her purse more tightly in her hands and then stormed out of the house.

Lily watched her mother-in-law go and wondered what on earth had gotten into Elizabeth. What invitations? And how dare she accuse Lily of being responsible for John's behavior?

The jail parking lot was mostly empty when Lily pulled into it on Friday afternoon. Her hands opened and closed as she approached the front door, hurrying past the rows of marigolds smiling brightly from either side of the sidewalk.

She walked through the front door to brown brick walls and red industrial carpeting. A metal detector sat just inside the door. Lily pulled her keys from her pocket, placed them in the bowl to the right, and then walked through and picked them up on the other side. She told the woman at the desk who she was, gave John's full name and inmate number, and then handed the woman her driver's license.

Lily rubbed her lower back while she waited. There were nearly two months left in her pregnancy, and she was already counting down the weeks until her swollen ankles and aching back would feel better. Her back pain had been growing in strength throughout the day, and now she was barely able to ignore the discomfort.

After a few minutes' wait, Lily was ushered into a small room with a chair set against a partition with a window. Another chair sat on the other side. There would be no physical contact with her husband. She wondered how private the conversation would actually be but decided she had so little to lose that it didn't matter.

It wasn't a long wait before an officer brought John in, wearing a white jumpsuit. The officer left them alone, saying he'd be in the other room and to call when she was ready to go.

John looked her up and down, his lips thinning in irritation. He was freshly shaven and his hair was combed, but he was still not as polished as usual. "How's the baby? Are you taking care of it?" His voice came through the sides of the window, though the trim didn't look like it should carry the sound that well.

Lily took a seat at the counter and motioned for him to do the same. "I'm taking care of myself just fine. The baby's fine." The man she had once been able to talk to so easily stood in front of her now, but she had no idea what to say to him.

John rolled his eyes and sat. "Why are you here?"

She blinked. Wasn't it obvious? "Did you really rack up all that debt in other people's names?" It was the only thing she could think to ask.

His response was a sigh and a bored look. "I pled guilty, didn't I? Do I seem like the kind of person who'd take a fall for someone else?" He paused a moment, then answered the question foremost on her mind. "It started out as a game, just to see if I could get away with it. I made the first few credit card payments, then decided to see how high the company would let me go." He smirked at her. "Pretty far, actually." It was a boast as much as anything. He didn't seem the least bit sorry about it.

"You don't feel guilty about messing with someone's credit like that? Many people's credit, it sounds like. How could you do that?" All of the hope inside her seemed to shrivel up. Didn't he understand that what he had done was wrong?

He looked almost bored as he settled back in the chair. It made a scraping sound against the floor as he shifted. "It was easy. I stuck to children and never used the name of any child over the age of six. I figured by the time they turned eighteen, any credit problems I caused would be wiped off and no one would ever know." He leaned forward and tipped his head to the side, one of his signature charming smiles sliding into place. "No kid was hurt by what I did; I was careful not to hurt anyone."

"Nice justification." She knew the disgust was evident in her voice and didn't care. *Children. He used children. And he doesn't feel the least bit sorry about what he's done.* "And how did you get your hands on all of that stuff? Some of those names were female."

He smiled again, obviously pleased with his own cunning. "The Internet is an amazing thing, you know. I realize you are far too puritan to ever come up with a plan like this yourself. I couldn't let you know how valuable some of those pretty trinkets I brought home were, and I certainly couldn't have them delivered to the house. I had accounts at every UPS Store within thirty miles. They took the shipments, and I signed for them when I picked the package up. The whole process was simple. I could have done it for years if I hadn't tripped a time or two." He sighed. "It was sloppy of me."

Her stomach was tying in a knot to match the growing ache in her back. "And the sofa set? That wasn't a gift from your parents, was it?"

"No, I took cash advances from a couple credit cards, then paid the remaining few hundred with our own money. It looked aboveboard enough to the store." He got a wistful look on his face. "I miss that television. The one here's a joke. Do you think federal facilities take donations?"

Lily stood and turned away, but she couldn't take more than a step in the tiny room. She wasn't ready yet to leave but couldn't stand looking at him any longer. What was wrong with him? Didn't he get it? This wasn't a joke, it wasn't a game. It was fraud, it was stealing—it was federal prison for him and penury for her. She would be left with next to nothing. Hadn't he considered how this would affect their son and their unborn child? She placed a hand on her stomach and rolled her shoulders; the stress was getting to her.

"Come on, Lily. You can't say you didn't enjoy the way we lived. All that money was making life run awfully smooth. You loved the big house and fancy kitchen, the beautiful yard and pretty trinkets every bit as much as I did."

She whirled back to him. "Trinkets are little miniatures of monuments you buy in gift shops and key chains that say 'I love New York.' A three-thousand-dollar pair of candlesticks does not qualify." She was dumbfounded at his attitude. "I admit I enjoyed having beautiful things. My parents' house was cramped for six, but it was fun. We didn't need to have a lot to be happy. I would rather live in a cardboard box than live like a queen on someone else's money."

He rolled his eyes. "Those credit card companies make millions of dollars off of Joe Schmoes like your parents every year. So we got a little of it funneled our way. It's not like it hurt anyone. I'll do my time and let the government pay for my education. Although I won't be able to do real estate anymore." He pressed his lips together, obviously resigned to reality. He glanced back up at her and tilted his head. "And you'll do what you need to do. I wish you luck."

Lily's knees felt weak and she slid back into the chair. "You wish me luck?"

He rolled his eyes. "It was a fun ride, Lils, but seriously, the bloom's been off the flower for some time now—surely you've noticed." John tapped his fingertip on the small counter in front of him. "I want regular pictures and updates on the children. They're still my kids, but you're never going to fully forgive me. And frankly, I'm tired of being bored."

"Bored?" It was a knife to the heart. The pain in her chest was even stronger than that in her back. Her lungs tightened, and she was unable to take a full breath.

"Out of my mind. I already talked to my attorney. Expect him to bring over the divorce paperwork sometime in the next week. You'll get all of the assets, of course."

"Assets?" Disbelief ran through her. This had to be a joke!

"What, is there an echo in here? Assets. You know, valuable goods. And you call yourself a college graduate. It's a good thing you never became a real teacher. You're obviously not any brighter than the average first grader." He looked her up and down again, this time with a condescending air. "Weren't much of a society wife, either, actually."

As if he hadn't made that painfully clear on a regular basis. She closed her eyes to block off the pain his words thrust into her with every turn. Sucking in a breath as her anger took over, she counted to ten and then glared at him. "There are no assets, you idiot. Do you honestly think the government is going to let me keep one thing you own when it was purchased with stolen money? The only asset in my name is my car—which, I might add, I'm going to have to sell to pay the credit card debt you racked up in my name without my even knowing you had applied for the cards.

"The house, furniture, every account that ever had your name on it has been frozen to pay back your debts. After buying diapers, groceries, and putting gas in the car since you were arrested, I have seven hundred dollars to my name. Seven hundred to start a new life with your children—and you dare speak of assets."

"Don't get all bent out of shape. A sweet little Mormon girl like you shouldn't have trouble finding a new husband. You've already proved you're fertile and a passable housekeeper." He looked no more than irritated by her fury. "I'm sure your parents will come through until then. They'll have that big new house soon."

Ignoring his snide comments on her likelihood of remarrying, she reminded him, "My parents and two sisters are living in a two-bedroom apartment that's smaller than the great room and kitchen of that monstrosity we live in. There's no room for us. Your parents blame me for your being here, so they won't help. And that reminds me, what is this about invitations we didn't accept?"

He ignored the last question. "You said you'd rather live in a cardboard box. I guess you're about to get your wish." He smirked at her.

Lily reflected that it was probably a good thing there was a sheet of glass between them; she had never wanted to throttle anyone so much in her life. This was their family he was talking about. How could he be so blasé about the whole thing? "I never knew you at all, did I?"

He sighed. "We have different agendas, Lily. I wish I'd realized that before we married. I wish you the best of luck. Don't forget to send pictures and updates on the kids."

Lily shot out of her chair, swore, and whirled around to the door. Tears stung her eyes, but she wasn't showing him one more moment of weakness.

She couldn't remember walking from the visiting booth to her car, but when the tears stopped falling, she vowed never to cry over him again. Then she bent over the steering wheel as another bout of sobbing overtook her.

CHAPTER SIX

Lily's eyes were gritty when she went to bed that night. Whenever Denise was upset, she found solace in cleaning, and after returning from the jail, Lily had taken a page from Denise's book. She'd spent several hours cleaning and organizing the house, and the ache in her back had grown stronger through the day until she fell into bed at eight, exhausted and praying for some relief.

When her water broke half an hour later, Lily realized relief wasn't in her immediate future. She groaned as a contraction ripped through her, and she fumbled for the phone by her bedside.

Denise sounded half asleep when she answered the phone but soon became more alert as she realized what was going on. "I'll be there in twenty minutes," Denise promised. Even at that time of night, the drive from Orem to Highland would take at least that long.

When another contraction ripped through Lily, she changed her mind. It had only been a couple of minutes since the last one. "I don't think I have that much time, and I can't drive myself. I'm calling an ambulance. Meet me at Utah Valley?"

"I'll be there. Let me know if they take you somewhere else. See you soon." Denise hung up and Lily called 911. Once the ambulance had been dispatched, she made her way down the hall, clutching at the walls as she crossed to Stephen's room and threw a few things into the diaper bag. She was not ready. *It's too soon*, her mind screamed. But there was little she could do but hold on until the EMTs arrived.

Red and white lights flashed through the window as the ambulance pulled silently in front of her house a few minutes later. Lily crossed to the front door and let the paramedics in to load her on the gurney.

Stephen's cries filled the ambulance as they weaved through traffic to Utah Valley Regional Medical Center in Provo—the only hospital in the area with a neonatal ICU. Lily couldn't reach out to her son where he sat in the child seat behind her head, but she watched one of the paramedics talk to him and try to distract him from the noise and confusion. The effort went unappreciated by the toddler.

Worry washed through Lily as she wondered what was going to happen. Her baby was still six weeks early. It was far too soon. She knew they couldn't stop the delivery now that her water had broken, but would her child be okay? Even with the miracles of modern medicine, babies died every day—and her mother wouldn't be there with her this time around.

Denise was in the ER when the ambulance arrived. "How are you doing?" she asked Lily. She took Stephen from the male paramedic who happily handed the crying child over.

"Never been better," Lily said with a grimace as another wave of pain crested over her.

"I'll take Stephen to the car. Rich and Cam will take him home tonight. We've already called your parents. I'll be right back," Denise said.

"Hurry." Lily panted as the pain subsided again on the other side of the contraction. The gurney was rushed down the hall toward delivery.

The doctor came into delivery right behind Denise and checked Lily out. "Looks like you're nearly there. Have you been taking shots to make the baby's lungs develop faster?"

"No, my son was born two weeks late. This pregnancy has been going along normal enough until now." At her last appointment, the doctor had mentioned she seemed stressed and needed to take things easy, but she hadn't thought about it again since. Stress had pummeled her from every side. Why hadn't she even thought about how it was affecting her baby? Was she so caught up in her own life that she could ignore her child's needs?

"It's all my fault," she muttered under her breath as the doctor spoke in low tones to a nurse who had just entered the room.

"Hey, hold on, everything's going to be all right," Denise told her, pushing back the hair from Lily's sweaty forehead. "You're in a great hospital. They'll take good care of you and the baby."

As another contraction pulsed through her, Lily gritted her teeth and prayed Denise was right.

The next day, Lily lay in the hospital bed when Denise came in. "Hello! How's the new mommy doing today?" Denise asked as she set a cheerful vase of daisies and alstroemeria on the side table.

"Better. It was easier than with Stephen—you know, if you overlook the terror of giving birth nearly two months early and the worry about my baby lying in the NICU with tubes and monitors covering her whole body."

"Your daughter *is* half the size of Stephen when he was born, so the actual delivery should have been a little easier." Denise opened a bag she'd brought with her and pulled out a brush and small makeup kit. Obviously she was going to overlook Lily's sarcastic comment. "I thought you'd be in there with her now."

"They kicked me out for a little while. Nurse rotation or something."

Denise nodded and picked up the brush. "Stephen and Cam are having a ball together."

Guilt swamped Lily when she thought of her little boy at someone else's house, and it got even worse when she thought of her new daughter, Sophie, lying alone in the Neonatal Intensive Care Unit. "Good, I hope he's behaving for you." The words sounded listless, even to her own ears.

"He builds block towers, Cam knocks them over. If anything, Cam's the troublemaker." She brandished the hair brush. "Now, how about we fix you up before I wheel you down to see your little girl? Any changes since this morning?" Denise nudged Lily into a sitting position and started brushing her hair. Her chatter about their little boys would normally have calmed Lily and set her at ease, but this time it did not. As usual, Denise was quick to notice. "Hey, want to talk?"

Lily covered her mouth with her hand, trying to hold back the worry and anger that threatened to overwhelm her. Tears poured from her eyes, but she managed to clear her throat enough to get words out. "It's my fault my baby is in the NICU right now. If I'd handled the stress of the past week better, if I'd kept a closer eye on what was going on in my own house. If I hadn't been so naïve, so trusting, I wouldn't have been so shocked— John demanded a divorce at our meeting yesterday. I didn't expect it. If I hadn't been so stressed, I wouldn't have gone into early labor."

"You idiot." Denise's voice was soft and affectionate as she gathered Lily in her arms. "It's hardly your fault you trusted your husband. You were supposed to trust him; otherwise, what kind of life would it be? You couldn't have anticipated the things he did or his sudden decision to divorce. Anyone would have responded to the tension. If it was Sophie's time to be born, it would have happened one way or another."

Lily didn't mention the stress she had experienced before the world had shattered around her. Things hadn't been right in her marriage for a long time. John got that part right, at least. "I felt the back labor all day, but I didn't pay attention. If I'd focused and listened to my body, my baby wouldn't be in some artificial womb now. I've made so many mistakes."

Denise moved to look Lily in the eye. "Then it's time you faced your future and tried to rectify those mistakes. First, let's get you fixed up so you feel human. We'll go see your new angel, and then you'll start making plans. Your babies need a home, and it looks like you're the only one who can provide that." As if she'd settled the question, Denise returned to brushing Lily's hair.

A short time later she pushed Lily into the neonatal unit and wheeled the chair over to the incubator where Sophie lay.

Lily couldn't believe how tiny her baby girl was. She looked like a little doll lying in the bed, though the tubes attached to her arms and legs belied the image. There were too many tubes to be able to pick her daughter up, but Lily adjusted the tiny pink cap on Sophie's head and rubbed her fingers over the little girl's face and arms. After a moment, the nurse and Denise moved away, giving Lily some privacy—a move Lily appreciated. Her heart felt full, torn between joy at the precious child she had given birth to and the guilt and anger that still haunted her. The jumbled emotions were an ache in her chest and a lump in her throat that threatened to choke her.

When she had cleared her throat enough to speak, she whispered to her daughter. "You've had a pretty rough time, sweetie, but Mommy promises to do better. It's not going to be easy, but you, your brother, and I are going to be just fine," she promised the sleeping child. "This world must seem confusing with all the light and noise and the activity swirling around you. I think I have an idea how that feels. The doctors say you're really strong and your lungs were pretty well developed, considering how tiny you are. If you do really well, you might be out of here in a few weeks. I know your brother's anxious to have you home." She forced away the question of where that home would be.

Lily sat with her baby for a long while, telling her all about her plans and her family, whispering reassurances while Sophie slept. When she finally let Denise wheel her from the NICU, Lily knew she would do everything possible to provide stability for her children.

Lily stepped out of the elevator onto the ground floor of the hospital and passed the gift shop, headed for the cafeteria. It had been four days since she'd given birth to Sophie. Lily had checked herself out of the hospital the previous day. Now a steady stream of patients and hospital staff poured around her as she dragged her exhausted body to get something to eat.

A smile brightened her face as she saw her younger sister, Shelly, walk in the front doors across the long reception area, carrying a backpack. Lily waved at her sister, who was visiting for the weekend. It was only a moment before Shelly spotted Lily and hurried over. She threw her arms around Lily's shoulders and stood on tiptoe to hold her tight. The fact that Shelly was barely over five feet meant she had to stand on tiptoe for a lot of things. "Hey, how are you holding up? I got here as quickly as I could."

"Thanks for coming. How was your trip?" Lily asked.

Shelly shrugged and adjusted her backpack over her shoulder. "Long. I wish I could have come sooner."

Tears squeezed from Lily's eyes and she wiped them away. "How's Utah State treating you? Are you hungry? I was just going to grab something to eat."

"I'd like that. School's fine, but it's still too cold." Shelly squeezed Lily's upper arm. "Where's the cafeteria?"

They made small talk until they got through the line and then settled with their food at a corner table. "How's Sophie doing?" Shelly asked.

Lily rubbed her eyes. It had been too long since she'd gotten a decent night's sleep. "She's doing really well. The doctor hopes to take her off some of the machines in a few more days. She's so tiny. It makes me sick to think of her lying up there alone, even for the few minutes it takes for me to come eat."

Shelly twisted one frizzy brown lock around her finger. "Where's Stephen through all of this?"

"With Denise. She's been so wonderful to take care of him and a hundred other things this week. Actually, she's been amazing ever since John was arrested." Lily noticed what Shelly was doing to her hair and took a closer look at her sister, taking real note of the change in her appearance. She tried to come up with a tactful way to ask about her hair, then settled on, "Been wearing corn rows lately?"

With a snort, Shelly shook her head. "Unfortunately, no. Remember me telling you I wanted to get a perm? Never again. Look at this frizzy mess!" She gestured to her shoulder-length mop. "It looks like I stuck my finger in an electrical outlet."

Lily couldn't help but laugh at the apt description. When her laughter turned to the familiar burn of tears, she forced it back. "Thanks for coming. I needed you more than I knew. I wish you lived around here."

"You could always move to Logan. Then I'd be nearby to help babysit." Shelly looked hopeful.

Lily smothered some fries in fry sauce and shook her head. "No, it's too far away. I haven't figured out what I want to do yet, but don't start making plans for me."

"You want to stay here?"

"Not really, but . . ." She trailed off, thinking of the funny looks she got at church and even the occasional lifted brow some of the hospital staff displayed when Lily gave her husband's name. She shook her head. She could move home to Ephraim, except it would be nearly as bad there. She'd know everyone and they'd all know what had happened. They would care about her and commiserate, but it wasn't what she wanted. Since she couldn't move in with her parents, it wasn't as though she had free rent as an incentive. Still, Logan . . . ?

"Think it over." Shelly reached into her backpack and pulled out an adorable pink teddy bear with a little note attached to it.

"You're really sweet. I know how tight things are for you." Lily took the bear and nearly sighed at the feel of silky fur between her fingers. The eyes and nose were embroidered on, rather than parts that could fall off, so they were safe for a baby. It was so perfect.

"I'd love to take credit, but Curtis asked me to give it to you."

Pivoting her head in surprise, Lily blinked. "Curtis? Denise's brother, Curtis?"

"Yes, Curtis—the really tall basketball player who lives downstairs from me and is related to Denise," Shelly said with a smile. "He caught me in the halls a couple days ago and asked all casual-like if I was coming down to visit. I said I was. This morning he asked me to give you and Sophie the bear. Since Sophie's probably not allowed to play with toys yet, you'll have to do."

"How thoughtful." Lily ran a finger over the bear's soft face and tried to speak around the lump in her throat.

A couple hours later, the two sisters emerged from the NICU. They stripped off the gowns the hospital required. Lily thought she'd go get Stephen, and maybe they could eat some mac 'n cheese and watch a mind-numbing toddler movie before bedtime. She had felt torn between her two children all week. She wanted to spend every waking minute with Sophie but knew Stephen must be confused and upset to have her gone so much, especially with John's disappearance. "I guess we ought to get home. You probably have stacks of homework to do."

"Always. But I'm happy to visit anyway."

A dark woman walked over and introduced herself. "Mrs. Drake, when you have time on Monday, could you take a few minutes to swing by my office to discuss payment arrangements? There seem to be some irregularities with the insurance."

Lily felt her stomach clench. The last thing she needed to worry about right now was hospital bills—not that the thought of them hadn't been rippling through her mind for the past several days. She had no idea how she would manage to pay for everything. "What kind of irregularities?"

The woman's eyes flicked toward Shelly and back. Lily shook her head. "Go ahead. What kind of irregularities?"

"Well, it seems the policy was cancelled when your husband, um, stopped working for his company a few weeks back."

It was like another punch to the gut after everything else she'd gone through. "But—but the premium was paid out of his last check. I mean, I saw the stub they mailed out." It had been in the large stack of mail she brought home the first time she had gone to the post office.

The woman's brows lifted. "Then we should be able to work around that. If you can bring in your paperwork on Monday, we'll see what we can do for you."

Lily leaned against the wall behind her. Their co-pay on the hospital stay was going to add up into the thousands by the time the doctors released Sophie. What if the insurance company refused to pay for anything? How would she cope? Despair washed over her.

Shelly wrapped her arm around Lily and led her toward the elevator. "Hey, it's going to be all right, somehow."

"Is it?" Lily felt the tears welling in her eyes again. "Is it really? Since John was arrested nothing has felt right or okay. How can I deal with this on top of everything else?"

She waited until they stood alone in the elevator before turning into her younger sister's shoulder to sob out her anger and frustration.

Chapter Seven

Lily couldn't sleep that night. Instead, she lay in bed, thinking of everything that was happening in her life and what she was going to do about it. Sometime after midnight, she decided she could use a glass of milk and headed for the kitchen. The hall light reflected off a picture frame in John's office as she walked past. Lily stopped when she realized the frame held an award he'd earned the previous year for ethics in real estate.

Angry, she picked up a small box from the floor and tossed several of his framed certificates into it. Every instinct inside her demanded his lies and pretenses be erased from her life. How dare he put on such a good front when he wasn't what he pretended to be? How could he betray her like that—because it was a betrayal to her, as well as to everyone else whose identity he had stolen.

Mad, disgusted, and overwhelmed, she carelessly threw pictures on the stack. Tears streamed down her face, but she only swiped at her cheek with the back of her hand a few times, otherwise ignoring them.

When Shelly showed up at the office door a few minutes later, Lily had nearly emptied the walls and desktop of his personal possessions—those inexpensive enough that no one would think she was stealing. She didn't care if the load went to an incinerator—she didn't want to look at it one more time as she passed the room.

"Um, are you okay?" Shelly's tone was tentative, as though she were afraid Lily might start throwing some of those things at her.

Shoving a paperweight on top of everything else with a satisfyingly loud crash of glass below, Lily turned to her sister. "I couldn't sleep. It seemed like a good idea." The words came out fierce, and Shelly lifted her eyebrows at the response. Though the box wasn't large and it wasn't full yet, Lily felt exhausted and flopped into the desk chair. She still ached from the birth. She ached all over, but the worst ache was in her heart. Everyone kept telling her everything would be okay—it would all work out in the end. Right now, however, all she saw was a big question mark blocking her way, and she didn't know how to get past it.

After a long moment of silence, she sighed. "I'm going back to bed." She picked up the box and set it in Shelly's arms. "Put that in the garage, would you? I'll have to finish the rest later."

She would let John's parents worry about his things. Right now she just wanted the box out of her sight.

On Monday Lily was able to hold her daughter for the first time. Several of the tubes and monitors had been removed, and Sophie—who was still so tiny Lily could hardly believe she wouldn't break at the slightest touch—snuggled up to Lily when she pulled her close. As she touched her baby's velvet cheek, Lily felt awed.

Yes, it would have been better if Sophie hadn't been born so early, but Lily couldn't help but feel amazed the little girl had lived. She was the miracle in all this mess. She was such a special spirit, a huge blessing. Since she had a moment of peace, Lily sang softly to her baby.

When she finally left the NICU and went out for a break to stretch her legs, she headed for Ms. Carlisle's office, the copies of her papers stuck in her back pocket.

The heavy weight on her shoulders seemed to get larger as she thought of the bills accruing each day Sophie stayed here. She had no idea how she would cover them. It seemed an impossible task at the moment, but she could only take things one step at a time.

Lily knocked on Ms. Carlisle's open door and was welcomed in. She settled on one of the nondescript gray office chairs and looked the olive-skinned woman in the eye. "I have the check stub." Lily reached into her pocket and slid it across the desk.

After a moment, Ms. Carlisle nodded. "With this, I believe we can arrange for the insurance company to ante up their portion of the expenses. What confuses me is why the broker at the office called to cancel the policy if they pulled it from your husband's check."

Feeling light-headed, Lily tried to wet her dry mouth. "The broker did? Ross Drake? Are you sure?" How could he have done that to her, knowing she was so close to her due date?

"That's what the paperwork said. Is Mr. Drake a relation?"

"My father-in-law." Lily's stomach felt sour, and she wanted to break something. Father, mother, or son—any of the three's necks would do for her right now. She was infuriated. Did they really have to make it all worse for her? Wasn't it bad enough already?

"I suppose it might have been a misunderstanding?" The woman ended the sentence with a lift in pitch, turning it into a question.

"Sure, that's it. A misunderstanding." But Lily knew it was pure spite. Apparently, Ross blamed her for what happened to John every bit as much as his wife did. But still, how could he do such a thing, knowing his grandchildren would be the ones to suffer?

"Now, how much do you think you'll be able to pay on your portion each month? Three hundred dollars?"

Fighting the tears that were again filling her eyes, Lily shook her head and explained the whole situation in detail. When she finished, she accepted a tissue from the box the financial planner had handed her. "So you see, I might scrounge fifty dollars some months, once I get a job, but right now, I can't even come up with that." The impossibility of it all poured over her some more.

There was empathy on the woman's face as she studied Lily. "I'll have to look this over and see what we can do for you. Right now, don't worry about your bill. Just focus on your little girl and on getting your life in order. I'm sure we can work out terms."

Doubting it would do much good, but willing to take anything she could get at this point, Lily thanked her and left the office, taking a circuitous route back to the NICU to visit Sophie again.

When she arrived, Elizabeth was holding a heated conversation with the nurse on staff. "She's my granddaughter and I don't understand why you won't let me in. Do I need to talk to your supervisor?"

"I'm sorry, only the parents are allowed to let in visitors. As the mother isn't here right now—"

"And why is that, anyway? Where could she be? Probably off shopping or getting her hair done. It's not like she cares about anyone but herself!" Elizabeth took a step closer to the nurse and compressed her lips into a thin line. Before she could say anything more, Lily spoke.

"Just so you know, I was in the financial office trying to straighten out a problem caused by your husband." When Elizabeth's head whipped around to face her, Lily pressed a fingertip into her mother-in-law's shoulder. "He cancelled our insurance after it was paid for, even though he knew I was late in my pregnancy and needed it more than ever. After your son left me facing the imminent loss of everything I thought we owned. And why? Because John had to prove to his daddy that he could succeed in life and do better than anyone else.

"Do you think John's concerned about his baby? If he is, he has a strange way of showing it. But then, I guess you could say like father, like son, couldn't you? Neither of them cares the tiniest bit what happens to the children."

"That's not true," Elizabeth said, brushing Lily's hand away. "You can't keep me from my grandchildren. I have a right to see them."

Feeling more than murderous, Lily moved forward until they were nearly nose to nose. "Even if we're stuck living on the street, you already said you wouldn't buy us a loaf of bread—not even to feed your only grandchildren, whom you are apparently so concerned about—there is no way on this earth you are going to get into that room," she gestured wildly at the NICU doors, "to so much as breathe on my daughter. I cannot believe your nerve, thinking you can just run the world any way you want. You can't have your cake and eat it too."

"We'll see about that. If I have to take it to the hospital director himself, I'll see my granddaughter."

"Good luck with that," Lily said as she watched the woman rush haughtily away. She turned back to the nurse. "If she returns, I want security called." Lily grabbed a pair of booties, a gown, and a mask from the pile and started putting them on. Now that Elizabeth was gone, Lily felt a rush of tears but welcomed them this time since they accompanied a feeling of elation at having spoken her mind for the first time in three years.

The nurse stuttered an agreement and hurried away.

Another week passed, and Lily had nearly cleared John's things from the bedroom and his office. She only had the strength to work for a few minutes a day, but she found the act of packing his things to be therapeutic. Bit by bit she was putting away the past and working toward a future. Anything in drawers or closets that she didn't open regularly could stay there until it rotted for all she cared, but the trappings of his personal life were now out of sight. She hadn't heard anything from her in-laws—a fact that relieved her. If Elizabeth had taken her suit to the hospital director, she had obviously been turned away.

Lily had spoken to her family several times on the phone, and her mother had made three trips to visit with her and Sophie. Denise was still helping out with Stephen.

When she stepped away from the NICU at lunchtime, needing to stand and walk for a few minutes before returning to her baby's side for the rest of the day, she had a message on her phone. "Mrs. Drake, this is Carl McFadden, John's attorney. I have the divorce paperwork filled out. I need to meet with you to get everything signed. Please call me." He listed his phone number and the address to his office.

Lily stopped and leaned against the wall as she replayed the message. It wasn't as though she hadn't expected a call or a letter. John told her it was coming, after all. Still, signing paperwork would make it all real. She pushed back the tears that were always close to the surface these days and forced herself to pick up the phone. She had been meaning to get her own attorney but hadn't gotten that far. There was no point putting off the meeting. She didn't have to sign anything, after all.

Two hours later Lily greeted the receptionist at McFadden's palatial office. The woman sitting behind the polished granite desktop asked her to sit while she waited.

A tall, middle-aged man entered the front office. He smiled, but there was no friendliness or mirth in it, only studied politeness. "You must be Mrs. Drake." He paused. "I'm Carl McFadden. Come on back. I have your paperwork ready."

Lily stood, feeling very underdressed in her jeans and T-shirt when she compared her outfit to the designer suit on the attorney and the receptionist's perfectly tailored dress-suit. She sat in a deep leather chair at a large walnut table. He indicated where she should sign the documents. "Everything's set out in your favor. You'll retain custody of the children and receive virtually all of the assets. John's being very generous."

Lily snorted at the apparent generosity. She took the pen he handed her, then set it on the table beside the papers. "You may want to work on other things while I read this." She didn't look at him but continued to study the document.

The attorney sat across the table from her. "It's all very straightforward. I'd be happy to explain it to you, if you have any questions."

He seemed rather too anxious to get her signature on the page. She flashed him a friendly smile, though she felt anything but friendly at the moment. If the fact that John had requested a waiver on the ninety-day waiting period wasn't enough, the man standing over her was just a little too intense for comfort. "I'll be sure to ask if I have questions. If I'm in your way, I'd be happy to take the papers home. We can discuss particulars tomorrow or the next day."

"Actually, I'm going to be out of the office for a few days, so it would be best if we finished this up now. I do have another appointment in a few minutes, and I'd like to have these filed today." He picked up the pen and offered it to her again. Rather than take it from him, Lily stood, her anger rising. She was not going to be rushed. "I wouldn't want to make your clients wait. I'll look his offer over, meet with my attorney," *who doesn't actually exist yet*, she added to herself, "and return it in the morning. I'm sure someone else can file them. Surely you don't do that yourself." It was all she could do to keep her voice calm as she collected her purse. What was it with the pushy Drakes and their pushy lawyer?

"Oh, no need to rush." He gestured her back to her chair. "I'm sure you're worn out from all the time you spend in the hospital with your daughter. Take your time."

Lily lifted a brow and knew something wasn't right about the agreement he was trying to rush her into. She may have acted like an idiot over the past few years, but she wasn't going to be taken for a ride this time. After considering for a long moment, she sat again and picked up the papers.

It took several minutes of looking over the agreement before Lily realized what was wrong with it. In her exhausted, keyed-up state she might have missed it if he hadn't been so pushy, she thought, as angry with herself as she was with the attorney. When she finished reading the terms of the divorce again, she slapped the pages onto the desk and snatched her purse from the table. "I'm afraid these terms are unacceptable. There's no provision for child support. I want thirty percent of John's earnings, beginning six weeks after he's released from prison. I've been asking around and the number seems about right for two children."

"Now, Mrs. Drake. You must understand that he's giving you all the assets—everything. He's walking away from this with nothing, and it's bound to take him quite a while to settle into a new career. You can't expect him to fork over such a large portion of his paycheck."

It took all her effort to keep her voice down so the receptionist wouldn't hear every word. "You keep speaking of assets, but we both know everything in his name belongs to the courts. Once I sell the car to pay off the debts he incurred in my name, and without my knowledge, I'll have next to nothing left over. It's not going to support the children until they turn eighteen. He must be an idiot if he thinks I'm going to agree to this."

"You have to be realistic. He's asking nothing from you." His face was calm, his tone placating, which only infuriated Lily more.

"There's nothing for him to take!" She slapped her hand on the papers in front of her. "You can tell John where he can put this agreement. I'll have my attorney contact you soon so you can iron out something reasonable." Lily slung her purse over her shoulder and marched out of the office.

CHAPTER EIGHT

Later that night, as the time approached when the nurses changed shifts, Lily could feel her eyes getting heavy. There was so much to do, and yet she wanted to be at the hospital with her baby all the time.

"Hey," Denise walked into the NICU in her smock and booties. "How's Sophie doing today?"

"Much better. The doctor thinks she'll be released in a couple of weeks. That means she'll go home three weeks before she was supposed to be born. Very good news." Lily talked about Sophie's improvements and rubbed the tip of her finger along her daughter's face. "Do you want to hold her?"

"For a minute. You need to go home soon."

Lily nodded. She transferred her daughter to Denise and then stood. Her muscles protested from sitting in the same position for so long. Other than her short packing sessions and the few minutes she spent with Stephen in the mornings, she had been living at the hospital. Right now she wanted to take her baby home, snuggle up in bed with her kids, and sleep for a week.

All too soon, Lily and Denise were asked to leave for a couple of hours, and Lily trudged down the hall toward the elevator. Denise tucked a lock of hair behind her ear and eyed Lily. "What's going on? You're awfully quiet tonight."

Lily sighed. "I should've known you'd notice. I got two bits of news today. One is wonderful, the other, considerably more than irritating."

"Good news first," Denise said.

"I spoke with the finance lady today. She said the hospital's going to comp my co-pays—all of them. I don't have to worry about paying a dime of the hospital costs. That doesn't mean I won't pay for the ambulance, or the odd specialist who bills separately, but it's a huge relief."

"That's wonderful!" Denise poked the elevator button and then turned to give her friend a hug. "So what's the other piece of news?" The elevator doors opened and they stepped in.

Lily kneaded her purse and fought the urge to bite her lip. "John's attorney called me. I went to his office this afternoon to look at the divorce documents. John asked for the waiting period to be waived. I guess even in jail he can't wait to be rid of me." Lily heard the note of bitterness in her own voice but ignored it. "There were no provisions for child support, not even after he gets out of prison. The idiot attorney kept trying to convince me to sign without reading the papers, and then he told me I was getting all the assets in the divorce and should be happy with that. As if."

"You've got to be kidding me. Seriously? What did you do?"

"I told him he'd be hearing from my lawyer. No way am I going to let John out of all responsibility to care for his kids. He demanded pictures and visitation once he gets out but doesn't want to pay a dime to feed or clothe them." Lily pushed the hair back from her face and tried to calm the anger throbbing through her. "Now I have to get a lawyer." She felt her lips twist. It was the last thing she wanted to deal with on top of everything else.

"I'll be happy to do some checking around for you. I have a friend who was recently divorced," Denise offered.

"I'd appreciate it." When she felt the lump rising in her throat, Lily swallowed and then changed the subject. "Do you mind if I leave Stephen with you tonight? I'm too tired to get him before heading home. I'm sure he's already asleep."

Denise said nothing for a moment, but once they stepped out into the snowy parking lot, she nodded. "You know I'm happy to take care of Stephen, but, Lily, I'm worried about you."

Lily rubbed her eyes and pushed back her exhaustion. "I'll make it home safe enough. I'm just counting down the days until I can take Sophie home with me."

"That's kind of what I wanted to talk to you about."

Lily lifted an inquiring eyebrow.

"Look, I can only imagine what you're going through. Still, your son needs you. You have to be out of your place in less than three weeks. You don't have a job and I know you want to spend day and night in the hospital with your baby, but you need to make some decisions, get things ready to move."

"Wait." Lily stopped in her tracks and looked at her friend in disbelief. "You're giving me a lecture on taking charge of my life when my baby is in the hospital? Don't you think I miss spending time with my son? I treasure every second with him, but he's not alone; he has you. Sophie is in there alone more than half of the time because I can't live in the NICU."

"I'm sure it seems cold-hearted, but you have things that need to be done. Do you need help packing? Have you thought beyond the next two weeks?"

Icy wind blew through the openings in Lily's coat, and she hugged her arms closer, trying to keep the chill at bay. "I've begun packing a bit each day." She didn't bother to explain she had hardly packed any of her own things. John's things would undoubtedly arrive at his parent's house wrinkled, jostled, some of them broken—that was if his parents got up the nerve to collect his belongings.

"Good. And have you thought much about a job?"

Lily shrugged. "I'm almost done with my recertification papers. I've been taking them into the hospital with me sometimes."

Denise nodded. "That's something, then. I'm sorry to nag at you, but time's running out fast and your son misses you."

That brought a pang of guilt to Lily's chest. Of course Stephen was confused and upset. His father disappeared, and she had been either away from home or asleep twenty-three and a half hours of the day. "You're right. I just hate to leave Sophie alone in there."

"So let me arrange for some people to sit with her when you can't be there. We can take care of a few things next time your mom comes to visit too. I just want to help."

Tears left icy lines on Lily's face. She turned and continued walking toward her car, moving slowly until she knew Denise was walking with her. "It's so overwhelming."

"I know. It's okay." Denise slid an arm around her friend's shoulder. "I'm just giving you a little nudge. I could come in tomorrow evening while you spend some time with Stephen. Rich and Cam will have a manly night together without me."

"Thanks." Lily turned and gave her friend a hug. She wished Stephen would have a chance for a manly night with his dad, but as that was out of the question, she'd have to make up for John's lack by being the best mom ever.

The ball flew from Curtis's fingers as the bell rang, signaling the end of the first half. The net swished as the ball fell through and the scoreboard recorded two more. Utah State University 45, UC Davis 38. Curtis loped across the floor to the coach when he was benched for a breather.

His gaze roved over the stands and caught on a small poster with his name on it. "Go Werner #12," it said. He grinned. Though the signs had started appearing a couple of years earlier, it still amazed him that people bothered to make them.

Then he realized who held the poster and his grin slid away. Though his half sister Kaylee had been at Denise's and Cliff's weddings, he hadn't spoken with her or anyone else in her family. Despite the distance he put between them, she often attended his games.

Curtis pulled his eyes away when Kaylee smiled at him. He still wasn't sure what he wanted to do about her. He didn't need any external distractions, and thinking about his convoluted family was definitely a distraction. Three years earlier, he had no interest in meeting his birth family—he had his twin and a great adopted family. Though Cliff had periodically brought up searching for their biological family, he hadn't searched because Curtis hadn't wanted to know.

Then Cliff's future sister-in-law, Denise, had pieced together the information she had and realized they were siblings—well, half siblings. Their birth mother, Daphne, had never been good about keeping a husband but she had given birth to four children: Denise, the twins, and Kaylee, who had been adopted by Daphne's brother and his wife. Though Curtis eventually accepted his relationship with Denise—they had already been friends, after all—he never wanted contact with the rest of his biological family, especially Daphne, who was now in prison. Kaylee respected his decision, to a point. Her appearance with the signs at his games ensured he knew she was still around, still wanted contact with him.

After a few minutes, he was sent back in and played hard, putting the crowd into the background as he focused on the ball. The game was tight during the last half as their opponents inched up toward USU's score, though the Aggies pulled it off in the end with four points to spare. The Mountain West tournament was coming up as the season ground down, and another win hopefully meant a better seed.

Unable to stop himself, Curtis let his eyes drift back up to the stands as he returned to the locker room. Kaylee watched him as she stood to leave. She lifted her hand in shy greeting, and he found himself holding her gaze and extended his hand in a half wave.

The team's spirits were high as players talked about the game, laughed and ribbed each other over stumbles, and generally wound down. Curtis, however, remembered the bright smile that had broken over his youngest sister's face at his simple acknowledgement. It made him feel a twinge of guilt for holding back, but he wasn't ready to get to know her yet.

Lily moved three days before Sophie was scheduled to be released from the hospital. Her home teachers, Denise, and Rich came to help, and Curtis and Shelly even came down together for the day. The weather was warmer again as February came to an end, though another storm was supposed to hit town that week. The final boxes and few furniture items Lily felt comfortable taking with her had been packed.

All personal papers had been sorted and either shredded or boxed, and the fridge was empty. As far as Lily was concerned, the house was ready for the Feds to take possession. She took a long look at the backyard. She'd spent hundreds of hours in this yard, adding new flower beds, agonizing over shrub and tree choices, and playing with landscaping options.

"It's a pretty incredible landscape. I bet it's amazing in the summer." She turned to see Curtis walk up behind her, his hands in his jacket pockets. "Denise said you did all of it yourself."

"Yeah. It was a lot of fun. It'll be a long time before I get a chance to play in the dirt again, I'd bet. Unless Denise lets me put in a flower bed at her house." She smiled but knew it was weak.

"You have a pretty good eye for design. Or did you have help?"

"I did talk to a landscaper about feasibility a couple times when I was working on the plans, but it's mostly my brain child." She felt warmed by his compliment since he was studying to be a landscape architect and had much more training than she did.

"I like the forsythia there in the corner." He pointed to the plants. "And are those lilacs?"

"Yes. Hard to tell when they don't have any leaves, isn't it? But they'll be blooming before you know it. My favorite is the tricolor butterfly bush in the nook over there." She gestured toward the corner behind a low stone wall. They talked shrubs and flowers as they ambled back to the front of the house.

Denise waited at the side of her car, bundled in a warm coat. "Your stuff's taken care of, and Rich just called the Drakes and told them where he left the key so they can come for John's things. You ready?"

Lily nodded and took a last wistful look at the house and the broken dreams it represented. "Yeah, let's go."

Curtis climbed in beside Denise, and Lily followed them to the free-way in her own car. She didn't look back.

That evening after settling the children into bed, Lily sat at the table with Denise, Rich, Curtis, and Shelly. Lily was settled into the spare room for the next few weeks while she tried to decide what to do with her life. She couldn't afford to wait much longer before she made a move.

"Did you get your application in?" Denise asked as she snitched the olives Rich had picked off his pizza.

"Yeah. Little good it'll do me." Lily felt her anger rising as she thought of her encounter at a local school district office.

Shelly's eyebrows lifted. "That sounds like a story. What happened?"

Lily took a sip of her root beer and carefully set her glass back on the table. She had several options but decided honesty wasn't going to hurt anything but her pride. "The woman glanced at the name on the top of my resume, looked at me, then back at my name. Then she asked if I was related to the Drake guy who stole the kids' identities. Stupidly, I told her I was. She gave me one of those fake smiles and said she'd pass the application on."

"Well, it's too bad she made that connection, but it doesn't mean they won't call." Rich reached for another slice of pizza.

"I might believe that, if I hadn't seen where she filed the papers. I doubt the garbage man does the hiring." Lily clamped down on her anger.

"I can't believe that. It's like, discrimination or something!" Shelly pounded a fist on the table.

"Can't she get in trouble for doing that?" Curtis asked.

Wishing she hadn't told them, Lily rubbed at the pain in her temple. "Her boss might not appreciate it, but she didn't do anything illegal. Wives of felons are hardly a protected class." However, it underscored the difficulty she was going to have finding a job—and her need to return to her maiden name of Cox on all future applications.

Chapter Nine

Lily gave the melting butter a quick stir in the saucepan, then returned to chopping her cooked chicken. Her cell phone rang, and with a sigh, she wiped her hands on a nearby towel and then fished the phone from her pocket.

"Hey," Shelly's voice greeted her. "I found the perfect apartment today."

"I thought you were happy at the dorms." Lily cradled the phone between her ear and shoulder and picked up the knife again.

"Not for me, cheesehead, for you. It's a two bedroom. It's tiny, but it's only a few blocks from me, and the price is great. It's in a nice quiet neighborhood, with plenty of young families too."

"Shel, you bullied me into applying to the school districts up there, but I put in applications at a lot of places. Don't get your hopes up. I could end up nearly anywhere at this point." Lily was glad Shelly wanted to have her close—she'd like nothing better than to be near her sister—but after her experience at the local district office, she wasn't holding her breath.

"I bet I could round up a couple guys to help unload your stuff. Curtis would probably help, if he doesn't have a game that day, and Rob, of course." Rob was a guy Shelly was "friends" with from her student ward. "There are others. We could have you settled in no time."

With a sigh, Lily began whisking the flour into the melted butter. "You know I'd love to live close to you—"

"It's going to work. I can feel it."

Since Shelly seemed determined to believe in her plan, Lily decided a change of subject was the easier course. "So how are classes going?" She began adding milk to her white sauce.

"Same old, same old. Rob and I are doing a duet in our ward in a couple weeks." Shelly talked on about college life and her classes for several minutes, then ended the call so she could run to a study group.

After slipping the phone back in her pocket, Lily added the chicken chunks and poured the white sauce into a large casserole dish filled with cooked rice. She wiped her hands again and then stepped into the living room to check on the boys, who were making a lot of noise. Cam and Stephen sat in the living room, surrounded by scattered blocks.

"Momma," Stephen said when he saw her. "Store go boom!" He dropped a large wooden block on a small stack of blocks, making an exploding noise when they collided. Cam laughed and clapped his hands, trying to imitate Stephen's sounds.

She smiled, then glanced around the room to make sure everything was fine. There weren't any signs of the boys getting into anything they shouldn't have while she was on the phone. When she was sure all was well, Lily returned to the kitchen.

Stephen followed her in a moment later and asked for hugs and kisses, then jabbered at her, one hand wrapped around her leg so she couldn't move without fear of tripping over him. She was grateful he wasn't insisting on being held—yet. Though she couldn't blame him for being clingy and irritable lately, it did make it harder to get anything done.

After finally convincing him to join Cam in the living room for a few more minutes, Lily began chopping florets from a head of broccoli. Denise walked in a moment later, her arms full of grocery bags. She grinned at Lily as she dropped the bags on the countertop. "I should keep you around. Do you know how great it is to shop without a child in tow?"

"I've nearly forgotten those glorious days of shopping solo." Lily smiled and scooped up the broccoli, dropping it in a dish with the chicken and rice and mixing it all together.

"And you cook. Rich will never let you go if you aren't careful." Denise began unloading the bags.

"You cook."

"When I must. When Rich threatens to order a week's worth of pizza if I make him eat another turkey and avocado sandwich."

Lily laughed. "He'll be home soon, right?" She put the lid on the casserole dish, then set it in the microwave.

"Ten, maybe fifteen minutes."

A little boy began wailing in the next room. The two women looked at each other and said together, "Cam."

Lily stopped at the table where Sophie lay in her car seat, still fast asleep. She touched her baby on the cheek and smiled when Sophie let out a sigh. With joy at having her angel home, Lily followed Denise into the living room where a little-boy brawl was in progress.

When Rich came in a few minutes later, both boys were sitting in their highchairs at the table with toys, perfectly happy again. He lingered over a kiss with Denise, then glanced out the kitchen window, which faced the front yard. "There's a cop car on the street."

"Did you get caught throwing snowballs at old ladies again?" Lily asked, lifting a brow at him.

"I'd never do that," Rich protested as he snitched one of the carrot sticks Denise was cutting.

"That's not what your mother told me." Lily held back a grin as she set the table.

"Hey, Mom started it. Besides, that was nearly twenty years ago. It's not like she was an old lady then, even if she did claim otherwise during the fight." He pushed the last bite of carrot into his mouth, then scooped his son out of the high chair, pausing to press kisses all over the giggling boy's face. "That's the only time I've ever heard her admit she wasn't young anymore—and she still was at the time."

The doorbell rang and Lily exchanged a surprised look with her cousin. Rich returned his son to his chair, then walked to the front door. When he opened it, the man asked for Lily.

A deep sense of foreboding filled Lily as she walked to the door. "I'm Lily."

"I have these papers for you." He had her sign her name and handed over a manila envelope. The exchange was over almost as soon as it began, and Lily walked to the sofa, pulling the sheets from the envelope. She stopped in her tracks when she read the first sentence of the court document. She didn't move or say anything until she finished the entire thing.

"You've got to be kidding me." Lily slapped the papers onto the coffee table and turned toward Denise and Rich. "You're never going to believe it. You know how it's taken three weeks to hear back from John, despite his desire for a speedy divorce? His parents have decided to sue for custody of the children." It was a fight to keep her voice low, but Lily didn't want to upset the boys or wake Sophie.

"What? How can they do that?" Denise picked up the stapled sheets.

Lily stalked across the room and back a couple of times while she waited for Denise and Rich to read the document. The thought of possibly losing her children to her frigid in-laws made Lily sick. What kind of people were they to even consider taking the children from her? Why would they want to take the kids? It wasn't like they ever came over to visit. John had made it clear his mother didn't like the noise and confusion, so they rarely visited his parents either.

When Denise finished, she turned to Lily. "They've got nothing on you. You have a place to live—you're living here for the moment. It's not like you're on the street." Her words made Lily cringe, reminding her about the cardboard box comment she'd made to John.

"But I don't have a job or a prospect of one. I have nothing to live on. They have a ton of money and could fight me on this for years if they wanted. They know I can't afford to pay an attorney, and their grandchildren will be the ones suffering if I have to pay someone to help. I just can't believe they'd do this. It's all because I expect their precious son to take financial responsibility for his children. It's not like I'm asking all that much. I realize I'll get nothing until he's out of prison. I'm not even expecting back child support for that time. The requests my lawyer and I have made are totally reasonable—too reasonable, probably."

"You have plenty of prospective jobs," Rich said, placing a calming hand on her shoulder. "And you're going to get one sooner or later. It's just a matter of time. It's not like you've had much chance to look for one with everything going on. And this bit about you being an incompetent mother is total garbage. You're one of the best moms I know."

Lily sat on the sofa with a plop. Just when things began to look like they were getting better, they always took a turn for the worse. "Well, one thing's for sure, I'm not giving into them. No matter what I have to do, there's no way those people are getting their hands on my children. My babies will not be their second chance to prove what horrible parents they can be." She wiped at her tears and took a deep breath, trying to calm the anger pouring through her.

"We'll do anything we can to help." Denise set a hand on Lily's shoulder. "They'll be sorry they messed with you."

Though Lily had no idea how they would manage to fight the powerhouse of attorneys the Drakes could hire, she felt reassured.

Lily spent the next few days in constant prayer as she tried to figure out what to do next. She couldn't take a minimum-wage job and still pay rent anywhere, since the entire paycheck would be soaked up by child care. She kept applying for jobs and hoping for a miracle or a sign of what direction the Lord wanted her to take.

Meanwhile, she began learning more about the legal system and with her lawyer, formulated a response to her in-laws' attorneys.

She was out walking with Sophie one balmy afternoon while Denise watched the boys when her cell phone rang. She didn't recognize the phone number. "Hello, this is Lily."

"Yes, this is Tavonny Hope from Little Grove Elementary School in Logan. I've been looking for a substitute teacher, and the district office gave me your name. They said you were just cleared with the state. I have a three-week position I need filled. It's a second-grade class. If you think you can make arrangements, the job starts on Monday."

Elation and terror warred in Lily's chest at the idea. Elation because three weeks was enough work to justify a move to Logan. If she could arrange more work for some of the other schools while she was in the area, she would actually be able to make a living. Terror came in when she thought of finding an apartment, child care, and moving her family to start work in three days' time. Could it even be done?

"Monday, that's awfully soon. I want the job, but . . . wow."

"One of our teachers has had to schedule surgery for Monday morning and will be off work for three weeks while she recuperates. I have a few other substitutes on my list who might be able to do the extended period, but they aren't licensed teachers, and I hate to have them in a classroom for such a long time." The woman went on with a few more details, including the possibility that the job could last a little longer than the three weeks requested and lead to more work with the school if they were happy with her performance.

Lily said a quick, silent prayer of thanks and told the woman she would be there first thing Monday. As soon as she hung up her phone, Lily called Shelly. "Hey, about that apartment you said you found. Could you check and see if it's still open?"

Shelly's squeal of excitement was enough to make Lily grin, if she hadn't already been grinning like a fool. It looked like she was moving to Logan after all.

The apartment Shelly had picked out for her was bright and friendly, but cramped. Lily resigned herself to that fact as she dropped a load of baby clothes in the corner of the kids' bedroom. She knew anything even close to her price range was going to feel tiny after the huge house they lived in before. There was a little consolation that at least she didn't have much furniture to squeeze in.

Her parents brought up their truck loaded with her things, as did Rich. Her own car was packed to the gills between bags and kids, but she had most all of her belongings now. She turned back to the door in time to see Curtis and Shelly's friend Rob carrying a hideous sofa that even Deseret Industries should have rejected in Lily's opinion. But as Shelly had managed to snag it for twenty dollars, and the cushions were in decent shape, Lily wasn't about to complain. Not aloud anyway. Ugly could always be covered up.

"Where to?" Curtis asked as he turned his head toward her.

Lily pointed to the only wall in the living room that was big enough for the monstrosity. "That would be great. Thanks, guys." While they slid the sofa in place, Lily took a moment to study Rob, the man Shelly had referred to as a Dean Cain look-alike. He had the same dark hair and eyes, and his face had just a hint of roundness to it and a great smile. He probably wasn't as built as the actor had been during his stint as Superman, but it was obvious Rob hadn't been living like a couch potato, either.

"Are you kidding me? Both my brothers would beat those guys hands down," Denise told Lily's dad as they came into the kitchen with a last load of food from Denise's car. "The only reason Carmichael gets any baskets is because the rest of the team practically gives them to him on a platter. Isn't that right, Curt?"

"You bet. He's such a slacker." Curtis grinned. His tone and expression said he would have agreed even if she had said grass was purple, just to humor her. Denise pulled a face in response.

"I think you may be a tad prejudiced," Lily said, smiling at her friend's enthusiasm. Curtis's twin, Cliff, was in the NBA now, playing for the

Chicago Bulls, and Curtis had finally decided to declare himself eligible for the NBA draft right after he competed in the Mountain West tournament next week.

Denise didn't deny her bias toward her brothers. She beamed instead and returned to arguing with Lily's father. Lily knew he only brought the subject up to poke at Denise.

Positive feelings surrounded Lily as everyone finished unloading her furniture and the family helped her empty some of the boxes. After devouring a stack of pizzas, her family and friends trickled out that afternoon, leaving Lily alone in her place with a fussy baby and a curious toddler. The creamy walls turned dreary in the evening light, and the cold air that whipped around outside seemed to seep through every crack. Lily hadn't bothered to buy a television yet, so she turned on the clock radio she had grown up with and settled Sophie to bed.

Stephen entertained himself with the blocks he found in one of the boxes while Lily put sheets and blankets on his bed. When she returned to the living room/dining room/kitchen, he was rubbing his eyes.

"Hey, kiddo, ready for your bath?"

"No bath. Barney!"

Lily smiled at him. "How about Barney in the bath? I found him when I unpacked." She scooped her son into her arms and carried him to the bathroom. They laughed and giggled together as she soaped him down and washed the pizza sauce from his hair. "Does Barney like to have his hair washed?" she asked when Stephen complained.

"No. Barney no like."

"Really? Do you think he'd cry?" She took the rubber miniature in hand and looked it in the eye. "I bet you wouldn't cry over a little water in your face, would you?" To prove it, she took some soap suds from Stephen's hair and rubbed it on Barney's head, then down his back. "Do you hear that? No crying! Wow, Barney doesn't mind his hair being washed."

Stephen took the toy back and shook his head. "Barney no like."

"Maybe not. Can you tip your head back so I can get the soap out of your hair? I bet you can be brave like Barney and not cry, even if you don't like it." She used her hand as a shield across his forehead and rinsed his hair out with a cup. He only whined a little bit—something she was grateful for.

After the bath, Lily tickled and teased Stephen as she rubbed lotion on him and dressed him in his pajamas. Their usual games were cut short by Stephen's exhaustion, and she only read him an abbreviated version of *Green Eggs and Ham* before tucking him into his bed.

Once both kids were asleep, the quiet echoed around her. She heard the sound of tires on pavement and honking in the distance. Though she'd been a single adult for far more years than she'd been married and her children were asleep nearby, she had never felt so alone.

With nothing better to do and no enthusiasm to do anything anyway, she changed for bed and crawled between the covers before nine.

CHAPTER TEN

On Monday morning, Lily stood at the front of a classroom of tiny desks grouped together in pods of four. It seemed like ages since she had finished her student teaching. Her knees quaked as she looked across the room, checking to make sure everything was ready. If only she felt prepared to take on the group of children.

As the first few students began to trickle into the room, she found herself facing mixed reactions. Some of the kids smiled shyly. One gave her a guarded look, but most fell somewhere in between. She greeted everyone with a bright smile, learned their names, and directed them to their seats.

Her stomach felt like a hoard of angry birds was flying around inside it as she looked out at the group. The bell rang and she called the class to order. Most complied, but she noticed a dark-haired boy named Colton had his brows lowered and his lips puckered in defiance. Lily smiled and directed him to his desk again. He shuffled over to his seat, mutiny in his eyes. She sighed inwardly. This was going to be a very long day.

As the hours passed, she learned how right the premonition had been. The group seemed to be keyed up, and Lily had more trouble keeping the children in order than she remembered having when doing her student teaching. As they waited for the final bell, she tried to answer one girl's questions, but then a fight broke out in the back of the room.

When she pushed through the huddle, she faced Colton and Jacob, their eyes angry, fists flying. Thankful neither had drawn blood, Lily pulled them apart just in time for the bell to ring. Most of the other children in the room seemed to hang around for a moment, as if unsure the excitement was really over.

"Go on," she directed the class, while holding tight to the angry boys' jackets. When the others began to file out, she turned back to Jacob and Colton, studying them through narrowed eyes.

"I have to go or I'll miss my bus," Jacob protested when she tried to direct the two to the principal's office.

"Me too," Colton chimed in.

Lily didn't know if they even rode the bus, but she was too tired to deal with it right now. "Tomorrow, first thing, we're going to have a chat about this." She walked them out to the front doors of the school and watched each of them step onto their busses, though not without pulling faces at each other. Then she headed to the front office.

Tavonny, the head secretary, smiled at Lily as she came in. "You look ready to drop. Did they give you a rough time?"

"Not any more than I expected. Except for the scuffle at the end of the day."

"Already? Lucky you."

"Tell me about it. Can I get files on a couple of boys from my class? I need to give their parents a call." She pushed the hair back from her face as Tavonny motioned her over to the computer to retrieve the information.

When Lily called, no one answered either phone. She wrote their numbers on a bright green sticky note and slid it into her pocket. She'd try again in a couple hours.

Thinking of the spelling words she had to give out the next day, the math quizzes to correct, and the kids' daily journals to check, she wondered how she would keep up with it all. Still, it would be good to have something new to think about. She stopped in surprise when she reached her classroom, then smiled to see Shelly sitting behind the desk, leaning back in her chair and munching on a chocolate chip cookie. "What are you doing here?"

"I wanted to congratulate you on surviving your first day. Besides, I needed an excuse to buy cookies and put off my homework." Shelly stood and took a step to the side, choosing to sit on the edge of the teacher's desk. "They're not as good as homemade, but I don't have an oven so they'll have to do."

Lily sank gratefully into the chair and rested her tired muscles—she hurt all over. Picking up a cookie, she took a big bite. "The only thing better would be—" She stopped when she saw the small jug of milk and sighed in contentment. "Bless you." She took the container from her sister, noting another was already opened on the desk. She took a long swig of milk and a second bite of cookie, savoring the crunchy, chocolatey taste on her tongue.

Shelly laughed. "You'd think you hadn't eaten in months."

"Oh, today felt like months. Then to top it off, I got to split up a fight as the bell rang. I spent more time working crowd control than actually teaching today. What was I thinking when I became a teacher?" She closed her eyes and settled the back of her hand over them to block out the light. Her head was pounding.

"I don't know. That you like munchkins?" Shelly earned a wan smile. She stood, took a drink of milk, then tossed the empty carton into the garbage can. "Now, what do we have to do to get you out of here?"

Lily pointed to a stack of math papers. "Those have to go with me."

"Grab them, we'll swing by day care for the kids, and do some homework at your place while dinner cooks." Shelly straightened a couple of desks while Lily stood wearily to her feet.

"Who's making dinner?" Lily asked, wondering if she had the strength to do it.

"For a change, I am. I even brought some food. Don't look at me like that. Just because I've been in the non-cooking dorms for more than a year doesn't mean I've forgotten how to boil water."

Lily laughed and stood to collect her papers. Shelly might be insanely busy, but she knew when to pick her breaks. Right now, Lily couldn't be more grateful.

The next two days passed somewhat better as Lily learned the children's names and began settling into a routine. The children were filing back into class from their afternoon recess, the boys jostling each other and the girls giggling in little groups, when the intercom went off. "Ms. Cox, you have a phone call," the front office manager's voice boomed.

Lily felt her pulse jump as she wondered what the emergency was. She turned to the two parents who were there to help with stations and asked one to get the class sorted into groups. When she reached the office, she was directed to a telephone. "Hello, this is Lily Cox."

"Lily, thank goodness. This is Loralee from the Primary Colors Day

Care. It seems we've got a problem. Your children are fine, but we need someone to come pick them up." The sound of children talking and crying and excited shouts filtered through the telephone line.

"What do you mean? What happened?" Lily's mind began to race as she thought about everything that could have gone wrong. She couldn't leave in the middle of the school day. What was she going to do?

"We're unfortunately going to be closed for a few days, but I'll explain everything when you get here. I have a dozen more calls to make."

"But everyone's okay, though, right?" Lily's mind began to race as she wondered if Shelly would be out of class, and what the chances were that she'd be able to find a new day care facility before the next morning. She felt the muscles along her shoulders and the back of her neck tighten as she worried about this new problem.

"Everyone's fine. Don't worry about the kids, but we're at the park down the street and someone is going to have to come for them."

Lily got the directions from Loralee and wrote down the number to the cell phone she was calling from. "I'm going to try and reach my sister, Shelly. She's on the list of people I approved to pick up the kids."

"If you can't reach her, please let us know who will be picking them up," Loralee requested.

"Of course."

As soon as she hung up the phone, Lily lifted it again and dialed her sister. "Hey, Shel. I need a favor."

When she finished that call, Lily let out a sigh of both relief and consternation.

"Trouble?" Tavonny asked.

"You don't know of any good day care that has room for a toddler and an infant, do you?" Lily turned to the woman behind her. "Something's happened at their current location and my sister has classes."

"I might know of a few." Tavonny jotted something on a sticky note, her thick black hair falling in front of her face like a curtain.

Principal Nader breezed through the office from the front hallway. "Tavonny, did I receive a fax from the district on the anti-drug plans?" She nodded to Lily in greeting, then directed her attention to her office manager again.

Tavonny's assistant came from the back office, scooped the pages from the fax, and handed them to the principal. "Right here. Any ideas for the assembly yet?"

"No, but tell me if you think of anything." She bustled into the back office, already scanning the printouts.

"Here you go, Lily. I hope one of them works out for you." Tavonny handed Lily the note.

"Thanks, I really appreciate it." Lily tried to refocus her mind as she returned to her classroom. She still had over an hour until school got out, and since her kids were taken care of for the next few hours, she needed all of her attention on her students, or at least as much as she could muster.

When school ended, Lily grabbed her cell phone and began dialing the day care centers to verify space and prices. She picked up the name of another place from one of the first grade teachers and found three centers that could take her children.

The first center she looked at wasn't very well maintained. It wasn't the punch spills on the carpet or scattered toys in a corner that bothered her—spills probably happened daily, and toys, well, what was a day care center without toys? The problem was the water marks on the ceiling and walls indicating a leak in the roof, the cloudy front windows caused by air leaks between the panes. It was a new business, so it might have simply been a matter of needing more capital to fix things, she admitted to herself. The woman in charge seemed nice enough, but Lily could just hear the barrage of complaints her in-laws would launch if they ever saw it.

That was enough to have Lily determined to at least look at all of her options before committing.

The second place was nice and neat, the equipment was in good repair, and the location was convenient, but Lily saw the way the kids looked at the director. She was an authority figure, not someone they ran to give hugs and kisses to as they trickled out of the building with their tired parents. Though she didn't want to jump to conclusions, Lily just didn't feel right about it.

As she pulled into the parking lot shortly before the last day care closed for the evening, Lily prayed this place would feel right. At the very least, she hoped it would look good enough to chance leaving the kids there for a few days while she explored other options, if necessary.

"You must be Lily Cox," the petite brunette said when Lily came through the door.

"I am. I guess that makes you Courtney." Lily smiled as she saw a little girl call out to a woman coming into the room behind her.

The golden-haired toddler squealed and jumped into the woman's arms. "Mama, I made a necklace for you!" She held up a colored macaroni necklace for her mom.

"It's beautiful. You are so talented, sweetie." The woman bent and let her daughter drape the string over her head. "How did things go today, Courtney?" she asked the director.

"Excuse me for a moment?" Courtney asked Lily, and when Lily nodded, she approached the other woman. "Better. The fish oil seems to be making a big difference." The women talked for a couple of minutes about the day, and then the little girl leaned over and gave Courtney a hug.

When Courtney came back over after the mother and daughter had left, Lily couldn't help but ask, "What was that about fish oil?"

Courtney smiled. "Lyndsey is extremely ADHD, and her parents have been worried about medicating her. I read fish oil is effective to calm the condition a lot of the time. It's worked out great. I hate to have the kids medicated unless there really is no other option." She picked up a stuffed puppy from the floor, and they walked across the room as Courtney talked about the daily routine, introduced Lily to the other workers, and showed her around.

When Lily left the day care half an hour later, terms all worked out, she was so grateful to have found the place and prayed the next day wouldn't be so chaotic.

CHAPTER ELEVEN

Lily was exhausted from a long day, though happy about the progress she was making with some of the kids after a week in the classroom. She walked out to her car and settled her things in the passenger seat. She glanced at the bits of refuse on the floor in front and the thick coating of dust on the dash and made a mental note to clean her car this weekend. She had sold the Lexus before her move to Logan and traded down to an old Honda so she could pay off the bills John had racked up in her name—or most of them. She was left with one credit card payment and a few thousand to keep her financially afloat for a little while.

It seemed her life was spent running from place to place with hardly a moment to pause and take a deep breath. While she had plenty of time to make the car a mess, she hadn't quite found enough time to clean it up, especially since she always seemed to have one arm filled with a wriggly infant and her other hand restraining a curious toddler.

She turned her mind to the dozen things she needed to accomplish that night before bed while she inserted her key in the ignition. She turned the key and got nothing. No clicking, no grinding. Nothing. The car had worked fine that morning. Surely the battery hadn't gone dead in eight hours. She checked to make sure the top light was turned off and the headlights hadn't been left on. Reassured, she tried again. Still nothing.

Lily set her head on the steering wheel, wincing slightly when she hit it harder than she'd planned. She really didn't have time for this. Courtney would be expecting her to pick up the kids any minute, and Lily had errands to run and copies to make . . . . The list went on and on.

She sighed, then got out of the car. It was useless to expect that look-ing under the hood would solve her problem. Since the only things she knew how to do were to hook up jumper cables and check the fluids, she had no hope of finding the answer on her own. "So much for thinking I could buy Stephen new clothes." Just having the car towed would eat into her tight budget. The public transit system in Logan was nonexistent, so she really had to have her car.

She dug into her purse for her cell phone. Miraculously, Shelly was at her dorm room and free to rescue her.

"You're a saint," Lily said when Shelly arrived twenty minutes later.

"I know. You can pay me by making some of your famous chocolate chip cookies." Shelly eyed the closed car hood. "Do you have any idea what's wrong?"

Lily sent her a disbelieving look. "You're kidding, right?"

Shelly laughed. "Sorry, stupid question."

"You had the advantage of a boyfriend who taught you a few things about basic car repair. I'm lucky if I can figure out how to work the jack." Maybe it was time she learned something about basic maintenance, she thought.

They transferred all of her work papers to Shelly's car, along with both car seats, and then took off to pick up the kids. "It's going to be a couple days before your car's fixed, isn't it?" Shelly asked after Lily finished filling her in.

"If I'm lucky," she grumbled. "Don't grow up and take on responsi-bilities, Shelly. All they do is suck the fun out of life."

"Tough day?"

"Not really, just a lot on my plate tonight. Things have been going reasonably well in class, actually."

"Good. I was thinking—I won't need my car for a few days. If I really need a ride somewhere I can always beg one. You should take my car until yours is fixed." She sent a quick sideways glance at Lily. "Do you have money for repairs?"

Lily didn't bother to answer. Her financial state could certainly have been worse, but it was still too depressing to think about.

After a long pause Shelly nodded. "That would be a no then."

"Depends on what's wrong. I could scrounge the cash, but it might not leave me anything to live on once this teaching job ends."

With the addition of Stephen and Sophie to the car a moment later, and Stephen's incessant chatter about his day, they waited to continue the conversation until they were at Valley View Towers, the dorms where Shelly lived.

"Thanks for loaning me your car. I really appreciate it. I'll try and get things straightened out with mine as soon as possible." Lily got out of the car after Shelly parked it.

"I'm sure Dad would loan you the money."

"Yeah, I know. I just think it's time for me to try being an adult for a change. I'm almost twenty-seven, and here I am running back to Daddy for money every time I get a hangnail."

"Hey, it's not that bad. It's not like you've got any debts, right?" She was well aware of the financial troubles John had caused. "I mean, not anymore."

Lily stared out the window, not wanting to meet her sister's eyes. There was that one card left, but the payments were minimal. Thankfully the balance was low as well. She would have gone through the whole process of getting the card included in the court case, except for the fact that she had actually taken the card out herself and spent the money on it—regardless of the fact she had thought she was paying it off each month. "My credit's decent, but it's not like I can just shut the door on that part of my past and walk away."

"Once the divorce is final—"

"I'll still be dealing with what he left behind. I have his children, Shelly. He's never going to let things be. I have to share custody, or at least give visits once he's out of prison, and I think his parents are hoping to drag the custody battle out until he's released." Still burning inside over their suit, Lily rubbed a hand along the back of her neck and felt guilty. "I'm sorry for snapping at you. You dropped everything to come get me and then offered to lend me your car. I shouldn't take my frustration out on you."

"What's a sister for?" Shelly's smile was faint but filled with understanding.

Lily pulled her sister in for a tight hug, grateful she had someone to turn to. "You're the best."

"I know." Shelly's smile was impish.

"Hey, ladies. I haven't seen you for a while, Lily. How's the teaching gig going?"

Lily turned to see Curtis Werner, his dark hair wet and slicked back from his face, and a light jacket on his lanky frame. He had a gym bag slung over his shoulder. She figured he must have come from basketball practice. "It's going well enough. How's the team phenomenon? I heard you guys cleaned up at the tournament last weekend. You played great!"

He shrugged self-consciously, and Lily gave him points for humility—something John had severely lacked. "Players don't win titles, teams do. I haven't seen you around since you hit town, but Shelly mentioned you were keeping pretty busy. I promised Denise I'd check in on you." His eyes slid over her, as if taking in every detail. A smile hovered around his lips.

"I'm fine, thanks. I'm sure your schoolwork and basketball keep you more than busy enough without worrying about your sister's cousins." Though she loved Denise to pieces and was grateful her friend was watching out for her, she was embarrassed to be a topic of discussion between Denise and her brother.

He grinned. "Yeah, but if you're my sister's cousin, doesn't that make you mine, too?"

"Something like that." However, her feelings for him had never taken on the sibling-like quality she had always felt with her real cousin, Rich. Lily smiled weakly, then turned her head back toward the car when she heard Sophie fussing. "I'd better be going. It's dinnertime."

"Hey," Shelly turned toward Curtis. "If you are sort of our cousin too, do you think you could spare an hour or so to help a damsel in distress?"

Lily forced a smile and elbowed her sister in what she hoped was a discreet manner. "No need to bother him. I'm fine."

"What's going on?" Curtis asked

"You're good with cars, right? Lily's wouldn't start when she got off work this afternoon." Shelly wasn't about to back down.

"Yeah? What's wrong?" He turned to Lily.

She shrugged. "Who knows? I got nothing when I turned the key—not even a click. I can have it towed tomorrow. I know how busy you are."

"Hey, it's no problem. I have a couple free hours in the morning, I'd be happy to take a look at it. If it's something simple like battery cables, it would be a crime to pay for a tow truck." He held out his hand. "Give me your key. What school do you teach at again?"

Shelly piped up and told him, describing the car and where to find it. Seeing she was outmaneuvered, Lily pulled her car key from the ring and handed it to Curtis. "I appreciate you taking time to do this."

His grin disarmed her. "No problem. That's what family's for."

It took some effort not to shake her head, but Lily managed to smile until he turned and walked away. She sent Shelly an exasperated look but didn't say anything, not really put out by Shelly's pushiness. "Good night, Shelly, and thanks again."

The next day Lily was returning with her class from a trip to the school library when Tavonny stopped her. "I think you should know a tall, handsome man is looking under the hood of your car. He looks vaguely familiar. Is he a boyfriend?"

Lily held back the smile that threatened to erupt. The thought of her dating anyone long enough for him to be called her boyfriend was so removed from her current life plan it was funny. "My cousin, of sorts. He's helping me out." It may have been a stretch, but in an odd Southern kind of way, it was true. At least her real cousin, Richard, would have twisted the logic until he made it true.

"Too bad. He's a cutie." The woman winked and then headed back into the office.

"Yeah, I think one failed relationship is enough for me, thanks," Lily mumbled as she herded the kids back to the classroom. Still, she paused to glance out the window and see Curtis lower the hood of the car. If she hadn't already sworn off relationships, she might have admitted that the sight of him, even at seventy yards, made her want to bite her lip in appreciation.

Once the kids had gone home for the day, Lily walked to the office to see if Curtis had left her a note. After nearly two weeks of teaching, Lily felt she was getting back in the groove, and though she was tired from crowd control, she really enjoyed working with the children and seeing the lightbulb flash on in their eyes when they managed a difficult word or math problem.

She smiled wearily at Tavonny. "Did Curtis leave a note for me? He said he might."

Tavonny's brown eyes grew big, and she smacked her palm on the countertop. "Curtis? I knew there was a reason he looked so familiar. He's Curtis Werner from the USU basketball team." She shook her head in amazement. "I didn't know he was your cousin. All the rumors say he's going to join his twin in the pros next year. Has he said anything about it?"

"I know the possibility's been tossed around. Did he leave a note?" Lily was amused by the woman's reaction. Having known him for several years now, she found it hard to idolize Curtis. He was just a man, even if he was sinfully handsome. And incredibly nice. And totally talented. And knew a ton about plants.

One of the teacher's aides walked in from the back room, a stack of papers in her hand.

"Can you believe Curtis Werner, the basketball player, is related to Lily?" Tavonny rushed to tell the woman, as if afraid Lily might beat her to the gossip. "He fixed her car today."

"Curtis Werner? Wow, could you introduce us?" the aide asked. "I've always admired his . . . basketball skills. He's single, isn't he? He dated someone last year, but they broke up."

It was all Lily could do to hold back the laugh that threatened to escape when she thought of the forty-something woman flirting with Curtis. Not that the woman wasn't attractive, with her wide-set blue eyes and salon-perfect hair and makeup. She was sure to turn heads, but still—she was nearly twice his age. "I don't believe he's dating anyone right now. I haven't pumped him for information lately," she answered dryly. Who knew Curtis had a fan club of enthusiastic older women? She wondered what he'd say if he could hear the conversation.

Tavonny looked at the paper in her hand with a dreamy expression on her face, then reluctantly handed it to Lily. "You're so lucky, Lily. I wish I had someone like him at my beck and call—even if he does happen to be related to you."

Lily smiled and said good-bye. "Yeah, real lucky, that's me," she mumbled under her breath, though she did feel blessed he was willing to help her out with the car. When she opened the note and learned the problem was minor and inexpensive to repair, she said a prayer of thanks and relief. Perhaps she was lucky after all.

Chapter Twelve

Curtis walked into the chapel after Sunday school. His smile felt pasted on after all of the congratulations he'd received since church began. The invitational had been held earlier in the week, but with preparation for the Mountain West tournament and class work, he'd been swamped, spending hours hiding away in his dorm room or in a remote corner of the library to catch up.

He appreciated the support of his ward. There were always a few friends at his home games, cheering him on. The sisters even decorated the outside of his dorm door before games, which was pretty nice most of the time.

Since he was so tall, he stood a head above most everyone in his student ward. That meant he couldn't hide well in a crowd, so Lacy Dunkin was still across the room when he saw her turn and spot him. She always used ward meetings as opportunities to get closer.

He hurried to look away, pretending not to see the mahogany-haired girl he'd been avoiding all morning—all year, actually. With a sharp pivot to the right, he turned toward the back, hoping for a single seat to slide into. Bumping into someone in his rush to get away, he glanced down to apologize. "Oh, excuse me. I can be such a klutz." He looked into a pair of familiar brown eyes and couldn't help but smile. "Lily, what are you doing here? I know you're single now and all . . ." he trailed off, feeling his attempt at light teasing going awry.

"No problem." She juggled a car carrier with her daughter in one hand and held her son on the opposite hip. It looked like a good bump would send all three of them rolling. "I'm here to listen to Shelly and Rob sing. I guess I found the right ward, huh?"

"Yeah, let me give you a hand." Not sure how Stephen would accept him, since he'd only met the tyke a few times, Curtis took the covered baby carrier from Lily and the large diaper bag she'd slung over a shoulder. He caught a glimpse of Lacy from the corner of his eye and directed Lily to a bench. Then he had a quick and totally internal debate on whether or not to make a request of Lily. "Save me, would you?"

She sent him a curious look but sat down. "What am I supposed to be saving you from?" she whispered as she sat Stephen on the bench.

Curtis didn't have a chance to respond before he felt a hand on his shoulder and looked up to see Lacy. He forced himself to keep smiling. "Hi." He glanced away long enough to set the baby seat next to him, so he was book ended by Lily and her daughter. This position had the added advantage of leaving nowhere next to him for Lacy to sit, if she were so inclined.

"That was a great game Wednesday. Your three-pointer was terrific. I saw it on ESPN," Lacy gushed. "Oh, who's your friend? I'm Lacy Dunkin, the Relief Society president. I thought I knew all the girls in our ward." She reached past Curtis to shake Lily's hand, her arm brushing against his chest. He squished himself back against the bench tighter, trying to avoid her touch.

"I'm sure you do. I'm Lily Cox, Shelly's sister, and I'm just here visiting."

"Well, you're welcome here, of course." Lacy retracted her arm and set her hand on Curtis's shoulder in a proprietary manner. "How do you know Curtis?"

Curtis hurried to slide an arm across Lily's shoulder and pull her close. "Oh, we've known each other for a long time. She's a close family friend." He sent Lily an adoring smile. "And her kids are so sweet."

Stephen took this as his cue and climbed onto Curtis's lap, taking Curtis by surprise.

Not wanting the kid to fall off, Curtis withdrew his arm from Lily's shoulder and focused on the toddler. "Hey, Stephen, it's good to see you too. We men, we've got to stick together."

Lily caught on quickly. She smiled at Lacy without giving away a hint of her real thoughts. "Oh, yes." She reached out and patted Curtis's cheek. "He was barely more than a pipsqueak when his sister first introduced us. It's so nice to be living in Logan now where we can see each other more often." She fluttered her eyelashes at him, laying it on just a tad too thick in his opinion.

"You're married, then?" Lacy asked Lily, still smiling brightly.

"Divorced. Being a single mother can be difficult sometimes, but Curtis has been so generous with his time and talents to help me out." The look she gave Curtis was tender, but he could see the laughter in her eyes. "I don't know what I would have done without him."

Lacy's eye narrowed and her smile became brittle. "Yes, well, come back any time. See you later, Curtis." She walked away, sliding her fingertips along his shoulder. He held in a shudder—Lacy was very pretty and he'd heard nothing but good about her work in the Relief Society, but something about the territorial way she acted around him turned him cold. Lily on the other hand . . . he pushed that thought away. She was still technically married, after all.

"She seems nice," Lily said, obviously trying, but failing to conceal a grin. "And cute too."

"Yeah." Curtis didn't realize how flat his response must have been until he heard Lily's quiet snort as she tried to hold back a laugh. He couldn't feel anything but relief to have gotten out from under Lacy's thumb so easily—at least for the moment. "Your mom," he said to Stephen as he tapped him on the chin, "is a more than passable actress and a very good sport."

Stephen simply beamed and accepted the plastic cow his mother handed him. "Moomoo. See, moomoo."

"Yes, it is a moomoo. Very good. You must be a genius," Curtis agreed.

"It looks like you have a fan club. Judging from the large number of jealous looks I'm getting from the girls in your ward, I'd guess it's got more than one member in it." Lily's face was serious, and her tone was so light that it took the sparkle in her eye to tell him she was teasing. "I know a couple of older women who want to meet you too. One is old enough to be your mother, but I told them I'd be happy to introduce you."

"Nice. Just what I need. Why is it you're Denise's best friend again?" he asked dryly.

This time she really did laugh but kept her voice to no more than a whisper. "Come on, Curtis, you're a strong, tough man. Can't you handle the women on your own without resorting to deception?"

"Some women are more tenacious than others. Lacy won't take a hint." He knew his voice sounded weary, a perfect response for the way he'd felt the instant before he had run into her. "Thanks, by the way. I owe you."

"I'll make sure and collect someday." She cleared the laugh from her throat and faced the front as the bishop opened the meeting.

The kids kept both Curtis and Lily busy for the hour, but Curtis felt comfortable in the role of mother's helper. It didn't hurt that he found Lily attractive, friendly, and not the least interested in him as more than an acquaintance. It was a bonus that she was willing to help him fend off Lacy.

When the meeting ended, he walked out to the foyer with her, still holding Stephen. They made small talk while they waited. When Shelly and Rob managed to navigate through the throngs of students, he sent them an easy grin. "Hey, you guys were great. This singing together in church stuff is getting to be a habit, isn't it?"

"A bit, and we've just been asked to sing for something else, so you might hear us again pretty soon," Shelly said. "I saw you being all cozy on the bench and Lacy's reaction." Shelly's eyes twinkled at them.

Lily cleared her throat, as though she were covering up a laugh. Curtis rolled his eyes.

"That's a story we'll have to share later." Lily smirked at Curtis before she continued. "I have to get going. Dinner's at six, Shelly. And, Rob—good luck dealing with my sister here. I know her schedule's impossible."

"You're telling me. Trying to coordinate practice time can be insane—she's always got her nose in a book at the library." His smile at Shelly was indulgent, however. It was obvious his feelings for her were more than those of a friend.

"If you weren't taking off to go skiing so often it would be a little easier," Shelly teased back as they turned away. The two of them wandered off.

"Thanks for bailing me out, and good luck with your class this week," Curtis said to Lily as they continued to the parking lot, walking much slower than Shelly and Rob.

"Anytime, and thanks. I appreciate your help with the kids and with my car this week. You saved me a bundle." Once the kids were loaded in the car, she waved good-bye and slid into the front seat.

On Tuesday, Lily ate her sack lunch in the teacher's lounge. She'd seen her class safely into the lunch lines and then disappeared, grateful for a few minutes of peace and quiet to recharge for the afternoon. She was congratulating herself for the headway she'd made with some of the kids when the door opened.

One of the sixth-grade teachers, Mrs. Trost, and the principal, Mrs. Nader, came in, talking about the anti-drug event they were planning. Lily tuned them out and focused on the book she was reading until she heard her name come up.

"Is it true, Lily? Do you have an 'in' with the university basketball team?" Mrs. Nader asked.

Lily squelched a wince and turned, forcing a smile. "I don't know that you could call it that. I know one of the players, but that isn't the same—"

"See, I told you," Mrs. Trost interrupted. "I bet you could get a couple players to come speak with the students about staying drug free. We really need good examples, people the children can look up to. He's practically a legend, this Curtis Werner of hers."

"He's not my Curtis—"

Mrs. Trost didn't wait to hear what Lily had to say. "They would probably do a whole series of visits to area schools if Lily asked them to. Isn't that true, Lily?"

Lily stared at the two women and wondered what she'd gotten herself into. "I don't know if I could get them to do anything. Curtis is so busy with school and the upcoming—"

"But he'd be happy to help us out, don't you think?" Mrs. Nader got on the band wagon this time. "After all, it's for such a good cause, and people in a position like his have a responsibility to make a positive impression on students. It's his duty. You understand that, don't you?"

Why did I eat in here today? Lily fervently tried to think of a good reason to keep her from having to ask Curtis for another favor. "I'm sure he agrees they need good role models, but—"

"See!" Mrs. Trost said with a big smile. "I told you she was our woman. You'll be happy to take care of it, won't you? And I'll see if the district would like him to do other assemblies. Oh, it's going to be so wonderful."

"And you coming up with the idea for the whole thing has got to weigh in with the district," Mrs. Nader added. "I'm sure we could continue to find employment for you if you pull off something like this. It shows real dedication, don't you think? Just the kind of teacher the district would want to have working for them next year." Her look was innocent, even if there was a warning edge to her tone.

"I'll let you know how my call goes before the day is over." Mrs. Trost jumped up and hurried out of the room.

"He's really busy right now, Mrs. Nader, I don't know how—"

"That's why it's even more impressive that he'd be willing to help, dear. You're such an asset to this school." Mrs. Nader beamed at Lily, patted her on the hand, and left.

Lily was speechless, but she moaned as she closed her eyes and let her head fall back onto the top of the chair. What had she done? How had that happened? This wasn't a one-time talk to a couple dozen kids. This was at least six schools—maybe more, if Mrs. Trost got completely out of control. Lily knew Curtis's schedule was packed, even if the basketball season was officially over. And was that more than a friendly observation Mrs. Nader made about her getting hired next year, based on her ability to get Curtis on board with this idea? Surely not. They couldn't possibly put her job on the line based on someone else's actions.

The afternoon seemed more out of control than usual as Lily wondered how she would ever approach Curtis about this "opportunity." But she couldn't put it off—she had to talk to him right away. Tonight, if possible.

When the last child left for the day, Mrs. Trost came in, clasping her hands in pleasure as she went on about how excited the other schools sounded at the prospect. "It'll be so nice, I even spoke with some people from the Cache County School District, and they think this is a wonderful idea. I'm so glad you're going to help us with it."

Cache County? That was a completely different district. Was she trying to get Lily killed? "Wait, Mrs. Trost. Please." When Lily was certain she had the woman's attention, she stood and took a deep breath. "I don't know if he'll be able to help us. I'm sure you can appreciate the kind of schedule these students keep with finals just around the corner. This is asking an awful lot of these boys."

Mrs. Trost's eyes gleamed, and she clasped her hands in front of her in excitement. "Oh, well, I wasn't just thinking boys. Don't you think it would be a great thing to have one of the female players there as well? Or maybe two. After all, we need to show the girls that they can do great things too, even if the women's team didn't do nearly as well as the men's this year." She waved that little detail away and spread her hands apart.

"Anyway, I'm sure you can straighten everything out for us. Contact the coaches and set it up, will you? I'll have a schedule of visits ready for you by the end of the day Monday."

"Wait. You can't expect them to drop everything at this time of year. They have responsibilities." Lily couldn't believe it. The woman wasn't listening to a word she said.

"Oh, dear. I'm sure it won't cut into your time with him that much. You can sacrifice for the children, can't you?" She patted Lily on the arm.

"It's not me I'm worried about."

"Good, very good. I'm glad you can be so unselfish with your young man." The other teacher clapped her hands and beamed. "Now, I'd better be going. So much to do. So much planning." She turned and headed toward the doorway. "I'm simply swamped with lists to put together for these things." She was still talking to herself as she walked out the door.

Lily fell back into her chair and covered her face with her hands. She wondered what had just rolled over her. After a long moment, she sat up and looked around her, then pulled her cell phone from her purse.

Dialing the number didn't take nearly long enough, and unfortunately he picked up instead of letting it go to voice mail.

"Hello, Curtis, this is Lily."

"Hey, Lily, what's going on?" The warm friendliness of his voice made her wince. He was not going to be happy about this.

"Do you have plans tonight? I have to talk to you, and you'll want to be face-to-face for this one."

"Uh, sure. I can meet you in an hour."

CHAPTER THIRTEEN

When Curtis walked into Wendy's, he found Lily already sitting at a booth with extra food set out across from her and Stephen squishing French fries in the high chair beside her. She swirled a fry in her Frosty and grimaced. He wondered why she was so upset and why she thought he'd be upset too.

He stopped next to her and caught her gaze. "Are we expecting someone else? Or is this little guy up to eating monster-sized burgers these days?" He tapped Stephen on the head and got a French fry-packed smile in return.

She shook her head. "No, I ordered for both of us. I hope you don't mind. I owe you."

He lifted a brow but slid in across from her. "What do you mean, you owe me? I thought I owed you."

She nudged the burger, a drink, and large fries closer to him. "Oh, if you help me out, you'll have paid me back with serious interest. I guess things got a little out of control today. I don't know what to say or how to fix it or quite how it happened in the first place."

He reached out and covered her shaking hand, his apprehension growing. "What got out of control?"

She met his eyes and swallowed, then began filling him in.

When she got to the part about his name coming up, he removed his hand and sat back on the bench in horror. He hated speaking in front of crowds. His hands always got sweaty, his heart raced as if he was working out, and it wasn't uncommon for him to become nauseated. "No. Say you didn't volunteer me."

"No, I didn't. I swear. I wouldn't volunteer you for anything like that.

I know how busy you are." Her answer was resolute and sincere, but there was still fear in her eyes.

Relieved but guarded, sure there was still something more he wasn't going to like, he sent her a measured look. "Okay, so you didn't volunteer me. How does this affect me?"

She licked her lips and winced, but she didn't break eye contact with him. Then she finished the story. By the time she finished, he was staring at her in disbelief. The food in front of them was completely forgotten as he tried to accept that he'd been volunteered for something he not only didn't want to do but couldn't imagine squeezing in time for—and that was ignoring the possible puke factor.

"I'll just tell them I can't. It isn't possible, not with everything I've got going on. My professors have let me put off some big projects because we were on the road so much, but there's only a few weeks of school left to get it all turned in. We're in the middle of end-of-season tournaments, and I have a ton of credits."

"I know. I told them that." Lily bit her lip and sighed.

He studied her for a moment and saw the worry in her eyes. "What haven't you told me?"

There was a long pause as Lily seemed to be trying to decide what to say, then she shrugged. "Mrs. Nader implied that my future work with the district would be influenced by whether or not I was able to get you and the others to help." She didn't meet his gaze.

"Oh." He turned his attention to his cold fries, dipping them in the ketchup but not eating anything. This would have been so much easier if he could just say no with only the tiniest twinge of guilt attached. But how could he say no if it risked her job?

His stomach turned over, and for an instant he wondered if she was using him as a stepping stone as some had tried to do, or if the principal was really using him as the crowbar. He knew Lily wasn't like his social-climbing ex-girlfriend Natalie, though. Denise would never have put up with someone like that as her best friend.

Still debating inside himself, Curtis met her gaze and gave her a half smile. "Didn't something similar happen when you were student teaching?"

She covered her eyes with one hand. "I can't believe Denise told you about that or that you remember. I don't know how it happens." She looked at him earnestly. "It's like I have big neon lights on my head that spell out, 'I'm a chump. Dump on me.' " She bracketed her forehead with both hands, as if holding up a sign.

Curtis couldn't help it; he began to chuckle. When he looked up at her, she started laughing with him. Then Stephen got in the act, laughing like a wild man. Everyone around them was staring and giving them odd looks, but Curtis didn't care.

After catching his breath, Curtis opened his sandwich. "I seriously doubt the coach would let the others help out, even if they were dying to. Maybe if we'd had more notice, but term's about over and nearly everyone's behind on their work."

"Can you tell me where to reach him, though? I have to at least try."

"No problem. I'll get the number for you before we leave. How do you manage these things?"

"I don't know. It's like when my friend Larisa decided we needed a ballroom dance club in high school. I knew the steps from classes at the college, so I ended up teaching this whole group of teenagers. I don't even know how it happened. One minute I'm signing up to join, and the next I'm in charge."

Curious, Curtis gave her a close look. Did the woman's talents never end? "You ballroom dance?"

"It's been a long time, but I remember a few things. Why?"

He held back a smile and shook his head. It wasn't as if he was likely to have an excuse to see how good she was. "Just wondered. What other scrapes have you gotten yourself into?"

Curtis's roommates started to snore in the hotel room, but even though it was late, he was too keyed up to sleep. The NIT tournament would finish the next day, but his team had played off for third place and won only that night. His college basketball career was officially over, and, though he knew his basketball days were nowhere near their end, he still felt a touch of melancholy. He'd played for Utah State for five years now, and he would never have a need to suit up in his jersey again.

He didn't like the feeling, so he got out of bed and moved to the little table in the corner where he'd left his laptop before the game. Maybe there would be a note from Denise or his mom—though he had already spoken with them that night, so the likelihood wasn't great.

A new message from Kaylee blinked at him when he logged in. She had written a short email just before he left for the conference, but he never answered. He didn't know how. A response was bound to encourage her, and he wasn't sure if he was ready for that yet.

He clicked on her name and anxiously read her note.

CURTIS,

I RECORDED ALL YOUR GAMES SO I COULD WATCH THEM THIS WEEK. GREAT JOB! I KNOW WE'RE ALL REALLY PROUD OF YOU. I'M GOING TO MISS BEING ABLE TO DRIVE ACROSS TOWN TO WATCH YOU PLAY IN PERSON NEXT YEAR, BUT I'LL STILL BE CHEERING YOU ON FROM HOME. CONGRATULATIONS! THIRD IS NOTHING TO SNEEZE AT (THOUGH I'M SURE IT WOULD HAVE BEEN FIRST IF THOSE REFS HAD CALLED FOULS BETTER DURING YOUR LAST GAME).

KAYLEE

He had to smile at her comments. It probably wouldn't have made much of a difference if that extra foul or two had been caught, but he thought it funny that she mentioned it. She had been there for so many of his games that year. He'd miss her face in the crowd too—a realization that had surprised him when he found himself scanning the stands during his first turn on the bench. On impulse he hit reply.

KAYLEE,

THANKS FOR YOUR SUPPORT. IT WAS NICE LOOKING UP AND SEEING YOUR SIGNS ALL SEASON. YOU'VE BEEN A GREAT CHEERLEADER.

TAKE CARE,

CURTIS

He hurried to send the message before he could think better of it or stop himself.

Curtis's back ached and his shoulders were sore from hunching over his laptop as he worked on a landscape schematic for class. The load had been heavy the past few weeks with the professors gearing up for finals, and he was grateful to have one of the few private rooms in Valley View

Tower. If he'd had to work around a roommate's music, noise, and telephone conversations, he'd have gone crazy long ago.

As it was, he could hear music blaring from the next room and voices laughing in the common area. He wished he dared go out and join them, but if he didn't get this assignment finished and emailed to his professor tonight, he'd be toast.

He growled under his breath when he heard his cell phone ring and almost didn't pick it up. Knowing he should at least check who was calling, he flipped it over. Denise's name was on the caller ID. There were few people he would allow to interrupt his work, but she was one of them. He smiled and answered it. "Hey, gorgeous, what's up?"

"Not much here. How's your homework coming?"

He stood to stretch his legs. "It never ends. I keep thinking I'll get a little ahead, but it never works. How about you?"

"We're good. I heard you used Lily to scare off a girl in your ward. Very manly of you," she teased.

Curtis pulled open his mini-fridge and pulled out a half-empty bottle of Powerade. "If you'd done your duty as older sister and raised me right, I'd be better at letting them down easy." He ignored the fact they'd only met a few years earlier.

"You didn't seem all that shy when we met. What's wrong, can't take the attention? I hear you have quite a following. Most guys in your shoes'd be in heaven."

"Lily must have exaggerated. And since you've known me all of three years, I'd have to say your experience is lacking. I'm not shy—I just don't like to hurt people's feelings. Especially the barracudas—they tend to retaliate." He took a deep swallow of his drink, guzzling the rest of the bottle.

"Afraid she'll eat you whole?"

"It's not me Lacy's interested in, it's the basketball player. I prefer to deal with women who know the difference."

"Ah, so that's why I never hear about you dating since you broke up with Natalie."

"No, you don't hear because I don't tell." He shrugged one shoulder and admitted. "Not that there's a lot to say. Basketball and school have taken over my life and women are nothing but trouble." He dumped the empty bottle in the garbage can and sat back at his desk.

"I've heard that before, and I didn't believe it the first hundred times, either."

Rolling his eyes, he decided to change the subject. "So, to what do I owe the pleasure of your call? Just decided to nag me on my dateless life?"

"No, actually I called to invite you to our place for dinner Saturday since Cliff is playing in Salt Lake on Sunday. Paige is coming to visit while his team's here." Denise's adopted sister, Paige, had married Cliff a few years earlier. "I'd invite Kaylee too . . . ."

"Don't push it, Denise." Irritation shot through him. Her nagging about Kaylee was worse than her questions about females. He understood where she was coming from, but he wasn't ready to break through that particular barrier—not yet.

"That's what I figured. I won't invite her this time, but it kills me to have to choose between you guys." There was a long pause. "So will you come?"

Curtis turned and looked at his calendar, even though he knew it was wide open. It wasn't that he didn't want to go, he just felt somehow out of place there alone when everyone else was married. But he couldn't really turn down the opportunity to see his brother and sister. He could use a break, and he rarely saw his twin during basketball season. "I'll be there. What time?"

"We'll eat at five, but come early. I'll let Lily know you'll pick her up."

"I should have known. Denise, you aren't trying to fix me up with your best friend, are you? Cause not only is her divorce not finalized yet, but you know how I feel about that."

"She's having car trouble and you're coming from the same city. It doesn't make sense for you to drive separately. Besides, I thought you liked her, and her kids are adorable."

She made her point and it was reasonable. "I do like her—she's nice. Her kids are adorable, and I'll be happy to give her a lift—just as long as you don't get any ideas."

"Ideas? Who, me?"

"Right," he mumbled.

When he hung up fifteen minutes later, Curtis felt relaxed and ready to return to work. In another hour he could have his assignment done. He glanced at the clock and his smile faded. Of course, then he'd have to hit the sack if he wanted to be alert for class in the morning.

The brief message Denise left on Lily's phone was a nice surprise. They hadn't spoken in a week and Lily was happy to have a break.

After settling Stephen in front of *Finding Nemo*, she sat at the bar in her kitchen and glanced at the stack of papers she needed to correct, along with the visual aids she still had to prepare for the next day. And then there was dinner to make. She considered the list of things she needed to do and reached for the phone instead. The phone rang twice before Denise answered.

"Hey, you called?"

"Yeah, you didn't just get home from school, did you?"

"No, I had some errands to run before I picked up the kids. It was a crazy day." Lily opened the fridge to consider dinner ingredients.

"Your class is a handful, huh?"

"A couple of the kids are. Of course, there are still plenty of cute ones who make every minute of it worthwhile. There's a really shy girl who's starting to open up with me a little. On the other hand, there's Colton—I don't understand what's going on with him." She moved the milk out of the way on the top shelf to peer behind it, but the bag of limp green salad did not bode well.

"Is he a little devil?"

"He could give Dennis the Menace a run for his money. I wish I could find a way to help him, but I won't be teaching the class much longer."

"You can only do what you can do."

"Yeah. Poor Stephen's been fussy too—whining, jealous of every minute I spend with Sophie the past couple of days. Anyway, that's not why you called me. What's going on?" Sighing inwardly, she pulled bread and cheese out. She just didn't have the energy for anything more complicated than grilled cheese tonight.

"Cliff and Paige are going to be in town for his game next weekend and we wanted to meet for dinner on Saturday. Say you can come. You haven't seen them in ages."

Lily paused and thought about everything she had to do. "I could work it in, but I'm not sure if my car will make the trip." She pulled the nearly empty tub of butter from the fridge and made a mental note to buy more soon. "I might be able to borrow Shelly's, I guess."

"Don't worry about it. Curtis said he'd be happy to bring you down with him. I suggested it, but if you're both coming you might as well ride together and save the miles and gas. At least you'll have someone to talk to. I know how hard it is to drive with small children."

"Denise?" Lily rocked back on her heels. There were definite undertones in her friend's voice. "Are you trying to set us up?"

"Set you up? Why? Just because you are two eligible young people? Just because you're my close personal friend and cousin, and he's my close, personal, um, brother? Why would I do that?" Her voice was just a little too cool, too casual for Lily to believe a word she said.

"That's the problem with you happily married people. You all think everyone else is dying to get married too." Lily pulled a knife from the drawer and opened the butter tub. "My divorce may not be final for months now that I'm fighting John on the child support issue. Men are totally off the list for me at the moment."

"Did I say anything about marriage or dating?"

"Of course not, you wouldn't say anything like that—it would be too direct. What time are we meeting?"

When Lily hung up the phone, she had promised to call Curtis right away to arrange a ride. She needed to tell him how things had gone with the basketball coaches anyway.

CHAPTER FOURTEEN

Curtis was in his dorm room after dinner when he remembered to check his voice mail. He generally kept his ringer off during the day, so incoming calls would be saved but wouldn't disturb him. Four messages replayed for him: a reminder about a church service project the next morning; a request from a classmate asking to borrow notes; a message from Lacy asking if he was going to be at the dance that night; and Lily wanting to know about arrangements for the next day. He felt a twinge of guilt that he hadn't contacted Lily yet. It had been on his mind all week, but he'd put it off.

He figured he might as well call her back now. Since he had no intention of playing Hide from Lacy all night, the dance was out. As he waited for Lily to pick up, Curtis pulled his school books out of his backpack and turned on his laptop. Five rings later, her voice mail came on. "Hey, Lily, this is Curtis. I'll have my phone on for the rest of the night, so call me back." He hung up and returned to the computer, glanced at the reminder for the basketball team banquet on his desk, and nudged it away. The coach's note at the bottom that he should bring a date made Curtis want to squirm. He didn't need the pressure to find someone to go with him.

A moment later there was a knock at the door.

Thinking of all the work he had to do, he answered the door to find Lacy standing outside. "Hey, Curtis. You look great tonight. Are you coming to the dance?" She twisted a long lock of shiny brown hair around her finger.

"I'm sorry." He tried to sound like he meant it. "I have a ton of homework to do."

"But you've worked so hard all semester. Don't you think you deserve a break?" She batted green eyes at him and smiled flirtatiously. She was cute, and he knew several guys in the ward who would've been thrilled to be the object of her attention. He just wasn't one of them.

"I have a big project due Tuesday and a family thing tomorrow, so I need to study tonight." He tried inching the door toward her a little, though she still stood in the hallway. He wouldn't shut it in her face, but he didn't want to encourage her, either.

"Come on, it'll be fun. You don't get out often enough."

Curtis was trying to come up with a response when he saw Shelly and Lily come around the corner of the hallway. Shelly had a bundle of blankets snuggled against her shoulder, and Lily held Stephen on her hip. The two sisters laughed and shared a conspiratorial look. He saw his salvation. "Hey, Lily, I was trying to reach you. You must not have your cell phone with you."

Lily smiled at him, then glanced over at a miffed-looking Lacy. "Hi. Lacy, isn't it? It's good to see you again." She turned back to Curtis. "What's up?"

"I was just telling Lacy how sorry I was that I couldn't spare the time to go to the dance tonight. I have homework coming out my ears."

"Ears!" Stephen said loudly and pointed to Curtis's ear.

Lily grabbed one of Curtis's earlobes and pretended to look in his ear. "Yeah, I can see it. There's a shovel and a backhoe in there. Looky, Stephen, isn't that scary?" She spoke to her son in a lower voice, making him giggle, then returned her gaze to Curtis. She kept a straight face as she looked him in the eyes. "You're in serious trouble. You're going to need some minor surgery for that. I happen to know a really good specialist."

"You dork." He pulled her into a hug, careful not to squish Stephen. "I've been thinking about you all week." Curtis looked down at her, his arm still around her waist, and they locked gazes. He thought he saw something flash in her eyes for a moment, and he felt his throat tighten. He took a deep breath and caught the scent of lilacs. His mouth felt suddenly dry.

A slow smile spread across her face, and she tilted her head to the side as a playful look entered her eyes. "Yeah? I've wondered why you haven't called me. I've been waiting to hear about our plans tomorrow."

"You'll have to check your voice mail." His heart began to speed up as their flirting continued. He was standing entirely too close for friendship and was secretly glad Lacy was giving him an excuse to do so.

"Looks like you're busy tonight," Lacy said in a huff. "I'll see you later, Curtis." She turned and stalked down the hall.

Curtis looked at Shelly and saw her struggling not to burst into laughter. When Lacy disappeared from view, he eased his arm from around Lily and stepped away. He did his best not to show his reluctance.

"Now you owe me again. And I know just what I want in return." Lily lifted an eyebrow at him. "I know you're swamped, but do you mind if we come in while I discuss some business with you?"

"Business? That does sound serious. I can't spare much time, but the two of you are welcome to come in." Curtis held open the door and motioned for them to sit on his bed while he took the only chair in the room. "Now, what's going on?"

"First off, why can't you just tell Lacy you're not interested? Why the charade?" Shelly asked. "You're not setting a very good example for Stephen here."

Stephen smiled and clapped his hands.

Curtis let loose a smile of his own. "Just spineless, I guess." He paused for a minute and then remembered the "business" Lily had mentioned. "So, Lily, you need some guy discouraged or something?" He reached out and grabbed one of Stephen's waving fists. Stephen's other hand latched onto Curtis's watch. "Aren't you doing your job, protecting your mama?"

"Not everyone has their own fan club. Quite the opposite, in fact." Lily readjusted Stephen on her lap. "No, I spoke with the basketball coaches this week—men's and women's. They both love the idea of their players getting involved in an anti-drug campaign. They're going to, um, suggest strenuously that their team members help out with the project."

"But they can't make me get involved. I'm no longer part of the basketball program, now that the season's over." He saw the question in her eyes and took a slow, deep breath. He knew why she was here—he couldn't forget that her school principal might make things difficult if he didn't come through for her.

"Yes, but if you could at least do a couple of schools, it would really help me. At least my school. I know how busy you are. I'm even willing to help you write your speech or whatever."

"Is your job still on the line, then?" And an even better question, "Are you sure you want to work with a principal like that?"

"I wouldn't necessarily teach in her school next year if I get hired by the district. I don't know. Look, if you really can't, just say so. I know you're overwhelmed right now." She didn't meet his eyes but instead kept her attention riveted on the toddler in her lap.

Curtis fought with himself as he remembered she was not like Natalie, no matter what this request looked like. It wouldn't kill him, really, and he could make it work, if she helped with the speech. He glanced at the desk and saw the invitation for the banquet sitting there. "I might be able to work something out, if you'd do me a favor."

"What?"

He told her about the banquet and the not-so-subtle request for him to bring a date—only he didn't call it a date.

Lily's eyebrows lifted as she repositioned Stephen in her arms. "Why me?"

"We get along well enough, and you know I'm not interested in a relationship."

Shelly looked incensed. "Are you saying my sister isn't good enough for you?"

Curtis rubbed a hand over his face. "That isn't it at all. I just—" Everything he thought of to explain sounded worse and worse. "There's no good way out of this, is there? Look, I don't want some girl to get ideas about a grand future together because I took her to one event. I don't want to sit through the whole evening bored out of my skull because I have nothing in common with the person I take, and I don't want to make a big deal out of this."

He looked at Lily and remembered that sizzle of awareness that had passed between them out in the hall, but he pushed it away. This had nothing to do with that. "We're friends, right? Wouldn't you like an evening of adult conversation and a meal you don't have to make yourself while your sister generously offers to babysit?"

"Thanks for volunteering me." Shelly's smile said she wasn't angry. "I would, of course, adore a chance to teach Stephen important skills like how to flush half a roll of toilet paper in one go and that cigarette lighters make a bright light." The innocent expression on her face lasted only half a second before her lips began to twitch.

"You're pushing your luck if you actually want to watch my kids, you know." Lily gave her sister a look of mock censure, then turned to Curtis. "You realize I'm still married, right?"

"This isn't a date. It's two friends having dinner together. I'll help you out of your spot; you can help me out of mine. We're even."

"Dressed to the nines and attending an important event together with a fancy meal and dancing," Shelly clarified.

With a look of alarm on her face, Lily glanced at her sister, then back to him. "How dressed up are we talking about?"

"What you wore to church last week was nice." He couldn't care less if she came in a brown paper bag as long as he didn't have to ask anyone else. Besides, he'd enjoy the otherwise long and dry evening if she were with him.

She still looked wary. "And you'll be willing to speak at a few schools?"

"Absolutely. You said you'll help me with it, right? Is your offer still good? Give me the schedule and I'll sign up for a few assemblies. Do you have it with you?" He'd have done it even if she hadn't agreed to attend the banquet with him, but he wasn't going to complain.

"I'll bring it with me tomorrow when we go to Denise's." Apparently satisfied, Lily stood and Shelly followed suit. "I thought I heard something about homework. We'll clear out and let you get back to it, unless you want to catch that dance, after all." Laughter bubbled in her eyes. "I'm sure Lacy would be happy to entertain you."

"Thanks, but I'd better stick to my homework tonight." His answer was dry. "I'll pick you up tomorrow at two then?"

"I'll be ready." Lily took a note from her back pocket. "I wasn't sure if you'd be here, so I wrote down my address, in case you didn't remember from helping me move in."

A moment later, Curtis was alone again.

The scent of lilacs seemed to linger in the air for hours.

The next day, after strapping Stephen and Sophie into the back seat, Lily got into Curtis's car with the awkward feeling of going on a blind date. Not that this was a date. He wasn't her type at all, but Denise's hints seemed impossible to forget, and it made Lily uncomfortable. She didn't remember Denise being that slick before. She must have been taking lessons from Rich.

Rich was the sort who could charm a canary into a cat's mouth. Luckily, he was harmless. Usually. In any case, Lily liked Curtis so it wasn't as though it would·be a hardship to ride with him. Curtis grinned at her when she looked up from snapping her seat belt into place and her heart raced. She was grateful when Stephen distracted her by demanding a toy.

The black Ford Thunderbird was old, probably near forty years or more, but immaculate. Lily lifted a brow as she looked over at Curtis. "I know guys can be funny about their cars, but I was under the impression you're too busy to polish up a car like this. How do you afford gas for this monster?"

He grinned back at her then pulled away from the curb. "I'm too busy to mess it up too. A summer job bought my wheels and pays for the upkeep. Scholarship pays for school."

"You wouldn't have time to work anyway." She wasn't a car buff, but she had to admire this one. It was sleek and shiny, and the engine purred where her car's engine roared.

"And no boss would put up with my schedule even if I did find the time. Speaking of work, how's the teaching going?"

She set her head back against the seat and looked out the front window. "I finished up the last day of substituting for that class. Their regular teacher will be back Monday, and I have something set up for Wednesday. I think the district will probably keep me fairly busy."

"And every class will have its own terrors, I guess."

Lily thought of Colton and smiled despite herself. "One or two, but nothing I can't handle." She glanced over at Curtis's profile and took in the confident grip he had on the steering wheel as he pointed the car south. "I bet you were a handful in school—charming the office staff, giving off vibes of wide-eyed innocence while you planned your next prank."

He grinned again. "You're off there. Well, on some of it. I did charm the office staff. My practical jokes weren't as well developed back then as they are now. Mostly my teachers wanted to pull their hair out because I was always in the middle of any fight on the school grounds. I've always had a bit of a temper, though I learned to control it by the time I hit junior high."

"And where was Cliff in all of this?"

"He had my back . . . or he was the one I traded punches with. He was my best friend, but we got on each other's nerves too. Yeah, my teachers were probably glad to wave good-bye at the end of the year." His smile faded, and he looked a bit sorry for his actions.

Sophie began to wail and Lily reached back, inserting the pacifier in the little girl's mouth again. She turned to look at Curtis while she held the pacifier in place for a long moment. Sophie would spit it out otherwise, then start fussing all over again. This put Lily in the perfect position to study Curtis and appreciate his casual good looks. "You must like landscaping if you're studying it. What kind of jobs do you want to do?"

He started talking about his dreams and plans. They discussed plants and design for a long while. Eventually they segued into her work at the school and the plans that were coming together for the anti-drug assembly and activities. She was surprised when he really listened and asked relevant questions—John never would have. The next thing she knew, they were looking at signs for the Orem/Lindon exit. The trip seemed to take no time at all.

Coming back into the area where she had lived for so long brought up unhappy memories. She pushed them back. There was no way to know how the divorce settlement and custody suit would go, and she didn't plan to dwell on it today.

Chapter Fifteen

Curtis smiled when Denise greeted them at the door, offering hugs and gushing over Lily's children. She sent Stephen down the hall to play with Cam. Then Rich walked in and stopped behind Denise, putting his hands around his wife's waist in an embrace. She looked back at her husband and gave him a kiss. It sent a little jolt of wistfulness into Curtis's heart, as it always did to see them together and so happy. Not that he had time for a relationship, or the inclination, really—he just wondered what it would be like to be as happy as Rich and Denise.

Curtis's smile broadened when Cliff appeared from the other room.

"Hey, frog face, it's about time you got here." Cliff pulled Curtis into a back-pounding hug.

"Yeah, I would have been here earlier, but I had to wait forever for Lily to get ready." He turned and caught the pillow she threw at him.

"Not true. He was late and I waited for him," Lily defended herself.

"Oh, right, I forgot." Curtis turned back to his identical twin. "Good game last night. Too bad you have such an ugly mug the camera avoids you."

"Speak for yourself, Dog Breath." Cliff put a hand on Curtis's shoulder and gave it a squeeze. "Good job at the tournament. I miss playing with you."

"Yeah, well, with a little luck, I'll be slaughtering you on the court again soon."

"Boys, boys. Can't we all just get along?" Paige intervened. It had taken Curtis a while to get to know Paige enough to be comfortable with her. At first she'd seemed the least likely candidate for his brother to marry. But since she was also Denise's adopted sister, the five of them, with Rich, had spent quite a bit of time together before Cliff went pro. Once he got past the public façade she wore, Paige turned out to be pretty nice, and she clearly adored Cliff.

"Yes, Mom." Curtis pulled his sister-in-law close for a hug, then set her back and looked at her. "You get more beautiful every day. What are you still doing with this loser?"

"Wondering if the two of you will ever grow up."

"Not a chance." Curtis dropped a kiss on her forehead and released her. "How's everyone at home?"

Paige walked over to coo at Sophie. "Great. You've probably seen Gerald around campus now and then," she said to Curtis, who nodded that he had seen her brother. After a moment she had the baby out of the carrier and returned to her seat on the sofa with the little bundle. Cuddling the baby close, she continued, "My parents are doing great, but they had an emergency come up this morning, so they couldn't be here, and . . ." She paused and looked around, waiting until every eye was on her. "We'll be having a baby of our own in September."

Everyone swarmed around, offering congratulations and more hugs. Curtis saw the excitement shining in Cliff's and Paige's eyes and felt another twinge of jealousy. He knew they'd had their share of difficulties, what with Cliff's NBA schedule and Paige's many committees and her work with their ward in Chicago, but they seemed to make it work.

Dinner was noisy and filled with laughter. Curtis was glad Lily slid almost seamlessly into the family party. When he looked at her sitting beside him, their gazes met and he smiled. He was glad she'd come. He was enjoying getting to know her better more than he'd expected.

They were all sampling a slice of pie and glass of milk an hour later when Lily looked up from where she was feeding Sophie a bottle. "Gerald couldn't come?"

"He wanted to, but he said he's going home to meet Rachel's family this weekend." Denise grinned and wiggled her eyebrows.

"I met her a few weeks ago. She seems really nice," Curtis said.

"Speaking of family," Denise said in a deceptively casual tone. "Kaylee said you emailed her back after your invitational." She lifted her eyes to look at Curtis, sending him a hopeful look.

Curtis shifted his gaze to the pie in his hands, not wanting to get into it. "Yeah, I couldn't completely ignore her. It would have been too rude after she wrote me." Twice.

Denise played with her own pie, acting as though she were focused on the dish. "I wondered if it was another step toward letting her in." Denise's voice was light and casual. Too casual to be natural. The air seemed to prickle around them all as they carefully picked their way through the conversation.

"It wasn't that big of a deal. Don't make anything out of it." He looked back at his sister, hoping she didn't sense the confusion warring inside him.

A lifted eyebrow said she knew he was wavering on this issue, but he shrugged and looked away.

"Coach has seen tapes of us playing together," Cliff intervened. "He wants us both on his team. One of our guards is retiring." Curtis was grateful for the subject change. Even though Cliff kept in touch with the whole tangled family and emailed Kaylee regularly, he claimed he understood Curtis's reluctance.

"Tell your coach he'll have to fight everyone else for me." Curtis gave Cliff a wry grin. "I'd love to play ball with you again, but I'd rather not end up in Chicago."

Cliff's grin was huge. "Guess we'll see what happens."

Curtis knew most people thought he had wasted time not jumping into the NBA when he had the chance two years earlier. Recruiters had tried to get him to apply for the draft. Who knew how long he would be able to play, they pressed. He was twenty-five now. If he was lucky, he'd have a good decade of ball in him before he retired.

The previous spring he had nearly applied because Natalie pushed so hard, but it felt all wrong to him. He loved basketball. It was much more than a scholarship or a hobby, but he hadn't been sure if he was ready for the lifestyle choices it would require—the distance from home, the many days and nights on the road, even more traveling than he already had with college. It was a big step. Now he was making it, and he hoped it wasn't a mistake.

It was nearly 10:00 PM when Curtis and Lily began their return trip to Logan. It had been nice for Curtis to spend time with his family, but there were enough questions raised at the get-together to leave him unsettled.

It wasn't that he hadn't wanted to go pro two years earlier, he thought as he listened to Lily singing Stephen to sleep. There were plenty of aspects that appealed to him—the game, for one. The paycheck was another bonus. And though traveling was mostly a pain, he would get to see a lot of cities around the country he hadn't seen yet and probably wouldn't otherwise. It was a great dream that so many people shared—including his ex-girlfriend, Natalie. If Curtis hadn't overheard her talking to a friend about his prospects, he might not have realized that her potential status as an NBA wife was the real reason for her interest in him.

Then there were the drawbacks. No life of his own for six months out of the year—and that was if they didn't make it to the playoffs. And there was the superstar lifestyle with drugs and booze and women that many athletes still found time to indulge in despite the crazy schedules. Then the working on Sunday thing. Granted, he would usually be able to attend church wherever he went, and Sunday games were only once or twice a month. Still, he really struggled with those issues.

He knew a lot of LDS athletes were able to make a positive contribution to the Church through their examples, but he didn't want to be that candle on a hill. He just wanted to be Curtis.

His thoughts were interrupted as they passed through South Salt Lake when Lily broke the long silence. "What's it like to be a twin?"

He glanced at her in surprise, noting the wistful look on her face. "What? I mean, that's a hard question to answer since I don't know what it's like not to be a twin." He'd heard the question before, but it surprised him this time. Coming from her, it didn't feel like idle curiosity.

They sat in silence for a moment as he tried to come up with a better answer. When she spoke, her voice was soft, and he had to strain to hear it over the sound of tires on concrete and the hum of the engine. "I was born a twin. My brother, Joel, died of SIDS when we were two months old. I've always wondered what life would've been like if he'd lived, how it would have been to have a brother around—I have all sisters."

That made more sense. "I'm sorry about your brother."

He caught her shrug from the corner of his eye. "I don't remember him. All we have are pictures, a couple of baby outfits he wore that my mom couldn't get rid of, and a grave marker. Sometimes I feel like part of me is missing because I didn't have him growing up. What did I miss out on?"

"I can only tell you what it was like for me. Cliff was my best friend and my favorite nemesis. Without him to compete with, I doubt my basketball skills would be what they are, since he pushed me constantly to try and beat him. I guess it worked the other way with school. I was always a little better at book work, though that didn't come easy to me. When I needed someone to talk to, someone to support me against everyone else, he was there. Yes, we fought sometimes—a lot of times—but he always had my back."

"It must've been hard to have so much distance between you since you graduated from high school, though—different schools, different countries for your missions. Now he lives halfway across the continent and you hardly ever see him." Her voice was calm, but when he looked over at her, there were tears on her cheek, glistening in the lights on the side of the highway.

Uncomfortable with the emotional display, and the fact that it tugged at his heart, he was quick to return his gaze to the road. "You look upset enough for both of us."

She laughed and wiped her cheeks. "You probably think I'm one of those wimpy, weepy females. I'm not usually like this."

He allowed a smile to form on his face. "No, I don't think that. I can only imagine how you must feel, and you can only imagine how I feel. It's hard having Cliff so far away, especially with his crazy schedule. Basketball has kept us both hopping. I'm glad he has Paige. She seems to accept the job and all it includes and doesn't think it's all about her." He realized his past experiences were starting to influence his words, and he fought to put those memories behind him.

"I'm sure it helps make things more normal for him, to have someone to come home to. But I got off topic. Cliff and I keep up with each other through email and phone calls. Mostly we leave messages because we never seem to be available to talk at the same time."

After a brief pause, he continued. "There are disadvantages to being a twin too, you know. You have to share your birthday." She laughed at that. "Being identical meant we didn't really have our own identities. I've been called Cliff almost more times than I've been called Curtis. A lot of girls in school liked the Werner twins—"

"So humble." Sophie began to fuss and Lily turned around to check on her, sticking the pacifier back in her mouth for the fiftieth time that day, it seemed.

"Let me finish." He smiled despite himself. "They liked the twins.

They didn't care that Cliff and I were totally different people with different interests and personalities. It was like we were just carbon copies of each other. It wasn't until I got to Utah State that people started seeing me as Curtis, instead of as Cliff-and-Curtis. Even then, whenever we played together, they made a big deal about it in the press—the Werner Wonders." That nickname always made him feel like people expected far more of him than he would possibly be able to fulfill. "Now it's 'why didn't you go pro like your twin?'"

"Why *didn't* you go pro like your twin?"

Usually the question irritated him, but she seemed so genuine he couldn't refuse to answer. "I wanted to finish my degree, to make something of myself besides my basketball career. Cliff has been able to take his last year of classes through independent study and via the Internet. That wouldn't work as well for me, but I am planning to do most of my masters through distance-learning." Of course, this was only part of the reason he hadn't gone pro, but he wasn't about to get into the rest of it with Lily.

"And . . . ?"

Curtis glanced over and caught her patient stare, one arm stretched over the seat to soothe her child, her body turned fully toward him. He wasn't getting anything past her. "And . . . it didn't feel right. Not yet."

A lifted eyebrow indicated she thought there was more, but she didn't push him. "But now it is?"

"This is it for me. If I don't join up this year, I won't be able to later, I'll be too out of practice. It was time to make a decision. I love basketball."

"You don't sound thrilled about the pros, though. What is it? The money? The travel? The fame?" Her voice was a bit bitter, but the dark made her face unreadable.

"If it were just basketball—just playing and making a nice income, it would've been easy to go pro a long time ago, but there were a lot of other things to consider."

The only sounds that came between them for the next several minutes were the swish of tires on concrete, the humming motors on the freeway, and music floating from the radio.

"So, tell me about your family," he finally said. "You and Shelly seem to be great friends. Has it always been that way?"

"Not always. We've had our disagreements, but I don't remember us ever getting into brawls." He held in a smile as she continued. She talked about her sisters, Kellie and Danyelle, who were still in high school, about summers with Rich at her house and the crazy things they had done in her hometown of Ephraim. They discussed his mission and favorite classes. Before they knew it, they were home again.

After carrying Sophie inside, Curtis returned to the car to remove Stephen's car seat. When he reached the front door again, Lily had already eased Stephen into his toddler bed. "Thanks for the ride tonight," she said as she watched him set the seat in the living room.

"No problem. It was good to talk to you. Maybe Denise wasn't totally off when she asked me to give you a ride." He smiled at her, noticing how tired her eyes looked. "That would have been a long, lonely trip without you—and the kids."

"I thought she was trying to nudge us together when she called," Lily said, hooking her thumbs in her back pockets. "She didn't seem that way tonight, though."

"I had the same idea." His gaze slid down to her lush, soft-looking lips. When he realized he was wondering what it would be like to kiss her, he blinked and stepped back. He was so not going there, no matter how good a time they'd just had together. "I'll, uh, call you in a day or two about the banquet."

"We'll have to get together to write your assembly speech. Maybe you can get a study room at the library."

"Yeah. If not, we can probably find a table. I'll call. Good night." He stepped out on the porch and turned toward his car, hearing her call good night to him. *That way lays madness, Curt. She's a friend, and that's the end of it.* He pushed the momentary insanity from his mind and began working on a garden plan in his head.

CHAPTER SIXTEEN

On Monday morning, Lily was cleaning up the kitchen from a late breakfast when there was knock at the door. Finger-combing her hair back from her face, Lily stepped around the piles of clothes she'd stacked in the front room to take to the laundromat, and then opened the door. A young woman wearing a coral sweater and tan pants stood on the other side.

"Hello, can I help you?" Lily asked.

"Yes, are you Lily Drake?" The woman hitched her brown leather purse further up her shoulder.

"I am."

"I'm Melinda Drizzle, the caseworker who's been assigned to your children during the custody suit. May I come in? I know I don't have an appointment, but we like to pop in sometimes to verify the condition of the house and how the kids are doing. Is now okay?" The woman's manner indicated she had every expectation of being allowed inside. She handed over an agency card with her name and office information.

Her fleeting perusal of Lily's appearance may have been nearly fast enough to miss, but it made Lily think of her messy hair, the sloppy clothes she wore, and her lack of makeup. Feeling like a frump, she smiled and stepped back into the room. "Come in. Now's fine, of course. You're lucky to have caught me. I'm going to the laundromat in a little bit and won't be home again for a few hours."

After taking a quick glance around, Lily was glad she hadn't let the condition of the apartment slump much. John had always wanted every-thing perfect, and while she didn't keep things to his exacting standards now, it wasn't a mess either. She introduced the woman to her children. Then, at Melinda's request to spend a few minutes alone with Stephen,

Lily returned to the kitchen to finish drying the dishes.

By the time Lily finished cleaning and was ready to tackle her appearance, Melinda had finished with Stephen and Sophie. She asked to be shown the bedrooms and bathrooms, checked to make sure chemicals and other toxins were out of reach, and looked for other hazards.

Sophie began to fuss and Lily picked her up, knowing the baby was hungry.

"If you wouldn't mind, I have a few questions for you." Melinda motioned toward the sofa.

"I'll need to nurse while we talk. Sophie's ready for lunch." Lily tried to put on a big smile, while her stomach felt like an entire swarm of hornets flew around inside it.

Melinda agreed, and once Lily settled Sophie in to eat with a baby blanket covering her for modesty, the caseworker began. "Your apartment seems fine. It's clean and orderly, considering you've got a toddler. I don't see any issues there. I'll have to make several visits over the next little while to ascertain the quality of care your children are getting. Now, I understand you're employed."

Lily stammered out an explanation about her work situation and day care arrangements. Then she answered what seemed like hundreds of questions about the children's daily routines.

When the caseworker finally left, Lily wasn't sure if she'd done well or not. Though she knew her in-laws could provide everything the children needed materially, she wasn't as certain about the time and attention they required. Her biggest fear was that Melinda wouldn't understand that or see how cold her in-laws could and would be to the children. What would she do if she lost her babies?

Curtis and Lily spent the next two evenings poring over information for his speech. He set up his laptop in a library study room as they wrote and polished, and he found he enjoyed the time with her. On Tuesday he was impressed with how contentedly Stephen sat on the floor playing with Sophie while they worked. On Wednesday they weren't so lucky.

Lily hurried in, apologizing for being late. "I think Stephen's coming down with something. He's been a real pill today. Sorry." She bounced the toddler on her lap while they discussed the changes she'd considered the night before.

Stephen was so whiney that Lily finally laid him on a blanket on the floor. She gave him something to play with, then told him it was time to sleep. He whimpered for several minutes, but she ignored him and then, miraculously, he slept.

Sophie began fussing after a little while. After ten minutes Lily was unable to calm the baby so Curtis offered to take her. Lily typed for a moment then looked up, her eyes narrowing as she focused on her silent infant. "You just had to show me up, didn't you?"

"What can I say? Females love me. It's the animal magnetism." He glanced up at her from playing with Sophie's nose, grinning until he saw the telltale shine in Lily eyes.

She blinked back tears and passed a hand over her face, which was turning red with mortification. "Sorry, not enough sleep, too much stress." She took a deep breath, then looked at him again. "Where were we?"

"Quitting. We're almost done, anyway. You're too tired for this. I'm sorry to drag you into everything. I forget how busy you are." He didn't do well with crying females—not when the tears were genuine. He felt guilty pulling her away from home when her kids weren't feeling well and she had worked a long day at school. It was a marvel she managed so well.

"I think you have that backward. I got you into this, remember?"

"Have you worked much this week?" he asked.

She looked away and nodded. "Every day, which puts the kids out of sorts as much as me. It's just that Stephen's being fussy and Sophie's colicky. She isn't sleeping much, so then I don't sleep much. Her crying keeps Stephen awake, and he's difficult enough to handle without being worn out."

After a couple more tears squeezed from her eyes, she put out a hand, stopping his next comment. "They're behaving now. Let's finish this— we're nearly done. You don't mind holding her a little longer, do you?"

"No problem." Curtis watched Lily compose herself and focus on the laptop again. He told himself to remember how much she had on her plate in the future and maybe to drop a bug in her sister's ear about giving her a night out from time to time.

The mail came Saturday morning with a large manila envelope from her divorce lawyer. Not wanting to look at it quite yet, Lily set it on the counter while she flipped through the stack of mail. It was mostly junk.

Stephen began crying from his room, and she gave him mommy kisses for a bump on the head after he rolled off the bed. Sophie began that fussy whine that meant she needed to eat, and then Stephen was crying, hungry, and needed breakfast. By the time Lily returned to the mail, she was snacking on a graham cracker to bolster her own flagging energy.

Clenching her teeth against whatever news it contained, she opened the envelope and found a new copy of the divorce documents in her hands. A small envelope fell out with the legal papers, and she opened it to find a sheet of paper with John's handwriting on it.

Lily,

I decided it was easiest just to give in on the child support issue. It won't matter since the Feds will be taking most of my paycheck for years and you won't see a dime of child support until they're satisfied. Besides, when my parents win the custody suit, you'll be paying them. You really are a pathetic mother. Take what you can get, I guess. It's always been my motto.

John

The rage that filled Lily's chest was enough to make her want to rip all the documents to shreds, but she couldn't do that. She wanted the divorce over with so she could stop worrying about it. She'd been working on her defense against the Drake's suit, but the fact that she had barely worked that week and didn't have anything scheduled for the next week either didn't help. When it wasn't the kids keeping her awake, it was the stress and helplessness of her situation. If she filled out one more job application in the next few days, she thought she would scream.

After putting the children down for their afternoon naps, Lily read the document front to back and then signed it. As soon as she dropped it back in the mail to the judge, she would start preparing for the banquet that night. She wasn't going to lose her children, and she wouldn't let John's nastiness get her down. She'd just won a fight in the divorce against him. It was a day to celebrate. With any luck, she'd be legally unshackled from him before the month ended.

CHAPTER SEVENTEEN

Lily knew Curtis had told her she could wear Sunday dress to the basketball banquet, but she wasn't about to choose a denim skirt and pink T-shirt for something this nice. She spent considerable time debating between several formal dresses that hung in her closet, things she'd ignored since John's arrest.

Though she told herself it wasn't a real date, she spent more time than usual teasing her hair into submission and making up her face. She still felt woefully inadequate as she looked in the full-length mirror on the back of the bathroom door. Her black sheath dress was a little tighter than before her recent pregnancy, and she was about to try on something else when the doorbell rang.

Dodging toy trucks and scattered crayons on the living room floor, Lily crossed the room in her nylon-clad feet. "Please let it be Shelly!" she whispered before putting on a smile and opening the front door.

Both Shelly and Curtis stood on the other side. "Hey." Curtis smiled at her, his eyes flitting over her in appreciation. "You look great. That's definitely not what you wore to church the other week."

Lily felt color bloom on her cheeks and worked to keep her expression calm. "It's not too dressy, is it?"

"No, it's perfect. I brought Shelly with me. It didn't make sense for both of us to drive." He still hadn't taken his eyes off of her.

"Of course not." Feeling herself blush, Lily invited them in. She went in search of the black heels that matched her dress and threw a few necessities into a coordinating clutch. She could hear Shelly talking to the kids before she joined Lily in the bedroom.

"You really do look great," Shelly said when they were alone. "I thought his eyes were going to pop for a minute there."

"Don't be ridiculous," Lily whispered back under her breath, though the growing heat in her cheeks said she was blushing—again. "I'm sure you're exaggerating. Now, you know where the formula and diapers are. I'm taking my cell phone, so you can call me if there's a problem." She headed back to the main room. Shelly trailed behind her as Lily lectured her on the locations of the first aid kit and emergency phone numbers.

"Yes, I know. Go on, get out of here. How do you expect me to teach Stephen to cut his own hair if you're in the way?" She shooed them toward the door.

Lily rolled here eyes at her sister. "Behave for at least the first five minutes, will you?"

"I only promise good behavior until the car pulls out of the parking lot." Shelly fluttered her lashes. "After that, it's party time."

"Party!" Stephen cried out. Then he seemed to realize his mom was leaving and began to wail.

"Cut the innocent routine," Lily told Shelly. "We already know what a devil you are. Thanks for your help." Lily gave her sister a quick one-armed hug, smothered both of her kids with hugs and kisses, then allowed Curtis to lead her out the door.

Stephen continued to fuss and wail, but she gritted her teeth and let it go. He was bound to stop crying in thirty seconds. The day care provider swore it happened that way every day.

She turned back to look at her door before they reached the parking lot, then caught Curtis's eye. "Sorry. I guess I'm an overprotective mother," she said, following Curtis to his car.

"You don't really believe Shelly when she says things like that—about the hair cutting and toilet paper flushing?" He lifted an eyebrow at her.

"No, she's a great babysitter. You'd think I'd be used to leaving my babies with someone else after leaving them at day care when I work, but I hate it. I don't like leaving them at day care either. I'm just a bit neurotic, I guess." She laughed it off and slid into the car as he held the door for her.

He shut her door and came around to the driver's side. "Not so neurotic. My sisters are every bit as worried when they leave their kids."

Lily knew he was trying to comfort her, but she still felt guilty. Sophie was on formula half the time anyway, so it wasn't as though she had to nurse every two hours. And Shelly would take great care of both children.

Pushing the thought away, she determined to enjoy herself this evening. She asked him about his school projects, and he began to tell her about the landscape he and a couple of classmates were putting together for a new senior housing project in town.

Lily enjoyed the evening without her children. They were never far from her mind, but she felt reasonably confident Shelly could handle anything that came up.

The food was good, the others sitting at their table were nice, the awards speaker was entertaining, and Curtis won the MVP award for the year—something Denise was bound to brag about to all of her friends and family for ages to come. The thought made Lily smile even wider when Curtis returned to their table with the statue.

When the program came to an end, music started and Curtis asked her to dance.

"I don't know. It's getting late." Lily looked at her watch and noticed she was wrong. It wasn't even nine yet. She hoped he didn't think his company was boring her. When she looked into his eyes, he smiled down at her, his eyes teasing but intent. It made her breath catch.

"It's not that late," he wheedled. "Besides, it'll be nice to cut a rug with someone who's taken ballroom dance. Just a couple songs?"

Lily knew it wasn't the smartest choice. She was far too attracted to him. Still, even a married woman was allowed a dance—maybe two— with a man other than her husband. And she could imagine what his arms would feel like wrapped around her. She kept her tone light, hoping to mask her thoughts. "It's been years, almost forever."

He lifted his brows and studied her for a moment. "Funny, you don't look that old. I could swear we were about the same age."

She felt her lips twitch and held back a smile. "Sometimes I feel ancient." Still, she allowed him to lead her to the dance floor.

"Compared to that son of yours, anyone's bound to feel ancient from time to time." He swung her into an easy two-step. "You seem light enough on your feet to me. Not like a decrepit old woman at all."

She had been wrong; dancing with him was even nicer than she imagined. "I didn't know you could dance—ballroom, that is. You never said anything." She felt his hand on her shoulder, smelled the musky scent of his cologne, and noticed his smile. It had been ages since she'd felt this way in a man's arms—long before John went to jail. What a sad commentary on her marriage.

"It hasn't come up between landscaping, anti-drug speeches, and broken-down cars."

"I could swear I mentioned that I dance. You didn't say anything about it then." Lily felt as if they were wrapped in a bubble. The music swelled, and the rhythm flowed through them. She couldn't tear her gaze away from him. She felt a tug of sadness. She had dreamed of a moment like this with John, but nothing like it had ever happened.

His voice was low and just a trifle husky when he answered. "A guy has to keep a surprise up his sleeve once in a while. I wouldn't want to bore you."

"I hardly think that's possible."

The music changed, and he swung her into a waltz. Though they weren't facing right into each other's eyes in this stance, like they had been in the two-step, there was something very intimate in the way they were positioned to look over each other's shoulders.

Then she turned to look into his eyes. It was as though time hung between them. There was a tingling of awareness and a tightness in her chest as their gazes held and they whirled around the room. The waltz had never affected her like this before, but then she'd never danced it with Curtis. She was close enough to smell his cologne and she enjoyed the fact that he had the correct form and was skilled at the dance, leading her through the steps flawlessly, though they didn't try anything complicated. She knew from experience that a good partner was hard to find.

When the song ended and a fast one began, she hurried to step back and he glanced away, mumbling something about it being time to get her home. She agreed, looking toward the door as she tried to settle her pounding heart. She was still officially married, and despite her growing interest in Curtis, she wasn't sure she wanted to risk her heart again so soon.

Back in the car, he asked about her plans for the summer, as if he needed something to wash away the awareness Lily still felt flowing between them.

It took a moment for her to pull her attention to the subject at hand. "I'm applying everywhere. Summer teaching jobs are few and far between." She stared out the front window and tried not to think about her rapidly shrinking checking account; it would be a shame to end the good feelings by thinking about reality. "I don't have a lot of marketable skills, but I'm sure something will come along."

The drive was a short one, but by the time she reached home, the air was a little easier to breathe. She waited for him to come around to her door, reminding herself that the strong attraction she felt was certainly all in her head. It had just been too long since a man treated her right.

They walked to her front door, but when she lifted her hand to open it, his hand closed over hers. "Thank you for coming with me tonight. I had a really good time."

She lifted her gaze to his. "Thanks for asking me. It's been a long time since I had an enjoyable evening away from the kids. Congratulations again on your award."

He shrugged and then reached out to touch her cheek with his thumb. A sizzle passed between them again, and Lily wished John could have been more like Curtis—she had thought he was once. Thinking of John reminded her again that she was still married, and she blinked to clear her head. She removed her hand from under Curtis's and reached for the doorknob again.

When she opened the door, she found Shelly sitting on the sofa with a sleeping baby in her arms. "I was wondering when you'd get back," Shelly said.

Lily was grateful for her sister's presence to distract her from her racing heart.

CHAPTER EIGHTEEN

"Hey, man, it's just a bunch of rugrats. Don't let it bother you none," said Reggie, the teammate who'd be speaking with Curtis at his first appearance. The two of them sat in front of the school in Curtis's car.

"I know, it's crazy."

"If you can't make it through these assemblies, what're you going to do about the media circus at the draft?"

Curtis put a hand on his sick stomach. "Don't remind me. Public speaking was never my strong suit." He'd done a couple of quick interviews for the news here and there over the past couple of years but rarely any that lasted more than a couple of minutes, and he always sweated and sounded like a moron.

"You'll be fine. Come on, man. Let's get moving."

Curtis followed his ebony-skinned co-speaker out of the car. They had played together for a couple years and both were eligible for the NBA draft this year.

Reggie's confident air and smooth strut to the school's front door left Curtis following along while his stomach did somersaults. Lily wasn't working that day, but she'd gotten permission to be there. Knowing she'd watch him stumble over his words only added to his nerves.

When they entered the school, the light scent of lunch still floated in the air—tomato sauce and the sweetness of dessert mingled with the usual school smells of cleaners and dirt. They checked in at the front office, and a youngish woman who introduced herself as Tavonny walked them back to the gym. Thanking her, Curtis thought he could still hear the squeaking of sneakers on parquet floors, the call of kids tossing balls back and forth. All school gyms seemed to hold that quality for him. He and Reggie made their way up front to the microphone and stands, where the two players from the women's team waited.

Lily was already there with her kids. She looked lovely, as she always did. Curtis felt something twist up inside him, so he scooped up Stephen, swinging him through the air until he giggled. "Hey there, kiddo. How are you doing today?"

"Curtis! Fwy more, fwy, fwy!" He held out his arms to let Curtis know he wanted to be an airplane. Curtis was happy to comply. It gave him a moment to push back the memory of Lily in his arms at the banquet. He couldn't remember the last time he'd responded to any woman so strongly.

He and Stephen flew down the length of the stage and then back to where Lily cuddled Sophie. "Lily, I'm glad you could make it." He fought to act unaffected by her.

"I wouldn't miss it." Lily had Sophie in one arm and a trickle of drool glistened on the little girl's chin.

They chatted for a moment, and then Lily took her seat and waited for the kids to file in.

"Man, you're good with those kids. Too bad you didn't decide to be a kindergarten teacher instead of a farmer," Reggie said as they waited for everyone to settle down.

"Not a farmer, a landscape architect. Someday when you're rich and famous, you're going to build some ridiculously huge house—because I know you will, man—and you'll need someone to design the yard. Someone like me."

Reggie pushed Curtis's shoulder. "But you'll be too busy spending all your dough from your own fat contract. There won't be time for you to do plans for the likes of me."

Curtis tried to imagine being too busy to squeeze in time for garden design and couldn't. "Oh, I don't know. We'll see about that. There is an off-season, you know."

The wait was nerve-wracking, and the tension rose as the minutes ticked past on the clock. The four university students stood in the back behind a curtain, and Reggie kept up a comfortable patter, taking Curtis's mind off the growing crowd outside, though the roar of children's voices made it impossible to forget them completely.

Curtis would be the first speaker after Principal Nader introduced them. He preferred it that way, since it meant he could get it over with, then stand on the sidelines to watch the others. *Quick and painless*, he kept telling himself. Twelve minutes—ten if he talked too quickly. He always talked too quickly in front of crowds.

He felt like a fool being so nervous to stand and speak. After all, on his mission he'd talked to people about the Church, street contacted, held discussions, gone door to door. This shouldn't have been such a big deal, but for some reason looking out over hundreds of children seemed ten times more difficult. He said a quick prayer for strength and peace, then came out from behind the curtain when Principal Nader introduced him.

The sea of faces was even more intimidating than he'd expected, but he smiled and waved, then moved to make room for Reggie, who came out next. While he waited for the two women who were speaking that day, he scanned the audience, not realizing he was looking for Lily until his eyes stopped on hers. Her smile was brilliant, and it gave him peace, calming the fears that rolled inside him, if only a little.

The whole program went well. The children responded to what he and the other athletes said and kept their little eyes and faces turned toward the speakers, giving their full attention.

When it ended and the children's applause thundered around them, Curtis wondered why he'd ever questioned the decision to do this. Sure, he'd been given opportunities to speak to groups before, but nothing had been so important or so impossible to extricate himself from.

He glanced at Lily again and remembered the time they had spent together, planning his speech. Then he remembered twirling her around the dance floor at the banquet. At that moment, he was glad he hadn't felt like he could back out. He wanted an excuse to keep spending time with her.

The principal came back behind the curtain after the student exodus had begun and thanked them all again for coming and being willing to make a difference for her students.

Curtis smiled and said all the right things, but he couldn't wait to be released. When he stepped off the stage, he was happy to see Lily waiting. A bolt of something much stronger than friendship shot through him when she smiled in his direction.

On Wednesday, Curtis and his landscaping classmates took a trip to the local nursery, Kilpack Gardens, to select plants for their project. They chose some trees and shrubs, a collection of perennials, and a few annuals to provide color all summer long.

Curtis helped load the plants and trees into the back of two trucks as a clerk invoiced the purchases for the retirement center.

"Anything else we can get for you today?" the harried clerk asked when the last plant had been loaded.

"No, thanks. Busy day, huh?" Curtis glanced around and noticed a number of customers wandering the walkways on the other side of the fence. Several of them already had a wagon full. He noticed the "Now Hiring" sign in the front window and lifted a brow, looking at the man who was double-checking the invoices. "You hiring full time or part time?"

"Last I heard he wanted to add a couple more part-timers." He passed Curtis the papers to sign. "Looking for a summer job?"

"No, but I know someone who is."

Before John's arrest, it had been years since Lily needed a resume. She'd gotten very good at writing them lately.

She hadn't expected much at the nursery Curtis told her about, but she applied anyway. It had been a pleasant surprise to receive a request for an interview a couple days later.

Now facing the nursery, Lily pasted on a smile, ran her sweaty hands over her khaki pants, and stepped forward. The heat and smell of plant life filled her senses as she walked into the building, making Lily feel right at home. It was early yet, but she'd planned to give herself a few minutes to become familiar with their products and the layout of the business. She loved the gift shop with the funky flower-themed tea set and the little statues that would dress up a secluded corner. As she wandered, she compared the selection to other nurseries and considered what kind of displays she might put together, if given a chance.

Everything was ordered and made sense, and, though it was still early in the season, Lily noticed several customers walking through the aisles. She was approached once by a busy employee putting out new stock in the garden decoration section, but Lily could see they were understaffed. She wanted this job so badly—just being able to work around all of the plants and flowers and share her love of gardening with customers would make up for not having anywhere of her own to weed and plant this year.

She smiled as she approached the teenaged girl at the front counter. "Hello, I'm Lily Cox, and I have an appointment with Louis."

The girl smiled. "Right, he's waiting for you in his office. Let me show you." She led the way, her auburn ponytail bouncing from side to side.

A wooden porch swing hung beside the office door, which stood open, showing a couple desks with multiple computers and telephones. A sixty-ish man with salt and pepper hair sat behind a desk, a telephone cradled in the crook of his shoulder while he typed on a keyboard. He ordered some aquatic plants and three pallets of vermiculite before noticing the women standing in the doorway.

He gestured for Lily to wait a moment and wrapped up his call. Lily took a moment to inspect the man and his office. The desk was covered in papers but wasn't too disorganized. She noticed a vase with three leafy branches poking out of it and a bonsai on a nearby table. He hung up the phone and turned to her, extending a hand. "Hello, I'm Louis Kilpack."

"I'm Lily Cox." Lily took his hand and hoped hers wasn't too sweaty.

The man's eyes seemed to study her. His brows lowered, though his friendly expression remained. "Sit down. Your resume says you're a schoolteacher."

"I'm certified, but I haven't done much since my student teaching. I've been substitute teaching lately, but unfortunately the district won't be hiring for a while yet." She glanced out the office door at a vine that clung to a nearby railing. "I love your business. I took a look around before our appointment and really like the way you've set things up." Lily was anxious to turn his attention away from her dubious teaching career and focus on the nursery, but Louis wasn't cooperating.

"So if you have a teaching degree, why are you here? I have to wonder what the draw is for you. I don't want to offend you, but it can take a while to train new employees. I need to know you'll stick the summer out. I see from your resume that you haven't worked for a few years."

Lily moistened her lips, anxious at his no-nonsense approach. He was still being perfectly cordial, but she wondered if he'd already decided against hiring her. But if so, why did he bother to interview her? "I got married and stayed home with my baby. Since I'm getting a divorce," the words were still hard for her to say, "I need to get a job again, and I love gardening."

"I see you've never worked in a garden center before. Your resume said you've done a lot of gardening and studied botany. Tell me more about your experience."

With a smile, Lily began discussing her background, her college botany class, and her experience with landscaping her home in Highland. She pulled out several photos she'd taken of her yard the previous year and slid them across the table.

Louis took a long moment to study the picture before meeting her gaze again. "You did this yourself?" The note of curious respect in his voice relaxed her.

"I spoke with a landscaper. He provided the major muscle for the job and consulted with me on bedding shapes and plant suggestions. I picked most of the plants myself for each spot. I also did nearly all of the maintenance."

The man looked over the photos again, then handed them back to her. "Kilpack's is a family-owned nursery, and we only hire people who know what they're doing. If customers want someone to give them advice about where and when to plant their flowers and bushes to get the most out of them, they come here—not the big box stores. All of my employees, including the girls at the front counter, have to know plants, or they don't get hired."

It made sense to Lily. She nodded and lifted an eyebrow when he reached for the vase with the three branches in it. It had seemed like a strange decoration for his office. She seriously doubted he did any major propagation in there.

"If it were March, I'd take you out back and have you identify a few trees for me based only on structure and bark. Since they've all leafed out, however, we'll try something different." He set the vase between them on the desk, challenge in his eyes. "I want you to tell me what plants these branches came from if you can, and everything you know about them."

Confidence filled her as she looked them over. She was relived to be able to show him she really did know what she was talking about. The three branches in the vase were obviously from different plants. Lily could tell that now that she had them in front of her. None of them had flowers, though one showed signs of budding at the end of the branch. She reached out and took that one from the vase.

A close inspection confirmed her first impression. "This is lavender. It looks more like Munstead than the Hidcote or French lavender plants I had in my yard. Lavender not only smells sweet, but it's edible and lends a very classy touch to desserts." She looked at Louis. "Even my picky ex-husband couldn't find fault when I cooked with lavender. It requires only moderate watering—a couple good dousings a month, usually—and likes to sunbathe."

"Very good." Louis reached out and accepted the branch she offered back to him. "You really cook with it? I've met one or two people who do, but most people only dry it."

"It's a great addition to cakes and lemonade. I have a lot of recipes for it." Lily smiled and pulled the next branch from the vase. She turned it over in her hands and inspected it closely. This one was a bit tougher, but she had it in her yard in Highland, so it was familiar. "Perovskia, also known as Russian Sage, right?"

He nodded his head.

She continued with the details she recalled from her research, feeling more confident by the minute. When she had finished with the third branch—heather—Lily returned it to the vase and hoped she'd given Louis enough to satisfy him.

Louis sat back and studied her. "Most people don't get that last one."

"I made the mistake of ordering seeds for it my first year, and then I found out it doesn't like hot summers much. I tried to compensate by putting it on the east side of the house so it would get shade during the hottest part of the day. It did okay, but it never thrived, so I pulled it out after a couple years and put in something else. Summers are cooler here, so I imagine it would cope better."

He smiled at her explanation. "Yes, though I still suggest people give it afternoon shade."

"I'll remember that."

"Right now, the position is four days a week and we'll have to cut that back as fall approaches." He named an hourly wage, which seemed fairly generous, even if it was less than she made substitute teaching.

Lily had to hold back a laugh of relief. After paying for day care, she'd only make enough to cover rent and some of her utilities. Still, with her savings, she might be able to stretch things until she got a teaching contract—if she was very, very careful. She shook Louis's hand. "I look forward to working with you."

CHAPTER NINETEEN

The Logan High auditorium brimmed with the chatter of students. As Curtis was introduced, he smiled and waved at the mass of faces in the audience. He knew this was Kaylee's school, though he hadn't realized which schools he was signing up for originally. He wondered if she was out in the audience, nudging a friend and whispering that he was her brother. Or maybe she was too embarrassed. He didn't know what she was thinking, but with the stage lights blinding him, he couldn't see faces anyway.

The presentation went well, and the general reception was favorable, though Curtis figured most of the kids who needed to hear the message were probably out somewhere getting high. When the assembly ended and the hordes hurried to lunch, a number of students approached the stage where the basketball players still stood.

Curtis shook hands and talked his way through the crowd, using nearly the entire lunch break until the numbers trickled to only a handful. He wondered why Kaylee hadn't come up too, though he wasn't sure if he wanted her to or not. He still didn't know if he was ready to speak to her, to take that irreversible first step into her life.

Then he felt a nudge at his left. Reggie motioned to a single girl standing alone and uncertain under a beam of light. Meeting her face, Curtis found himself looking into Kaylee's eyes. She stood more than twenty feet away, indecision on her face as she watched him.

The recessed light shined on her light brown hair, picking out coppery highlights he would have missed otherwise. It had been a couple of years since he'd seen her up close. Gone was the awkwardness of the new teenager who had attended Denise's wedding.

His eyes flitted over her features, picking out the family chin and the same blue eyes they all seemed to share. She studied his face, as though memorizing every detail, uncertainty hanging there. He was sure she wanted to talk to him, but after his edict a few years ago that no one contact him, she wouldn't approach without encouragement.

He'd kept his distance for so long that the thought of crossing that final line made his mouth go dry and his heart pound in his chest. The memory of his older adopted brother, hunched and dejected after being turned away by his biological family, flashed through Curtis's mind. He didn't think he could stand to be turned away by his birth family once he had made the effort to get to know them. It was the reason he had held back, despite the warm reception Denise and Cliff had both received.

He could ignore Kaylee. He could pretend not to know who she was, as though she were just any one of the teens he'd greeted that day, but they both knew that he knew who she was. And it was too late to pretend anyway. As he stood hesitating, he saw her face fall as hope slipped away from her. She had been there for him so many times, even if only on the sidelines. Seeing her pain now felt like a stab to the chest, and he moved without making a conscious decision.

He felt full of nerves as his legs ate up the distance between them in a few quick steps. His hands began to shake. It was worse than standing in front of hundreds, he decided. "Hi, Kaylee. I was starting to wonder if you'd gone to lunch." The steadiness of his voice surprised him.

There was no bolt of recognition, no tug of familiarity like he'd had when he first met Denise. But then, he didn't need it. It was enough to see the happiness and yearning in her eyes seeming to war with uncertainty. He reached out to shake her hand and wondered if she felt as wrong-footed about all of this as he did.

The silence lengthened as he continued to hold her hand for far longer than necessary. She nodded. "Yes. I wasn't sure what you would do or think, even though . . . ."

He released her hand self-consciously. "That last home game. I was starting to wonder if you'd come. You were late."

She smiled, obviously pleased he noticed. "I was at work." She mentioned a burger place on the other side of town and told him she had a part-time job there. "How did you know it was me in the stands that first time?"

"I might have avoided talking to anyone at Denise's wedding, but I paid attention. And of course, Denise always has pictures of you around her place." He kept his voice low, hoping not to attract attention. There were still far too many students and teachers milling around for his comfort. "You have the Callister chin." He reached out and touched it with an index finger, his stomach knots unraveling. "I'm sorry," he said with regret at her being stuck with his chin.

She laughed nervously but with obvious relief. "I kept telling myself if I was patient, if I just didn't give up, you'd want to know me some day." Tears came to her eyes and she blinked rapidly, but one tear slid onto her cheek. She brushed it away. "I don't understand how you feel or why you feel the way you do, but I want to understand."

He slid his eyes away from her, feeling guilty for putting her through all of this waiting and uncertainty. She seemed to sense his feelings and picked up the conversation again. "I listened to all of your games, when I couldn't be there. You're really an amazing player. I wish I'd gotten some athletic ability." She let out a nervous laugh.

He met her eyes again. "But you play the cello, don't you? Denise and Cliff brag about you all the time."

She blushed and averted her eyes, and Curtis realized they were drawing attention. He shifted his weight from one foot to another and stuffed his hands in his pockets.

"They're too nice. It really means a lot to me that they keep in touch," Kaylee said.

Her eyes returned to his, and he saw both courage and fear in them. His guilt rose again, so he looked away. "I'm glad. I think I'd like to hear you sometime—when you have a concert again."

"I'd like that a lot. I'll probably be so nervous, I'll faint." This last part was muttered under her breath, so low he wondered if she meant for him to hear.

"What are you talking about? Callisters don't faint. You'll be fine. Let me know when you perform next. You have a spring concert coming up, don't you? Denise mentioned it." Denise always seemed to mention Kaylee, and her adoptive parents—who were really their biological aunt and uncle. "You still have my email address?"

"Yeah." She beamed up at him.

They both smiled nervously and then stood looking at each other without saying anything else for a long moment. Unable to stop himself, Curtis reached up and ran the back of his knuckle over her cheek. "You're beautiful, you know that? The females in the family certainly got their share of the beauty genes." He set his hand on her shoulder, not ready to offer a hug yet. He squeezed her shoulder, and she nodded as if she understood what he was trying to say, tears in her eyes again.

"You probably need to get some lunch. You'll need to feed those cello-carrying muscles. I'm surprised a tiny thing like you can even lift one of those."

She giggled and said good-bye before she walked away. Curtis turned and smiled at a boy getting Reggie's signature. A moment later, the paper was thrust into his hands. He glanced up again and watched Kaylee exit the room before putting pen to paper.

The boy seemed to notice his gaze. "That Kaylee Callister is pretty hot, huh? I think you're too old for her, though."

Unable to help himself, he laughed. "I'd have to agree—if I wanted to date her. But she's my half sister."

The kid's eyes got big as he looked at Curtis closer. "No way. She's your sister? Kaylee? Wow."

For once Curtis didn't mind the little bit of hero worship he saw in the kid's eyes, not if it helped Kaylee.

When they finished up and walked back out to the car, Reggie gave Curtis a gentle punch on the shoulder. "What was all that with the cute little high school girl? It was some intense conversation. You been robbing the cradle and not telling the rest of us?"

The jab was intended to be good natured, friendly, even teasing, but Curtis realized what the exchange with Kaylee must have looked like to everyone else. He smiled and forced a casual act. "She is pretty cute, isn't she?" He turned and spoke conspiratorially, "All the cutest girls are related to me. It's just disgusting."

"She's related to you?"

"Yeah, she's my sister. My aunt and uncle adopted her years back." He stumbled over the sentence, pushing back his natural inclination to avoid the subject entirely.

Reggie's brow furrowed, and he gave Curtis a questioning look. "Um, I don't know about you, but where I come from, that would make her your cousin, not your sister."

Curtis reached out and clapped a hand over Reggie's shoulder. "Not in my family, man."

Study time that evening was almost a complete wash for Curtis. He stood and walked over to the window, looking down three stories to the large field of grass below. He'd met his sister face-to-face that day. He could still take a step back, but he knew it would be too hard. Besides, he ached to find the answers to his life, to know where his family was, to know about them. And he feared the answers more than he dared admit.

He'd been putting off the inevitable—contacting his birth mother's family—for four years now, or very nearly, and had insisted that Cliff only get to know their birth mother's family, though both of them were curious about their birth father—if anyone even knew who the man was. Curtis wouldn't put it past his birth mother to have lied to Denise.

He knew if he took that final step and accepted Kaylee and everyone else, he would need to know about his birth father too. He couldn't wait around any longer. Once the bridge had been crossed, that would be it.

Though Cliff had always wanted to search for their biological family, once he had found Daphne's family, he had become content with his limits. But Curtis knew that now that he'd spoken with Kaylee, he wouldn't be able to hold back much longer. He would have to take steps to meet his other aunts and uncles. He had several other cousins—some of whom had given him less than friendly looks at Denise's wedding. He knew his anxiety had alienated them somewhat. Still, he'd have to cross the same invisible line to them that he had crossed to speak with Kaylee today. He prayed it would be easier and the outcome as satisfactory.

The result of today's adventure was inevitable. Now he needed to be careful not to rush headlong in the search for his birth father.

At the knock on his door, he pushed away from the window. Lily stood on the other side, as pretty as a picture, with her hands clasped behind her back and without her children.

"Hey, I just stopped in to see how it went today. It was your third assembly, wasn't it?" She smiled at him, then reached out and touched his arm. Her shrewd brown eyes studied his face, and she tipped her head to the side. "Are you okay? You seem . . . pensive."

Lovely and discerning—a dangerous combination. "Yeah. Want to find a quiet corner to talk for a few minutes?" He knew he shouldn't tease himself by spending time with her, however innocent. She was still married, and it was growing increasingly difficult to remember that fact.

"Sure."

Curtis checked to make sure his key was in his pocket before he led her to the end of the hall, where they could have some privacy. He leaned back against a wall and slid to the floor, settling his arms across his knees. Lily followed suit and sat next to him. Noises from the common area in the middle of the floor echoed back to them, and they saw people walking between rooms and the bathroom, but there was a little privacy in their corner of the hall—at least enough that they wouldn't be easily overheard.

"Where're the rug rats?" he asked.

"Shelly and the other girls on her floor are spoiling them." Lily's smile lasted only a few seconds before she became more serious. "Did something happen today?"

"I spoke with Kaylee after the assembly." He knew he wouldn't have to explain to her who Kaylee was or why this was momentous. He probably ought to be unhappy that Lily knew so much of his business—things he hadn't told her himself—but it made this so much easier.

"Really? How did it go?"

"Okay." He nodded, reminding himself that it had been fine, that the rest of it would go fine as well. It had to. "It was the right thing to do. The best thing. The worst thing. The next step." He let out a shaky breath and ran a hand through his hair. Just thinking about it brought his irrational anxiety to the surface. He hated looking weak in front of Lily, but she seemed to accept him—irrational fears and all.

"Isn't that good, though, making that first step? It's not like any of them are going to turn you away. You know they've accepted Cliff and Denise."

Curtis took a deep breath and cleared his lungs. "You know, I'm a lot more like Denise than like Cliff when it comes to this issue. Cliff can look at the family we have, the biological one as well as adopted, and be happy with what he has. With me, I always knew if I found one member, I'd have to find everyone.

"With Denise, I could just pretend that she married into the family or something, but I can't do that if I let in Kaylee and everyone else. Once I accept them, I'll have to try and find my birth father. I won't be happy going halfway." He wasn't going to dwell on whether or not they would all accept him.

He turned to look at her, willing her to understand. "That scares me more than anything. I already know enough about my birth mother to be pretty sure I won't be happy with what I find." He knew Denise's encounter with their birth mother hadn't been wonderful, even if mother and daughter were developing a tentative relationship. When Lily picked up his hand, he wrapped his long fingers around hers. It amazed him how easy it was to talk to her, to share his worries and fears—despite the fact that he didn't want her to see him at less than his best.

"You're strong, though. You'll be fine."

Her face seemed to glow, so he had to reach out and touch it to be sure it was real. It was real, and petal soft. It scared him that he was growing so attached to her, but he let his finger trace over a few freckles dotting her cheek and enjoyed her sharp breathing, which signaled that his touch might affect her at least a little bit too. Then he pulled back. "Thanks for being there for me, Lily. You're a great friend. I have plenty of pals on the team and friends on the floor here, but I can't talk to them about this."

She smiled, though it looked a little forced. "You're welcome. I'm glad to be here for you. You're a . . . good friend too. Thanks."

When he watched her walk back down the hall a little later, he pushed away a vague hollow feeling inside him.

CHAPTER TWENTY

Lily had nearly convinced herself that everything would be smooth sailing from here on out. She had a job that would keep her busy for the next few months. Shelly was being super helpful, watching the kids half the time Lily worked, so that her child care bill would be lower than expected—this month, anyway—and Lily also substitute taught two or three days a weeks.

It was a Saturday, the end of her first week at her new job—which she really enjoyed. What she hadn't known about the nursery's stock, she had picked up quickly. Shelly had offered to care for her children, and Lily felt good about the bright, sunny day ahead of her. The kids were healthy and happy, and she was certain nothing was going to get in her way. Then the phone rang while she prepared for work.

"Hello?" She applied eye shadow as she put her cell phone to her ear.

"It's Elizabeth. We're going to come visit the children today. We should be there about noon. Have them ready for an afternoon at the park, will you?"

Lily's hand grew lax, and she fumbled the makeup brush when she heard her mother-in-law's voice. "I'm sorry, what was that? You want to come today?" The caseworker had mentioned at her last visit that John's parents would need to be given a chance to spend time with the children. When Lily objected, she'd been told the visit could be supervised, if she liked.

"That's what I said, isn't it? Today. We'll pick them up and take them for a few hours. I'm sure you can find something to do while we're caring for them." The word *properly* was insinuated on the end of her frosty sentence.

"I'm afraid I'll be at work today. I won't be able to join you, so you'll have to arrange another time." She intentionally ignored Elizabeth's comment about taking the children alone. There was no way she was letting her children go with them unsupervised. It never even occurred to them to offer to babysit when she lived near them. Not once in the past two years had they watched Stephen for her, even when Lily asked.

"Since you won't need to be there, I don't see a problem."

"Since I won't let you take them without supervision, it is a problem. My sister is watching them today. I might be able to arrange for her to meet you somewhere and stay while you spend time with them, but you won't be putting them in your car. If you like, I can check with her plans and see if we can accommodate you."

"You're being completely unreasonable."

"I'm sorry you feel that way, but it doesn't change anything." Lily carefully put away her eye shadow and powder, not wanting to fumble and drop them in her frustration.

There was a low murmur as Elizabeth spoke with someone in the background—probably her husband, Lily figured—then she came back on the line. "Fine. Call me right back." She hung up without saying good-bye.

Lily let out a long, controlled breath and then called Shelly. "Hey, Shell," she greeted her sister. "I have an issue."

"What's going on?"

"The Drakes have kindly decided to grace the children with a visit today. Elizabeth is being very insistent, but I don't want them to be alone with the kids."

"Um, yeah. I can't blame you. So you want me to tag along?" Shelly asked.

"Actually, I don't want the kids in their car, either. If you're willing to deal with them, you'll drive the kids wherever they want to go and stick by them like glue. Bring your homework or whatever if you want. You might get some studying done, but don't let them out of your sight. Do you mind too much? I can always tell her no."

Shelly snorted. "And have her complain that you refused to let her see the kids? Not likely. I'll take care of everything. Where do you want me to meet them?"

"I'll have her give you a call, if that's okay." Lily felt really guilty, certain the Drakes would be thoroughly nasty to Shelly.

"No problem. Don't worry about it, seriously."

"I owe you big time."

"Yeah, yeah. Just make sure to keep plenty of chocolate chips on hand."

"You got it." Lily hung up with relief and phoned Elizabeth back.

"Yes? What did she say?" Elizabeth said in lieu of "hello."

Lily fought the urge to grit her teeth and used her sweetest voice. "She'd be happy to work things out with you. Let me give you her cell phone number and when you get close, you can give her a call and make arrangements to meet her." She rattled off Shelly's number and ended the call. "What a great way to ruin a lovely day," she said to herself.

She took a deep breath and then opened the mascara tube. Shelly would be there any minute, and Lily wanted to be sure she had time to go over some ground rules for the visit before she had to leave for work.

CURTIS,

YOU ASKED ME TO LET YOU KNOW WHEN THE SPRING CONCERT WAS BEING HELD. I JUST FOUND OUT TODAY, IT'S MAY 11 AT 7 PM AT MY SCHOOL. DO YOU THINK YOU CAN COME? IT WAS GREAT TALKING TO YOU LAST WEEK.

Kaylee's email went on to talk about a few other things that were going on in her life. Curtis smiled as he typed out a reply and sent it. He'd taken a few minutes' break to check his email after his fingers started cramping up from the paper he was writing. There was only a week of school left before finals and then he'd graduate. The teachers were piling on the work, and he couldn't wait until it was finished.

After deleting the junk mail in his inbox, he stood and stretched. He walked over to the window to look down at the students clustered in groups on the lawn. The weather was beautiful, and he wished he could be out working in the dirt instead of being cooped up in his room with his thoughts. That reminded him that he'd planned to check on the landscaping project his group had finished the previous week.

Deciding he needed to get out for a while, he grabbed his car keys and headed for the door.

The landscaping looked good, and Curtis checked on several plants to make sure they were getting enough water and to verify that the sprinklers had been set correctly. When he finished, he still wasn't ready to go back to his dorm, so he turned his car north to enjoy the spring weather a while longer.

Ten minutes later, he approached Kilpack Gardens and noticed Lily's car in the parking lot. Unable to help himself, he pulled in. It had been over a week since they'd spoken, and he wanted to see how she was doing.

The store was busy with a line at the cash register and more customers milling around. He enjoyed the sights and smells of plant life as he wandered up and down the aisles, watching for Lily.

When he did finally stumble across her, she was helping a young woman with pond plants. She bagged the water lily, then sealed it and handed it to the customer. "Keep an eye out for frost. If it looks like it'll be too cold, you'll want to bring these in for the night, but otherwise they should do great."

"Thank you so much," the woman said. Then she hurried off with her purchases.

Lily's smile vanished, and she turned back to straighten the stack of plastic bags. Her face had a pinched, worried look about it.

"Hey, I had some questions about lilies. I was looking for one. Do you think you can help me?" Curtis asked, sauntering up from just outside her line of vision.

She smiled even before she fully turned and saw him. "There are lots of lilies here. Any type in particular?"

He loved her smile, and even more he loved that he could bring it so easily to her mouth. "I like mine tall, over five feet, with a bright smile and a drooling baby. Speaking of which, how are your kids?"

Her smile dimmed. "They were fine when I left home this morning."

"Are you afraid Shelly's teaching them how to use hunting knives?" he teased, trying to bring a smile back to her face.

"That would be the least of my troubles. My in-laws decided—this morning—to drop in and see the kids. Elizabeth was angry when I told her she wasn't taking them anywhere in her car. Shelly was supposed to meet them at a park about an hour ago." Lily hugged herself, as if she were cold despite the unusually warm temperatures outside. "I wish I were there so I could see what was happening. I feel bad Shelly has to deal with everything."

Curtis reached out and brushed back a lock of hair the breeze had blown in her face. "She won't let anything happen to them. You know that."

"I know." Lily met his gaze for a heart-stopping moment. Then she turned and organized a few more things on the counter behind her. "It's just maddening, knowing these people never cared about my kids when we lived nearby, but suddenly they want to take full custody, to visit them without me there. I just—" she broke off and her hands balled into fists.

Curtis reached out and put a hand on each of her shoulders, giving them a squeeze. "I can only imagine what it feels like, but I'm sure Shelly will keep a close eye on them. When do you get a break? Have you eaten lunch yet?"

"Yes, I just got back from lunch a little while ago. I work until four."

"Then I'll see you when you get off." She turned toward him, and he tapped her on the nose with his finger. "Stay tough. This place looks busy enough to keep your mind focused for the next little while."

"Yeah. I better get back to it."

"All right. I'll talk to you later." He stuffed his hands in his pockets and turned to complete his circuit around the nursery. His mom was talking about changing up a corner of her yard, and he'd have plenty of time on his hands once school got out. Maybe he could get a few ideas while he was here.

Lily worked extra hard the rest of the afternoon and was almost surprised when four o'clock arrived. No one had said anything to her about Curtis's visit, so she hoped it hadn't lasted long enough to be noticed. She really enjoyed her job and didn't want to mess things up.

As she returned to the front counter to clock out and hang up her large green apron, she saw Curtis leaning against his car, talking on his cell phone. She doubted he could see her through the window, but she patted her hair to make sure it wasn't flying every which way from putting away the new selection of shrubs.

"See you Monday," the young cashier said with a smile as Lily headed out.

"See you." Lily dug her keys from her pocket and headed straight for Curtis.

He hung up the phone and then turned and smiled at her. "I just spoke with Shelly. She said the Drakes took them to Carl's Jr. and would probably be another half an hour. Sophie's had her bottle and a recent diaper change. She'll bring the kids back when they're finished. Care to grab a bite, since the kids are eating? I know a great Mexican place not far from here." He seemed to sense her hesitation. "We can go as friends. Otherwise you'll go home and worry about what's going on. Maybe a little distraction is what you need."

Lily considered his offer for a moment, feeling a little let down at the word *friends*, but she nodded. "I'll meet you there."

He gave her directions, and she hurried to her car.

Dinner was comfortable, and Lily enjoyed the time with Curtis. It had been a long time since she'd been to a Mexican restaurant because spicy food had caused her terrible heartburn when she was pregnant. Lily also hadn't felt comfortable eating out much since her financial situation had changed. She wouldn't have done so today, but Curtis had been right, she did need a distraction. And turning him down was nearly impossible.

She tried to hold onto that calm feeling when she arrived back at her apartment and noticed her in-laws' car in the guest parking lot. Putting on a smile, Lily opened the front door. Elizabeth stood on one side of the room, looking at a family picture that had been taken the previous fall before Lily had put on weight from the pregnancy. She'd thought about putting it in the children's bedroom so she wouldn't have to look at John so often, but hadn't moved it yet.

"Hello," Lily said. "I thought you'd be on your way home by now." From down the hall, she could hear Shelly's voice, accompanied by little-boy giggles.

"I was waiting for you," Elizabeth said. "Ross is checking out the playground equipment." She gestured to the community park half a block away.

This seemed strange to Lily as Ross never did handyman work around the house. She doubted he owned a hammer and screwdrivers, and she couldn't picture him testing the swing set or slide for safety. "That's thoughtful of him. Did you have a nice afternoon?"

"It would have been nicer without your sister shadowing us every step of the way. She may have had her nose in textbooks, but I know she was watching every move we made. It's insulting.

"And this place, this . . . hovel you're living in, after the beautiful home you had in Highland. How can you even think of raising your children in a place like this? Don't you think they deserve better? You can't care for them properly, and your sister isn't suited to this kind of work. She hardly interacted with them at all. And who knows what's going on at that day care center you take them to!" Elizabeth gestured with her hands to make each point.

Lily moderated her tone and tried her best to be calm, though as she spoke, she realized she was not succeeding very well. "Shelly held back today to let you interact with the children. I was under the impression that was the whole point of the visit. She was there to assist you if you needed it and to make sure everything went well, but it was your visit, and I asked her not to interfere too much." She set her purse on the sofa with more force than was strictly necessary.

"This apartment is in decent condition and it's all I can afford right now, but I know the district here is getting ready to hire next year's teachers soon, and I'm in a good position to get one of the jobs. Within a year we should be in a much nicer place. The day care center is quite nice, but you're welcome to check it out if you like. I understand the caseworker plans to do so soon."

Not mollified, Elizabeth continued with her list of complaints. "Stephen was nervous and uncomfortable with me today. I don't know what you're telling him about us, but I don't appreciate it." Lily found it convenient that Elizabeth forgot how Stephen had always acted that way on the rare times she had stopped in.

"Maybe if you'd bothered to spend any time with him before now, he'd be more familiar with you. Since it's too much for you to remember he exists most of the time, you shouldn't be surprised that he isn't comfortable with you now." There was nothing placating in Lily's tone.

"I can't help it if you moved half a state away. You're just trying to keep us apart."

"Then who do you suppose is to blame for your not seeing them much while we lived nearer to you? Don't come in here and start blaming me because you took no interest in them. If you care so much about them, you could have tried to be there for them, instead of finding fault with all my efforts." She took several steps in Elizabeth's direction. "It's no picnic for me either, you know. I didn't ask to be put in this position. If you want someone to blame, you'd better start looking at your son." Lily balled her hands into fists and held them at her sides while her voice grew louder. "If you haven't said good-bye to your grandchildren, now is the time. If you have said good-bye, you're welcome to leave."

The woman huffed in outrage. "You show no respect whatsoever. What kind of parent are you going to be with that kind of attitude? You can be sure I'll speak to the caseworker about this!" Elizabeth grabbed her purse from the end table and stalked out of the apartment.

Lily listened to the front door slam and fought back the tears threatening to fall down her face. She hurried into the bedroom where Shelly was putting clean clothes on Stephen. A dirty diaper sat balled up on the floor beside them. "That woman is . . . I can't even say a word that bad. How did you put up with her all afternoon?"

Shelly laughed. "She is a pill, isn't she? I just ignored her. There's nothing she can do to hurt me, after all. The kids were regular tyrants this afternoon. Weren't you, babycakes?" She said the last bit in a singsong tone to Stephen, then turned back to Lily. "I've rarely seen them so out of sorts. Maybe she and Ross will decide they don't want to take the kids after all."

"That's a little more than I can hope for at this point. The other possibility is that they'll be so certain I'm being a horrible mother they'll fight twice as hard." Lily plopped down on Stephen's bed and looked at her daughter, sleeping peacefully as though no one was ranting and raving in the room.

"Well, they'll be worn out at least." Shelly gave Stephen a pat on his rear end. "You're set to go, kiddo."

He jumped up and ran to his mother, climbing into her lap. "Mama, we pwayed on the swings. I missed you."

Lily smiled at him and hugged him close. "I missed you too, sweetie." As he slid his tiny arms around her neck, she rubbed a cheek over his silky head. There wasn't anything she wouldn't do for him or any fight she wouldn't fight. Holding him in her arms provided a bit of the calm she needed so badly.

"Soooo, you were gone a long time. How was dinner with Curtis?" Shelly wiggled her eyebrows. "He told me he was taking you for Mexican."

After putting Stephen down and watching him run out to the living room, Lily shrugged her shoulders but allowed a small smile to blossom on her face. "It was good." She eyed her sister. "Don't go getting any ideas. We have a nice time together. That's all."

"Yeah, uh huh."

Uncomfortable, Lily turned the questioning back on her sister. "And what about you and Superman? How is that going? How many times have you sung together this semester?"

Shelly focused on cleaning up the diaper wipes and dirty clothes. "We're fine. Good and stuff."

"And stuff? Come on, Shelly, what's going on? I see the way you are with him."

Shelly turned back and headed for the hallway. Lily followed her into the hall, and then Shelly pulled the door closed behind them. "I don't know," Shelly said. "He's a great guy—really great. How could I go wrong? But I still love Jimmy."

"Who comes home from his mission in a few months."

"Exactly."

Lily wanted to laugh, but her sister seemed too uncertain. "When it rains, it pours, right? Come on, I stashed a few of those chocolate-chocolate chip cookies in the freezer for a stressful day. Share a couple with me?"

"Oh, yeah."

CHAPTER TWENTY-ONE

When Curtis checked his email again, there was another note from Kaylee. He smiled to himself, then shot back a reply, as happy with the direction their relationship had taken as she was. He still wasn't sure how he felt about meeting the rest of the extended family, but no doubt that would come soon enough.

He sat for a long moment after he logged off, thinking about the next step he needed to take: contacting Daphne and finding out who his biological father was. The issue had been running through his mind since he first talked to Kaylee, but now it felt urgent. This was something bigger and more serious than stepping across the room to speak with Kaylee. He had known she wanted to meet him. There was no reason to believe Daphne would feel the same way. Then there was his birth father—did he even know the twins existed? Would he turn them away?

There were far too many questions to unravel right now, so after Curtis debated for a long while, he flipped open his phone and began to dial.

Denise picked up after only a couple rings and he smiled when he heard her voice. "Hey, how are you doing?" he asked.

"King Frog Face," she greeted him, "I was just thinking about you and wondering how you were doing with all the changes going on right now."

"Great. Better than I expected, actually. I do have a dilemma though, and I wanted your input. I . . . ." He let out a disgusted huff. "I can't believe I'm saying this, but I need to get a hold of Daphne. I don't want to see her, but I have some questions."

Denise was quiet for a long moment, and then she chuckled. "I should've known it would be you who finally decided he needed answers.

Cliff's just a little too complacent—either that or he's been waiting for you to come to your senses."

"I can be a bit hard-headed."

"I know how terrifying this next step is. It's huge, really huge, and I'm sure you wouldn't be making it if you could see any way out of it."

"You know me too well. I'm such a wimp."

"There's nothing wimpy about what you want to do. I have the name of your birth father, if you're ready. But you should still write to Daphne yourself if you want to. It might help. Then you can decide where to go from there."

Curtis began and tossed out a dozen letters, then finally decided on a wording that was as good as he could manage. His stomach felt like it was filled with a slick ball of grease, making him slightly nauseated. He didn't want Daphne to know where he lived, so he'd need a safe way to pass mail back and forth without giving too much away.

Hello, Daphne,

I'm your first son, the oldest twin, and I admit I don't really know what to say to you. First, I guess, is thanks for giving birth to me. Thanks for giving me the chance to live with my adoptive family, who has been so good to me. Though we were never rich, they gave me everything they could and all the love I could wish for.

I find myself at a crossroads. I'm about to finish school and go into a world that might be bigger and crazier than I expected. Though it's taken me longer than my twin, I've finally decided to meet the family, to meet Kaylee. I haven't met the others yet, but, I'm sure that'll happen soon.

I'm trying to learn more about my past now, and I wondered if you have anything to share about me. What were you doing when you had me? Do you have more information about who my birth father is than what you told Denise? I realize I offer little in return and you may feel like I'm just asking without having any-thing to give. But please try to understand that I need to know

about my history, and I'll try to give you any answers I can. I'm
sure you have plenty of questions for me too.

Curtis

Following Denise's example, Curtis rented a box to receive his mail.
Since school would be out so soon, he drove to Ogden to rent the box near
his parents' place. He wavered back and forth before dropping the letter
in the mail slot and turning his back on it. There was nothing more he
could do. He'd have to wait.

Anxious about the letter and confused about his own need to search,
he hurried back to his car. A stop to visit with his parents might be just
what he needed.

Curtis pulled up in front of his parents' home and wished, not for
the first time, that Cliff didn't live so far away. If he were closer, Curtis
wouldn't worry about telling his parents of his intended search for his
birth father. He knew they would be supportive, but it still tore at his gut
when he thought of his search. Somehow he'd always considered searching for his biological family to be a betrayal. And his past had never mattered to him before. Why should he care now? It wasn't logical.

But then, Curtis thought, *nothing about this is logical, is it?*

He got out and shut the door behind him. His mom's car was in the
driveway, and suddenly, despite his reluctance to face the reason he was
here, he was anxious to see her. He took the last few feet to the house in
long, ground-eating steps and pushed through the front door. "Mom, you
home?"

She called back to him from somewhere deep inside the house.
"Curtis?" There was a pause as he followed the direction of her voice.
"What are you doing here?"

He came around the corner and threw her arms around him.

"I had a free afternoon and couldn't stay away. That, and I miss your
home cooking." He pulled back from the hug and pushed a lock of graying hair away from her face. Somehow, despite raising him and Cliff,
along with the other five kids, she still looked younger than her contem-
poraries.

"Lucky for you, I haven't started cooking yet, or there wouldn't have been enough. You might have gotten stuck with peanut butter sandwiches."

"You wouldn't do that to me—I'm your favorite son."

"Of course you are—just like Cliff, Andrew, and Lance."

"Aww, Mom. You can admit I'm your favorite. It's just me here now. I won't tell the others. Not right away."

"Yeah, I bet. Come into the kitchen. I'm making cannelloni."

"You must have ESP. You know that's my favorite." He followed along behind her to the kitchen.

"Everything I make is your favorite."

"True, but if I had to choose a favorite of my favorites, this would be a serious contender." He picked up an olive and popped it into his mouth.

"Sorry, this is for a sick neighbor."

He let out a pathetic sigh and she laughed. "I suppose we could make a double batch, just for you."

He leaned his lanky frame back against the cupboard, feeling more than a little oversized in the tiny room. She moved around the kitchen with ease, adding this and that to the bowl, stopping to double-check the recipe. He asked about each of his siblings—she always had more current information on everyone than he did, with the possible exception of Cliff. She talked about the neighborhood news and what she had been up to, and she put him to work chopping fresh parsley and mixing the cheese stuffing while she organized everything.

His father walked into the room just as she was putting the dish into the oven. He saw his son and a smile broke onto his face as he pulled Curtis into a hug. "Hey, I didn't know you were coming tonight."

"I didn't warn Mom because I didn't want you to come up with an excuse not to be here."

His father pulled back, a twinkle in his eye. "Well, I guess it's too late for me to claim a prior commitment."

"Way too late. You're stuck with me now. Mom's making cannelloni for dinner. Even if you did have to leave, I'd be taking the food with me."

"I thought we were past the stage where you were supposed to eat us out of house and home."

"Not quite. School gets out soon, and you'll be stuck with me again for a while," Curtis reminded him.

"It's a good thing your mother put in a garden." Then, as if mentioning his wife reminded him she was in the room, he turned and pulled her into his arms, giving her a lingering kiss. "Hi, honey. How was your day?"

Curtis watched his parents greet each other. Their complete love and acceptance, the easy romance and commitment—he wanted that. With Lily. Desperately. He couldn't be certain she felt the same, but he was very encouraged by the way things were headed.

"So what brings you here, son?" his father asked when he pulled away from his wife. "You and Lily get engaged?"

Curtis wondered how long his parents had been expecting that news—and more important, who they had been talking to. His mom always seemed to know when something was going on in his life, even if he wasn't the one to tell her. "Her divorce isn't even finalized. We haven't discussed our relationship yet, either." He grabbed a carrot stick from the bag beside him on the counter. "Besides, if I were going to make an announcement like that, I'd have brought her along."

"You'd better," his mom said. "But you never answered his question. Why the sudden visit?"

"Mooching dinner off of you isn't a good enough reason?"

"No. I've been waiting to ask until your dad got home. Spill." She pointed to a chair at the kitchen table. "Dinner's got to bake for a while anyway."

Curtis took his usual place to the left of his dad, feeling like a little boy facing the consequences of bad behavior. Would his parents always be able to do that to him with just a look? "Well, if you know things are progressing with Lily, should I assume you know about me and Kaylee getting in touch?"

"Yes," his mom said.

"How did you find out, anyway?" His eyes narrowed at them.

"Our sources are confidential. I can't divulge them," she said seriously.

"Whatever. All right, then you can probably guess where this is going." He really didn't want to bring it up himself. He was such a pansy sometimes.

"Probably," his dad agreed. "But why don't you spell it out for us, just to prevent confusion."

"You like to see me squirm, don't you?"

"Immensely."

Curtis ran a hand through his hair, though he couldn't help smiling. "I feel pulled to search for my birth father. I don't want to, but I can't seem to ignore the draw. I wrote my birth mother this morning and asked for more details. I'm not sure what I want to hear, but I really feel like I need to find him."

His dad took his mom's hand on the table and gave it a squeeze. "We thought this might be coming. Even though we're concerned about how this might affect you, you know we love and support you, just the way we did Andrew and Leslie."

Leslie's search for her birth family had gone well enough. Andrew's, not so much. Curtis's other two siblings who were adopted hadn't chosen to search, and he doubted they ever would.

"If you feel drawn to do it, you can't ignore the feeling," his mother added.

Relief poured through Curtis. "Thanks. I love you guys. Cliff and I don't want this to change anything between us and you guys. We're not trying to replace you or anything."

"We know that," his mom said, standing and coming around to hug him. "You'll do what you need to do, and it'll all work out."

"Love you, Mom." He stooped over and gave her a gentle squeeze. As long as his parents were on his side, the search didn't look nearly as daunting.

Chapter Twenty-two

Sophie's wailing rose in pitch as Lily walked the floors with her. It was four in the morning, and two hours had passed since the baby's fussing began. "Shhh, baby girl. Come on, settle down, will you? We're both tired, and I have a long day at school tomorrow—or is it today?" Exhaustion warred with irritation, and Lily fought to maintain her patience.

Her mind wandered back to the call she'd received from the caseworker the previous afternoon. The day care had passed inspection. Doubtless her in-laws would still think it was substandard, but at least the judge would see a satisfactory report.

"Mommy?" Stephen's tired voice came from the kids' bedroom door. "Why Sophie crying?"

Lily let out a slow breath and walked over. "She's not feeling well. I'm sure she'll feel better soon. Do you need a drink of water?"

Stephen nodded and Lily put a little water in a cup. He usually used a sippy cup but did well enough with a regular one. She wasn't about to mess with anything more at this hour—a tablespoon or two of water on his pajamas wouldn't hurt him. Stephen took his drink, then gave his screaming sister a kiss on the cheek and returned to bed.

The baby coughed and Lily wondered if the cold medicine she'd given Sophie earlier was even helping. She wished she could go to sleep, then decided to try lying down with Sophie. Maybe she would relax if she got horizontal.

Eventually Sophie settled down, and Lily finally began to drift into sleep, minutes before her alarm clock went off. It was time for a new day to begin.

Sophie was still warm when Lily got up to get ready for work, but thankfully, the fever was low-grade now. Still, the coughing worried Lily too much. There was no way she could leave her baby at day care.

With a sigh, she picked up the phone and called to get a replacement substitute teacher. She wondered how many times they had to find a substitute for the substitute.

The woman who answered the phone sighed when she heard Lily's request. "Are you sure your kid is really sick? You know how they like to fake it."

"She's an infant who was born premature. I need to take her to the doctor right away, and I don't have anyone available to take her for me. I'm really sorry to leave you in a bind, but there's no way day care would take her like this, even if I wasn't worried that it was serious."

"You didn't give us much notice," the woman complained.

"It was just a runny nose last night. Sorry." Lily checked back on her daughter and realized Sophie felt even warmer than before. Her worry increased, and after settling Stephen in his seat, Lily scooped her daughter into her arms and hurried to the car. "What kind of parent am I?" she berated herself as she buckled Sophie's car seat in next to Stephen.

"Sophie sick?" Stephen asked.

"Yes, sweetie, Sophie's sick. We're going to the doctor now."

"No shots!" Stephen hugged himself, as if he could ward off the imaginary needle.

"No shots for you. Don't worry, kiddo. You're fine."

Sophie began coughing again, and Lily felt her pulse pick up slightly. It didn't sound good at all—the coughs were coming from deep in her daughter's chest. Lily headed straight for the emergency room.

The morning passed in a haze as they did tests and started an Sophie on an IV. Once they were settled into a hospital room where monitors were running and a humidifier whirred nearby, Lily tried to keep Stephen sitting still and reasonably quiet. Her efforts weren't terribly successful.

When Shelly walked into the curtained area late in the morning, Lily let out a sigh of relief. "You're such a life saver. Thank you. I'll never be able to repay you for all the help you've given me." She felt a bit weepy, both because of the stress of being in the hospital with her daughter and for her sister's willingness to drop everything to help. She knew Shelly had been out of class less than ten minutes.

"You're welcome. I'm here for you—always. How's she doing?"

"It's pretty bad. She has croup. They're saying I shouldn't send her back to day care for at least a month because she's susceptible to getting sick. She's not in the ICU again—that's a good thing." Lily tried to look at it positively, but she couldn't help worrying about her daughter, the medical bills, whether the school district would let her work for them again after she ditched out today, and what she would do about child care while she worked.

Shelly reached over and gave Lily a tight hug. "You focus on her. I'll take care of the tyke. Katie will help out if I need her to." Katie was Shelly's roommate and best friend since elementary school. "I have an early final on Tuesday—it's at 7:00 AM—and then another two on Thursday afternoon, but other than that I'm wide open to babysit next week. Just don't be surprised if you come home to find your kitchen slightly messy and your chocolate chips all baked into cookies." Shelly smiled and bent to pick up her nephew who hung onto her leg.

"Cookies! Can we eat cookies?" Stephen asked, looking into Shelly's face.

"Maybe later, kiddo." She turned back to Lily. "I'll just take this guy back to the apartment for now."

They made arrangements, and Lily watched her sister go, Stephen on Shelly's hip and the diaper bag over her other shoulder.

Lily could hear the clatter of the lunch trays being delivered and stretched her back muscles. Her whole body protested against the hours she had spent sitting in the chair. Sophie had been much more alert that morning but had just fallen back asleep. Since her stomach was rumbling, Lily considered going down to grab something from the cafeteria. She was still weighing the value of eating against the chance that her baby might wake up alone when she saw movement at the door.

"Hey," Curtis said, clutching a bunch of white daisies and purple Dutch irises in a vase. "How's she doing?"

I must look awful. My makeup's probably smeared all over my face. Lily tried to hide her embarrassment, even through her surprise at seeing him there. "She's doing better. The doctors think she'll be able to go home later today." She motioned to a chair, and he took it, handing her the flowers.

"Wow, Sophie's only three months old and she's already getting flowers from men. She's going to be a handful by the time she becomes a teenager." She sniffed the flowers and touched a soft petal. "It was very thoughtful of you. Thanks. How did you know?"

He shrugged, as if to say it wasn't a big deal. "After I saw Katie without Shelly at two meals in a row, I asked if Shelly had gone home for the weekend. Katie told me what happened. You should've called me. I'm happy to help out in any way I can."

Tears pooled in Lily's eyes, and she pushed them back, looking again at her baby. She'd wanted to call him, had considered it several times, but hadn't known what to say. She wanted much more from him than she dared ask. Instead she tried to make light of his offer. "You shouldn't say things like that. You might get stuck babysitting." She let out a half-hearted laugh.

He covered her hand with his own. "I'd be happy to help if you need it. Friends lean on each other, Lily. And besides, I've changed a diaper or two in my day, so don't be afraid to call me anytime—even after I go back to Ogden for the summer. It's not that far away. And," he paused for a moment, "I'm going to miss seeing you around."

Lily's eyes found his, and she felt her heart pounding in her chest. It had been a long time since she felt like this for anyone besides her husband—and a long time since she had that heart-pounding, breath-stealing experience, even with John. "I really appreciate it. I'm going to miss you too."

The moment held and lengthened until she started to think he was leaning closer than before. She tipped her head up toward him, then realized what she was doing and backed away. She turned to check on her daughter again, trying to even out her breathing. Desperate, she searched for a neutral topic. "So, are you all ready for finals?"

There was a long pause before he answered. When he did, his voice sounded strained. "Yeah, more or less." There was another pause. "Hey, have you eaten? I could grab something while you stay with Sophie if you'd like. You probably haven't left her side in hours."

"You're right. I'd appreciate it. I was thinking about eating when you walked in. I'm not too picky right now." Her stomach growled audibly, agreeing with her.

He laughed and squeezed the hand he was still touching, then let go. Her hand quickly felt cold. "I'll get you something and be right back."

Lily took a slow, deep breath as he left the room. Things were getting more complicated with their relationship—she hoped that could-have-been kiss was all in her head. The last thing she needed right now was another relationship, even if Curtis was sweet and thoughtful, good with the kids, down to earth, handsome as sin . . . . The list was really too long to mention. She fisted her hands on her lap and shook her head. He'd be moving far away in a matter of months, so holding out any hope that something was going to happen between them was ridiculous.

Sophie sighed and Lily turned back to her baby. Here was someone who would stick by her through everything—at least until she became a teenager. The thought made Lily smile, even as she ached, knowing that day would come all too quickly.

CHAPTER TWENTY-THREE

After two days in the hospital, Sophie was doing much better, and the doctor released her. Lily was grateful to return home. She didn't want to think of the medical bills they had just accrued.

True to Shelly's word, there were fresh-baked chocolate chip cookies bagged up on the counter. Lily smiled wanly to herself and moved zombielike through the apartment to put Sophie to bed. Stephen was already down for an afternoon nap.

After thanking Shelly for her help, Lily turned on the nebulizer the hospital had sent home with her and snuggled down with Sophie in her own bed. She knew her daughter wouldn't sleep long before waking, and Lily hoped this way she could get a few minutes' nap as well. She also didn't want to have her baby too far away.

Lily had missed half a day of work at the nursery and a full day at the school. Again, these were details she'd have to figure out later. Tomorrow. With a sigh, she let all of that go and drifted into sleep.

The following week was relatively quiet, considering Sophie's ongoing illness and Lily's busy work schedule. She and Shelly struck up a babysitting bargain that left Shelly with time to study and a little extra money to pay her school expenses. Shelly offered to sit with the kids for less than the day care charged—not much, but the extra bit of money would come in handy for Lily.

Even if Sophie had been well enough to go back to day care, Lily felt much better about Shelly watching her than a busy stranger who had several other children to care for.

On Thursday, Lily was rushing around simultaneously looking for her shoes, wiping drool from Sophie's smiling face, setting up a movie for Stephen, and trying to fix her hair and makeup when the doorbell rang. "Thank you, Shelly!" If she had someone else there to watch the kids, maybe she could find a moment to finish curling her hair and put on some mascara before work.

When she opened the door, she didn't find Shelly or Katie. It was Curtis. Lily froze. "Hi."

"Shelly and Katie both had finals this afternoon. I volunteered to help out." He stepped closer and Lily gave way, letting him into the room.

Lily became even more aware of her appearance and that she hadn't brushed her teeth after breakfast. She felt herself blush as she noticed he was all casual masculinity in his faded blue jeans and hunter green polo. *Dang.* Did he always have to see her looking awful when he looked so great? "I . . . are you sure? I mean, they can be a handful."

"I've got a lot of nieces and nephews, remember? I can warm bottles and make peanut butter sandwiches or mac 'n cheese. I've changed many a diaper, and Shelly said Sophie was feeling much better now."

Though she managed to hold back a wince at the idea of Curtis seeing her cluttered apartment, she nodded. There was no choice—she really had to work today. Had to. And he did seem to be good with the kids. She considered for a moment and then nodded. "Okay. Promise you'll call if you have any problems?"

"Of course. Go ahead and finish getting ready for work. I'll just hunker down with Stephen and play cars." Curtis folded his long body into a sitting position on the floor.

Lily nodded, then turned and stepped back into the bathroom. Pulling the door shut behind her, she noticed the big wet spot on her shirt left from Sophie spitting up on her earlier. She saw her harried and disheveled appearance in the mirror—and what was that on her cheek? She took a cleansing breath, then picked up the curling iron again. If he'd been harboring any romantic interest in her, it was surely over with now.

She told herself that was the way she wanted it anyway, but she didn't believe it.

Stephen and Sophie both went down for naps several hours later, and Curtis cleaned up from lunch. He'd forgotten how exhausting it could be to take care of little kids. He rarely handled any kids for more than a couple of hours and even more rarely one as young as Sophie. He couldn't help but smile when he thought of Lily's children, however. They were both so cute and funny. After she had been so sick the previous weekend, Curtis had expected Sophie to be fussier.

As he finished drying and putting away the dishes left over from breakfast and his adventure in toddler lunch-making, he thought of the look in Lily's eyes when she'd opened the front door. It was clear things had been a bit insane that morning. He had nearly reached out and wiped away a smear of something from her cheek—probably strawberry jam. But as his hand had begun to lift toward her, he'd caught himself and stuffed it in his pocket instead.

He was far more attracted to the messy, harried Lily than he had been to the self-possessed, organized woman he had known the past several years. Curtis couldn't be sure if it was simply because he hadn't been look-ing at her that way before because of her marriage or if he'd been blind. Then he remembered the interest she had piqued in him when they first met and he smiled to himself.

He heard Sophie crying and hurried to the kids' room to pick her up. Stephen had only been sleeping a few minutes and Curtis didn't want to wake him. He cuddled her close and with a sniff knew what the problem was. He'd told Lily he could change diapers, but he didn't say he enjoyed it. Stinky ones like this were even less enjoyable.

Curtis completed the smelly task, which included a full change of clothes, but Sophie didn't stop crying. She coughed several times deep in her chest, loud and raspy. The sound scared him, but it seemed to clear whatever was in her lungs. He decided to settle down with her near the humidifier and keep a close eye on her. Shelly had mentioned Sophie had a nasty cough.

After checking her temperature to make sure it wasn't rising, he walked around and bounced her for a few minutes, then decided it had been a couple of hours since her last bottle. Maybe she needed more to eat—or drink, in her case. He fumbled one-handed as he opened the container of formula and added warm water to the bottle. He shook it and adjusted Sophie in his arms to feed her.

She latched on immediately, and he wandered to the sofa to wait while she ate.

It didn't take her long to finish it off, and he wondered if he should fill another one. "Hey, sweetheart. Are you still hungry or are you finished?" He tilted her up and settled her on his shoulder, then twitched a burp cloth under her face and began patting her back. "You have a very healthy appetite. I guess a growing girl needs to eat though, doesn't she?" He continued speaking nonsense to her while he worked on getting the bubbles out of her stomach.

When she was finished and smiling again, he settled her on his lap so she faced him and continued talking to her. She gurgled and cooed and grinned up at him—at least he told himself it was a grin. She couldn't help but like him. After all, he had just changed her diaper and fed her. What more could a baby want? A moment later he realized a full stomach wasn't all it was cracked up to be as she spit the contents of her stomach onto his shirt.

Curtis let out a groan. "Was that really necessary? Huh?" He wiped at his shirt with the burp cloth but kept his voice soft and low, more teasing than anything. He picked her up and carried her to the kitchen, tucking her carefully in one arm as he dampened a cloth and blotted at his shirt. "That's what I get for being so self-confident, isn't it, honey? You're just keeping me in line. I appreciate that in a woman." He looked down at her, and she burbled some more.

A warm, tingly feeling filled him, and he pressed a kiss to her soft face. He didn't know how anyone could help but love this little girl. He was totally lost in her blue eyes.

They were nearly as enchanting as her mother's.

Lily entered the apartment to find Curtis standing at the sink, holding Sophie and dabbing at a wet spot on his shirt. Just then, Stephen tore around the room with a car in his hand. "It's not very attractive when grown men slobber on themselves," Lily said to Curtis, sure her little girl was actually responsible. Lately Sophie had been spitting up more than usual.

Curtis looked up at her, a sheepish grin on his lips. "What can I say? I'm just a slob. Good thing Sophie doesn't seem to mind."

"She's not very discerning." After setting the grocery bags in her hands onto the sparkling countertops, Lily touched her daughter's face. Sophie jabbered and reached out toward her mom.

"First she spits up on me—and this is not the first time today, I might add—then she deserts at the first opportunity. There's just no loyalty anymore." He said the last bit to Sophie, then glanced back at Lily.

"How did it go? I thought Shelly might beat me here to let you off the hook." She shifted Sophie onto her shoulder and rubbed soothingly across her daughter's back.

"She called about half an hour ago, but I told her not to worry about it. Other than an abundance of baby spit up on my clothes, everything's gone well enough."

"Well enough? So they were both angels with no issues all day?" She lifted her brows at him, certain he was smoothing things over.

"Perhaps not that well," he admitted. "But it was fine. Nothing I couldn't handle. Is that all of your groceries?"

"No. I expected Shelly to be here, so I spent a little time at the store before coming home. You might have noticed the cupboards were getting bare. I'll just settle Sophie in the baby swing and go get the other bags."

"Don't worry about it. I'll bring them in. Is your car locked?" Curtis moved toward the front door.

"No. The bags are all in the back seat." She buried her face in her little girl's neck and smelled the sweetness of baby. "What a nice man that guy is." She pressed her lips against Sophie's silky skin and then leaned away to look at Stephen, who was tugging on her pant leg.

When Curtis came back in, she had a child in each arm. "I think I got the easy load," he said. He set the bags on the counter and then placed the milk in the fridge. "Everything's out of the car, and I locked it behind me."

"I appreciate your help." She set Stephen down and moved to her purse. "I'm sure you could use some gas money."

"Don't worry about it. I had a good time this afternoon."

"Come on, Curtis."

He set a large hand over hers on the purse, stopping her from opening it up. "I was happy to help. Seriously."

"I always pay Shelly and Katie." She caught his gaze and felt her breath hitch in her chest at how close he stood. His hand was warm on hers, and she felt a light tingling up her arm.

"Lily, humor me, will you?"

She let her arms sag. "You won't let me thank you for your help?"

His smile dazzled and his cologne tempted her. When he spoke softly, his voice sent shivers down her spine. "You're welcome to say thank you. And if you want to do more, I wouldn't turn down dinner. My meal card ran out two weeks ago."

"I can't promise much of a meal."

"I'd settle for peanut butter and your company if that's all you're offering."

She allowed her lips to twitch up. Really, it was the least she could do, wasn't it? "I can probably do better than peanut butter. And it would be nice to have some adult company while I cook. How does pasta sound?"

"Perfect."

CHAPTER TWENTY-FOUR

The music at Kaylee's concert was surprisingly interesting. Curtis enjoyed the melding of instruments nearly as much as seeing the blush that covered Kaylee's cheeks when everyone applauded for her solo.

He stood in the back by himself, not wanting to be noticed by her parents. He was tempted to sneak out when the show was over, rather than talk to her and her family, but he couldn't bring himself to walk out without telling her how great she had done. Would she believe that he came if she didn't see him? What kind of coward would that make him, anyway?

So he hung out, waiting as the crowd bustled in around the musicians, offering hugs and kind words. He saw her parents flank her with her brother beside them. Though he felt his own version of stage fright, he pasted on a smile and made his way through the crowd.

Kaylee saw him before he reached her, and her face brightened into a big grin. "Curtis, I'm so glad you could come." She all but launched herself into his arms when he got close enough, and he thought of the difference a few dozen emails had made in their relationship. The last time he'd stood in this auditorium, it had been awkward and uncomfortable between them.

"You were wonderful. I'm even more impressed than I expected. I'll have to tell Denise she wasn't complimentary enough." He tried for an easy grin but wasn't sure he'd managed it.

Kaylee laughed and moved away. "You really liked it?"

"How could I help it?" He watched her eyes dance with joy and was glad he had come. His smile dimmed somewhat as he turned to her parents, but he fought to keep his expression looking more than just polite. "Derrick and Sue, right?"

Sue smiled and greeted him happily. Derrick was a bit more cautious about his welcome. Kaylee's brother, Luke, was even less welcoming, but he shook hands with Curtis and was perfectly civil. Awkward didn't even begin to describe it, but Curtis kept his focus on Kaylee for several minutes as she chattered and Sue took more pictures than he could count. Finally he felt safe excusing himself, citing the long drive as his reason for leaving.

"I need to go too," Luke said. "I'll walk out with you." He gave Kaylee's arm a squeeze. "I guess being your brother isn't too embarrassing. Good job." The tilt of his head and quirking of his lips belied his show of nonchalance.

"Thanks, Luke. Thanks for coming, Curtis. I really appreciate it." She hugged them both.

"I'm glad you invited me. Will you email me a picture of us together and one of just you?" Curtis asked when he pulled back after their hug.

She beamed at the suggestion. "Of course, if you want. Good night."

Curtis said good night to everyone and followed Luke out, sure Kaylee's big brother had words for him that he didn't want Kaylee to hear. Curtis recognized the set jaw and determined expression on the boy's face. From what Denise had said, Luke graduated from high school the previous spring and was preparing for a mission. This might be his last chance to play protective older brother for a while.

When they were clear of the building and crowds, Curtis shoved his hands into his pockets and glanced over at Luke. "So, was there anything special you wanted to say, or did you just want to spend an extra couple of minutes in my fascinating company?"

Luke's mouth firmed into a thin line. "It's been almost three years since Denise told you about the family, and you never cared about meeting us then. What's different now?"

Curtis studied his cousin. "Kaylee got under my skin. I know I haven't exactly been approachable, and I don't blame you for being wary."

"This isn't about me. You're welcome to come or go—whatever. Cliff is pretty cool and I like having him around, but he hasn't been dragging my sister through years of hoping and worrying. That's been all you."

"Are you worried I'm not going to stick around?" Luke's silence was answer enough, so Curtis continued. "I'm sorry I didn't jump in with both feet like Cliff. I have my own issues I've had to deal with. I promise you, though, I'm not going to disappear on everyone now. If I wasn't going to stick things out, I never would have crossed the stage to talk to

Kaylee a few weeks ago. I've seen what that can do."

Luke studied Curtis with serious brown eyes. "You promise?"

"Absolutely. You're welcome to wait and see how things go before you accept my word, but I'm not going to hurt Kaylee anymore." He thought again of the way her face had lit up when he came into view. "She's sweet and I could use another sister who doesn't have memories of me tormenting her when we grew up." His lips twitched into a smile.

Luke chuckled. "You're welcome to stick around, if you promise I get to keep all the rights to making Kaylee miserable."

"Deal." Curtis took Luke's hand gladly.

The air was cool when Curtis exited his car a little later. A gentle breeze ruffled the new leaves on the bushes and trees. The sweetness of spring called to him, teasing his senses. Winters in Logan were frigid and discouraged loitering outdoors. Now that it was warmer, he wanted to soak in the evening air, so it seemed natural to invite Lily and the kids to take a walk, despite the late hour.

"How was the concert?" Lily asked when the children were settled into her double stroller and they had turned onto the sidewalk.

"It was really nice. I expected to be bored, but I actually enjoyed the music. Kaylee's solo was really good. She's amazing." He maneuvered the stroller over a crack and listened to Stephen exclaim about a wave of peach tulips bordering the sidewalk.

"Pretty, Mom. Pretty fwowers. Wook, a dog. Hey, doggie!" he called, waving madly at the terrier on a leash in the front yard.

Lily laughed at her son, and Curtis caught her looking his way as they wandered from one block to the next with no particular direction in mind. "I don't see you so carefree very often," he said.

"I don't feel that way much. The kids were good this afternoon, though, and it's a lovely night." She brushed a lock of hair from her face. "So you decided you like classical music after all?"

"In moderation." They exchanged a look of understanding. It felt so good here in her presence, calming—even with Stephen calling out greetings to the gray and white striped cat in the nearby bed of ivy.

A cool breeze blew by them, and he saw Lily shiver. "Cold?"

"Just for a minute. It's already passed."

He stopped the stroller and crouched down on the side to look into Sophie's seat in back. She was sound asleep, so he tugged the thin blanket up to drape softly across her face and block the breeze. Her fist curled against her cheek, and he couldn't help but reach out and stroke the tiny fingers. She was so perfect. He stood and returned to pushing the stroller. "She's already asleep. I guess it's tough being a good little girl."

"Yeah, poor thing has her big brother trying to either take her toys or haul her around the house like she's one of the toys."

He laughed. "That sounds about right." He asked about how her parents' house was coming, and she talked about the landscaping plan she was helping them put together. It was nice to be with her. Though he and Lily kept in touch with calls and emails, he hadn't seen her since he'd babysat the kids two weeks earlier.

After a lull in the conversation, she asked, "What's going on? You've been quieter than usual."

"Nothing much. Things have been uneventful. Workouts with the various basketball teams don't start for a few weeks, so I've spent a lot of time tweaking my parents' landscape, keeping in shape . . . nothing much to say, I guess." Except that he'd had plenty on his mind—specifically the empty mailbox taunting him every day. And Lily.

"So you haven't heard from Daphne yet?"

"No. I know it probably came out of the blue for her, but I'm anxious to have the information. I'm kind of nervous about what she'll say to me—if she'll get nasty or be nice about it." He felt his face scrunch up. "I know Denise said their relationship is coming along all right, but I can't help but worry."

There was a long pause, and he glanced over at her thoughtful expression. She looked straight ahead with one hand on the stroller, though he did most of the pushing and guiding. He thought she was beautiful. Every time he saw her, he was more drawn to her. "How about you? Have you gotten anything important in the mail lately?" He knew she would understand his question.

She shook her head but didn't look at him. "I haven't heard anything about the divorce. I expect something soon, but it could be months before the judge rules on the custody issue. I just want it all over with. Wondering what will come up next is wearing on me." She flashed him an impish smile. "On the other hand, I swear Sophie said 'mama' yesterday." Lily laughed. "I know she's way too young to speak. It was probably just gas."

He laughed with her and their eyes met. Their gaze held for a long moment, and he wondered if he could stand living halfway across the country from her next year. He knew now that he didn't want to, but he wasn't nearly as certain of her feelings.

"Wook, pretty fwowers," Stephen exclaimed, pointing to a few daffodils spiking up through the dark earth around them. They would be the last this spring.

"Very pretty flowers," Lily said.

Curtis agreed as he turned his attention back to pushing the stroller. He had plenty of time to decide what to do about Lily later. First, he had to wait for her divorce to go through. He enjoyed working on their friendship—for now, anyway. The bitterness toward relationships he'd developed the previous year had eroded under her warm smile.

Daphne heard the muttering of voices in the next cell and her cellmate's snoring. She looked at the letter in her hand again. She'd put off writing back to Curtis for more than two weeks, justifying to herself that she didn't want to pay to send it. She had more urgent people to write with the few free envelopes and postage the state provided each week.

She knew it was simply an excuse. At first she'd used it because she was mad at him for offering next to nothing in the way of a relationship in return for the information he sought. He didn't seem to want to get to know her at all—he just wanted information. She pushed the thin gray hair back from her face and sighed as she felt a remnant of the hurt that had brought on her anger.

When that first burn of anger had passed, she'd still wanted to write a scathingly nasty letter—had written it, in fact. Then Daphne had remembered how far that kind of thing had gotten her with Denise and knew sending a note like that would almost certainly damage the tentative relationship she was building with her oldest daughter and ruin any chance of something with either of her sons.

She smoothed the sheet of paper on the notebook as she decided where to start and what to say—their relationship would always be affected by what she wrote now, and she wanted to get it right.

CHAPTER TWENTY-FIVE

Lily returned home after a day of substitute teaching. Her back ached, her feet hurt, and she needed some cookies ASAP, but it had been a good couple of days. She was looking forward to having a class of her own—hopefully next year. She doubted there would be many more substitute teaching jobs that year since school was nearly out.

Shelly called to her from the kids' bedroom. "It figures you'd show up as I finished changing a poopy diaper."

"I lingered a few extra minutes for that very reason," Lily teased as she dropped her bag inside the door and then headed to the room.

"I suspected as much. You're remarkably good at it." Shelly settled Sophie onto a blanket on the floor and then picked up the dirty diaper. "The day care said the kids did great this morning."

Shelly had morning classes during the summer session, so she could only watch the kids for a couple of hours in the afternoons, but Lily appreciated her willingness to help out. Both Stephen and Sophie seemed a lot happier now that they rarely went to day care. Stephen's clingy behavior was improving, and he seemed just a tad less jealous of his sister—most of the time. "How were they this afternoon?" Lily picked Stephen up and gave him a big hug before settling him on her hip.

"Great. They both went down for naps right after we got home and haven't been awake long. I picked up the mail for you—Stephen insisted. It's on the counter." Shelly avoided Lily's gaze as she walked past her to the bathroom to wash her hands.

The key to the cluster box on the street hung inside the front door, and Stephen was always anxious to pick up the mail, even though there was nothing in it for him. Lily figured it was the excitement of seeing things magically appear in the box each day, though it was junk most of the time. Then again, he was always allowed to open the junk mail.

She walked to the kitchen and found the envelope under a grocery store ad. It had her attorney's return address on the top corner, which made her breath catch. She felt the bottom fall out of her stomach as her trembling fingers reached for the envelope. Lily had been waiting anxiously for this. She hoped it was the divorce decree. She ripped the envelope open and pulled out the sheet.

It was official—she was a single woman again.

Tears clouded her eyes as she read the lines a second time. Yes, she had wanted it over with, but sadness, defeat, and a wave of discontent flashed through her. She wasn't supposed to be in this position now. Her plans and dreams had been interrupted in one of the worst ways. Then Stephen ran over and hugged her leg, and she smiled. Not all of her dreams had gone awry. She did have her beautiful children.

"Is that what I think it is?" Shelly asked, carrying Sophie in with her.

"Yeah." Lily blinked back the tears and pushed away the unhappiness that flooded her. There would be time to mourn her lost illusions when she was alone and the kids were in bed. "What do you say we order a cheap pizza and celebrate my singleness?"

Shelly pushed a lock of hair behind Lily's ear and smiled. "I think that sounds fantastic. I'm buying." When Lily tried to protest, Shelly held up a hand to stop her. "Hey, it's my turn. Especially after all of the cookies I've baked and eaten here in the past few months—a trend that is not likely to end anytime soon."

Lily laughed and hugged her sister. "You're the best. That sounds great."

Curtis opened his mailbox the next day and found a letter with the state correctional facility's return address and an inmate number. He stopped and stared at it for a moment as he felt a rush of adrenaline pour through him. He'd about given up on receiving anything from Daphne after nearly a month had passed. Denise had enough information to begin a search. She could have started by now—but it would be easier with a little more information, assuming Daphne had anything else she was willing or able to share.

He ripped open the envelope and pulled out two sheets of paper. It was normal ruled white paper. The handwriting was uneven and sloppy and only covered one side of each sheet. Denise had warned him Daphne's speech and writing were choppy—a result of too many years of doing drugs.

Curtis,

I took long to write because I wanted to get it right. You asked about Alex. I didn't think you would be the one to ask. Cliff has been visiting the family longer, I hear. I thought it would be him. Congratulations on the NBA draft. I've seen some of your games. You're good. I've much reason for pride of my kids. I want to see you and Cliff play each other again. I watched when you played him in college.

You ask about Alex. I not seen him since before you were born. Met him in Evanston. Don't be rough on him. Tough time. Heard he moved, can't remember where. Has a son, about your age, maybe a bit older. He was maybe two years older than me. Or a little more. Think he grew up in Arizona. Memories fuzzy. Good luck with search. Please write this old lady again sometime. It's very lonely here.

Daphne

Curtis stood in front of his mailbox for a long moment before he noticed the sounds of someone moving around. He folded up the letter and closed his box. He'd have to call Denise with the information so she could begin the search.

He also wanted to talk to Lily.

When her cell began to ring, Lily stood at the bottom of the slide, waiting with her arms extended to catch Stephen. She felt her phone vibrate in her pocket as she scooped Stephen up and gently deposited him on the ground so he could run back up the play set to slide again. She dug into her pocket and pulled out the phone, smiling when she saw Curtis's name on the display. She tucked her hands-free earpiece into her ear and answered. "Hello?"

"Lily, how are things going?"

His voice sent a little thrill through her. She wondered if part of her excitement was tied to knowing she was single now. Would he care? Had she been reading him right? "Great. I had the day off for once, so I brought the kids to the playground. You?"

They made small talk about his family and her kids for several minutes before she brought up her letter. She hadn't called him the previous night but had wanted to talk to him about it. He'd asked a couple of times in the most casual way possible.

"Really?" he said when he found out the divorce had been finalized. There was a long pause and his tone changed when he spoke again. "That's great. I got a letter of my own." He went on to talk about the letter Daphne had sent.

While they talked, Lily caught Stephen at the bottom of the slide several more times and picked up Sophie, who was fussing. Thankful for her earpiece, she continued speaking with him as she loaded the tired kids into the stroller and headed back to her apartment. Conversation always seemed to flow easily between them, and he made her laugh several times.

When she reached home, she lingered on the shady doorstep while a liberated Stephen ran in and grabbed a toy truck. Her breath caught in her throat when Lily realized the only thing that would make the moment better would be if Curtis was actually beside her.

The day turned hot. Lily dabbed sweat from her brow, then continued shifting the perennials to fill holes left behind by customer purchases. June was well underway, and though sales had slowed, her work hours at the nursery were still going strong. Often as she worked, she thought about discussing the plants with Curtis. They had spoken a few times since she had gotten her divorce papers, but life and the children kept their calls further apart and shorter than she would have liked.

She was grateful for the work and loved her job. Every day when she was surrounded by the trees and flowers, she dreamed of planting this or that. She imagined her parents' new yard and what other suggestions she'd make for the landscaping. There were a few more weeks before the house would be habitable, but as soon as her family was settled, she'd take the kids to visit.

With a nod, Lily finished straightening the table she was working on and moved to the next one.

"Oh, these are nice. I've always had a thing for yarrow. What do you think, honey? They'd go great in that bed by the poplar." A woman's voice broke through Lily's thoughts and shattered her concentration. That voice was more than a little familiar. In fact, if she didn't know better . . . she turned and looked at the couple bent over the selection of plants on the next table. The woman flipped another plant tag over and commented on it.

Dang! She couldn't believe it. What were the odds that Elizabeth's best friend would show up at Lily's place of employment? Suspiciously astronomical, considering the couple lived in Utah County. A moment later, the woman looked over and seemed to see her for the first time. She pressed a hand to her chest and blinked. Lily didn't find the move the least bit believable. "Well, if it isn't Lily Drake. Honey, isn't this a nice surprise?" The woman tugged on her husband's business suit with a manicured hand.

Lily wracked her brain, trying to remember the couple's names. She and John rarely went to his parents' house for gatherings, and she'd only met them a few times. "S" something. Sara, Sarina, Sariah? It wasn't coming, but she couldn't just stand there like an idiot. She forced a smile onto her face that was as false as the other woman's and walked over. If the socialite had ever picked out a plant in person before, Lily would eat the yarrow they were looking at. Or not—yarrow might be safe to eat, but it probably wouldn't taste very good.

"How strange to bump into you here," the woman said, walking over to Lily. "And don't you just look the picture of health and prosperity? How are your little angels?"

The woman's tone was toothachingly sweet—even more than usual—but Lily managed to smile anyway. She hoped it was a smile and not a grimace. "The kids are doing just great. Thank you."

Sandra-Sasha-Savannah took Lily by the arm like an old friend and then waved over her shoulder to her husband. "Bring two of those, Roger." She turned back to Lily and began leading her to the front door. "Things back in Highland are lovely this time of year. I was driving past your old place just a few days ago. The roses were gorgeous, of course, but it sure looks neglected without you there to take care of things."

They were approaching the check-out counter when Sadie-Selene-Sally shifted the topic of conversation again. The woman spoke in a louder voice as they approached two employees who had been talking at the register but who had stopped to listen to Elizabeth's friend's monologue. "You sure did land on your feet compared to John. Imagine, your poor husband going to prison for fraud and you not having a clue the whole time. It's almost past believing." She said this as they reached the counter.

Of course they've stopped their gossip to listen to everything the old hag says. Lily tried to keep her face impassive as the woman released her arm. The damage had been done. No need to keep Lily so close now.

The dutiful husband set two pots of pincushion flowers on the counter while his wife gushed about the quality and selection the nursery offered, apparently oblivious to the fact that they were buying something completely different from what she had picked out.

The woman continued chatting about home and friends and how devastated the Drakes were at the situation with John, inferring again that Lily must have been aware of his actions.

Lily felt her cheeks redden as she repeated in her head, *I mustn't punch the evil woman and cause a scene at work.* It was a sore temptation.

"Well, good luck, dear. But then again, who needs luck when they have your many wiles?" The woman laughed insincerely and breezed from the building, leaving Lily to grind her teeth.

As Lily walked back to her work, she heard the girls begin to whisper.

CHAPTER TWENTY-SIX

Curtis's gym bag hit the floor, and he flopped onto his bed at his parents' house. He hated flying sometimes. The airport had been noisy and crowded, and the lines seemed to take forever. He had to fold his tall body into the tiny space they referred to as "leg room" and squish into those narrow seats.

There would be perks in being drafted to the NBA—one of which would be the cash to go first class so he didn't feel so crowded.

The workout in Denver had been good. He liked the coach well enough and the facility was nice. Perhaps there were nicer ones out there, but at least being drafted to Denver would mean he was relatively close to home, even if it was half a continent from his twin. He wondered—not for the first time—what Lily would have thought of the city and if she'd ever been there.

She was never far from his mind as each new sight in the city, every glimpse of a playground made him wonder how she would fit in, if she would like it there—if, that is, he was able to convince her to marry him. He laughed at the direction his thoughts had taken. She was barely divorced. He needed to give her a little time before springing a proposal on her. And they hadn't even kissed—yet. Though he was pretty sure she was interested in him, there was no guarantee her feelings were anywhere near as serious as his.

After sprawling on the bed for several minutes, Curtis leaned over and pulled his laptop from his carry-on. A minute later he was checking his email.

CURTIS, I FOUND SOME INFORMATION YOU SHOULD FIND INTERESTING. TAKE A LOOK.

DENISE

There were several attachments, so he downloaded and opened them. The first one was details she'd been able to confirm about Alexander Grayson Fields. Curtis was so engrossed in reading it that when his cell phone rang, he answered without looking at the caller ID. "Hello?"

"Curtis, are you home?" It was Denise. "Did you get my email? I haven't heard from you and thought I ought to give you a heads up since you were so anxious about it."

"I pulled it up just a minute ago. I haven't really had time to look it over yet." He switched from her documentation of the search to a copy of a newspaper article.

"I think I found him," she said. "He's about the right age, has the right name, first, middle, and last. He was married when you were born, and he has a son just months older than you. That's what I learned from his community newspaper, anyway. He has a phone listing in Rock Springs, Wyoming."

Curtis pulled up one of the other attachments she'd sent. "Give me a second." His eyes skimmed the text, picking up basic data that confirmed this was probably the Alexander Fields they were looking for, unless Daphne had given them the name of someone she had just known about. "He was a widower when the story was written. No shock for his wife anyway, and his son lives out of state. It looks promising."

"There's something even more promising. Look at the picture I attached—the one called Young Alex."

He clicked on the name and took a shocked breath when it came up. It was only a black and white newspaper clipping, but the man looked just like him. "Holy cow."

"Yeah, Daphne led us right. Who would've thought?"

Curtis ignored the flippant tone that underplayed her words. It took him a moment to begin breathing again and get his brain in order. "Where is he? Where did you find him? Do you have an address?"

There was a brief, uncertain pause. "Curtis, you're not going to just barge in on him, are you?"

"I don't know. I'll have to think about it for a while. I haven't had time to catch my breath." He was reeling and a little freaked out now that the information was right in front of him.

She seemed to consider that for a moment. "The address and phone number are in one of the attachments. Call me before you do anything. Give me a chance to talk you out of it."

"Denise, I'm not some baby who doesn't know right and wrong."

"You'll do whatever you need to do. Just give me a chance to make sure you aren't jumping into things."

Several seconds stretched between them, but he knew she was right. It wouldn't hurt to talk it over with her first—whatever he ended up doing.

They hung up after a moment, and Curtis decided he wouldn't get anything else done without a break, so he shut down the computer and went for a walk. He wanted to call Lily, but he wasn't sure what to think yet. He felt anxious about the search, but he also felt a sense of urgency. Though he'd promised to call Denise, he knew he'd make the trip to Wyoming soon. He needed to see what he could find out.

He remembered the file that held Alex Fields's phone number. Denise was right to make him promise not to rush into things, but he had nearly hit his limit already.

After several phone calls back and forth with Cliff and after the better part of a week had passed, Curtis's gut feeling that he should drop by Alex's house had only increased. He knew it was risky—the chances of things going south were high—but he had to meet the man, and everything inside him said not to put it off. He couldn't send a letter and take the chance that the wrong person would read Alex's mail. He couldn't allow the man to ignore him or deny him the chance to speak face-to-face. Even if the only result was rejection, he had to make an attempt.

The thought of rejection terrified him—it was the main reason he hadn't looked before—but he wasn't going to let his fears rule him this time.

Though Denise tried to get him to let her call Alex as an intermediary, Curtis couldn't accept it. His sense of urgency was growing stronger every day. Cliff tried to waylay Curtis too, but he couldn't put it off.

Curtis knew he was looking at an all-day trip, maybe overnight if things went well. He wasn't going to count on either outcome, so he planned to pack a bag, but he wouldn't make a reservation. If things went awry, he'd turn around and come home that night.

He pulled his cell phone from his pocket and stared at it for a long moment. He'd memorized the phone number after looking at it so many times. After a moment of deliberation, he flipped the phone open and dialed Alex's number. He could always claim he misdialed, right?

He pushed *send* and then lifted the phone to his ear—only to hear tones saying the number had been disconnected. A moment later he verified that he'd dialed correctly. *Alex isn't living there anymore? Where do we go from here?*

He dialed Denise. He was relieved when she picked up right away. "Hey, sis. I have a question for you—what do I do if Alex has moved?"

"Why do you think he's moved?"

He could hear Cam making car noises through the phone, and he imagined them playing together on the floor. "Well, when I called just now, it was disconnected."

"You did what?"

He explained, then asked what was next. When Denise made her suggestion, Curtis nodded to himself. It made sense. He could pay someone to see where Alex had gone or what happened to him. However, he didn't want to sit on his hands and wait for news.

With his decision made, he dialed Lily's number.

Curtis walked through the door of the nursery where Lily worked and glanced around. He smiled and greeted a young woman behind the counter, then walked to the right, wandering down the aisles looking for Lily. Over the past few weeks he'd made several trips to Logan to hang out with her and the kids and get to know her better. Though he'd spoken with Lily several times while he was on the road the past week, he'd been anxious to see her again.

He walked through the area where the pond plants were located, noticing how few were left, and wandered through the roses, small shrubs, and then out to the trees. After following the trickles of water flowing from the large pots, he finally found her watering the last of them. She looked hot and tired as she rubbed a sheen of sweat from her forehead with the back of her arm. She shifted the watering wand to the next pot, then looked up at him and smiled when their eyes met. "Hey, what are you doing here?"

"You left your phone at home and Shelly answered it. She said you get off soon. Care to join me for dinner and some stimulating adult conversation?" This was the closest he'd come to asking for an actual date since her divorce was finalized. He planned to use this opportunity in more ways than one.

Several emotions seemed to fly over her face, including interest and uncertainty. "I ought to hurry home and give Shelly a break. She's been great at babysitting for me, but I shouldn't take advantage of her."

He stepped closer and brushed a hair from her face. Her skin was so smooth and she still smelled of that lilting, floral perfume she always wore. "Take advantage—she insists."

"She does?" She lifted an eyebrow at his declaration.

"Yes. I asked if she minded. She insisted she does not. I think she said something about 'more cookies for her'? I'm afraid she's going to run through all of your baking supplies well before summer ends." He thought the constant talk about cookies was funny and had decided it was more of a joke between the sisters than anything.

"It's strange, I come home to fresh cookies at least once a week, but I rarely notice more than a few eggs missing. And I haven't bought chocolate chips in ages." She moved a bit closer. "How was your stop in Denver?"

"About like the one in Chicago and L.A. How are the kids today?"

"When I left them to come to work they were doing great. I'm sure they're nice and sugared up now that Shelly's in charge."

He grinned at the glint in her eyes and noticed she'd forgotten about the watering wand. Though he would have loved to continue monopolizing her attention, he redirected it. "I don't think the rocks need water." He held in a laugh when she looked down and shifted the wand so the stream returned to the pot.

She seemed confused and a bit out of sorts when she focused on her work again. He could practically see her gathering her wits about her, and he hoped it wasn't wishful thinking on his part.

A moment later she switched to the next pot. "So what brought you up to Logan today?"

"Denise found some information for me. I wanted to talk about it with you, and I wondered how things were going with your legal mess."

She pursed her lips together. "We just keep shooting documents back and forth. Our lawyers are having a grand old time of it. I'm not worried about the caseworker anymore. If they'd just leave me alone, it would all turn out fine." Lily looked up at a couple of her coworkers talking a few rows over. They eyed her and Curtis and then giggled to each other. She returned her attention to the pot in front of her. "The legal fees are killing me."

Two other employees walked by, speaking in low tones. Curtis glanced over and saw them look pointedly at him and Lily. One muttered something that sounded like "she can sniff out money." Her companion giggled and shot Curtis a flirtatious look before they turned down another aisle, heading away. He turned back to Lily.

She flushed and explained, "Everyone knows about John. It's been . . . uncomfortable."

Angry that the girls were making things difficult for Lily, Curtis decided to ignore them and focus on their previous discussion. "I think I might have a solution for the legal fees issue—a small one. A Band-aid, really."

She turned the water off at the wand's switch as she finished the last pot, then folded her arms over her chest. "Do tell. Band-aids are at a premium at my place."

"Only if you'll have dinner with me." He smiled in his most charming manner and stuffed his hands in his pockets before he gave in to the urge to touch her again. He was mesmerized by the tendril of hair that had escaped her ponytail and curled sinuously along her cheekbone.

"Charm doesn't work on me, you know." Still, the corners of her mouth twitched.

"It doesn't?" Her comment amused him, especially since charm had seemed to soften her up on more than one occasion.

"No, I'm immune now. I fell for charming once, so I won't fall for it this time."

"So what does a guy have to do to get a promise of dinner?"

She walked around him, wrapping up the hose as she made her way down the row of trees. He followed, waiting for her to come up with some answers.

She walked about fifteen feet before she turned and looked over her shoulder. "A promise of Mexican wouldn't go wrong. I liked that place you took me last time."

He laughed. "Mexican it is."

The restaurant was noisy and crowded, but the server arrived with their drinks quickly and took their orders. Lily sipped her drink, focused on Curtis. Why did he have to be so dang good-looking? "So, what's this big news you've got?"

"Well, we're ninety-nine percent sure we found my birth father."

"That's great!"

"And then we lost him."

Her brow furrowed. "How do you lose a grown man?"

"He doesn't live there anymore—or at least, his phone's been disconnected. Denise suggested I hire a PI to find him." He leaned lazily back against the bench, his long legs poking into the walkway, even though his shoulders were on the far side of the seat. He was all easy grace and cool confidence—except for the way he moved his straw in the glass of ice. That was a sure giveaway that he was nervous.

"That's a good idea."

"Except they cost a lot of money, and I don't want to just hang out waiting forever."

The waitress brought a basket of chips and a bowl of salsa. When she left, Lily scooped some salsa up and then returned to the issue at hand. "So what are you going to do?"

"I thought I might pay someone to go with me. Someone smart, pretty, funny, with a good babysitter and excellent people skills. Someone who occasionally finds herself roped into things she never planned on."

Lily narrowed her eyes at him and retracted her hand from the chips. "Ah, so this dinner was to soften me up so you could do me the great favor of digging me from my financial woes. That's very kind of you." Her mouth suddenly tasted bitter. Apparently she was a service project.

"There's no reason for you to get touchy about it. I know things are tight, and I'd love to help you out a bit. This way, you'll be able to earn it. It's not like I'm offering you money to sit home and look pretty—though I'm sure you'd do that admirably." His lips curved as he studied her. "I need help, and if you come with me, that'll mean you can't work that day."

"You seem to have forgotten I have two children. How much fun will they be to drag around?" She felt herself color at his flirty remark. When he had said similar things in the past, it had almost always been for Lacy's benefit.

"I mentioned the trip to Shelly, and she called your mom. Apparently they're dying to kidnap your children for a day, possibly overnight. Didn't you say you wanted to take the kids to see your parents' new place?"

Yes, I wanted to take the kids—to see it myself. Lily pushed the thought from her mind for a moment and focused on his offer. She really wanted to help him if it was practical, though she had no intention of accepting his money. "What do you need me to do?"

"You have Friday off, right?"

"Shelly's just a fount of information, isn't she?" Lily managed not to roll her eyes.

Curtis grinned. "I thought we might leave early. I could pick you up about seven. Rock Springs is only a couple of hours from here. That would put us there late enough in the morning to determine if anyone is living in the house or possibly ask neighbors for information. With any luck, we'll be home by sundown."

Lily considered what it would be like to spend an entire day with him—more or less completely alone. No children begging for her attention every ten minutes. No work. Just adult conversation and companionship with this fascinating man.

It was the most tempting offer she'd had in ages—and the most terrifying. She wasn't sure if she could stand the heartbreak if things didn't work out. He was going to move soon, and she couldn't go with him. The potential for problems was so great. But she wasn't going to worry about the future quite yet.

"It might be fun."

"Great."

CHAPTER TWENTY-SEVEN

When Lily returned home after a leisurely dinner, she found Shelly holding a sleeping baby and sitting on the floor watching cartoons with Stephen. He jumped up when she walked in and ran over to her. "Mama, we watching Nemo."

She scooped him up and gave him a tight squeeze. "I see that, honey. Were you good for Aunt Shelly?"

"Yes!"

Lily looked at her sister, who cocked her head to the side as if to say he wasn't too out of line. After giving her son a kiss on the cheek, she set him back on the floor and redirected him to the television. "How long has Sophie been out? It's still a bit early, isn't it?"

"She didn't have much of an afternoon nap. Stephen was reasonably well behaved. Sophie—not so much. She fell asleep about fifteen minutes ago." She offered the baby to Lily, who snuggled her little girl close.

"Why'd you agree to let me stay out longer if she was being a pill?" Sophie had recovered nicely from the croup, but she'd been fussy the past few days.

"You had a nice dinner, didn't you?" She sent her sister a meaningful look. "I expected you to stay out later or for Curtis to come here afterward. It's been a while since you've seen him."

"He has to get on a plane in a few hours—he's heading to Georgia this time, then New York, and I'm not sure where after that." She rolled here eyes at Shelly's speculative look. "And yes, before you strain yourself trying to keep from asking me, I agreed to help him in Rock Springs on Friday."

"Great! It'll be fun taking the kids home. Mom said she'd have a room all ready for us, and you know Kellie and Danyelle will spoil them all day." She gave Lily a long, appraising look and lifted an eyebrow. "So, how are things with you and Curtis?"

Lily smiled and tipped her head. "You know, sister, for a woman who has two guys on the string and never discusses them, you're remarkably curious about others peoples' relationships."

Shelly smiled mysteriously and grabbed her purse. "I suppose we're all entitled to our privacy. Can you make sure to come straight home from work on Thursday? I have a date with one of those men." She kissed her nephew and feathered a finger over her niece's hair. Then she said good-bye to Lily and left the apartment.

Lily shook her head and turned toward the kids' room. She'd have to remember to counter her sister's questions with some of her own more often.

Friday morning dawned sunny and warm. Lily was exhausted when Curtis pulled in front of her apartment, but she was ready to go. After spending the night on Lily's sofa, Shelly would take the kids to Ephraim in a couple hours. She sat with Lily on the porch, her morning glass of juice cradled in her hands and the baby monitor by her side to alert her if the kids woke.

"You could just come by tonight after you finish," Shelly said, when Curtis walked toward them. "You could bring Curtis along too. You know Mom would love to have him visit." She had a twinkle in her eye that made Lily want to cringe. Did she really have to make the suggestion in front of him?

"I don't know if Mom and Dad are settled that much yet. They only moved in a couple of weeks ago."

"And you inherited your organization talents from Mom. She even said to bring Curtis back with you, if you can. She hasn't seen him in ages."

Lily wondered what Shelly had told their mother. What kind of relationship did her parents expect? "I suppose we'll see. Thanks for taking care of the kids."

"My pleasure. This weekend I'm teaching them the art of playing with sharp, pointy objects. We may even move up to knives." She shot Lily a saucy grin.

"Fine, just don't forget to teach them basic first aid before the other lesson, okay?"

"First aid comes in handy throughout life. It's great for fixing bloody noses, bruised knuckles, torn skin—" Curtis grinned and dodged as Lily swatted half heartedly at him.

"My children are not going to be brawling on a regular basis, thank you very much. They are very well behaved." Lily shook the hair out of her face and stood up.

"You forget how much time I've spent with them. They're reasonably well-behaved—for their ages." He stepped back, grinning, when she glared at him. "But just wait. Boys are made for brawling. Of course, you wouldn't know that since you didn't have brothers."

"I don't believe for a second that you and Cliff are typical." Lily glanced over at Shelly and saw her smiling at them. "Try to keep the sibling carnage down to non-life-threatening injuries, would you? The phrase for the day is 'zero fatalities.' That applies to my little ones too." She sent her sister a mocking look and adjusted her purse over her shoulder before turning back to Curtis. "Shall we go then?"

After driving around town for fifteen minutes trying to find Alex's old neighborhood, Curtis pulled the car in front of the right house—at least, the address looked right to Lily. A red and white "For Sale" sign was posted in the front yard, perched above a pale green picket fence.

Lily watched Curtis as his eyes wandered over the property. Then she took a closer look herself. It was a comfortable-sized home—not too small but not overly large either—with white clapboard siding and pale green accents that matched the fence.

They got out of the car and walked up to the gate.

"Mature trees, nice bushes. He had a good eye for landscaping. Someone did, anyway," Curtis commented.

"I love the bench there in the corner, but the butterfly bush looks like it hasn't been trimmed back in a few years. I bet it's spectacular in August." She glanced over, met his gaze, and warmed under his regard.

He broke eye contact and pointed. "It could use some hardscaping in the corner. You could build up a bed along the fence and put in a small patio to enjoy the shade."

She could imagine that, the two of them sitting around a table while Sophie and Stephen played at their feet. "And a pool-less waterfall into a bed of gravel or a fountain under the maple tree." She could almost hear the music of water falling on rocks. The intimate scene in her head only strengthened her awareness of his warm, long body beside her. She caught his eye again and felt a breath hitch in her chest.

He reached out and traced her cheek bone and then along her jaw. His grin softened into something more serious as his fingertips brushed across her bottom lip. "That's one of the many things I like about you—you speak my language. And you have great taste." His voice dropped in pitch and volume. The tension thickened between them as the moment stretched, each focused on the other as they swayed together, as if drawn by magnets.

Lily's throat began to tighten from the intensity of his gaze. She licked her lips and swallowed as he drew closer. Her heart pounded as she realized that after all this time, he was really going to kiss her. His fingers slid down the side of her throat, and his hand settled on her shoulder just before his lips pressed to hers. Lily reached out to steady herself against him, her hand flat on his chest. *Finally.* The word echoed in her mind as she inched closer and his hand slid around to cup the back of her head. His other hand found her waist, drawing her in.

The kiss ignited a zing of electricity that bounced around inside her. She breathed in the musky scent of his cologne. Curtis shifted his head in a silent request for more.

Lily trembled when he eventually drew away and then stood dumbly, reeling from an experience that was so much more than any kiss she'd ever shared with John—or maybe the kiss had just blown memories of any other man's kisses so far away, she couldn't recall them. She doubted she would ever forget the feel of his lips on hers.

He let out a long, jagged breath. "If I'd had any idea kissing you would be like that, I'd have done it months ago." His was face flushed. He rubbed his thumb over her bottom lip again before releasing her, though his gaze never strayed from her face.

Lily felt her heart soar when she heard his words, but it only made it harder to catch her breath. "Well, feel free to indulge again sometime." At the moment she couldn't think of all the reasons their relationship might not work out. She was having trouble processing anything at all.

"I will." He smiled, then glanced toward the sign and pulled out his cell phone. "Let's start with whoever's showing the house. Hopefully we'll be able to gather a little information."

No one answered and there was no voice mail, so the two of them decided to go knock on a couple doors in the neighborhood.

"It might go over best if we pretended to be a couple looking for relatives who used to live there," Curtis suggested as they headed up the first walk. "Or do we want to pretend to be interested in the house?"

"Play it by ear?" Lily asked.

Curtis knocked on the door. When a young mother arrived, Lily asked if she knew anything about the house, who owned it, who was showing it.

When the neighbor knew nothing useful, they moved on. It wasn't until the fourth house that they learned anything valuable.

"Oh, sure," a grizzled, white-haired man said with a nod. "Myrtle across the street there's showing it for them. She's out for her daily tatting class, piano lessons, or whatever keeps those cackling old hens busy at the senior center, but she'll be home after lunch. Right around one, I guess. You wantin' to buy?"

"It's a nice-looking place." Curtis shrugged. "I'll be relocating soon."

"Couldn't find nicer people than those Fields. Kept their house and yard up real good. You give Myrtle a visit or call in a bit. She'll get you in to see the house." He started to swing the main door shut, signaling the end of the visit.

"We will. Thanks." Lily waved and turned back to the street.

As they approached the car, Curtis took Lily's hand. "It's not even ten yet. Care to drive around for a while and grab lunch while we wait?"

"That sounds great." Lily squeezed his hand, loving the feel of his strong fingers intertwined with hers. Three hours of shooting the breeze with Curtis and no responsibilities. It sounded like heaven—just as soon as she called her mom to check up on the kids.

When Curtis and Lily returned to the house later that afternoon, they stood in front of it for a minute, just looking.

"Are you interested in this old house?" an elderly female voice asked behind them.

Lily stepped back and turned to look at the woman. "Yes. It's a lovely little place. Has it been empty long?"

"What makes you think it's empty?" Her eyes narrowed into slits and she seemed to puff up to her full height—which couldn't have been much over five feet.

"Lots of weeds in the flower beds, the grass could have used a mowing days ago and there's nothing personal spread around." Curtis waved toward the long front porch. "It has a lot of potential, though."

"It's a nice house for a growing family. Have any kids?" The old woman studied them for a long moment.

"Two," Lily said. She felt a bit guilty letting people think she and Curtis were married, but it seemed to be the easiest way to get information without drawing too much attention, and they hadn't exactly lied. "It looks like someone used to take great pains with the yard. How long has it been since that was true?"

"Alex loved to garden. He always had the nicest place in the neighborhood and was happy to help others with their yards when the need arose. I can't tell you what a help he was when I was down with a broken ankle a few years ago. Then the cancer came, and he got to where he couldn't even live alone. He oversaw the yard work for as long as he lived here, but he moved away last fall. Where you folks from?"

"Utah," Curtis said. "I'm going to be relocating for my job soon."

"Well, would you like to see inside? I have the key. Old Lester across the street phoned and said you'd been looking for me."

When Curtis met Lily's gaze, she nodded at him. They might as well take a look. They'd already gleaned quite a bit of information from this woman. Maybe she'd continue to be chatty and tell them what they needed. Besides, Lily was curious and could tell Curtis was too.

"I'm Myrtle West, by the way, and you folks?"

"Curtis and Lily Cox," Lily intervened. True enough as far as it went—even though it wasn't precisely accurate. She glanced at Curtis, who looked amused.

"I'd love to know more about the history of the place, the people who lived here. That kind of thing fascinates me." Lily did her best to look fascinated. "How many kids did they have? The house looks big enough for several."

"It is at that, but his poor wife had difficulty conceiving among other tragedies. Just the one son, Grayson, is all they were able to raise, but they loved him like none other." Myrtle kept up a constant monologue, talking about the family, the barbecues, the crazy things the son got up to with his friends. "He works for one of them big movie companies in Hollywood now. His father sure is proud of him."

"So, where's Alex now?" Lily asked as she peered into a closet. It really was a nice home, and she wouldn't have minded living in it under different circumstances. "Oh, I love the space here."

"There is room to spare, isn't there?" Myrtle said with a satisfied smile. "He's living with his son. When the doctors gave him six months to live, he planned to stay right here for the rest of his days; he didn't want to burden anyone. But his son wouldn't have it. He wanted his father close—like any good son would—so after some time, he convinced Alex to move in with him. Last I heard, he wasn't doing so well." A worried, pensive look came over her face. "I don't know how much time he has left, poor man. He's far too young to die."

Lily glanced back at Curtis and saw his face tighten. That put a wrench in the works. Would they find Alex before it was too late?

CHAPTER TWENTY-EIGHT

As they drove down Lily's street several hours later, Lily tried coming up with excuses to have Curtis hang around longer. It was barely dinnertime and she still had the long trip to Ephraim ahead of her, but she wasn't ready to say good-bye yet.

She huffed in irritation at the thought and gazed out the window. They had finally left Myrtle West behind with a noncommittal comment on the home and excuses about not knowing for sure where he'd be transferred. Curtis had called Denise the moment they drove away.

Lily was sure Denise was now deep into search mode and would come up with answers soon. She was a pro at this, and they didn't have months or years to find Alex—it sounded like they would be lucky to have days.

"So, you're going to Ephraim tonight?" Curtis asked. "Not in your own car—the engine that likes to quit?" He reached over and squeezed her hand for a moment before returning it to the gear shift to slow down in front of her building. He'd held her hand nearly the entire way home, releasing it when he had to change gears at every corner and red light in town.

"My car's doing fine. Lately." It didn't always start for work in the morning, and she'd run out of gas a couple of weeks earlier—thank goodness Shelly had been able to bring her gas to fill it. "There's nothing to worry about."

The car slowly came to a stop and Curtis turned, lifting his eyebrows. "Nothing to worry about? Of course not. My mistake." He lifted her hand in his again, playing with her fingers but slanting a look at her face. "What would you say if I invited myself to visit your parents' place with you? Shelly did mention your mom was anxious to see me."

"My car's fine. Really. You don't have to feel like you need to take care of me." One part of her wanted to dance in circles like a little girl after everything that had happened between them, while another reminded her that bringing him home would raise expectations—hers most of all.

"But you don't seem to understand. I do feel like taking care of you. I always do—not that you need help most of the time. You're very capable, but I want to make things better for you." A wry smile slid onto his face. "Besides, I'd love to spend the weekend at your folks' place. I believe I still owe your sisters a game of two-on-one."

"Ah, so it'll be a service project and a chance to follow through with a promise?" She hoped it wasn't true, but she couldn't totally convince herself.

He turned her chin so she looked into his face. "You could never be a service project to me, Lily. I asked to go because I want to spend time with you, and my future schedule promises to be . . . crazy." He leaned in and gently pressed his lips to hers just for a moment—only long enough to steal her breath.

The NBA draft was a week away and she'd done her homework. With post-draft tournaments and endless press conferences, she'd be lucky to see him at all in the next month. Put that way, how could she refuse? "I'd like that. I packed my bags last night. Let me go grab them."

Curtis sat in the seats at the NBA draft a week later. He felt jittery and anxious. What happened today would decide his future for the next several years. Of course, it didn't help that Denise had called that morning with news about Alex. She'd found Alex's son Grayson after a bit of digging and Cliff laying out a little cash for a PI. Then they'd verified that Alex was living there, but it didn't sound like things were going well at all for his health.

Curtis looked over at Cliff, who spoke with a few guys on the other side of the room. Curtis shifted, feeling uncomfortable in his blue pin-stripe suit. Despite the fact that he'd spent half his life in a suit—or so it felt sometimes—it felt constricting now, and he found himself tugging at the collar every few minutes. But he supposed that was only his nerves. He licked his lips and rubbed his sweaty hands against his pants.

Denise had called Cliff that morning about Alex, not Curtis. Curtis was still trying not to be offended by that, but as he'd been with Cliff at the time, they'd found out at the same time anyway. There was no telling if she'd have turned around and called Curtis after hanging up with Cliff or if she'd have waited until the draft was finished and he had some clue about his future.

And that brought him to the next issue: Lily. Would she want to live wherever he was picked to go? Would she want him, regardless of how far away it would be? Was she anywhere near ready to make a commitment to him or anyone else when the divorce was still so fresh? There were times when he was sure her feelings for him were serious and times when he felt her pulling back.

The visit to her parents' new house had been great. They had swung by his parents' house so he could pack a bag, and he came out of his room to find her deep in conversation with his mom. If he hadn't known for a fact that they had met only once before, and briefly at that, he would have sworn they'd been old friends for years.

Then her family had welcomed him with oatmeal-raisin cookies—Shelly claimed her sisters made it impossible to keep chocolate chips in the house—and offers of a quick pickup game on the new driveway. It felt like home, despite the weeds pushing through bare dirt in the yard, the walls that were still devoid of any decorations, and the fact that he'd had to squeeze his long frame onto a twin bed in the spare room at night.

And then there was the way Lily looked, how comfortable and relaxed she was when surrounded by family. Every glance between them, every touch had seemed heightened by the love that encircled them in that house. The idea of taking her across the country, so far from the family that loved her so much made his stomach twist with worry, but he honestly couldn't imagine living without her now. The last few days had been dreary without her smile to light up his days.

The NBA commissioner was introduced and stepped forward, interrupting Curtis's thoughts. The draft had begun. He tried to remind himself it could be hours before the thing ended and he might not be picked at all. On the other hand, free-agent status could have its benefits too, right? The knots in his stomach tightened, and he took a few slow, calming breaths.

He rubbed his sweaty palms on his jacket this time and turned toward Cliff again. Cliff looked his way and smiled, giving him two thumbs up. Curtis tried to smile back and willed his lunch to stay in his stomach.

Lily sat on Denise's sofa, the two of them glued to the television as they watched the draft begin. She was already wishing she hadn't eaten dinner—she felt nauseated. "Three hours. You said it could take three hours to complete?" She didn't think she could take the stress.

"Yes, but he's sure to be picked in the first half. I've been following the mock drafts obsessively." Denise munched on a handful of unbuttered popcorn, her eyes glued to the set.

Lily glanced at Denise and wondered if she even realized she was eating. Then again, maybe that was why the popcorn was plain—to minimize the guilt factor when the show was over. She turned back to the television as the camera panned the hopeful players. Curtis looked nervous to her, but she doubted most people would notice. He sat beside Reggie, who was trading comments with another neighbor, but Curtis's face was tight, blank.

She wondered why it mattered so much to her to know where he was going the moment it was announced. It wasn't as though they had a future—despite their amazing, delicious kisses. *Look at him, up there on the stage. What would he do with a wife who was bound to draw whispers wherever she went?* She pushed away her unhappiness on that front. The talking at work had grown worse—or perhaps she'd simply become more sensitive.

She'd been offered a contract in the Logan School District for that fall—a blessing she could not deny. And yet, she hated the idea of being stuck there without him. The trip to Rock Springs and weekend at her parents' had only intensified her feelings for him. There could be no doubt now, none at all, that she loved him. And the expression he wore sometimes when she caught him looking at her made her certain her feelings were reciprocated—at least a little. But there were still too many unknowns.

The first half hour of the show dragged as she stared at the television. Lily jumped when she felt a hand on her shoulder.

"You don't have to stare quite so hard. The announcement won't slip by you if you blink." Richard gave her shoulder a squeeze and walked around her. "For someone who isn't completely into basketball and who considers herself 'just a friend' of Curtis, you sure are intent."

"Hush, you're making too much noise." Denise didn't take her eyes off the TV, but she did smack her husband with her right hand and grab another handful of popcorn with her left.

"Now her insanity, I can understand." He grinned fondly at his wife.

Lily studied Rich for a moment, since the people on screen were interviewing the newest Blazer. "I've always liked basketball."

"Mmhm. And I've always liked bossy programmers who are obsessed with basketball and orange juice."

"Speaking of juice—get me a refill, would you, honey?" Denise picked up her empty glass from the coffee table and handed it to him, but never pulled her eyes from the screen. "Oh, there's Cliff. He looks almost bored. How could he possibly? Wait, the Bulls are up next."

Lily's attention pulled back to the proceedings. The Chicago Bulls was Cliff's team, and Curtis had worked out with them. Curtis hadn't talked like he was particularly taken with them, but she knew being with Cliff would cover a lot of ills. After a moment they announced that they chose someone else, and Lily settled back into her seat again.

The Denver Nuggets finally came up and Curtis eyed the manager, who studiously avoided looking in the direction of the draftees. This team was in his top three choices, one of which had already taken their pick for the night. Drawing number nine was a pretty good place for Denver, Curtis thought. It was high enough to get a good player, even if the best of the best were already gone. When he thought of one particular player who had been picked already, he got a funny taste in his mouth. Langley wasn't that good of a player.

Then the general manager called his name. His name. Curtis blinked as he felt Reggie slap him on the back in congratulations and push him to stand.

Curtis smiled so wide, he thought his face would pop. He was picked ninth? As he walked to the front he heard himself being praised for his strengths. He stopped to have a team cap set on his head. He was going to Denver.

"Denver's pretty close," Denise was saying. "Practically a hop, skip, and a jump from here. What is it, six, eight hours by car, barely an hour by plane, maybe even less?"

"Yes," Lily agreed woodenly. He was leaving the state, moving to Colorado. *Stupid. You knew it would happen. What's your problem?* "Much closer than Cliff. Hopefully he'll come home a bit more often." Still, she was dying inside because it was finally real. He was leaving.

She took the glass of celebratory juice Rich offered her and smiled. "To the number nine draft pick!"

"He should have been fifth instead of that Langley bozo," Denise said. But she lifted her glass anyway.

Lily looked at the screen where Curtis and Cliff were giving an impromptu interview and felt wistful. *If only . . . .*

CHAPTER TWENTY-NINE

Two crazy weeks passed as Curtis dealt with interviews, kept in practice, and tried to settle into some semblance of regularity. Lily, Shelly, and the kids came to celebrate in Ogden for the Fourth of July—though Shelly spent most of the day with Rob.

The Rocky Mountain Revue—one of several post-draft tournaments for newly picked players and those hoping to still sign a contract with an NBA team—was only a few days off. His mind turned to Denver and the research he had been doing on housing there, which naturally led him to think about Lily.

He had spent quite a lot of time looking at a variety of home listings online, unsure of what he should look for, what his circumstances would be in six months, a year. Nothing he looked at seemed right without knowing what his plans would be. As soon as he could get back to see Lily, he knew they needed to talk about their relationship and where it might be headed. Where he hoped it was headed.

His phone rang, interrupting his stuck-at-a-red-light reverie, so he glanced at the caller ID and saw it was Cliff.

Curtis answered and headed for the nearest parking lot as the light turned green. "Hey, Frog Breath, how are things going there?"

"Pretty good, snot-face. How is it going?"

"Keeping busy, as usual." Lily hadn't been the only thing on his mind lately—there was still the trip to meet his birth father. "Have you looked at the week after the Revue? You said you wanted to go to California with me. I should be free and easy for a while."

"Curt, I don't think we should rush this without preparing the way first. I told you."

"Yes, but we can't wait. I know we can't. I feel it in my gut, and that's the first time we're both free. If you don't want to come, I could go alone." Curtis rubbed a thumb over the steering wheel. He watched a young woman walk into a grocery store with a golden-haired toddler in tow. It made him wish even more for Lily.

"I'm not making you go alone. If things are that bad, we both need to be there. I just wish you would consider approaching him differently."

"If Alex weren't sick, I'd wait until August, feel things out. He is, though, so there's no point in wishing." Curtis tapped his fingers on the steering wheel.

"Right." Cliff's sigh was audible over the phone. "You finish at the Revue on Friday evening. Let's plan for Saturday morning."

"My game should be out fairly early. Why not leave Friday night?"

"If you're sure you can pull yourself away from Lily that soon. I haven't figured out why you're dragging your feet with her. You two need to talk."

Curtis grinned—he and Cliff had discussed the situation more than once. "Yes, we do. We'll have to see if I can't work things out before then." If he got his way, he and Lily would have a nice long talk—one even more important to his future than the draft or his family search. However, he didn't intend to let it wait until Friday night.

It was hot out, and Lily brushed the sheen of perspiration from her forehead. Curtis would be coming to Logan that afternoon. It had only been a few days since she'd seen him after his basketball game Saturday, but she always looked forward to seeing him again. Besides, there was something about him, about the way he took her hand when they were with his family and the feeling in his good-bye kiss before she had driven home from Salt Lake. She sensed something was on his mind.

Though she was nervous about making a move toward a more committed relationship, she couldn't help but hope he shared her feelings.

She shifted perennials and made sure every plant got watered properly, humming to herself as she went. It would be a short work day—only four hours. She was glad, since it would leave her time to shower and reapply her makeup before he arrived.

She pinched off a spent bloom when she heard someone approach from behind. She turned and caught the friendly face of a thirty-something woman. "Hello, can I help you find something?"

"Yes, I'd appreciate your help. I'm Scarlett Winters from the local newspaper, and I wondered if you'd answer a few questions for me." She pressed her sleek brown hair behind one ear.

Lily felt her chest tighten, but she forced a smile. "About our summer perennial sale? I'd be happy to discuss plants with you."

"No, Mrs. Drake. I wanted to discuss your husband. I understand he was convicted of fraud?" Scarlett pulled a little notepad and a pen from a hand bag.

Lily dampened her lips as her heart pounded and her stomach sank. "I believe everything you need to know about my ex-husband is available in the public records. It's a pretty old story, don't you think?" *Is this never going to end?*

"But it's never too late to get to the bottom of a story. For example, how could you not know something wasn't right in your finances? How could you not realize he was spending more than he made?" She flipped through a couple of pages and stopped at one, her pen poised. "It was pointed out to me that a wife living in such luxury is bound to realize something shady is going on."

Lily's stomach tied in knots and her mouth went dry. She thought of Elizabeth's friend just "happening" to stop by a few weeks earlier. Was Elizabeth responsible for this new interest? Lily would have said no, once. Ross and Elizabeth had always been so protective of their son and the family's good name. Then again, they were expending an awful lot of effort lately to cause her stress and trouble. "A lot of couples keep separate checking accounts for one reason or another. There's nothing remarkable about it. Now, if you'll excuse me, I have work to do."

When she tried to brush past, Scarlett reached out and snagged her shoulder. "Don't you want to defend yourself against the accusations that you're the one who demanded John provide you with the best of everything."

Lily hesitated for only a second—not because she agreed in the least, but because Elizabeth had used almost the same words to her to explain why she thought John had done it. It was a lie, of course, but that only made Lily more certain that the Drakes were responsible for this visit. "I have nothing to say to you."

"But inquiring minds want to know."

"Then they can read the *Enquirer*. I'm not interested in aiding your skewed reporting." Lily pulled away and headed for the potting room. Perhaps there was something she could straighten out in the employees-only area.

Everything was in perfect order, but Lily shut the door and slumped against it. Why had the reporter wasted her time chasing Lily down? It wasn't like there would be much interest in the story. She wasn't anyone special. Even if the Drakes were determined to make things difficult, why would Scarlett care enough to pursue it?

Then it occurred to her—Curtis would be a public figure, as much as any professional basketball player was a public figure. People would care what he did, and her actions could negatively affect him. This reporter wouldn't find an exciting story in the past, but someday, if her relationship with Curtis progressed and his career went as well as they expected, someone might find her history interesting enough to write about.

She choked back a sob as she realized it would never work. How would he feel about her after she ruined his reputation, even if it was only by association? She knew there was no way she could marry him—even if he did ask.

This knowledge was like a physical pain in her chest. Tears flooded her eyes, and she had to fight them back. Things at work were awkward enough without adding any more speculation to the mix. She was sure this wouldn't help.

She thought of Curtis's planned visit that evening and prayed she would be able to get though it without him realizing something was wrong.

When she exited the potting room a few minutes later, she ran into her boss. "Louis," she tried to put on a smile, "I'm nearly finished here."

"Good. Do you have a moment?" His brow was furrowed, and his look of unconcern wasn't completely believable.

Lily felt her stomach sour. Everything had been going fine—other than the whispers. Surely he wasn't upset about her work. She told herself she was being paranoid and smiled. "Of course."

He led the way to his office through the annuals and herbs and past the potting soil. When the door shut behind them, he gestured her to a seat and took his chair behind the desk. "There was a woman here today asking questions about you."

When Lily caught herself biting her lip, she took a deep breath through her mouth. "I'm sorry about that. I don't know what she was doing here."

"I've heard a few rumors, but they haven't bothered me. You're a good worker—always here on time, you work hard, and you're knowledgeable and friendly. But I don't want the business to get embroiled in some bad press."

She felt her heart plummet. Was he going to fire her? "I see."

"Can you tell me what's going on?"

Lily sat straighter in her chair and gave him the highlights about John's arrest and conviction, her move to Logan, and the fact that John's parents had been antagonistic. "I can't prove that they sent their friends here to start rumors or that they tipped off the reporter. I have the feeling that's what happened though. I'm sorry they're making you uncomfortable." Maybe the Drakes really could make life impossible for her. Would she be hearing from the district next, telling her they didn't want to hire her after all?

A long silence followed as Louis studied her. "It doesn't appear that you've done anything to bring this problem on. For the time being I'm just going to let it ride—so long as the business doesn't get any bad press."

Relief poured into Lily. It wasn't a full pardon, but at least she still had her job. For now.

She wasn't looking forward to seeing what else her in-laws might try.

Curtis watched Lily move around the kitchen, fussing over this and that after they put the kids to bed. It had been a nice evening with a trip to a local pizza place and then a stop at the park. He hoped it would stay quiet for a few minutes, at least.

He leaned a hip against the counter as she wiped at the non-existent dirt particles. "I never realized you and Denise had the cleaning compulsion in common. I thought she was the only one who scoured spotless countertops."

She stopped, looking abashed. "Sorry, I guess I've been distracted tonight."

So had he. His mind had been so preoccupied by what he had to say, or rather what he had to ask. Things between them had been awkward after his game Saturday—to which he had arranged tickets for family and friends. He attributed that awkwardness to the uncertainty of their relationship. But it was nothing compared to the tension in the air between them now. Something had been on her mind since he arrived, but she had danced around whatever it was that bothered her.

"Come sit with me." He took her hand and led her to the sofa. When she sat, he thought she looked uncomfortable, as though she was afraid of their conversation. Then again, maybe she was. What if she knew what he had to say and didn't want to marry him? What if she was trying to find the words to turn him down gently?

He screwed up his courage. No matter the outcome, he needed to know where they stood. "What's been distracting you?"

"Just some things at work. Nothing that won't take care of itself eventually." Still, she pursed her lips, worry clear on her face. She looked up at him and smiled wearily. "So the tournament has been keeping you busy this week."

"Not much more than usual. It's putting me through my paces, giving me a chance to play with a few of my teammates."

"You seemed to flow pretty well with your team Saturday." With her free hand, she picked at the flannel throw that was stretched across the arm of the sofa beside her.

He smiled and glanced down at their interconnected hands. It had meant a lot to him to look up in the stands and see so many supporters—and not just the fans, but people he knew and loved. He loved having her at his games. "I think it's going to be a good match for me. It'll be a while before we really get into the rhythm, but it'll be fine. I'm more concerned about other aspects of my life right now."

"Have you started making plans for your move?"

"Not really. I've looked at house listings, but nothing's struck me. I'll do some more looking later this summer, but I'm not sure what I'm looking for yet, so I haven't taken things too seriously."

She lifted her eyebrows. "You don't know what you're looking for?"

Now is as good a time as any. "I know what I want to look for," he corrected and gave her hand a squeeze. "I'm just not sure what I'll need." He felt his heart pounding in his chest. He was sweaty from nerves. "That's what I want to talk to you about."

"Curtis, maybe—" She closed her eyes as if she were in pain, then shook her head and focused on his again. "No, never mind. Go ahead." Still, she didn't appear to be looking forward to the discussion.

His anxiety increased at her comment. Why hadn't she wanted him to say it? "Lily, I love you. I love your kids and I want to marry you when you're ready. I know we haven't discussed our relationship, but I haven't been able to make any decisions about the future because we haven't talked about it." He hadn't expected the sharp ache in his chest when she looked away.

"It's not that simple. I've agreed to teach here this next year. There's the custody battle for the kids and . . ." she trailed off as though she couldn't come up with another reason. The ones she had given were plenty flimsy as it was.

He shook his head. "You've got to do better than that. Have you actually signed the contracts or just verbally agreed? I'm sure they'll understand that you're moving out of state. Especially since there's still more than a month before school starts." He pushed a lock of hair out of her face and trailed his thumb over her cheek bone. "And you know how I love the kids. What do the Drakes have on you besides money to back them up? If you're married to someone who will probably make more money this year than they'll see in several years, where will the argument go?"

His hand squeezed hers in reassurance. "Don't you care for me at all?" He caught her gaze and held it. "I thought I saw something more than friendship in your eyes, in your kisses." He trailed his finger over her soft, supple lips and wished they could have this conversation in a kiss. They didn't seem to have any trouble communicating then. The pain in her eyes made him hold back.

Her face seemed to crack and tears began trailing down her face. "Of course I care for you." She brushed at the tears.

He smiled, though he wasn't completely reassured. She hadn't said she loved him, only that she cared. He rubbed at her damp cheek with his fingertips. "Would you even go so far as to say you love me? Could you see us together and happy? Would you consider marrying me?"

She leaned into his touch, but her eyes were stark. "I do love you, but I can't marry you."

After hope had started to pour into him, hearing this was like being hit in the gut by a softball. "Why not?" He smiled slightly, trying not to show how awful he felt. And he had been worried about the pain of being rejected by his birth family. This was far worse than anything his birth father could do to him. He drew his hand away. "Did you make some unholy pact to marry only creeps?"

"No." She grabbed his hands and looked into his eyes. "Think about the publicity. Think of what other people will say when they realize you married me—a woman who was either too stupid to realize her husband was involved in fraud or turned a blind eye to it."

That was what was bothering her? "Who's going to know or care? What does that have to do with this?"

"A reporter who came into my work this morning was still interested in the story, despite the fact that I'm not important and there's no new angle to follow. You could turn out to be a very interesting angle for her. You're big news around here."

When Lily winced, Curtis realized he'd squeezed her hands harder than necessary in his surprise and anger. Why couldn't they just leave Lily alone? "Sorry." He let go and stood, pacing across the room—if you could call it pacing since the room was far too small for him to take more than a few steps in each direction. He whirled back to face her. "How could they still bother you about that? You're innocent."

Her voice raised in volume. "How do you know that? How are you going to explain that to them so they'll believe and understand? What makes you think they care that I trusted my husband and I was wrong?" She stood to face him across the short room. "They'll find out we're involved, and your name will be dragged through the mud with mine."

He took two large steps and stopped in front of her. "I don't care what anyone else thinks or says or does. Don't you get it? I love you! Do you think it'll be so easy for me to find someone else? Someone who loves me for me? Someone who wants to be with me and not because of whatever they think I can give them? How am I going to replace you—ever? I couldn't do it." He picked up her hand as he stood in front of her. His voice lowered as he infused it with all the feeling he could. "I can't imagine living without your smile and laughter, our quiet conversations, or those crazy kids of yours.

"I love you. I love you more than anything, and I don't want to lose you. I'll wait a while longer if you need more time. I know it hasn't been long since the divorce was finalized. I'll stand by you and be the support you need. If you want to teach, I'll support that. If you want to stay home with your darling angels—to make them our darling angels and add to the family, I'm more than willing to agree. In fact, that would be my first choice. I want what you want, so long as we can be together."

She looked him in the eyes. "But love and affection and a sizeable bank account can't solve everything." Her voice was low and heartbreakingly sad.

He reached out and touched a finger to the tear line on her cheek. His answer was soft and gentle. "I never said it would, but with you in my court, I know it would be enough. I know the kind of woman you are, and if everyone else wants to think I've been duped, so be it. I don't feel whole without you near me."

He saw her start to melt—just a tiny bit—and thought he was getting through to her. Then she stepped away and swiped at the tear with the back of her hand. "I think friendship's probably our best bet. I'm not ready to jump into anything else, and you may find absence won't make your heart grow fonder this time."

It wasn't what he wanted, but he hoped it would get him through for now. He prayed for strength and patience. "So long as we can be kissing friends, I might go along with that. I do love you, Lily." He leaned in and pressed a kiss to her mouth. It was short, but he infused it with all of the feeling he could muster. He didn't want her to be able to forget the way he felt. She was far too important to him.

Chapter Thirty

After Lily said good-bye to Curtis a while later, she sat on the sofa and leaned her head against the cushion. She wasn't sure she could stand to stay friends, not when even his casual kisses were enough to make her shiver in delight. When she dropped her hand to the cushion beside her, she touched a paper. Surprised, she picked it up. It was an envelope.

In the envelope was a stack of twenties and a note.

> Lily,
>
> I told you I'd pay fair PI wages for your help in Rock Springs. No one would have spoken to a lone guy like me, and you got way more information from Myrtle than I expected, or than a regular PI could manage. Accordingly, here's your weekend's wages. Sorry it took so long to get it to you. I had to wait for my first advance. This isn't charity, it's evening the score. Use it to pay your legal fees, like we agreed. I'm afraid it won't go as far as it needs to.
>
> Love always,
>
> Curtis
>
> PS, I would have given you this in person, but I knew you would have balked. Just be gracious about it, okay?

His final comment made her smile. He was absolutely right—it would have made her balk. And the legal fees for the custody battle were adding up. If she won the case, they'd be paid by the Drakes, or at least the court should require them to pay the fees. Whether they'd actually cough up the cash was another matter. She counted out the cash Curtis had left and goggled. A private eye made that kind of money for a day's work? Surely not.

She hurried to her laptop and did a little digging around. When she realized Curtis had been only a tiny bit more generous with her than a PI would have demanded, she decided to buy him a housewarming present with the extra. And he was right—the lawyer's bills were still more than the cash in the envelope, but at least she should be pacified for a while with this. She would have to live with the guilt of accepting the money—at least until everything was settled.

On Friday night Curtis came out of the team dressing room after a narrow defeat by the Georgia Hawks—his last tournament game—and grinned as he saw his twin standing near the exit. "What? Couldn't find anything better to do than hang around like a groupie? I know boneheads like you get a thrill out of it, but still—isn't that embarrassing?"

Cliff rolled his eyes. "Like you're ever going to have groupies. Obviously they'd rather hang outside my dressing room door. I suppose you may get some attention because we're twins. Don't hold your breath, though."

"You wish. Having me drafted has turned you into an egomaniac. What's up with that?" Curtis strode forward and pulled his brother into a hug. With everything going on, he was happy to see a friendly face. "Did you catch the game?"

"Yeah, I suppose you could have played worse. You might have once, back in high school."

Knowing his performance had been more than passable, Curtis punched his brother in the shoulder and good naturedly turned toward the outside door. "You got here earlier than I expected—Paige finally get sick of you and kick you out?"

"She'd never kick me out. She thinks I'm the sun, moon, and stars."

"What are you slipping into her food again?" Curtis ducked when Cliff threw a mock punch. He knew Cliff returned his wife's feelings in equal measure. They were nauseatingly cute together.

"We don't get together often enough. I've missed this." Cliff moved in and slung an arm around his brother's shoulder. "Paige had a thing tomorrow or she would've come with me for the weekend. Our plane leaves in three hours. Do you have your stuff packed?"

"I'm all set to go."

"No need to go find your lady love for a good-bye kiss?" Cliff slanted him a teasing look.

Curtis elbowed his brother in the ribs, albeit light enough not to bruise—probably. "Not all of us have women hanging on our arms." It hurt to admit it.

"No engagement rings yet? Are you slacking off? I thought you'd have settled all of that by now." Cliff's look was more than curious.

"Yeah, well. Some women are more stubborn than others. Come on. It'll probably take hours to get through the lines at the airport."

Curtis watched the mile markers as they approached the right exit the next morning. After their flight, they had spent a few hours sleeping before hitting the road again. And despite the fact he had long ago learned how to sleep on a plane, his eyes still felt gritty. He was glad Cliff was driving, since Curtis was afraid he'd have turned around by now if he'd come alone.

"What's this about—you know, with Lily?" Cliff asked, breaking the silence. "Denise said she thought things were developing there."

Curtis frowned as he felt the ache in his chest grow. He should have known better than to think Cliff wouldn't bring the subject up again. "Yeah, I guess. Things are a mess." He paused and affected a nonchalant tone when he mentioned, "I asked her to marry me the other day."

"I'd say 'way to go,' but apparently there's a problem."

"You could say that. I never thought basketball would scare a woman away, but that's what's happened."

"Basketball? That doesn't make sense." Cliff tapped his fingers on the steering wheel. "Do you think part of it might be the ex-husband?"

"Oh, yes. But not the way you're thinking. She's afraid his legacy will follow her and that she'll taint my image by association." Curtis tamped back the anger that bubbled inside him. He glanced at his twin. "She doesn't want to ruin my reputation. Bad media and all that." His hands balled into fists on his lap. "It makes me so mad."

"She does have a point about the media—hold on." Cliff held up a hand when Curtis whipped around and stared at him in disbelief. "I'm not saying she made the right choice. I'm just saying it could come back to haunt you, and you need to think about it."

"I don't care what the media says—she wasn't involved and I love her. How can I take that calmly? How can you expect me to think everything we have together is less important than an image?"

Cliff smiled as he flipped the turn signal on. "I didn't expect you to. I just wanted to make sure you saw things straight. And with the media, you never know." He guided the car off the freeway and waited while Curtis read him the next set of directions they had printed off the Internet. "We're not far now. How about if we put this issue away for the moment? When we finish up here, there'll be time to work something out with your lady love."

Curtis snorted, but he dropped the subject for the time being. Cliff was right—this time.

The neighborhood they pulled into was nice; the houses were a good family size but not mini-mansions—though for the price of a home in this part of California, Curtis knew he could buy a whopper of a home in most parts of Utah. On the corner near the end of the street, they pulled in front of a modest-sized clapboard home with two small levels and a detached garage in back.

The house was quiet, as if waiting for something, and set back into the small yard. There were a few trees and bushes and a couple basic flower beds out front. As he often did, Curtis automatically imagined the landscape as it could be, with a few changes. It could be a show place or a comfortable retreat. He shook his head to clear it when Cliff nudged him.

"Quit redoing their landscaping." He studied Curtis for a moment. "Now's the time to back out."

"Can't." Curtis glanced at his twin and then back at the house. "I'm terrified, but I can't change my mind now. Don't you feel it? The push to go in and meet him? The worry that it'll all go wrong?"

"I've wanted to meet him for years now, Curt. I'm just not sure about your methods." His expression became hopeful. "We could call first."

Curtis tightened his fingers in his lap and shook his head. "I have to see his face—this may be our only chance." Determined, he pushed open his door, trying to ignore his weak knees and the way his stomach tried to revolt. He said a quick prayer that things would go okay, and then he found himself at the front door, Cliff by his side.

Cliff was the one to lift a hand and knock. The twins exchanged a nervous glance, then returned to look in the window.

For a long moment Curtis wondered if the house was empty. It was a Saturday, but no sound echoed back to him from inside. He lifted his hand to knock again, but then he heard the thunk of rubber soles on vinyl flooring. The door was opened by a man close to his own age with dark hair, brown eyes, and a cleft in his chin. Before the man even opened his mouth, Curtis knew it was his half brother, Grayson.

"Can I help you?" Grayson asked.

"We're looking for Alex Fields. Is he home?"

The man's brown eyes slid over Curtis and then Cliff, his curiosity obvious. "No. Do you know my father well?"

Only biologically. "No, but we need to talk to him. It's important and rather private. I understand he isn't doing very well," Curtis said. He worried Grayson wouldn't let them in or that he was too late. And there were still a dozen other things that could prevent his meeting Alex.

A funny look crossed Grayson's face, but he beckoned them to come in. "Have a seat."

Curtis settled uncomfortably on the edge of the chair where he'd been directed, then took a look around him, wondering if Alex had been taken to a nursing home or if he might be in the next room resting. The house was less personal than a hotel room with only a picture of Christ on one wall and boxes ranging along a wall in the next room. "Just moved in or getting ready to move out?"

"I've been too busy to unpack." The man pursed his lips, then spoke, his words measured, "My dad's in a hospice center. He won't be coming home again." Pain radiated from his otherwise stoic face.

Curtis felt all the air leave his body, upset that things were so close to the end, though he was relieved they hadn't missed Alex entirely. "How long does he have?"

Instead of answering, Grayson looked between them. "Why do the Werner Wonders care about my father?"

Curtis stared dumbly at the title he'd heard bantered about when they were in high school and occasionally in college. There hadn't been the slightest twitch of recognition or surprise in Grayson's face when he'd greeted them. Curtis wondered if he'd seen them while they approached the house. "I'm not really sure where to start."

"I'm sorry we didn't notify you that we were coming by. You're

Grayson, right?" Cliff spoke for the first time. "We've come a long way. Could you tell us where to find him? Even if we can't speak with him, it would help if we could see him. Is he conscious?"

"He's in and out." Grayson pressed his lips together, offering no more details. "Do you want to tell me why you're here?"

Cliff answered in a soothing tone. "I'm not sure how to explain, not sure you're even the one I should explain to. It would be best if we spoke with your father first."

Grayson's eyes hardened. "You won't get past the front desk at the care center if I don't give them permission. If you want to see him, you'll tell me what this is about."

That settled the debate. "We've never actually met your father. I never even heard his name until a couple months ago." Curtis thought of the lonely little house in Rock Springs. "It took a while to track him down, to be sure it was him, and then to find time for the trip."

He wondered again if he had any right to alter this man's perceptions of his father. Probably Grayson had no idea about the trouble his parents' marriage had been in, if Daphne was right on that point. Did he have the right to put a mark on the man's name now? Everything seemed less black and white than it had only a few hours ago. Yet he had no choice; he couldn't back away now.

"Go on," Grayson said.

Curtis let out a slow breath and glanced at Cliff, who nodded in encouragement. "It's just . . . ." He looked Grayson in the eye and forced himself to be honest. "Twenty-five years ago, a woman named Daphne Callister lived in Evanston. She had a beautiful toddler and," he decided to soften the truth about her a little, "a need for male companionship. Apparently she met your father and they had a relationship." He saw the denial, hot and fierce, jump into Grayson's eyes. It actually made the telling easier. "Cliff and I are the result of that relationship."

"No. That's not possible." The denial was automatic and vehement, and Curtis couldn't blame him for it.

"There's no real proof, other than the word of a less-than-honest woman and the fact that we're dead ringers for your father when he was our age."

A muscle jumped in Grayson's jaw, and he shook his head. "My mother was pregnant with me twenty-five years ago. My father wouldn't have stepped out on her like that. They were devoted to each other. He was traumatized when she died. He never really got over it."

"I can understand you being upset."

Grayson's eyes hardened. "You're wrong about this. I'm sorry you drove all this way to learn you've been lied to. You can leave now."

Frustration spurred Curtis on. "We look like him, Grayson. When was the last time you looked at the family photo album? I saw a newspaper clipping. I know we look like him."

"Maybe your mother did know my father there. Maybe she lived in Evanston and she liked my father, but that doesn't mean he cheated on my mother. You admit the woman's a liar. Maybe she just figured you look enough like my old man to be believable." The expression in Grayson's eyes wasn't all anger; Curtis could see a terrible fear beneath it.

It made him ache to realize he'd brought this extra pain on Grayson when he was already watching his father die.

"That's a nice theory," Cliff cut in. "The only problem is, she gave Curtis and me up for adoption when we were hours old. She only realized who we were because she saw us on TV and we look like him. Since then genetics have won out. We play basketball—which your father played for years. Curtis is a landscape architect—"

"I've seen your father's yard in Rock Springs. He has a lot of talent," Curtis added.

"That's coincidence," Grayson insisted.

Cliff stood and shook his head. "We're sorry to have broken it to you like this when you must be in so much pain already. We can only imagine what you must be feeling. We'd really like a chance to meet him this weekend if his time really is so short."

Grayson stood as well, folded his arms over his chest, and looked at the twins, who each stood five inches taller than he did. "I suppose the only one who can send you packing is my father. I want to be the one to tell him. If he wants to talk to you, you can see him. Otherwise you'll go back where you came from and leave us alone."

Curtis wanted to snarl in protest. What right did Grayson have to keep him from speaking with his biological father, and would Grayson actually let them speak to Alex? Would he tell Alex they were here at all, or just pretend he had?

Cliff placed a restraining hand on his arm. "He's being more than fair, Curt."

"Fine. Where is this place?"

CHAPTER THIRTY-ONE

Less than fifteen minutes later, Curtis paced up and down the sitting area just inside the care center. Cliff sat in a nearby sofa.

"Will you cut it out and sit down? You're just like Denise. You're going to make me dizzy." Cliff's request had the sharp edges that told Curtis his twin was every bit as worked up about the meeting as he was.

Sitting was out of the question, but since he didn't want to antagonize Cliff either, Curtis walked to a window and stared out over the parking lot. "What if we're wrong? I mean, Grayson looks enough like us, but . . . ." He shrugged, uneasy.

"Yeah, I know. We could be wrong, but what if we're right and he doesn't want to meet us?" He rubbed a hand over his face. "I should be with my very pregnant wife, and you could be badgering Lily into marrying you right now."

Curtis let out a mirthless laugh and buried his hands in his pockets. "Yeah, like that'll help."

They lapsed back into silence, each wrapped in his own thoughts as they waited for an interminable half hour.

When Grayson came to the door, his face was pale from shock. He put a hand on the door jamb and gripped it until his knuckles turned white. "He wants to see you. I don't know how long he'll be awake." He turned abruptly and headed back down the hall. Cliff and Curtis exchanged a look, then followed.

The room Alex Fields lay in was painted a light gray and accented in subdued shades of lavender and green. There were pictures on the walls and mementos on one counter—a stark contrast to his son's house. It was clear Grayson had done everything in his power to make his father comfortable. Grayson stopped at the door and ushered the brothers in, but didn't join them. Curtis felt his pulse race as he approached the bed. Alex was in his early sixties, but the cancer made him look at least ten years older. His face was gray and his brown eyes sunken, his cheeks well lined. His eyes went back and forth between the twins, as though studying their faces.

When he spoke, his voice was low and a bit wheezy, as though it was difficult to speak. "I had no idea Daphne was pregnant." He looked sad. "Wish I had. Shoulda realized how much you look like me. I've seen Cliff play a few times." He smiled slightly and began coughing.

Cliff stepped forward, and then he and Curtis exchanged a look while the old man coughed and coughed. Curtis had no idea what to do. Could they help if they tried? They each approached, but Grayson came around them, lifted the glass of water from the nightstand, and supported his father's shoulders so he could take a sip when the coughing calmed.

"He's really not well." Grayson's mouth closed in a grim line.

"No, no. You all need to hear this. I'm not proud of what happened, son." Alex patted Grayson's hand, looking him in the eyes. "I screwed up. Your mother and I were struggling, and instead of being what she needed, supporting her, I was unfaithful. I told her later, after you were born, and we worked through it. I loved your mother. I still love her."

"You had a great way of showing it." Grayson's anger was palpable.

Curtis prepared to move back, sick at causing so much pain for his half brother. "I'm sorry. I didn't mean to cause you any trouble."

"I caused my own trouble, all those years ago. Lina and I were both worried and stressed, but instead of working it out, I made it worse. Of course, things grew better and I learned from my mistakes." He looked at Grayson and reached out a hand, placing it on his son's. "Now I can see small blessings in my mistakes. You have brothers. I won't leave you completely alone now—something that's worried me for a long time."

Grayson's face grew tight, and several seconds passed before he answered. His voice was controlled when the words escaped. "Great, Dad. You think of everything, don't you?"

Alex smiled and reached up to touch Grayson's face, cradling it in a withered hand. "I love you, son. You've always been a joy." His eyes fluttered, and he turned to the twins. "I'm very tired. Come back when I wake up. I want to talk some more." Then his eyes closed, and after a few minutes his breaths became long and regular.

Silence stretched in the room while the three younger men dealt with their reactions to what they'd just heard. Curtis turned toward the wall to try and regain control, wiping away a tear that slipped from his right eye. He'd found his father, but it was too late for a real relationship. Why had he dragged his feet?

He shot a look at Grayson and wondered. Maybe, just maybe, the reason he'd been led here was for Grayson and not for Alex. Grayson would be alone and might decide he wanted to be friends. It was unlikely considering his current attitude, but it was possible. Over the weeks since Denise had sent him the information about Alex, Curtis had thought about his half brother and how he would react. Would they have anything in common? Could they become friends? It looked unlikely at the moment.

Curtis knew he may never get another chance to speak with the man who gave him life. Now if he only had some idea what to say to Alex when he woke again.

There was a rustling sound as Grayson stood and motioned them out of the room. He told the nurse Alex was sleeping again and then led the way to the front entrance. When they had reassembled, he wasted no time. "I have no intention of keeping in touch once we all leave here to go back to real life. But for my father's sake, I'd appreciate it if you pretend to be open to the idea, and I'll try to do the same. Anything that will make his passing more comfortable at this point." His hard eyes and the anger in them belied his words.

"Grayson, I can't speak for Curt, but I do want to know you." Cliff shoved his hands in his coat pockets.

"I don't care," Grayson responded. "You'll always be a reminder that my father cheated on my mother. Do you honestly think I want you hanging around?" His hands balled at his sides, and he visibly fought for composure. "You can stay until he's gone. You can attend the funeral, if you choose, but then I want you both to leave me alone."

Grayson pushed the thick hair back from his face. "He'll probably sleep for a few hours—at least, he usually does. I'll let them know at the front desk that you can come and go. I've got a few quick errands to take care of. I'll see you later." He stalked from the room without making eye contact again.

The room seemed to reverberate with the silence Grayson left in his wake. "Guess we should get a closer hotel room, and I better call my wife," Cliff said.

"Yeah." Emotions pounded through Curtis so hot and heavy, he wasn't sure what was what. He turned and followed Cliff back out to the car. They stopped at the closest motel and Cliff went in to get a room. Curtis sat in the car waiting, his hands clenched in his lap. He should do something, but all he could manage was to hold on tight and try to keep from reaching for his cell phone. If he pulled it out, he would call Lily, and then he would blubber like a baby. He would rather not do that to her.

He pushed from the car in a burst of energy and strode to the end of the parking lot, then turned to come back, tears pouring down his cheeks. Was it relief that they had arrived in time? Gladness that his birth father accepted them? Mourning for a relationship he would never have a chance to have? Regret that Grayson wouldn't accept the hand of friendship and brotherhood they offered him?

He was so tied up inside that he didn't know which emotion dominated. He turned when he reached the car and made the circuit again. He hoped the motel had a gym or that there was one nearby. The stress was going to make him crazy if he didn't work some of it off.

Cliff met him back out by the car a few minutes later. Curtis had stopped crying for the moment, feeling better after the burst of emotion and activity. "All set?"

"Yeah. Called Lily yet? Denise?" Cliff asked.

"No, I'll take care of it soon. You?"

"Let's head up to the room, and then I'll call Paige."

Curtis removed their bags from his car and they took the stairs to the rooms on the second floor.

Three hours later they returned to see Alex. Grayson was by his side, though Alex still slept.

"I started to wonder if you decided to leave town," Grayson said. He sat with an artist's notebook on his lap and a pen in his hand.

Curtis knew he should have ignored the jab but couldn't quite manage it. "We'll be sure to let you know before we leave, so you won't have to wonder again." He kept his voice even as he took a nearby chair and slid it over to the side of the bed. Cliff did the same.

"Sounds like your mother was a wonderful woman. First having an affair with a married man, then failing to mention to him that she'd conceived." Grayson's tone was light, as if it was a friendly conversation, but the glint in his eyes was anything but friendly.

Curtis chose not to mention the fact that the married man in question was lying in the bed beside them and that Daphne hadn't forced him to break his vows. "Our *mother* was a paragon of virtues. We've never met the woman who gave birth to us."

"You said she told you my father—"

Cliff interrupted. "Our half sister has visited her a few times and Curtis wrote for information. We haven't met her face-to-face."

"Does she live in another country or something? I'm assuming you make enough to pay for a plane ticket just about anywhere." Grayson eyed Cliff, then Curtis.

Wanting to turn the subject before things got messy, Curtis said, "Your old neighbor told me Alex did all his own yard work. He has a great eye for design. I admired it when I was over there a few weeks back."

"You've been stalking him then?" Grayson focused on what he was drawing, as if the discussion didn't matter to him at all.

Curtis banked the irritation trying to rise inside him. "No, we knew he wasn't there anymore, but we weren't sure where he'd gone. My girlfriend and I went to check things out. The house was really nice, and your neighbors had nothing but good to say about him." It was strange referring to Lily as his girlfriend. He had never thought of her that way, not really, and there hadn't been much cause to call her that. He wondered what she would call their relationship. Friends probably. He was afraid he might grow to hate that word if things continued as they were for too long.

"Oh." Grayson paused for a long moment. "He's very good with plants, always has been. I didn't pick up his green thumb at all. Mother loved the flowers and he enjoyed caring for them. It was win-win. He's always saying things like, 'Foundation plants, my boy, they give the garden structure, but a clever plan can make the garden breathe.'" Grayson smiled to himself and picked up his father's hand. "It was irritating sometimes. He kept trying to tell me how to fix up my yard before he had to move here."

Curtis smiled as well. "He's right, you know. Basic structure first."

"Glad you approve," Alex said as he lifted an eyelid and looked at the three men beside his bed, his voice weak and gravely with sleep. "Always loved basketball too." He looked between the twins. "One of you plays for the Bulls, don't you? Grays loves that team. It's his favorite."

Sitting next to Grayson, Curtis was sure he was the only one to hear the man mutter that his preference had ended. Curtis managed to maintain the friendly smile he'd been wearing and not cuff his half brother over the head, but it was a near thing. He decided a little comic relief was due and hoped Cliff would play along. "I can't say I ever liked the team myself, but now if I can't catch the game, I always tape it. That way, I can razz Cliff about every mistake he made when we talk next. That's probably why he's so hard to reach after games these days."

"I watch Curtis's games too, but they hardly ever show him—they prefer to concentrate on the good players."

"At least I don't have two left feet. The only reason they bother recording you at all is to catch your mistakes."

"Funny, skunk-breath. Now you know why Kaylee wastes her time attending your games."

Curtis laughed and Alex joined in. "It's good to know you grew up to be friends. Poor Grayson didn't have anyone to tease growing up. I keep telling him to find a good woman and settle down, make some babies of his own, but he can't seem to choose one."

"So many out there, I just can't make up my mind." Though Grayson didn't roll his eyes, Curtis wondered how many times he'd had to fend off his father's demand for grandbabies.

"Too true," Cliff smiled. "Now if only Curtis could persuade his woman—"

"Cliff's wife is going to have their first in a few weeks," Curtis interrupted, not wanting the conversation to veer his direction. "It's nice Cliff met his woman when he did. Her adopted sister is our biological sister. That's how we found the family so quickly."

"Nearly broke Curtis's heart to find out he was related to the woman who fascinated him so much."

"Give it up. You're full of it." Curtis nudged his brother in the ribs with an elbow, though there was more than a grain of truth in it.

"I'm convinced that's why you wanted nothing to do with her for all those weeks. A broken heart."

"Gross! She's my sister! Besides, if Rich heard you say that, he might beat me up. I'm scared of him."

"Who's Rich? A body builder?" Grayson asked, a bit more interested than he had acted before.

"Computer geek—pasty skin, blackberry phone, understands binary. Terrifying." Curtis did his best to look terrified. It lasted all of two seconds before he had to grin.

The next thing Curtis knew, Cliff had told the whole story of how they came into contact with their maternal family line. Alex laughed several times, and even Grayson's lips seemed to quirk a time or two. Curtis allowed himself to be treated as the butt of the joke for a while before turning the attention back to Cliff.

Alex seemed thrilled to know one of his sons was expanding his family. He asked dozens of questions about Paige and the baby. Curtis watched Grayson's face grow more and more taut as the conversation continued. After a while, Curtis asked about Grayson's job.

"I draw animals for a living. Not very exciting when you think about it. If you'll excuse me." He stood and left the room abruptly, and Curtis wondered if they had alienated the man even more. He couldn't blame Grayson for being upset at having to share his father's last hours with strangers. When Grayson returned a few minutes later, Curtis excused himself and pulled Cliff into the hallway with him.

"What's going on?"

"I thought maybe Grayson could use a few minutes alone with Alex. Think of how you'd feel in his position. His dad may only have hours to live, but he can't spend any time alone with him because of us."

"I don't need your pity." Grayson spoke from behind them. "He's going to sleep anyway. I suppose I'll see you in the morning, unless you're leaving." He sounded almost hopeful.

He turned toward the front door, and Curtis grabbed his arm. "We're not trying to make this harder on you. I'm sorry if that's the way it's happening."

"Spare me. I'm going out for a few minutes. I'll see you both later." Grayson walked out the door, leaving the twins staring after him.

"Maybe you have a point," Cliff observed.

"Yeah, well. I could use some dinner. How about you?"

They stopped at the front desk on their way out to leave a number where they could be reached if Alex woke during the night or if his condition changed while they were away.

Chapter Thirty-two

The ringing phone woke Curtis from the depths of sleep, and he reached out for it. Cliff grabbed the cell phone first.

"'H'lo?" Pause. "This is he."

Curtis rolled back over in bed, then heard Cliff sit up, his voice considerably more awake. "Yeah, we'll be there right away. Thanks."

The phone hit the counter and Curtis squinted against the glare of the bedside lamp as Cliff turned it on. The clock said 4:39. "What's going on?"

"Alex is awake and he asked for us."

They both dressed quickly and hurried out to the car in the cool night air. After eating dinner the previous evening, they had returned to the care center to find Grayson at the bedside, drawing again. They couldn't see what he was working on, but he seemed wrapped up in his sketches. Since Alex was sleeping, they hadn't stayed long.

As they got in the car to return to Alex's bed, Curtis was curious about the notebook. Grayson had mentioned he drew animals all day, and Myrtle said he worked for a movie company. He wondered if the man was drawing for work or for pleasure. If he was lucky, it was both.

It wasn't long before they walked down the corridors to Alex's room again. Curtis rubbed at his gritty eyes and turned into the room where a nurse sat beside the bed, checking the machines that were beeping and flashing in the background. She smiled wanly at them, looking tired.

"Grayson only went home a little while ago. I'm sure he'll be right back. There we go, Alex. All done for now." She turned toward the doorway where Grayson now stood, looking panicked. "The doctor will be in shortly," she assured them as she passed.

Grayson crossed the room at a trot and touched his father's forehead. "Are you feeling worse? Is something wrong, Dad?"

At his evident worry, Curtis hung back, allowing a moment of time and space before he and Cliff intruded even more.

"I'm fine." Alex coughed several times. "Fine. Have a seat, boys. No time to waste."

He caught Grayson's hand in his. "I'm sorry for not being a better father to you, Grays. I'm so proud of you, of your work. Your mother would be proud too. I may not understand you all the time, but you've been a good son. Always. Don't think—" he lapsed into coughing again.

When he'd calmed down and taken a drink of water, he continued, "Don't think I don't know you're upset with me. Don't punish yourself. Give these boys a chance. You need a family."

The doctor came in, interrupting the conversation. A nurse brought something for Alex's cough and badgered him to take it while the doctor pulled the three brothers into the hall. "I wish I had better news for you. It's getting worse. He may have a few hours or he could linger a day or two, but I wouldn't count on it. Use what time you have." He left them in heavy silence.

After a moment, Grayson put on a forced smile and returned to his father's bedside. "Hey, Dad, do you remember when we stayed up all night to watch the comet when I was fifteen? We loaded up on popcorn and hot cocoa and told stories all night. We don't have the hot chocolate or the popcorn. Or the comet. Hmmm, maybe this night isn't anything like that one."

Alex smiled. "That was a good night—only I remember my thermos being full of coffee. Not you, though, boy. You had your standards. That's one more thing you have in common with your brothers. My Grayson's a Mormon too." He smiled while the twins looked at each other in surprise, then shifted their gazes to Grayson.

Curtis realized why Grayson had been so familiar with the term "Werner Wonders." It was more common in LDS circles than outside the Church.

Alex glanced at his three sons. His voice was thin and tired. "This is it for me, isn't it? The old final countdown?" He wiped a shaky hand over his mouth. "Well, how many men get to have their family gather around them for their last hours? Too many kick off alone in accidents or heart attacks. I'm lucky. Sit down, boys, and let me tell you about my army days."

Though his voice was weak, Alex seemed excited to tell stories about his time in the service—basic training, summer stints, and the horrible food he had to eat. He talked of meeting his wife and marrying her, of his joy when he saw his son born and his pride at high school and college graduations. He even spoke briefly of his excitement when his second son was born and his sorrow when the child died. No one said how the boy had died or how old he had been.

The hours passed as Curtis and Cliff listened to father and then son discuss their memories, learning more about the man in one day than some learn about their father in years. They took breaks while he rested, then woke ready to talk again. The sun rose, inched across the sky, and set again without any of the young men leaving the care center. When the memories ran down and Grayson's stories lulled Alex to sleep as the sun came up again, Curtis knew he had seen his father's eyes for the last time.

An hour later, Alex's body shut down, and the doctor pronounced him dead. While Curtis grieved for all he would never experience with the man, he sent prayers of thanks that he had been there for the end.

Grayson practically pushed the twins out the doors once everything was over. "Go home. You've done what you came to do," he told them. His face was haggard and worn. Tears continued dripping down his cheeks, though they had all cried off and on throughout the day.

"We can't just leave you to deal with everything," Cliff protested.

"I've been alone before. I'll be fine. I don't want or need your help preparing for the funeral. Please, just go away." There was desperation in his plea.

"There are so many arrangements to make," Curtis protested, though he hadn't a clue what preparations were needed for a funeral.

"He's made most of them already. I'll let you know about the funeral— he wanted to have it in Rock Springs. Go back to your homes and forget you were ever here. I wish I could." He turned and hurried off.

Two hours later, after calling Grayson and again being told he didn't want their assistance, Cliff and Curtis turned their car to the airport. But they both planned to return for the funeral, one way or another.

Curtis didn't remember flying over Nevada or Utah. He only remembered his exhaustion as the pain ricocheted through his chest while he tried to accept that the man who had given him life—a man he found he admired more than he expected—was dead. If he hadn't dragged his feet about finding Alex, if he'd searched earlier when they had first realized they were related to Denise, he could have had more time with him. It was Curtis's fault he and Cliff had lost that time.

If only.

Back in his own car in Utah, tears leaked from his eyes, and Curtis had to get off the freeway and find an empty parking lot to pull into until he could get himself under control.

He didn't know how long he'd been there when his ringing phone brought him out of his stupor, but he only looked at it next to him on the seat. He wasn't ready to deal with people right now. After wiping his face, Curtis pulled back onto the road and continued to his parents' house.

He pulled into the driveway around five. He hadn't stopped to eat or gas up on the way home. Both his tank and his stomach were on empty, but he didn't feel like bothering with either of those problems at the moment. Instead, he went up to his room and crashed for a nap. There would be time to deal with real life again later.

Lily sat at the table keeping an eye on the kids while she put together a schedule for the math book she would be teaching from in a few weeks. Stephen played with blocks in front of a cartoon with his baby sister. Sophie had begun pushing herself around on her belly like a worm lately. Lily knew it wouldn't be long before she started crawling. She could hardly believe her baby was nearly six months old.

Lily had been trying not to worry about Curtis's visit to his father, but it wasn't easy.

She shook her head to clear it and returned her attention to the pages in front of her. Long division wasn't a great favorite of hers—either for doing or for teaching. Not that teaching it strained her. She would never have made it through college if it did. Still, she hated it.

A toy crashed into her leg as the ending credits rolled onto the television screen and Lily looked at her son. Stephen walked toward her, his sister whining behind him. "Hey, kiddo," she said as she smiled at him. "What do you want?"

"Milk!"

Lily laughed and scooped her son up, then walked over and picked up her daughter. She held them both close, twirling with them in the kitchen. "You want milk, huh? Think you should have some of that?"

"Want some milk, Mama!"

With a shake of her head, Lily tucked both of them into their high chairs and walked to the fridge to get Stephen's sippy cup and Sophie's bottle. She added some graham crackers, since dinner would be another hour. In a moment, she settled herself at the table again.

When her mind drifted for the hundredth time, Lily reached for her cell phone with a sigh. She'd never get through this pile of papers if she didn't call and see if Curtis had returned.

CHAPTER THIRTY-THREE

At first Curtis wasn't sure what had pulled him from sleep. Everything seemed unnaturally quiet, and he wondered if his parents were still at work. He chose to close his eyes and try to sleep some more.

When his cell phone began to ring again, he recognized the tune as the one he'd assigned to Lily's number.

With a moan, he threw his arm over his face. He sat and tried to wipe the sleep from his eyes, putting his mind back in order. A glance at the clock told him he had only been asleep about an hour, which explained why his body called for him to return to bed. Instead, he rose and grabbed the phone. "Hello, Lils. What's up?"

"I haven't heard from you in a couple of days. I wondered what was going on, and how Alex was doing."

"Sorry, I'm running on fumes," he mumbled, wishing he could pull her close, bury his face in her hair.

"I take it things didn't go so well?"

"Could've been better. I haven't eaten anything but a donut since dinner last night." Curtis rubbed his stomach and headed for the kitchen.

"You need to take better care of yourself," she admonished.

He could have blessed his mother—there were leftovers. He had no idea how old they were, but lasagna never lasted long in their house. He cut a piece out and slid it onto a plate. "I need someone to help take care of me. Someone to make sure I eat right. Someone to talk to and cuddle with at night."

When she answered, her voice was flat and casual. "Sounds like you'll need a housekeeper and a dog. You can afford both now. Me, I could use a housekeeper too, but my kids are great cuddlers, aren't you, kiddo?"

"More cracker, Mama!" Curtis heard Stephen call out, and Lily laughed.

"Wouldn't you know food words would be his favorites?" Lily asked.

After a chuckle and pause, Curtis reverted to the subject at hand, putting the lasagna in the microwave. "Dogs might be great listeners, but they aren't great conversationalists."

"I doubt finding eager company will be a problem for you."

Curtis grabbed a bottle of water. He didn't look forward to keeping his own bachelor pad in the fall. "I know a great conversationalist. What do you think the terms would be to get her to be my housekeeper and companion?" He wasn't ready to let the subject drop, not yet.

"I don't know? What's the going rate for sixty-year-old widows to move across the country and take care of capable men these days? I bet you could find one who's willing."

"I don't know if I can wait for you to become a sixty-year-old widow. I'd be horribly jealous if you married someone else, anyway." His pseudo joke fell lame. The idea of her with any other man was too painful to consider.

There was a long pause. "Things must not have gone well or you wouldn't be avoiding the subject. What happened? You were gone too long for Alex to have just turned you away."

Curtis shook his head and pulled the lasagna from the microwave, forking up a bite but not eating it. "No. He seemed thrilled to find out about us. Cliff and I sat at his bedside with his son and watched him die. His son, Grayson, was at the house when we arrived. Learning about us only made it worse for him."

He walked across the room and looked into the backyard, absently noting that the lawn could use a mow. "I feel awful, dumping all of that on him. Even though his father was still alive when we arrived, Grayson was already in mourning. No one should have to go through all of that alone, but I get the feeling he is. No sisters or brothers, besides me and Cliff. I hope he has someone to turn to. He talked like he didn't, and no one else showed up at the care center."

"That must've been rough on all of you. I know you were hoping to make some kind of connection with your birth dad."

"I'm the one who didn't want to contact my birth family for so long. At least I knew they existed. It wasn't like I was taken by complete surprise, like Grayson. I can't blame him for not wanting to accept us. He practically kicked us out of town after . . . well, after everything this morning." It hurt too much to say it right out, even though he'd only known the two Fields men for a couple of days.

He continued, "Grayson didn't want help making arrangements. He said Alex made all the arrangements in advance, so at least he'll be spared most of that. Still, I wish he'd let us help. Cliff and I plan to go to the funeral in Wyoming later this week." Curtis heard his stomach growl and finally started eating.

"So where do you go from here?" Lily asked

"I try to forgive myself for waiting so long before we looked for him. I have to get some practice in today and tomorrow, tell my parents everything." He wasn't looking forward to that, afraid that despite their open attitude that they might feel hurt. He paused for a long moment as he fingered the window coverings. "I want . . . I'd appreciate it if you'd come with me to the funeral. Please come with me. I'll take care of any expenses—I'll even pay Shelly babysitting fees or whatever. I could use your support." The few days since he'd seen her seemed like forever.

There was a brief hesitation. "What days do I need to get off? I can't promise, but I'll try."

He let out the breath he hadn't realized he'd been holding and touched a finger to his reflection in the window, wishing it were her soft skin instead of cool glass. "Every day. Lily, marry me and move to Colorado. I could have all three of you to snuggle with at night."

There was a long pause, and when she spoke, her voice wasn't steady. "You're not going to make this easy on me, are you?"

Curtis crossed the room to the sofa, leaned back on it, and closed his eyes. He was so tired. "Not a chance. You just need a little time to get used to the idea and to realize I don't care about the media. I just need you by my side."

The ache in his heart burned a bit deeper, but he wasn't ready to give up yet. It had taken too long to find someone he could trust to see him when she looked at him. Someone who didn't care about the outer person that the world saw. He wanted to make things easier for her, give her all the things her first husband had tried to provide by stealing. And more important, he wanted to be the kind of man she deserved—the kind of husband he got the impression John had rarely been.

"Curtis." Her voice was even more choked up and he heard her sniff on the line.

He knew she wanted what he wanted and had to believe she would come around eventually. "I know, don't push so hard." He would have apologized, but he felt little more than a twinge of regret at making her uncomfortable. "I'll let you know when the funeral is." *And I have some shopping to do.*

"How did the trip go?" Curtis's mom asked as she checked the potatoes with a fork later that night.

Curtis shrugged. He had plenty to say to his parents—so much to tell them—but he hardly knew where to start. "I told you we met him. Alex was in a hospice center. He was really welcoming, wanted to know everything about us." He tossed the cherry tomatoes into the salad he had mixed up for dinner that night. "I listened to him and Grayson talk about old memories, laugh about the past. It was, I don't know . . . sad, but comforting. It makes me feel guilty that I held Cliff back from finding Alex for so long."

"He was in a hospice center?"

"He died early this morning." Curtis turned and leaned back against the counter. "We'll be going back for the funeral, whenever it is. Grayson doesn't want us there." He pressed his lips together for a long moment while his mom watched, letting him get it all out. "I know it was a shock for him. He had no idea his parents weren't always madly in love. I can't blame him for being upset, but I wish he could have been just a little nicer about it."

His mouth felt dry, so Curtis helped himself to some water from the fridge. "I know. I want things to be perfect right from the first—whatever perfect is. Don't worry, I'm not going to go into a funk like Aaron did." He knew his mom was worried about it. "We'll try again at the funeral. If things don't fly, I'll live."

"Of course you will." She leaned over and gave her son a hug. "It's amazing you're even upright after a weekend like that."

"Good thing there's a counter here, or I wouldn't be." He smiled to calm her worries. "Are you okay with all of this? It can't be easy for you to watch any of us look for more family, when you were such great parents. You know we love you more than anything, don't you?" He pressed a kiss to the top of her head—an easy thing to do when she was over a foot shorter than him.

"I know. I love you too. Both of you. You may have been a trial growing up," she didn't pause when he snorted at her understatement, "but you know I'd never have given you up for anything. I'm glad you had a chance to meet Alex before he died. I think it'll be good for you." She flipped the heat off under the potatoes and reached into the cupboard for plates, handing them to him. "Now, don't tell me you didn't call Lily and tell her everything already—I won't believe it!"

"She called me, actually."

"And will you take her to the funeral?" She eyed him knowingly.

He laughed. "That's the plan."

"Good, then you bring her back here again soon. It's been too long since I had a chance to talk to her. And I'm dying to meet her kids."

"I will, Mom, as soon as I can."

Neither Curtis nor Cliff had been able to get through to Grayson to find out about funeral arrangements. Lily had suggested they check online for an obituary at the local newspaper, but he'd been putting it off, hoping Grayson would call with details instead. Curtis had the sneaking suspicion Grayson was likely to wait until the last minute, however, to make it difficult for them to attend.

Giving up on being patient, he opened his laptop with a growl and turned it on. It only took a couple of minutes to track down Alex's obituary online at the Rock Springs' paper. He felt his heart squeeze slightly as he studied the photo of a much younger man, still in the prime of life and looking so much like himself. He turned his eyes to the text.

> Alexander Grayson Fields, 57, of North Hollywood, California, formerly of Rock Springs, Wyoming, passed away at a care center Monday, July 24.
> Alexander was born April 15, 1952 in Tempe, AZ., the second son born to Alexander and Ula Felton Fields.
> He attended school in Tempe and then went to ASU in Tempe, AZ, where he met his beloved wife Lina Marie Lymon.

They married June 8, 1978, and moved to Evanston in August of 1980, then to Rock Springs in 1985. He worked at Sunnyside Nursery for nearly twenty years before his health forced him to quit working. He was a great philanthropist, donating time and money to programs like Big Brother/Big Sister, the teen center, and junior basketball camp, allowing many who otherwise would never have been able to afford the fees to participate. He was active in Boy Scout leadership for ten years and loved taking the boys into the mountains to teach them about nature and wilderness survival.

He always said that difficult times in his youth impressed on him the need for community involvement in helping local youth to make good choices.

He is preceded in death by his parents; his sister, Clarice; his wife; and his son Michael. He is survived by his sons A. Grayson Fields of Bellmont, California; Curtis Werner of Denver, Colorado; and Cliff Werner of Chicago, Illinois.

The last sentence made Curtis stop in surprise. Grayson had included them in the obituary. He couldn't believe it. He had expected Grayson to pretend they didn't exist. A notice about funeral services that Friday ended the article, and Curtis reread the entire thing before saving a copy and emailing it to Cliff.

Curtis wondered what Grayson thought of some of the things the obituary had said about his father, especially now that he'd met the twins. Had Alex been in love with his wife? Had their marriage been good? Had he cherished her? He'd talked as though he did, but was it true? Had there been other women or had Alex devoted himself to his marriage after Daphne?

There were a hundred questions Curtis wanted to ask and no one to answer them.

Shaking his head, he turned and walked from the computer. He pushed aside the curtain and looked into the night instead. Resentment at himself and his fears flared again. With a huff of frustration, he sat back at his laptop, pulling up his journal to add an entry. Then he changed his mind and opened a different document.

He wrote with abandon, allowing all of his anger and frustration to bleed onto the computer screen, not paying attention to grammar or spelling, not worrying about anyone else seeing it. This version was for him and him alone. When he finished, the document was five single-spaced pages and completely disjointed. He didn't worry about that as he saved it. He closed the file, then lay back on the bed to stare at the ceiling.

He wished for oblivion—a few hours when he wouldn't have to think of anything. But he knew he couldn't sleep, despite the grueling basketball practice he'd pushed himself through that day. He opened his journal this time and wrote a calmer, slightly less self-castigating version. It had been over a week since he'd written last. He went back several days and poured out his feelings for Lily and their talk. Then he wrote about his experiences in California. When he finished, he felt better. After a prayer, he went to bed.

CHAPTER THIRTY-FOUR

Curtis's prediction that Grayson would hold back until the last minute nearly proved true. It was Wednesday night when he called to relay information about the funeral. "Sorry to call you so late, but things have been a bit hectic," Grayson apologized.

"No problem. I'm just back from practice. The location of the funeral hasn't changed has it? Friday at noon, right?"

There was a brief pause. "Yeah, it's there. Found out already, then?"

"Yeah, Cliff will be flying out tomorrow evening. His wife wanted to come but with her due date so close, they decided she shouldn't. We'll drive over together that morning. Unless you need us there sooner. We'd be happy to come early if you like."

"No need. If you've already made plans, I guess I didn't have to bother calling. See you Friday."

Hearing the click as Grayson hung up the phone, Curtis pursed his lips. Grayson had seemed a bit miffed. Curtis tried to be understanding about his attitude—after all, Grayson had been through a horrible few months and had just lost his father—but it was frustrating. Curtis had to remind himself it had taken much longer for him to come around to accepting his birth family—and he'd always known they existed.

Though Curtis was sorry he'd lost Alex so soon after meeting him, he realized his adopted father was his real dad. Getting the chance to know Alex was enough, even if it was brief.

Lily snuggled deeper into the arm Curtis had wrapped around her. She could sense the tension in both brothers that had grown as they neared their destination. Curtis had come up to visit her earlier that week, but it hadn't been nearly enough. She wasn't looking forward to having him move to Denver but reminded herself he would only be a phone call away.

When they reached town, Curtis read off the directions to the funeral home and they soon pulled in front of the building. Dozens of cars lined the parking lot. Lily had time to be grateful Alex had so many friends before Curtis helped her from the car and clasped her small hand in his large one.

"Don't be so nervous. We can slide into the back if you want," she said.

They arrived in time to catch the end of the viewing. Lily noticed many in the line but was sad to note few stayed around to talk. She thought of the funeral they had held for her grandmother less than two years earlier—how everyone had gathered around for a family prayer before the casket was closed. It had been a good-sized crowd, filled with the love and support they all needed.

Grayson stood alone to greet the mourners, his face drawn and pale with heavy circles beneath his eyes. He looked up and saw them. Some emotion flickered across his face but passed too quickly to identify it. He returned his gaze to the woman he spoke with.

When they reached the front of the line, Grayson didn't repeat any of the things he'd said to the visitor before them about being grateful they'd come. Instead, he looked at Lily. "Since you don't look pregnant, you must be Curtis's girlfriend; unless the apple doesn't fall far from the tree, after all." Bitterness all but poured from his face as he spoke.

There was a silent moment while they processed his meaning. Then Lily saw Curtis move in anger toward his half brother. "Cliff would never cheat on Paige—"

Cliff's hand shot out to grab his twin's arm to stop him, but his voice was hard. "Forget it, Curtis. It's been an awful week for him. Let it go." There was a tense silence between them for a long moment. When Cliff spoke again, Lily watched him as he faced Grayson. "We're sorry for your loss and the difficulties you've had to deal with. We'll overlook it this time. Neither of us would be generous enough to do so again."

"Since I'll never see you again, that shouldn't be a problem," Grayson said in a low voice. He turned and walked around them to greet the next people in line.

"He shouldn't have said anything like that," Curtis said when they reached the hallway a moment later.

"No, he shouldn't have." Cliff's face was grim. "He's lost and angry, and looking for someone to blame or lash out at. Let's go find a place to sit."

The funeral was beautiful. Lily didn't know if Alex had been LDS or if the son had altered a few basic things to suit himself after his father died, but it had a definite LDS feel to it—one of hope for the future and celebration of the life Alex had lived.

The pall bearers took the casket out afterward and Lily and the twins followed in their car to the cemetery, then watched as Grayson dedicated his father's grave. Not once did Grayson so much as glance their way.

Though the twins tried to stay unobtrusive, they drew some attention to themselves as they would in any crowd, considering their height. Several people came forward at the gravesite and greeted them. The obituary's surprise line at the end of the family member names had apparently caused a small furor. Cliff dealt with the niceties, while Curtis pulled Lily away, escaping most of the questions.

Myrtle West wasn't so easily put off, however. She walked toward them with determination and planted herself in from of them. "Why didn't you just tell me you were his son?"

Curtis looked a bit sheepish. "I'm sorry to have misled you. We couldn't be completely sure."

"Well, it certainly did come as a surprise to everyone who knew him. We had no idea he had . . ." She let her voice trail off meaningfully.

"It was a long time ago. People make mistakes all the time, and marriages aren't always smooth," he said. "It sounds like he made better choices afterward."

Myrtle eyed him up and down. "Don't have a clue how anyone tells you two apart. Darnedest thing I ever saw. I suppose you can tell which is which, can't you, honey?" she said to Lily.

"Yes, but that wasn't always the case." She smiled, then redirected the conversation. "Have you found a buyer for the house yet?"

"No, had a couple interested people come through—besides yourselves. I suppose you don't really have kids, then?"

"No, I do. They're adorable. My sister's watching them today." Lily,

Myrtle, and Curtis began walking away from the crowd. Lily talked of anything she could think of to take the topic away from the twins and their birth family, but there simply weren't enough acceptable details to please the old woman. She was relieved when Myrtle claimed to have other commitments and left.

After a slow circuit of the block of headstones in the newer section of the cemetery, Lily and the twins went downtown to find a bite to eat. If the local Relief Society hosted a meal, no one bothered to tell them.

Conversation turned to other subjects over lunch. The funeral and Grayson were silently agreed to be off-limits. Lily noticed the way they skirted the subject as they chatted about everything else in their lives.

It wasn't until they were getting into the car after lunch that Curtis told Cliff to head back to Alex's house. He'd decided he couldn't leave yet.

"What do you want to go there for?" Cliff asked.

"It would make sense for Grayson to go there one last time. I want to talk to him." It had taken the past couple of hours to convince himself he could do so without letting his temper take control.

"Grayson doesn't want to see us."

Curtis was well aware of that. "I know. I have to try talking to him one more time, though. I can't let it go."

"I thought you were mad at him." Cliff lifted his brows in surprise.

"I was. I am. I don't know. I just have to give him another chance." He sighed, tired of the whole situation, but he knew he couldn't walk away yet. "We're all he has left, Cliff. Maybe he won't want us now. Maybe he won't even want to get to know us in a month or two, but I have to let him know he'll be welcome if he changes his mind. Okay, and his attitude. It sickened me to hear him suggest that you'd step out on Paige, but he probably didn't think his dad would do that, either." He saw Lily's look of surprise and pulled her closer. "You don't mind, do you?"

"No, of course not." Her smile lightened his heart and gave him extra courage to see it through, even though he was sure the reception would not be positive.

"Fine, we'll go talk to him, but let's try to keep it short. My flight goes out at nine, and I'd like to be on it." Cliff pulled the key from the ignition and stepped out of the car.

"I doubt this will take long," Curtis said to Lily.

"Don't worry about it."

Curtis ran the back of a finger down her cheek. "Thanks." He used the finger to tilt her face up so he could drop a quick kiss on her lips. He loved her so much. As he turned away, he reached into his left pocket and played with the good luck charm he had wrapped in an old handkerchief he inherited when his grandfather died. He found himself touching the item often since he had acquired it a few days earlier.

Cliff murmured a comment about young love. Curtis pivoted and elbowed his brother in the ribs before they headed up the sidewalk to Alex's house.

"So what are you going to say to him?" Cliff asked, rubbing his side.

"I have no idea. I wrote down Mom and Dad's address and my phone number, though, in case he changes his mind down the road." He knew Grayson already had his and Cliff's numbers written down somewhere.

"He's never going to go for it, dude."

Curtis shrugged. He'd been too scared to get to know his birth family for too long. He knew Grayson didn't want anything to do with them, and maybe he never would, but Curtis wouldn't hide again. Never again. He saw Grayson walking in the shade under the trees. "Hey, Grayson," he called loudly.

Grayson turned at the sound of his name and frowned, but stood and watched as the twins crossed the grass to him. "What do you want now? Your share of the inheritance?"

Anger surged, but Curtis banked it back this time—mostly. "How did you know? I mean, NBA players make such a tiny salary these days. If we didn't each get a piece of the few thousand dollars you probably have to share, we'd go broke." He kept his tone flippant as he stopped a few feet away. He knew he would have been better off holding his tongue, but Grayson's attitude just got under his skin.

"What do you want, then?" Grayson's eyes were even more hostile now.

Curtis took a deep breath and looked him in the eye. "Why did you put our names in the obituary?" He hadn't known the question was in his mind until it came out.

"I didn't."

"Funny," Cliff interjected. "I could have sworn they were in the version I read."

Grayson let out a huff of breath and folded his arms across his chest. "Dad did it. After he first met you, before we returned to the hospital, from what I can guess. He called the mortician and told him to add you. I think he really *would* have changed his will if he'd known in time." Pain flashed across his face.

"We don't want any of his things, Grayson," Curtis said.

"That's fine, since you won't get any." Grayson's eyes hardened again.

"We'd like to get to know you, when you're ready to let us." Curtis figured he should earn lots of extra rooms in his heavenly mansion for holding back his anger when faced with such belligerence. Then again, he hadn't been exactly angelic with his responses.

He pulled a small square of paper from his pocket. "You can reach either of us through this address, if you decide you have any questions. Our family's large and eclectic, but there's always room for one more." Curtis extended the sheet of paper, but Grayson didn't take it, choosing instead to stare at Curtis and then Cliff, his eyes filled with contempt.

"Don't hold your breath. I don't need you or anyone else. Now, if you don't mind, I have a long drive ahead of me. Don't bother trying to contact me again." A muscle twitched in Grayson's jaw as he clamped his teeth together and moved toward the house.

Even though he'd expected this outcome, Curtis felt let down. He tried not to hold it against Grayson. Instead Curtis stopped him with a touch on the shoulder and slid the paper into Grayson's jacket pocket when he turned toward them. "Think about it."

As he and Cliff returned to the car, Curtis wondered about his half brother. It would be so difficult to have no one left to turn to. Grayson was the only one left in his family. Curtis hoped he had people back in California who cared about him—even if they did let him come to his father's funeral alone and were willing to let him watch his father die alone.

Chapter Thirty-five

Lily sensed Curtis brooding all the way home. He answered questions and responded to conversation, but there was a definite disconnect in his head. When she reached out to touch his hand, he grabbed on and held tight the whole way to Logan. From the front seat, Cliff teased them about feeling like a chauffeur.

Lily was glad when Cliff dropped them off at her apartment where Curtis's car was parked alongside hers. Curtis pulled her into a tight embrace there on the sidewalk. She leaned back enough to look him in the eyes. "Come in for a bit, will you?"

"Of course." He turned so one arm was around her shoulders.

"How are you doing? I know how worried you were about getting a cold reception from your birth family." She slid her arm around his back and allowed herself to enjoy the closeness.

"I was worried. I feel bad about Grayson, but I think it's more a matter of feeling bad that he's cutting himself off than any feelings of rejection. I'm sorry for what he's going through, but I wouldn't change things if I could—other than the fact that I'd have gotten in touch with Alex sooner."

That was a huge relief to Lily, who had been concerned about Curtis's response. She looked up at him as they reached her front door, and he leaned down to kiss her when a flash of light went off. She glanced over to be blinded by another quick flash. Then the reporter she'd brushed off in the nursery stepped forward. "Lily, how long have you and this hunk been a thing?"

"Who are you?" Curtis asked.

Lily had trouble grasping her keys in her rush to pull them out of her purse. She muttered under her breath, "Reporter. Just ignore her." Finally, she retrieved her keys and flipped through for the right one while Curtis deflected more questions from the nosy woman. Lily slid the key in and turned the lock. Curtis followed her in and shut the door behind them.

"Is she the same woman who bothered you before?" Curtis asked.

Shelly came out of the kids' room. "The same what?" She carefully shut the bedroom door behind her.

Speaking in a low voice so the kids wouldn't hear, Lily answered, "Reporter outside. She must have been waiting for me to come home." Lily felt her head beginning to ache. This was precisely the thing she wanted to avoid. "Your name is definitely going to be connected with mine now. We'll be lucky if they don't start making up all kinds of things about us."

Curtis pulled the blinds closed on the living room window, and Shelly collected her things. "I guess the day must have gone smoothly or you wouldn't be back so early."

"It went well enough." Lily put her handbag away and kicked off her shoes, then went to her room and peeled off her stockings. Through the closed door she could hear Curtis filling Shelly in. Lily slipped into a pair of cushy socks and changed to jeans before returning to the living room.

"The kids were good. They're still napping—it's late, I know, but they were unusually active. We'll see how long before they're running around again." Shelly shrugged and slid her purse strap over her shoulder. "I've got finals Tuesday afternoon—the end of my summer classes—so I won't be able to watch them, remember?"

"I've already arranged to leave them at day care. Thanks, Shelly."

"No problem, I appreciate you padding my bank account so much. I might not even have to get a regular job next semester if I'm careful."

"On the other hand, you may have a few one-time special expenses to worry about. September is getting closer," Lily said with a teasing tone. But instead of the brilliant smile Lily had expected, Shelly's lips barely tipped up.

"Yes. You never know. Good night." She turned and left the apartment.

Curtis peered out the window and watched Shelly reach her car and get inside. "No one stopped her to ask any questions." He stood and turned back to face Lily. "That was an odd response. What's the deal with September, anyway?"

"Her missionary comes home then." She picked up a couple of toys from the floor and tossed them into the toy box. "I wonder what's going on? I'll have to grill her later. I'm glad the reporter didn't bother her. You probably ought to go so you don't fuel the rumors and innuendo," Lily said, though she wanted him to stay.

"A little later, maybe." He walked over and slid his arms around her waist, pulling her close. "I sure have missed you."

She set her head on his shoulder and inhaled his scent. "You've been with me all day."

He poked her in the side, causing her to jump slightly from ticklishness. "You know what I mean."

"Yes. I know."

He leaned in and pressed his lips to hers, lingering over the moment. Lily enjoyed having him close, feeling his mouth brush across hers. She loved the tingle of excitement and happiness that filled her whenever he was near.

"I don't care what they say about us, you know." He spoke low between kisses, sliding his mouth along her jaw and trailing back to her ear. "I don't want to be separated from you."

After one more long moment, Lily gently pushed him away. "I'm not that spectacular. I'm sure you'll get over me eventually."

He touched her face. "We've been over this already, and your arguments aren't any more convincing now than before."

"Then why did you bring it up again?"

He grinned at her and dropped a kiss on her nose. "I was hoping you might find my arguments more sensible than you did before." He pressed a kiss to her forehead.

Stephen call out, "Mommy, Curtis, you come back!" A pair of little arms wrapped around her legs.

She pulled away from Curtis with more than a little reluctance and scooped up her son. He gave her a quick hug, then turned to Curtis and shook his finger at him. "I miss you. Where you been?"

Curtis took his turn getting little-boy hugs. "I've been working far away. I'm sorry. I missed you too."

"Don't go away again," the child demanded.

Lily watched Curtis turn to meet her gaze. "From the mouths of babes. I'd like to be close by all the time, but the decision isn't mine."

Curtis pressed one more lingering kiss on Lily before he left a few minutes later—a reminder that the choice was hers.

If only it didn't weigh so heavily on her shoulders.

There had been several phone calls from interested reporters and more than one photographer trying to snap pictures of Lily and Curtis over the next two weeks. The media just didn't know when to quit, Lily thought when she arrived at the family court a couple of weeks later.

Somehow a few enterprising reporters had managed to get her cell phone number, and she'd been forced to switch to a new one. Though they had left Shelly alone the first time, they had approached her several times since then in search of quotes for their stories. The calls and attention hadn't been as strong as when John was arrested, but it seemed to be lasting a lot longer.

The picture of Curtis kissing her on the doorstep—or rather, almost kissing her—had made it in one gossip magazine, and she'd heard it was posted around the Internet as well. Other pictures and articles had popped up, and she knew more were still coming. "Basketball Star Duped by Scheming Woman," one such headline proclaimed. It hadn't stopped Curtis from visiting her, but it had still been a strain. Lily kept her head down and her mouth shut and focused on getting through the day.

Shaking off her worries in the media, she greeted the woman at the front desk of the family court in Utah County. She was directed to sit and wait. Lily wandered the brown halls to a faded red bench and sat. The plate glass window provided a view of the parking lot, but it was better than having to see her in-laws sitting with their lawyer almost around the corner from her. Shelly had come for the ride to watch the kids, but she'd dropped Lily off and would take the kids to a park until Lily called to say court was over. She didn't want them exposed to any arguing that could occur.

Her parents walked in the front door a few moments later, shortly followed by the lawyer. Curtis had asked about coming, but Lily didn't want to make things any more dramatic than they already were. With the recent publicity, there was an all-too-high likelihood of his presence causing some kind of to-do—even if it was just her former in-laws causing the scene.

As the bailiff finally led them back to the courtroom, Lily's lawyer,

Jeneal, smiled and patted her hand. "Don't worry. They have nothing on you."

Still, with the daggers the Drakes were shooting at her, she couldn't feel so secure.

The judge, a dark-haired woman in her late fifties, entered and court began. Lily's parents were seated on benches near her. Her mother kept looking at Lily encouragingly, but her hands were rolling and unrolling her purse in her lap—a sure sign that the woman was anxious.

"Your Honor," the Drake's lawyer began when he had the floor. "My clients are very concerned about their former daughter-in-law's lifestyle, her ability to provide for the children, and frankly, her ability to parent them at all. She seems lost in a downward spiral of bad decisions."

It took great effort for Lily to keep her face impassive as the lawyer began detailing her many faults.

"Two young children can be a handful for a career woman," he began. "On the Drakes' last visit to see their grandchildren, the house was a shambles, the children were ill-behaved and dirty, and they acted as though they hadn't eaten all day. Even when she lived with her husband, she spent many more hours tending her flowers than in the care of her children."

Lily leaned over to Jeneal in panic and whispered, "I can't believe this. You know it isn't true."

Jeneal set a hand on Lily's arm and gave it a light squeeze. "Settle down. I'll have a chance for rebuttal. Just let them get it all out, and we'll take care of it."

"The day care provider she first chose," the Drakes' lawyer continued, "had to be closed because the facility was unsafe. The playground where the children go on nice afternoons is rusted with broken swings, and the apartment they live in is in a poor side of town where crime abounds."

Teeth gritting, Lily tried to keep an unconcerned expression on her face, but a glance at Elizabeth told her she wasn't succeeding. She picked up a pencil from the table and began fidgeting with it on her lap for something to do with her hands.

"Furthermore, Lily has shown an inability to keep steady employment as she worked a string of teaching jobs and sold plants and fertilizer in a nursery. Who knows the kind of debt she's had to go into in order to simply keep milk in the fridge. Stephen's eating habits were deplorable when the Drakes fed him—he refused to eat anything healthy.

"To top it off, even before her divorce was finalized, the defendant was seen in the company of a recently drafted NBA player. She's been in the papers and magazines for their illicit relationship, bringing attention to herself instead of focusing on things that matter most. She even took her new boyfriend home with her overnight."

Lily snapped the pencil in half in reflex. They had gone to her parents' house overnight with the kids. It wasn't like they'd had some tryst at her apartment.

She met Jeneal's gaze and leaned in again, "I took him to my parents' house. He played basketball with my sisters and helped my dad fix the gutter."

Jeneal rolled her eyes and faced forward again. Lily felt her shoulder muscles tense until she wanted to scream.

Finally, her lawyer was allowed to stand and speak. "Your Honor, I know you're familiar with the many allegations against my client. You have the caseworker's recommendation before you saying that the children are safe, happy, loved, and well cared for. Several surprise home visits have proven the house is clean and orderly and the day care is excellent. My client has obtained steady work with the Logan School District, and a report I submitted shows there is nothing overtly dangerous about the area of town in which she is living.

"The Drakes have shown little interest in their grandchildren over the years and have, in fact, only bothered to visit them on two occasions since their son was arrested seven months ago. Any child is going to behave badly with strangers." She shifted on her feet and put out a hand in supplication.

"If there has been an upswing in interest in my client's life, it will shortly blow over and is not of her doing. It would be a tragedy not only for this young mother, but also for the children if they were removed from her custody. Your proof that she's doing an admirable job is before you. This has been a frivolous suit, taken up out of spite. I ask you to leave things as they stand with regard to custody and to award the defendant all of the financial recompense we are requesting. Thank you." She sat and settled back into her chair.

Lily couldn't believe her representative had taken a mere minute to refute the ten or fifteen minutes' worth of complaints. How could that be considered sufficient? Was she going to have to hire someone else to fight this all over again?

The judge shuffled papers for a brief moment. "Miss Cox, would you like to respond to the issue with your first day care provider?"

Lily stood and smoothed the front of her skirt, mostly to wipe the sweat from her hands. "It turns out there was a leaky pipe in the neighboring business's suite. It broke, causing major flooding throughout their end of the complex. It was out of their control and was handled appropriately from the evacuation of the children to contacting parents immediately. Unfortunately, they were unable to resume business for several weeks, so I had to find a new place to take Stephen and Sophie."

Pursed lips and a look at the papers on the desk were the judge's response. "I remember when my children were young. Lauren was always dirty within seconds of getting out of the tub, or so it seemed, and they were all really picky about fruits and vegetables. They grew out of it, as I'm sure Stephen will. Can you tell me where the Drakes took the kids for lunch on the day of their visit?"

"My sister told me they went to Carl's Jr."

The judge muttered something too low to be heard, then set the papers on the table in front of herself. "You may be seated." A moment later, she addressed the court. "In the midst of the difficulties that have beset the defendant, I am appalled that such a malicious suit should be filed against her. It is clear that it was nothing but spite that drove the suit as not one shred of evidence has been found to support the claims brought against her.

"Therefore, I see no reason to remove custody from Ms. Cox. I grant her full remuneration for all legal fees and the pain and suffering costs for which she has counter-sued." She said a few more words and then closed the court.

Lily sat in shock as she tried to take in the fact that she'd been granted everything she had asked for. Everything. This nightmare was behind her, and she could finally get on with her life.

John's parents huddled with their lawyer. Elizabeth had tears on her cheeks, while Ross glared at Lily. Lily turned into her parents' loving arms and hugged them both in excitement and relief. She thanked her lawyer for the help, and they headed for the doors.

In no time she found herself walking out into open sunlight, feeling more free than she'd felt in a long time. She picked up her cell phone and called Shelly. Then she called Curtis. News this good needed to be shared.

CHAPTER THIRTY-SIX

The schools were all back in session for the new academic year. Lily enjoyed the challenge of teaching her own class—one where she set the tone and the rules. She hated having her own kids in day care most of the time, but it couldn't be helped.

Since Curtis had a couple of months' break before beginning practices for the fall season, he'd been staying at his parents' place in Ogden and had come up to visit her several times a week. He hadn't said another word about marriage, but it was in every look and kiss.

Friday night he couldn't come into town because of other commitments, but he called her after the kids had been in bed for a while. When they'd talked nearly half an hour, there was a knock at Lily's door. "No idea who that could be," Lily said as she saw that the clock on the stove read 10:27. She stood and opened the door to find Shelly, red-eyed and puffy-faced on the other side. "Curtis, it's Shelly. It looks like I better go. I'll talk to you tomorrow?"

"Is everything okay?"

"We'll see." Lily was certain something must be very wrong when Shelly hugged her.

"All right." He sounded a bit mystified but didn't protest. "I'll call if I can't come up. Tell Shelly hello for me. I love you."

"Yeah, me too, good-bye." She hung up the phone and pulled her sister closer. "What's going on?"

"Who'd have thought that after all those times you teased me about making a decision, it would be so hard? How could I have let this happen?" Shelly finally pulled away, then grabbed the box of tissues.

"What happened exactly?" All kinds of awful things poured into Lily's mind.

Shelly let out a damp laugh. "How do you choose between two men who want to marry you—especially when you love them both?" Then she burst into tears again.

This was serious—and Lily found herself seriously having to bite back a laugh for just a second as she thought of all the girls who'd love to have Shelly's problem. Two great, hardworking, sweet men who were dedicated to the gospel wanted to marry her. Either choice she made, she couldn't go wrong.

"Shel, what happened tonight?"

After a long moment, Shelly blew her nose and calmed down enough to speak, though her nose was still stuffy. "I had a date with Rob. We went bowling and stopped for ice cream at the dairy. Then we stopped to talk while we were walking across the grass to the dorms. We sat there, staring up at the stars and talked about the enormity of eternity when he tells me that when he sees eternity, he sees me there with him. Then he kissed me!"

Again that urge to laugh. "In all this time he's never kissed you?"

Shelly rolled her eyes. "Well, no, of course he's kissed me before. It's just that, well, it wasn't one of those kisses that follows The Rules, you know? A touch of lips, maybe a tiny nibble, then back away. No, it was . . . amazing. And I do love him. I love him so much. But I love Jimmy too, and he gets home from his mission in ten days. His last letter mentioned our wedding someday—which you know means like, this winter, because that's what I've been planning all along. But now I have this other option, and—stop laughing at me!"

Lily couldn't help herself. She was shaking all over, trying desperately to keep it in, to hide it away. It was all just too much. "I'm sorry. It's just you have too many marriage options, and most girls would kill to be in your position. But you and I, we're both being pursued by these men we won't be able to marry." Suddenly her laughter turned into tears, and she was sobbing in Shelly's arms. She had held in her emotions regarding her questionable future with Curtis, but now it poured out, tearing into her.

A year before, she'd thought life was great, though not perfect—it definitely had its trials—she had been happy enough and she'd hoped it might get better. Then it got worse—so much worse. Now that things were starting to even out again, she realized she wanted, more than anything, to be with a man she didn't dare accept. She knew he'd make her happier than John ever could have, simply because he cared about her—her feelings, her work, her interests.

Despite the way most men in his occupation acted, he wasn't so wrapped up in himself that he didn't see her. She doubted John had ever truly seen her for herself but only for what she could do for him. He wanted a sweet homemaker to hang on his arm, make the social rounds, and keep his life running smoothly.

In hindsight she could see John hadn't really cared about the things that mattered to her, and never had. It had taken months for her to break through the mental barriers being married to John had formed. Months to realize she could have a relationship so much happier and healthier than what he'd offered her.

"You can't marry Curtis? For heaven's sake, why not?" Shelly seemed to have calmed down as she held Lily and patted her back. "You and your kids are crazy about him. If he wants to marry you, what's stopping you?"

"I just . . . well, I love him so much, but the media circus we've been dealing with—can you imagine if we were married? What would the writers say then? How can I drag down his opportunity to be an example with . . . well, John?"

Shelly huffed in irritation and nudged Lily to sit up and face her. "You're such a hard-headed idiot! Have you even prayed about marrying him? Do you *know* you shouldn't—that it's a wrong choice?" Shelly wiped at the tear tracks on her face and sniffled.

Lily shook her head. "I know I should. I tell myself I should, but I think I haven't because if I don't pray, I can keep carrying this tiny hope inside me that it could work out. If I pray and He says not to marry Curtis, I'm afraid I'm going to have to end our relationship entirely," She sucked in a breath, fighting back another sob. "And man, I don't think I can do that. Talking to him gets me through all of the mundane tasks of the day."

"He gets you through your days, treats you like royalty, loves you no matter what bad press comes your way, and you love him? Sounds like you've already got your answer—you know your heart." She cocked her heart to the side and smiled. "But pray anyway. It never hurts."

Lily got up and moved to the refrigerator. She pulled out a bottle of chocolate syrup and a gallon of milk, then searched the cupboard for cups. If all else failed—and she knew she had eaten the last of her chocolate stash a couple of days earlier—chocolate milk was better than nothing. "And you? Have you prayed about it?"

They were both much calmer after the torrent of tears. "Not yet. I haven't even had time. It did occur to me that Rob was starting to think along those lines, but I talked about Jimmy so much I thought he understood. I told Rob I couldn't marry him—that I was going to marry Jimmy—something he's known from the first. It all started so innocently. Then he kissed me.

"For one amazing moment I thought of Rob and me, and I could see it—every day of our lives. It was wonderful, but it didn't feel right. I apologized, tried to explain, but he fumed and stalked off. I can't blame him. I should've broken things off with him ages ago." Shelly wiped the tears that started slipping down her face again. She pulled the tab from the new gallon of milk and began to pour.

"But, Lily, what if I made a mistake? What if he's the one and Jimmy isn't? What should I do if I pray about it and find out I was wrong? Worse yet, what if I don't get an answer? Or what if I'm told neither of them is right for me? I think I'd curl up in a ball and die."

"No, you wouldn't. You're a survivor, and you could live without either of them if you needed to." Lily smiled wryly as she added plenty of chocolate syrup to the glasses. "It may be miserable for a while, but you'd survive just fine."

Half an hour and two tall glasses of chocolate milk later, Lily reminded Shelly to start praying to make sure her decision was the right one, then sent her back to her dorm to sleep.

Before bed, Lily decided it was past time for her to put her own advice to the test. She would begin her prayers and hope for an answer she could live with.

CHAPTER THIRTY-SEVEN

Curtis had to hold back his fidgets as he stood on Lily's front porch. He would move to Denver in five days to start his new life. He heard Sophie cry and Stephen call out to Lily that someone was at the door. It brought a smile to his face, even as he ached inside at the thought of leaving them all behind.

He adjusted his hold on the pink rose and white daisy bouquet he grasped in one hand, then felt his breath whoosh from his lungs when Lily opened the door. She looked beautiful, as though she had taken great pains to prepare for his arrival. Then again, she always looked great. "Hi," he greeted her.

Her eyes softened when she saw flowers. "You shouldn't have." But a smile teased her lips even as she moved out of the way to let him into the apartment.

He let the door shut behind him before sliding one arm around her waist to draw her close. His flower-filled hand slid behind her back as he pressed a kiss to her sweet mouth. "Of course I should," he said when he pulled back after lingering for a long moment.

Stephen tugged on his pant leg, wanting to be picked up, and Sophie whined from where she sat in front of the sofa. Curtis handed the flowers to Lily, who buried her nose in them for a long moment, then thanked him. He picked up Stephen and flew him around the room like an airplane.

It felt good and natural to be here immersed in the love and laughter of this little apartment, even when he had to change Sophie's diaper while Lily tended to dinner and sent a tantruming Stephen to time out. He helped prepare the salad and set the table, taking Sophie around with him to keep her happy and babbling while he worked.

Through it all, he felt time slipping past. The time he would have to leave Lily was growing near. But this time it wouldn't be for the night, but for weeks. The doorbell rang, and he answered it to find a glowing Shelly and a young man on the stoop with her.

"Oh, hi, Curtis. I guess I should have seen your car out front. I wasn't looking. This is Jimmy." She pulled the man into the apartment behind her. "Don't worry. We won't interrupt your evening for long." She introduced Curtis to a brown-haired man with a dimple in one cheek.

Lily came back into the living room and smiled. "It's good to see you again, Jimmy." She pulled him into a hug. "Has it really been two years? It seems like only yesterday you were leaving." She winked at Shelly, who rolled her eyes. "I guess my sister doesn't feel that way, though."

He turned to beam at Shelly. "It was the longest and shortest two years of my life."

Curtis thought he understood completely. Shelly was unable to hold back a second longer and held out her left hand to show off the microscopic diamond to them. "Guess what?" she asked.

The sisters squealed together—a reaction Curtis hadn't expected. They both seemed so calm most of the time. "Congratulations," he told Jimmy, feeling a pang in his chest and unnaturally aware of the contents of his right front pocket. Lily had told him Shelly had a missionary, but he'd thought things with Shelly and Rob had progressed well beyond friendship.

"Thanks. It might seem too soon to some people, but I've always known I wanted to be with Shelly." He watched the sisters indulgently. "We're planning on marrying in December as soon as she finishes up school here."

Then Shelly was in Jimmy's arms again. If he had more to say, he forgot about it.

Ten minutes later the younger couple left, giddy and joyful and floating down the front walk. Curtis pushed away the envy that tore at his gut and allowed himself to be happy for them—though he imagined Rob wasn't going to be the least bit happy about the development.

Finally dinner was done and the kids were tucked into bed—for the moment, at least.

"Do you remember the first time we met?" Lily asked as they snuggled on the sofa in front of a movie neither of them was watching.

He played with her fingers in his lap. He shouldn't remember. It was years ago and he thought at the time that he was interested in Denise.

That was, of course, before he realized they were siblings. "Yes, you were all mussed because you had just woken up from sleeping all day—"

"Because I worked graveyards!" she protested.

He just laughed at that. "Yes. You wore pajamas with teddy bears on them. Your hair was a mess, and I think you had a smear of makeup under your eyes." He could see it clearly, as if it had been only weeks ago instead of nearly four years. "When we left your apartment a while later, I asked about you. I felt sad when Denise told me you were engaged."

"Don't be ridiculous. By your description I looked horrible. And how do you remember my teddy bear pajamas?"

"I'm serious." He rubbed his cheek over her silky hair and smelled the fruity scent of her shampoo mixed with her perfume. He ached at the thought of leaving her behind. "You always look good to me, even when you're not at your best."

He knew it was foolish, that asking her again when she had rejected his offer of marriage so many times was little more than masochistic, but he couldn't help himself. "Lily, you know I love you."

She seemed to sigh closer into his embrace, and her free hand fidgeted with his shirt. "Yes."

"And you love me?"

There was a short pause, but when she spoke her voice was sure. "Yes."

"Don't you think you might grow used to the idea? Do you think maybe, someday you might decide we can be together all the time?" He felt a lump in his throat. If she said no this time, he didn't know if he could keep coming back. It was madness to keep pursuing a relationship when she wouldn't commit.

He felt her fingers curl into a tight ball in his T-shirt, then slowly release. The moment dragged, and he prepared himself for the answer he dreaded. "Yes."

A moment of silence followed while he tried to decide if he'd heard her right. He turned her face up to his so he could see her expression and saw the tears glimmering in her eyes. "Yes? As in, yes, maybe someday?" He didn't dare hope. "Or . . ."

"As in yes, you're right. I've been holding out because I was scared— your reputation was little more than an excuse, though I was concerned about it. Mostly I wasn't able to totally let go of my guilt for the way my marriage turned out. I was afraid to try again. I trusted John so completely. How could I be sure I'd made the right choice this time? I was afraid to pray to see if my answer was right because I worried I'd be told no and then I would have to give you up. I just couldn't imagine not having you in my life in some way."

Joy burst in Curtis's chest, and he kissed her softly, drawing it out in celebration. "So you will marry me, then?"

She grinned. "Yes, as soon as possible. I know it will take a while to get my temple sealing canceled. I'll have to give notice to the school to find a new teacher. You'll need to find a home. Then there's the wedding to plan. You don't mind if it's just family and close friends, do you?"

He kissed her again, long and lingering this time, unable to believe he would finally have everything he wanted, everything he needed, when he started his new life.

"I suppose that answers my question," she said, dazed when he finally pulled back.

"The only thing I need is you, our families, and a temple sealer. Then my life will be complete." He dug into his pocket and pulled out the old handkerchief he'd carried around for weeks. "I bought this before the Revue, and I've been carrying it around ever since. I hoped it would be a good luck charm." He peeled back the final layer and revealed a simple emerald-cut diamond ring that was just a tad under a carat.

Lily gasped. When she looked back at him, he grinned at her. She touched his cheeks and kissed him, then allowed him to slide the ring onto her finger. It was a bit too big around, but that didn't seem to bother her. "I love it." She looked into his eyes. "I love you."

He tipped his forehead against hers, his heart filling to overflowing. "I love you back."

She touched the ring and looked up at him, tears hovering in her eyes. Her lip trembled slightly as she spoke. "This is your good luck charm?"

"It must have worked—you're wearing it, aren't you?" He pulled her onto his lap and slid his arms around her waist, drawing her even closer. He reveled in her soft warmth and buried his face in her neck for a moment, breathing in her scent.

When he pulled back, her eyes teased him and her lips tempted. "It took long enough to work, though, didn't it? It's been over two months." She bit her bottom lip.

He couldn't resist leaning in for another kiss. When he spoke, his words were muffled against her mouth. "You were worth the wait."

DISCUSSION STARTERS

1. How does John justify using minors' social security numbers instead of adults'? Despite his claim that he wasn't hurting anyone, how do his actions affect society at large?
2. Why do you think Lily feels guilty about John's crimes? How do we, as women, internalize others' guilt?
3. In what ways did gossip hurt Lily?
4. Why do you think Curtis constantly prays for strength, peace, and guidance? Does he receive those things? Does that kind of thinking usually result in instant answers or small whispers?
5. Curtis has several reservations when it comes to joining the NBA. What are they and what good or bad things would result from his various options?

ACKNOWLEDGMENTS

The more I work at this writing thing, the more I realize how many people have a hand in helping me reach my goals. Though writing is a very solitary endeavor in so many ways, this book would not have the polish or flow that it does without feedback from so many. A big thanks to my awesome critique group: Tristi Pinkston, Keith Fisher, Kim Job, Nichole Giles, and Danyelle Ferguson. Their feedback, brainstorming, and reassurance are always invaluable and prevent me from making a major fool of myself.

Thanks also to Holly Horton and Barbara Burgess for their critiques. Special thanks to Stephanie Eberle for reviewing the law enforcement scenes and to Kristi and Matthew Morris for their expert answers concerning all things basketball.

Thanks to all of the many people who worked on my book at Cedar Fort from editing to cover art to publicity. A special thanks to my editor, Heidi Doxey, who always has quick answers to all my questions and is so great to work with.

And, of course, a huge thanks to my husband, Bill, for all of his unending support through the hundreds (if not thousands) of hours I've spent writing, editing, and working on publicity for my writing. Without his help and faith in me, I couldn't have accomplished so much. I love you, honey!

ABOUT THE AUTHOR

Heather Justesen was born and raised in the heart of rural Utah. She spent most of her time reading and daydreaming as she grew up, much to some of her teachers' frustration. After attending Snow College, she transferred to Southern Utah University where she met her husband, Bill.

While living in Utah Valley after they both graduated, they foster parented fifteen children, and Heather worked for the newspaper and learned to love gardening. She now lives in her hometown of Fillmore, Utah, where she and her husband own a business, are both active on the local ambulance service, and raise a wild mix of cats, dogs, chickens, geese, ducks, and fish.

Heather's first novel, *The Ball's in Her Court*, was published by Cedar Fort in 2009. To learn more about Heather and her writing, visit her website: www.HeatherJustesen.com or check out her blog: www.HeatherJustesen.blogspot.com.